'Johns is one of Australia's most popular [...] reason—she tells great stories. She always [...] and then delivers them in a page-turning combination of heart, wit and wisdom ... *How to Mend a Broken Heart* is yet another cracking read from Rachael Johns ... in fact, it's her best yet.' —*Better Reading*

'Imbued with an adventurous spirit, and ultimately hope, this book transports you mentally to a vibrant and unique city a world away, yet strangely familiar. I highly recommend this book. I finished it feeling warm and cosy, if I'd just shared a wonderful adventure with two good friends.' —*She Society* on *How to Mend a Broken Heart*

'This was such a fun and rewarding read! ... If you are looking for a well-crafted romance novel by an accomplished Australian author, then Rachael Johns is your gal, and I heartily recommend this novel' —Victoria Brookman, author of *Burnt Out*, on *How to Mend a Broken Heart*

'A brilliant read from one of Australia's most popular authors, this will have you hooked from the very beginning.' —*Who* on *Flying the Nest*

'With her typical humour, empathy and wisdom, Rachael Johns has once again created characters you can't help but fall in love with and wish the best for. *Flying the Nest* might just be her best novel yet!' —Tess Woods, author of *Love at First Flight*, on *Flying the Nest*

'Writing with warmth and insight, Rachael Johns is brilliant at capturing the joy and sadness in all of our lives. I hope she has many more tales to tell!' —Anthea Hodgson, author of *The Drifter*, on *Flying the Nest*

'A really good book makes you feel like you've found a new friend—one that resonates with you, and one who you can learn from. That's exactly how I felt in Rachael Johns' new novel, *Flying the Nest* ... A disarmingly all-too-real portrayal of what happens when the traditional roles of wife and mother are turned on their head. This is a book that women will want to bond over, share laughs and tears over—a must read for every woman who has had their life take an unexpected turn.' —*Mamamia* on *Flying the Nest*

'Rachael Johns really gets women and is able to express the multilayered internal conflicts that so many of us experience, lay it all out on the page, and still make it deeply personal ... She's masterful at telling the stories of everyday heartbreaks ... *Flying the Nest* is wonderful—Rachael Johns never disappoints.' —*Better Reading* on *Flying the Nest*

'If you like your chick-lit with a dash of intelligent social commentary, *Just One Wish* is the perfect summer read. Rachael Johns's latest novel is sparklingly funny, quirky and totally of this moment.' —*Herald Sun* on *Just One Wish*

'Johns knows how to weave the experiences of different generations of women together, with nuance and sensitivity, understanding how competing contexts shape women's choices ... Exploring themes like motherhood, the roles of women, and lost love, *Just One Wish* will make you look at the women in your own life and wonder what stories they haven't told.' —*Mamamia* on *Just One Wish*

'Johns draws readers in with her richly complex characters.' —*The Daily Telegraph* on *Just One Wish*

'Rachael Johns writes with warmth and heart, her easy, fluent style revealing an emotional intelligence and firm embrace of the things in life that matter, like female friendship.' —*The Age* on *Lost Without You*

'Heart-warming and compassionate ... Any book lover interested in life's emotional complexities and in the events that define and alter us, will be engrossed in *Lost Without You*.' —*Better Reading* on *Lost Without You*

'Full of heartache and joy with a twist that keeps the pages turning ... *The Greatest Gift* will appeal to fans of Jojo Moyes and Monica McInerney.' —*Australian Books + Publishing* on *The Greatest Gift*

'Rachael Johns has done it again, writing a book that you want to devour in one sitting, and then turn back to the first page to savour it all over again. I loved the characters of Harper and Jasper; their stories made me laugh and cry, and ache and cheer and ultimately reflect on all the many facets of that extraordinary journey called motherhood.' —Natasha Lester, author of *The Paris Secret*, on *The Greatest Gift*

'The bond between Flick, Neve, and Emma blossomed as their sons grew up, but even best friends keep secrets from one another ... Fans of emotional, issue driven women's fiction will welcome Johns' US women's fiction debut.' —*Booklist* on *The Art of Keeping Secrets*

'... a compelling and poignant story of dark secrets and turbulent relationships ... I fell completely in love with the well-drawn characters of Flick, Emma and Neve. They were funny and flawed and filled with the kind of raw vulnerability that makes your heart ache for them.' —Nicola Moriarty, bestselling author of *The Fifth Letter*, on *The Art of Keeping Secrets*

'Written with compassion and real insight, *The Art of Keeping Secrets* peeks inside the lives of three ordinary women and the surprising secrets they live with. Utterly absorbing and wonderfully written, Johns explores what secrets can do to a relationship, and pulls apart the notion that some secrets are best kept. It is that gripping novel that, once started, will not allow you to do anything else until the final secret has been revealed.' —Sally Hepworth, bestselling author of *The Secrets of Midwives*, on *The Art of Keeping Secrets*

'A fascinating and deeply moving tale of friendship, family and of course—secrets. These characters will latch onto your heart and refuse to let it go.' —USA Today bestselling author Kelly Rimmer on *The Art of Keeping Secrets*

Rachael Johns is an English teacher by trade, a mum 24/7, a Diet Coke addict, a cat lover and chronic arachnophobe. She is also the bestselling, ABIA-winning author of *The Patterson Girls* and a number of other romance and women's fiction books including *The Art of Keeping Secrets*, *The Greatest Gift*, *Lost Without You*, *Just One Wish*, *Something to Talk About*, *Flying the Nest* and *How to Mend a Broken Heart*. Rachael rarely sleeps, never irons and loves nothing more than sitting in bed with her laptop and imagining her own stories. She is currently Australia's leading writer of contemporary relationship stories around women's issues, a genre she has coined 'life-lit'.

Rachael lives in the Swan Valley with her hyperactive husband, three mostly gorgeous heroes-in-training, two ravenous cats, a cantankerous bird and a very badly behaved dog.

Rachael loves to hear from readers and can be contacted via her website rachaeljohns.com. She is also on Facebook and Instagram.

The Work Wives

Rachael Johns

First Published 2022
First Australian Paperback Edition 2022
ISBN 9781867220275

Published by
HQ Fiction
An imprint of Harlequin Enterprises (Australia) Pty Limited (ABN 47 001 180 918), a subsidiary of HarperCollins Publishers Australia Pty Limited (ABN 36 009 913 517)
Level 13, 201 Elizabeth St
SYDNEY NSW 2000
AUSTRALIA

A catalogue record for this book is available from the National Library of Australia
www.librariesaustralia.nla.gov.au

Printed and bound in Australia by McPherson's Printing Group

This book is dedicated to working women everywhere. Women who are striving to keep kids, partners, houses and pets from falling apart, all the while trying to maintain a thread of sanity. Women who are climbing the career ladder and shattering the glass ceiling, so the next generation of awesome women don't have to fight so hard for gender parity. And also the women who support those women—to the mums, the grandmas, the mothers-in-law, the daughters, the sisters, the best friends, and of course … the work wives. You all rock!!

Prologue

When Shaun Reid, CEO of The Energy Co, summoned all employees to the boardroom just before close of business on Friday afternoon, neither Debra Fast nor Quinn Paladino had any idea that their worst nightmare and their greatest wish (respectively) were about to come true.

Like everyone else in the building they'd been counting down the hours until the weekend officially began and the last thing anyone wanted was to listen to Shaun wax lyrical about the qualities of the new guy.

Deb had a hot date to look forward to and Quinn had her parents visiting from South Australia. How the tables had turned—Quinn spending Friday night with her family and Deb out on the town!

She was grinning to herself when Quinn popped her head over the top of her cubicle at 4.45 pm.

'It's time,' her friend announced, tapping her smart watch.

Deb groaned as she closed the spreadsheet she'd been working on. 'Why couldn't this have waited until Monday?'

Quinn shrugged. 'That's one of the many mysteries of the world. Along with why Shaun has employed yet another man to fill the director of sales position. So much for gender quotas.'

'So, you think the rumour's true?' Deb asked—both she and Quinn clearly disheartened by the thought.

'Of that I have no doubt.' Quinn threw a hand in the air as if she were throwing in the towel. 'But you know Shaun's a man's man. Powerful women terrify him. Come on, the sooner we get to the boardroom, the sooner it will be over.'

'Just got to finish one thing and I'll be there.'

'I'll go save you a seat,' Quinn promised.

People were already crammed into the room by the time Deb arrived a few minutes later. The massive oak table that usually took pride of place in the middle had been pushed to the front, extra chairs had been brought in and were now lined up in rows like a classroom, but there weren't enough seats for everyone. She wouldn't mind standing at the back near the door to make escaping hastily once the meeting finished easier, but as promised Quinn was guarding a vacant chair beside her.

'Over here!' she yelled, waving her hands like they were at some kind of football match.

Deb apologised as she squeezed past Mikael from legal and Samira from customer service and made her way to Quinn.

'Where's Shaun?' called someone from the back. It sounded like No Mates Nate. 'Does he think we have all night?'

Murmurs of agreed disgruntlement echoed around the room as Quinn's phone pinged with an incoming text. She glanced at the screen then to Deb. 'Mam and Dad have landed. Hope this doesn't take long cos I wanted to be home to meet them.'

Before Deb could reply, the door at the front—the one that came direct from Shaun's office—opened and a hush fell over the room as everyone's heads swivelled towards it.

'Oh my God,' whispered Quinn, her jaw dropping as she gazed at the tall, broad-shouldered man who entered with Shaun.

Her whole face lit up and Deb immediately understood why. The new director of sales was without a doubt one of the best-looking men she'd ever laid eyes on; the problem was this wasn't the first time she'd seen him.

As the few other single employees—women and a couple of men—perked up around her, a chill snaked through Deb's body. Her heart thumping, she lowered her head and slid as low as possible in her chair.

'Good afternoon,' began Shaun, his smile so cheesy his artificially white teeth were in danger of blinding them all. 'I'd like to thank you all for coming to welcome our newest member of The Energy Co family, Oscar Darke.'

People started to applaud but every single cell in Deb's body froze. Despite the addition of beard and glasses, there was no longer any room for doubt.

'Oscar comes to us with an impressive resume of experience and lots of innovative ideas. I've asked him to say a few words, tell us a bit about himself and his vision for the future of the sales department.'

'Thank you, thank you.' Oscar clapped Shaun on the shoulder as he took his place, needing to stoop a little to talk into the mic that had been set up to add to the fanfare. 'I have to say I'm a little overwhelmed by such a warm welcome. I know you're probably all itching to hit the pub for happy hour so I'll try to make this snappy.'

With each smarmy sentence Oscar uttered, bile rose in her throat.

She silently willed him to stop talking so she and Quinn could escape without making a scene. Maybe Quinn would have some idea what Deb should do.

'I'm really looking forward to getting to know you all over the coming weeks,' he concluded. 'Have a great weekend.'

'Holy smokes,' Quinn hissed, leaning towards Deb and echoing her thoughts as everyone else stood. 'It's him!'

'What?' The hairs on the back of her neck prickled. How could Quinn possibly know? And then she realised … her friend's expression was one of glee, not horror.

'He's The One! I'm going to go introduce myself. Coming?'

Hell no!

Somehow, she swallowed those words.

'Are you okay?' Quinn asked, frowning slightly.

'Actually …' Deb put a hand on her stomach. 'I'm feeling a little queasy. I've got to get out of here.'

'Are you going to be sick? Do you want me to come with you?'

Deb shook her head. 'I'll be fine. I just need some fresh air.'

Without another word, she hightailed it to the elevators, almost tripping in her rush to get away. *Thank God it's the weekend.* She would need every second of the next forty-eight hours to work out how she was going to handle this, because one thing was certain.

She could not work in the same office as that man.

Debra

Three months earlier

Deb didn't know who was more nervous as she turned into the car park at Smythes Ladies College—her daughter or herself. Even though changing schools had been Ramona's choice this time, it was always nerve-racking starting at a new place, trying to make new friends, getting to know new teachers.

'What are you doing?' shrieked Ramona.

Clearly, Deb *wasn't* the only one on edge. 'What does it look like I'm doing?'

'No. No. No!' Ramona pointed ahead to where a row of SUVs that looked like they were fresh from the car dealership were cruising through the Kiss and Drive. 'Drop me off there.'

'But I thought I'd come in with you. Help you find the right classroom.'

'*Mum.*' Ramona groaned and rolled her eyes as if Deb had just suggested she wear a clown costume to school. 'I'm not in kindergarten. I don't need you to hold my hand anymore.'

'I know but …' Trying not to show her hurt, Deb looked anxiously towards the school's vast entrance. Surrounded by immaculate gardens, the main building with its sandstone walls, steep-sloping roofs and arched windows, looked like something out of Harry Potter—a stark difference from the local Catholic high Ramona used to go to. What if she got lost?

'Mum, *please*,' Ramona implored. 'I'll be fine.'

'Okay. If you're sure.'

As Deb relented and slowed her ancient Toyota Corolla in the Kiss and Drive, Ramona pulled down the visor and checked herself one last time in the mirror. Officially, make-up was forbidden at school, but when Deb had called her out for wearing foundation, blush, mascara and tinted lipstick, Ramona had told her to take a chill pill—that everyone did it and it was hardly visible anyway. Deb hoped she was right because the last thing either of them wanted was Ramona getting in trouble on her first day. Until this summer, she'd never even bothered with make-up.

'Let me stop the car before you get out,' Deb said as Ramona reached for the door. 'Having to call an ambulance on your first day would not for a good start make.'

She was trying to be funny, but Ramona didn't laugh. 'Thanks for the ride,' she said, grabbing her bag from the floor and opening the door in one fell swoop.

'Forgotten something?' Deb called.

'What?!'

Deb leaned towards the passenger side and tapped her cheek.

Ramona shook her head. 'Sorry. No time. Wouldn't want to be late.'

Deb jolted as the door slammed and the sound reverberated around the cabin. She watched as Ramona hitched her brand spanking new SLC school bag up her shoulder and joined the hordes of girls—all dressed identically in the uniform of blue-plaid summer pinafore, white short-sleeved shirts underneath and black shoes with white socks—swarming up the steps.

What had happened to her little girl this summer? Make-up, slamming car doors, no kisses—it was like someone had snatched her sweet daughter and replaced her with a stranger.

She jolted as a horn sounded behind her and glanced in her rear-view mirror to see a long line of fancy cars waiting to pull in behind her. Blinking back stupid tears, Deb pulled out of the school grounds and rejoined the morning rush hour traffic. It went against every bone in her body to leave her precious daughter alone on her first day, which was why she'd offered to take her. She didn't normally drive to work but thought Ramona would appreciate not having to navigate public transport.

Apparently not.

Her car came almost to a standstill in the traffic on New South Head Road and she switched on the radio to try and drown out her thoughts. The office wasn't far as the crow flies from SLC but at this time of the day she'd be lucky if she made it in less than half an hour. *And* she'd have to pay an exorbitant amount for parking.

By the time she arrived at the parking tower down the road from her building, she was in danger of being late. She made a mad dash down the street and was almost at the elevator when she remembered it was her turn to buy morning coffee.

'Dammit,' she muttered as she rushed to the café next door and joined the long queue.

'Double-shot skim latte and an almond cappuccino, please,' she asked when she finally made it to the front.

'Name?' barked the guy behind the till.

As if I don't tell you every second day. 'Debra.'

While she waited, she shot off a quick text to Ramona: *Hope everything going well, and the girls are nice. Can't wait to hear about your day tonight. Love you.* She knew how bitchy girls could sometimes be—especially to a kid from the western suburbs who could only afford to be at the elite school because she'd scored a scholarship. If it wasn't for the fashion program Ramona had been desperate to join, no way Deb would have endorsed this move.

Collecting the coffees, she headed up to the thirteenth floor in the painfully slow elevator, smiling at Lexi, the receptionist, as she entered. 'How's that bump of yours going?'

Lexi rested her hands on her burgeoning stomach. 'Giving me grief. And he kicks so much at night, I'm barely getting any sleep.'

Deb offered her sympathies and then continued, not wanting to linger long enough to get into proper conversation. As much as she liked Lexi, it got boring answering phones and directing traffic, so sometimes the receptionist resorted to gossip to pass the time.

'Hi, morning, hello,' she called to various people as she walked towards the finance department, detouring via digital marketing on her way.

'Quinn not in yet?' she asked Toby and Linc.

The two men in their early twenties, who both wore skinny jeans, black Converse and almost exactly the same shirts, shook their heads, not even looking up from their phones.

'She had a date last night. Maybe she finally hooked up with someone,' said Linc, exchanging a smirk with Toby. This was the only department where the employees didn't even bother trying to be surreptitious when on their mobiles in office hours.

Ignoring this remark, Deb put the almond cappuccino down on Quinn's desk. It was a miracle she could find a place among the clutter, which included make-up, bright-coloured hair accessories, a framed photo of her large family, tiny plush toys and other trinkets. The state of her desk was worse than Ramona's bedroom and that was saying something, but somehow Quinn managed to do her job, and do it well.

'See you later, boys,' she said as she left.

Neither of them replied.

There was a heated discussion happening in the kitchen between Sally, the NSW sales manager, and Steve from IT—probably The Mug Thief had struck again—but Deb kept her head down and continued to the payroll department. Her colleagues, Brendan, Garry and Ian—all middle-aged, semi-balding, married men—chorused a cheerful 'good morning' despite already being ensconced in spreadsheets.

Setting her latte on her desk, Deb slumped into her swivel chair. She couldn't stop wondering about Ramona—how her day was going, whether she'd found her first class okay, what the teachers were like, if the other students were being welcoming. Why didn't high schools have those apps where you could log in and watch your child through a camera? Lexi was constantly on her phone watching what her eighteen-month-old twins were getting up to in the day-care centre downstairs.

Then again, if SLC had such a thing, Deb would probably never get any work done. Speaking of … She switched on the computer and began going through her emails. About half an hour later, one popped up from Quinn.

Never have I felt more in dire need of caffeine. I owe you my life!!!
PS. How was Ramona this morning? Nervous?

Deb chuckled at Quinn's dramatic exclamation as she dipped into her handbag to grab her mobile. She sent the photo Ramona had reluctantly allowed her to take to Quinn.

Why the even-more-than-usual need for coffee? Big night?
Did you get lucky?
PS. No idea re Ramona, she barely said two words to me.
Sent photo to your phone.

Lucky? Lucky?! Simon was lucky I didn't stab him in the eye
with my chopstick before main course.
PS. OMG Ramona looks—ARGH—are you sure that's
really your daughter? She may as well be wearing a
straitjacket. I thought this school was supposed to be
fashionable?!!?!

Smiling, Deb took a sip of her latte. When not in school uniform, Ramona favoured vintage clothing, and would spend hours scouring second-hand shops. In the last couple of years, she'd even started making clothes herself, learning everything from YouTube videos. She had a style of her own and a flair for making old stuff look cool that impressed Deb whose wardrobe was almost entirely shades of black, something which both Ramona and Quinn berated her for on a regular basis.

What happened with Simon? I thought he sounded
promising.
PS. It's the program she's in not the school that's
fashionable. In terms of uniform, SLC is stuck in the dark
ages—or so Ramona told me when we spent an exorbitant
amount buying it.

That daughter of yours is a smart chicken.
Regarding, Simon. Rendezvous? Five minutes, usual spot!

It's a date.

Deb glanced at the time on her computer screen and decided to take an early break. The way she was feeling right now, it wasn't like she was going to achieve much anyway. Listening to Quinn share antics of her latest Tinder date—or was it Bumble or Hinge?—would hopefully take her mind off Ramona.

Quinn

'What took you so long?' Quinn asked, looking up briefly from her mobile as Deb entered the room where she'd been sitting atop a photocopier, scrolling Hinge on her phone and replying to messages from her mother.

'I was just about to come when Shaun sent me an email I had to reply to immediately.'

Quinn glowered—Shaun was *not* their favourite person and *not* someone to be trifled with.

'So, tell me about Simon?'

'God, you look shocking,' Quinn said, pausing in her message to Paul the Podiatrist to take a long hard look at her friend. Although dressed in her usual outfit of black business shirt and tailored black trousers, Deb's eyes were bloodshot, and she looked more harried than usual.

'Thanks very much,' she snapped. 'Who needs a teenage daughter when I've got you?'

'Sorry.' Quinn gave her a sheepish smile as she fiddled with her dangly earring. 'But you look like you got less sleep than I did. Have you been crying?'

'No. Well, not really.' Deb sniffed and shook her head. 'I'm fine. Just a bit glum. I made pancakes as a first-day treat for Ramona and she didn't eat any of them. She said she only felt like a banana, which I'm not sure she even ate. And I went out of my way to drive her to school but she didn't even kiss me goodbye.'

Quinn tried to focus on her friend's woes rather than the guy she'd just swiped right on; he looked like Ryan Reynolds' much younger brother. She loved Deb as much as she loved her family but if she had one flaw, it was that she was far too invested in her daughter's life. The term 'helicopter parent' had probably been coined for her.

'Ramona's fifteen,' she said tentatively. 'God, at that age, I never ate breakfast, never spoke to my mother, never mind let her *kiss* me, and was sneaking out at night to smoke weed with my friends.'

Deb visibly shuddered.

'Don't worry. Ramona's a good kid. She was probably just nervous. I bet tonight she'll be full of chatter about her day.'

'I hope you're right. Something changed this summer. She's suddenly wearing make-up and when I reminded her of the school rules, she told me to take a chill pill. A chill pill! It's like someone's snatched my sweet girl and replaced her with a stranger.'

'Everyone wears make-up at school these days. Unless she's wearing fake eyelashes and dark purple eyeliner, she'll be fine.'

Ew. Quinn screwed up her face and swiped left on someone who listed gambling and collecting *Penthouse* calendars as interests. Were they for real? Online dating was like panning for gold in a region that had been picked clean centuries ago.

'I still don't understand how you can do that. You take multitasking to a whole other level.'

Quinn looked up and winced. 'I'm sorry.' It was rude to be on her phone while having a conversation, but sometimes she couldn't help herself. There were so many possibilities, and she didn't want to miss any.

'Don't be.' Deb gave her a smile that looked like it took effort. 'I live vicariously through your sexcapades.'

'You know you don't have to do that. Now Ramona's getting older, more independent … you could join a dating app yourself.' She swiped left two more times, then hesitated on the third before swiping right. At twenty-seven she couldn't afford to be too picky.

'I don't need a man,' Deb protested. 'I got everything I ever wanted from the opposite sex when I had Ramona. Besides, between motherhood and work, when would I find the time?'

'I'm not saying you need to find a husband. Just have some fun. You know … some wink, wink, nudge, nudge. With someone like him.' She held her screen up to show Deb a guy who looked like something out of the 1970s romance novels her mam bought second hand from garage sales—dark hair, smouldering blue eyes, chiselled face.

Deb's cheeks turned beetroot and she shook her head. 'No way. I'd probably end up swiping the wrong way and connecting with someone from a bikie gang.'

Quinn snorted. 'I'm not sure bikie gangs use dating apps; I think their leather jackets, tattoos and hot machines do all the *wooing* for them. But I promise I'll help you set up your profile and give you a 101 on how to use the app. Or we could try eMatch. You don't even need an app for them—they still have a website, good for the oldies.'

'*Haha.*' Deb finally smiled. 'Thanks, but no thanks. Anyway, I want to hear about Simon.'

'Oh God.' Quinn slumped back against the wall, her legs swinging against the copier. 'Longest half hour of my life.'

'Your date only lasted half an hour?'

'Girlfriend, I deserve a medal for lasting that long.' She again angled her phone towards Deb. 'What do you think of this guy?'

'Quinn Paladino, will you concentrate for two seconds and just tell me what happened. Do I have to confiscate your phone?'

'*Sorry, Mum,*' Quinn sang as she reluctantly slipped it into her pocket. 'Okay, so to start with, Simon was fifteen minutes late. I was about to up and leave when he waltzed in the door and didn't even apologise. Unless the slimy kiss he planted on my lips was his attempt at sorry. *Ugh.*'

She grimaced at the memory. She'd kissed a few toads in the last decade, but Simon was the wartiest of all.

'Then we were sitting at the table reading the menu, small-talking about the weather, which should have been omen enough, when honest to God, he started drooling. Down his chin!'

'What?' Deb spluttered.

'I didn't know whether to say anything. It was such a lot I thought he must be able to feel it, but when he didn't do anything, I gestured to the serviette and mentioned he had something on his chin.' Quinn paused for effect. 'He lifted his arm and wiped his face on his sleeve.'

'No!'

'Oh yeah. When the waiter arrived, I'd pretty much lost my appetite, but I ordered a veggie chow mien out of habit. He kept drooling while we waited for our meals, so badly it started to drip all over the tablecloth. It was like having dinner with a Saint Bernard. All I could think about was what would happen if I ever let him go down on me.'

'Maybe he has a medical condition?'

Quinn slapped a hand over her mouth. 'Oh, I didn't think of that.'

The door opened and Lexi marched in carrying a thick stack of papers. She raised an amused eyebrow 'Are you two actually doing any photocopying?'

'Yeah, I was, but it wasn't working so Deb came to help,' Quinn lied, jumping down from the copier—funnily enough, that was how they'd originally met. On her second week in the office, she'd been photocopying some stuff for her boss and the paper had jammed. She'd been close to tears trying to fix the damn thing when Deb had walked in and saved the day.

Quinn was so grateful she could have kissed her, but instead she'd offered to buy Deb a coffee before work the following morning, thus kickstarting not only a ritual that had been going on almost three years, but also a friendship.

She had more to say about Simon, but no way was she spilling her 'sexcapades' in front of loose-lipped Lexi.

'Yes, paper jam,' Deb nodded, glancing down at her nails—she was a terrible liar. 'But I should be getting back to work now; payroll won't do itself.'

Lexi nodded and pushed past them to get to the copier.

'Catch ya later, Lexi,' Quinn said as she and Deb headed back to their respective offices.

Ramona

Ramona's stomach churned as the siren signalled the end of science class. Chairs scraped around her and the other girls rushed to collect their things and flee the room, but she wasn't in any hurry. She'd survived half a day, but lunchtime was always the worst for a new kid, something she knew all too well.

This wasn't her first rodeo—she'd lost count of the number of times she'd started at a new school. When she was little, she and her mum had moved almost every year, but when she started high school, she'd put her foot down.

No more moving. It's not good for my education.

Or making friends. At twelve this had been much more of a concern to Ramona than her grades, but in the end it turned out the problem was her, not moving around. Other girls thought her love of all things vintage weird when all they generally wanted to talk about was boys.

Her mum couldn't believe it when midway through last year Ramona had asked if she could apply for a scholarship at SLC. *What happened to staying put?*

That's when she'd told her about the special fashion program she'd heard about and how she'd die to be a part of it. As long as she could remember, she'd been obsessed with fashion and how it had changed through the ages. History was more interesting when you looked at it through the lens of clothing. And it wasn't like she'd miss anyone at her old school, or vice versa. Her mum had been reluctant at first, but when Ramona was offered a full scholarship, the fact she'd save on school fees—even though SLC was more expensive than her previous school—and the lack of boys had allayed any doubt she'd initially had.

Her being led astray by a boy appeared to be her mother's biggest fear!

Although the opportunity to do fashion as an actual school subject had been the biggest appeal, Ramona also saw this as a chance for a fresh start. This year she was determined *not* to stand out as weird, and hopefully even make some friends. At fifteen years of age, it was unnatural for your mother to be your BFF, even a nerd like Ramona knew that much. At this stage in the mother–daughter relationship, they should be hating on each other, having rampant arguments involving swear words and slamming of doors!

But so far it had been hard to even talk to other girls because most of the teachers here were so strict about silence in class. Her English teacher had been more relaxed, and in that class Ramona had tried to make conversation with the red-headed girl sitting next to her, but it was like she was mute or something.

'You're new, aren't you?'

Startled from her reverie, she turned at the voice of the person she'd been sitting next to this lesson. The girl, who had thick hair the colour of burnt leaves tied up in a high ponytail and boasted the kind of thick fringe that few people could get away with, had come to class late and the only seat available had been next to Ramona. 'Yeah. Hi.'

'I'm Kenzie,' the girl replied with a warm smile. 'You're in Drysdale too, right? Ramona?'

She nodded. Drysdale was the house she'd been allocated—SLC had six houses which according to the principal were the backbones of the school. She'd drilled this into Ramona at her interview—*Your fellow house members will become your family*—but that morning Ramona had felt anything but at home. Aside from Ms Stone, her Head of House, no one had given her the time of day. The other girls had been so busy chatting and laughing as they talked about school holidays that they hadn't paid one iota of attention to her.

'When Ms Stone introduced you this morning, I was jealous of your cool name. I used to read this old series when I was little about someone called Ramona Quimby. I loved it.'

Ramona couldn't believe it. 'I know it. My mum loved it when she was a kid too—that's who she named me after. I didn't think anyone our age had ever heard of it.'

'Most people haven't. But I'm not anyone. I'm a bit of a book nerd.' Kenzie winked as she pushed back her seat and picked up her things. 'Come with me. I'll introduce you to the gang.'

Stoked she wouldn't be sitting alone at lunch, Ramona tried to remain cool as they headed down the corridors towards their house.

'So what brought you to SLC?' Kenzie asked.

'The fashion program.' She chose not to mention the scholarship because she didn't want to sound like a povo or a smart arse. Her name had been listed in the school newsletter and on the website, but she doubted the kids bothered reading stuff like that.

'Oh *another* one. No wonder you look so polished.'

'I do?' Ramona wasn't quite sure what to make of Kenzie's tone. 'What do you mean another one?'

'My besties—Sydney and Nyra—are also in the program. I'm in specialist engineering. I'm not really into clothes but they tell me what's in and I get by.'

Kenzie seemed like the kind of person who did more than get by—Ramona could tell she was one of those people who looked glam even when she'd just woken up in the morning. The kind of person who looked good wearing daggie old trackies. Then again, maybe she didn't have any old clothes.

'You wouldn't want to have allergies here,' Ramona said as they headed into their house to dump their things. 'It smells like someone's let off a body spray bomb.'

'Oh my God, you're so funny.' Kenzie snorted and elbowed Ramona in her side. 'Sydney! Nyra!' she called, her voice carrying across the crowded house. 'You have to meet Ramona, she's hilarious.'

Ramona hadn't been joking—this school was so different to her last, and it was weird being surrounded by so many girls—but she glowed at Kenzie's compliment as they crossed the room to join her friends, one platinum blonde, one dark-haired. They were stuffing their laptops into their lockers but turned to scrutinise the new arrival.

'Sydney and Nyra, meet Ramona.' Kenzie gestured between the three of them. 'Ramona, meet Sydney and Nyra. We have science together but she's in the fashion program with you two losers.'

'Hi,' they said in unison, both looking Ramona up and down.

'Welcome to SLC,' added the blonde who turned out to be Sydney. She had an aura that told Ramona she was the leader of the trio.

If not for the different shades of their skin and colours of their hair, the three of them could be triplets. They had dewy complexions that only expensive product could be responsible for, all wore Tiffany studs in their ears and had the shiniest hair Ramona had ever seen. Sydney and Nyra flaunted the school rule about all hair longer than chin-length needing to be tied back in a ponytail and Ramona fought the urge to yank her own out of its scrunchie.

'Thanks. I'm excited to be here,' she said, before cursing herself. Did that sound dumb? Too enthusiastic?

If the others thought so, they didn't mention it.

'You coming to the cafeteria then?' Sydney asked.

Ramona nodded, too terrified to speak in case she said something else stupid.

Once she and Kenzie had put their stuff away, the four of them headed to the cafeteria, which looked more like a fancy restaurant than a school dining hall. Her old school had a canteen, but no designated place to eat like this. Ramona couldn't help noticing the other students moved out of their way as they walked—clearly these three were Popular with a capital P—and she couldn't believe her luck that Kenzie appeared to have taken a shine to her.

Do not *stuff this up!*

'Aren't you eating anything?' Nyra asked as the others collected food and all Ramona bought was an iced-tea.

She had ten dollars for emergencies in her bag so it was all she could afford and she'd left her embarrassing cheese sandwich in her locker. 'I'm not really hungry.'

'First day nerves, hey?' Kenzie wrapped an arm around her and squeezed her shoulder. 'No need to worry. You're with us now.'

Lunchtime flew by with Ramona trying her best to keep up with the conversation and not say anything stupid and then there were two more periods before the end of the day, the final of which was fashion class. Much to her relief, the room had long tables in rows, and Sydney and Nyra invited her to sit with them. Ms Rose, their teacher, dressed like she'd just stepped off the catwalk in Milan, and was unlike any teacher Ramona had ever met. There were no demands for silence and most of the lesson was spent playing getting to know you games. Everyone spoke over the top of each other, except the mute redhead who'd been in one of her other classes. Turned out she wasn't mute, but when she was forced to answer a question from Ms Rose, she stuttered.

Each time this happened Sydney and Nyra sniggered. Ramona felt bad for her but knew better than to speak up.

And it looked like her silence paid off because at the end of the day, when they were collecting their bags from Drysdale, Sydney said, 'Do you wanna come grab some food with us at the burger joint around the corner? It's kinda a first day back tradition.'

'Really?'

'Of course.' Sydney glanced up briefly from her phone where her thumb was flying back and forth across the screen. 'Unless you've gotta get home or something?'

'No. I can come.' Her mum wouldn't be home from work for another few hours.

'Awesome.' Kenzie grinned and hitched her bag over her shoulder. 'Let's go.'

The café was literally just around the corner, and it was decked out like an old American diner with black and white chequered flooring, red leather booths, lots of old neon signs on the walls and a jukebox in one corner. 'Under the Boardwalk' by The Drifters—one of Ramona's favourite songs—wafted from it. She instantly fell in love with the place, a popular after-school location if the fact that half of SLC seemed to be here as well was anything to go by.

'We already know what we're getting,' Nyra said, plucking a menu off the counter and handing it to Ramona.

'I recommend the peanut butter milkshakes.' Kenzie pressed her hand over her heart and moaned. 'They're to die for.'

'Oh, I um ... didn't bring enough money today. I'll just grab some water.'

'Hell no!' Sydney exclaimed. 'We'll shout you.'

The other two nodded.

'Consider it our welcome to SLC treat.' Kenzie hip-bumped Ramona.

She'd never met anyone so touchy feely but she kinda liked it.

'Thanks so much.' *Don't cry. Don't cry. Don't cry.*

'So, what's your Snapchat name?' Nyra asked once they'd ordered and found a booth. She sat across the table from Ramona and Sydney, next to Kenzie. All three of them had their phones out.

'Um ...' Ramona's stomach grew heavy as if someone had poured concrete down her throat. She wasn't on any social media. Her mum had always been adamantly against it, and she'd been something of a misfit at her old school anyway so never needed it. Most kids her age simply didn't understand her interests. Over the school holidays, she'd brushed up on what was currently cool in terms of fashion, music and TV, but why hadn't she thought of this?

'My phone got stolen,' she lied as she pulled it out of her pocket. 'That's why I'm using this shitty old one, and I can't remember any of my passwords so I need to create new accounts.'

Sydney eyed Ramona's second-hand Samsung like it was a relic from the past. She wasn't wrong. 'Your phone got stolen?'

She nodded, thinking how stupid that excuse was, but now she'd said it she had to go along with it.

'That sucks,' Kenzie said. 'My mum just upgraded, so we've got an iPhone lying around at home. It's last season's but aside from that it's in tip-top condition. You can have that if you want.'

'Really? I can pay you for it.' Ramona would rob a bank if need be.

'Don't be stupid,' Kenzie scoffed. 'I'll bring it for you tomorrow.'

'When exactly *did* this happen?' asked Sydney, as their milkshakes were delivered by a skinny guy who didn't look much older than them. He wore a white shirt, black pants, shiny black shoes, a candy-striped apron, a white paper hat and a flirtatious grin.

'Thanks.' Kenzie winked at him as he retreated.

'When?' Sydney prompted, taking a sip of her caramel shake.

Why did Ramona have the feeling she didn't believe her? 'Oh, uh … last Wednesday?' *Whoops*, she didn't mean to make that sound like a question.

'And you've gone without Snapchat *that* long?' This from Nyra. 'I would like, absolutely die.'

Ramona shrugged one shoulder. 'I've been busy. Why don't you all give me your deets and I'll friend you when I create new accounts tonight?'

She held her breath as she waited for their replies. Would this be where they tell her they'd made a mistake and didn't want to turn their terrific trio into an awesome foursome?

'What's your number?' Sydney asked eventually.

Relief flooding her, Ramona rattled it off and tried to tame her grin as her phone started beeping with incoming messages.

'Thanks,' she said as the waiter returned with their burgers.

'He's cute,' Nyra whispered as he left.

'Hey!' Kenzie elbowed her in the side. 'I saw him first. And besides, you already have a boyfriend.'

Nyra scowled. 'No, I don't.'

Sydney peered across her milkshake at Ramona. 'Nyra's parents had an arranged marriage, and they want her to marry their friend's son. He's studying medicine. I don't know why she doesn't just go along with it. He's super hot.'

'*If* I ever decide to get married it won't be to someone my parents picked for me.'

24

'Seems to have worked out okay for them,' Kenzie said, plucking up a fry. 'Maybe if my parents' parents had picked their spouses, Dad wouldn't be on marriage number two and Mum wouldn't change boyfriends more than she changes her socks. Honestly, I think dating apps have a lot to answer for.'

'I wish my parents would get a divorce,' Sydney announced. 'I can't wait till I'm eighteen and can move out of home with Blake. We're gunna get an apartment in Bondi so he can surf every morning.'

'Who's Blake?' Ramona asked.

'My boyfriend,' she beamed back.

'Oh *God*, don't get her started or she'll never stop.' Nyra rolled her eyes, then looked to Ramona. 'What's the deal with your olds? Do you have any brothers and sisters?'

'No. I'm an only child. My mum's single. I've never met my dad.'

'Seriously?' Again, she seemed to have perplexed Sydney.

She nodded. After that, the questions came fast and furious.

'Was it a one-night stand?'

'Ooh, did they have an affair?'

'She wasn't raped, was she?'

'No. Nothing like any of that. I'm a donor baby. Mum wanted to have a kid but wasn't in a relationship, so she went to a sperm bank and, voila, here I am.'

'Wow.' Nyra sounded impressed. 'See? No need for marriage anymore. Us girls can do everything on our own.'

'Still need a dude for the sperm,' Sydney pointed out.

'Is it weird not having a dad?' asked Kenzie.

'Not really. You don't miss what you've never known.'

That wasn't completely true—there were times in her life she'd felt the absence bitterly. Painfully. But she wasn't going to look like a sad sack by admitting it.

Thankfully, the conversation moved on, mostly to bitching about some of the teachers and warning Ramona who in their year to avoid like the plague—there was quite the list—then finally Nyra announced she had to be getting home.

As they stood, Kenzie said, 'You got plans Friday night, Ramona?'

'Um …' She racked her mind for something cool—the truth that she'd probably spend it crafting with her mother was anything but— yet cool eluded her. 'Nothing concrete yet.'

'Great, we're having a sleepover at Sydney's house this Friday to commiserate over the first week of school.' She looked to Sydney and Nyra. 'Ramona can come, right?'

Nyra didn't seem particularly pleased by the suggestion, but Sydney nodded enthusiastically. 'Sure. You're one of us now. I'll Snap you the details once you've friended me.'

One of us. It was everything Ramona could do not to burst into tears. How good did that sound? She'd never been one of anything before.

On the train home, she downloaded all the social media apps that her friends had, then friended/followed not only Sydney, Nyra and Kenzie, but—feeling bold—even some people she'd gone to her various primary schools with, some she'd barely even spoken to before. She didn't want it to look like her three new friends were the only mates she had. By the time she got to Granville station, she was following hundreds of accounts and her phone was beeping every few seconds notifying her that someone had followed her.

She even had people she'd never heard of sliding into her DMs and her cheeks were hurting from smiling so much.

Could another day *ever* top this one?

Debra

Finally. After a day that felt like it would never end, followed by navigating Parramatta Road in rush-hour traffic for well over an hour, Deb arrived home, vowing never to drive to work again. She parked in the car park on one side of their late sixties, red-brick apartment building—the one Ramona called retro, but she simply thought of as old—then grabbed the takeaway bag she'd picked up from the Thai restaurant around the corner. Her stomach groaned at the spicy aromas wafting from the containers. Hungry and desperate to hear all about Ramona's first day, she couldn't get inside quick enough.

One of her neighbours was coming out and held the door for her as she went inside. After climbing the stairs to their second-storey apartment, she nudged the doorbell with her elbow. Already juggling the takeaway, her handbag and laptop, it would be easier for Ramona to let her in than trying to dig her key out of her bag.

But her daughter didn't come. Deb tried again, but … nothing.

Trepidation shot to her heart—what if Ramona hadn't made it home safely on the train? She thought of the dodgy-looking people she saw every day on her own commute. Or maybe she missed the bus that took her to the station. But then why wouldn't she have called?

Dumping the takeaway on the floor, Deb fumbled for her key, shoved it in the lock and stumbled inside, almost tripping on a pair of shiny black shoes.

Thank God. Usually the sight of shoes strewn across the floor infuriated her, but they couldn't have made it home alone.

'Ramona?' she called as she retrieved the takeaway and closed the door behind her.

Their apartment wasn't huge, so it only took a few steps before she arrived at her daughter's bedroom. Sitting on her bed, laptop on her knees and phone in her hand, Ramona didn't even look up when Deb appeared in the doorway.

She cleared her throat. 'Doing homework already?' She swallowed the urge to remind her that homework shouldn't be done in bed. Ramona's bedroom wasn't big enough for a desk, but they both liked working alongside each other on the dining table, so it had never been a problem.

'Oh, hi, Mum.' Ramona snapped her laptop shut. 'I didn't hear you come in.'

'I know,' she said, trying to hide her irritation. 'Anyway, I've got chicken satay, pad Thai and that sticky rice you like. Come eat and you can tell me all about your day.'

'I already ate.'

'What?'

'I got milkshakes and burgers with some girls I met at school.'

It was getting harder not to be annoyed, but this sounded promising. 'So, you had a good day then? How was the train?'

'Train was fine, and the day was *the* best. Everyone is so cool and so nice. And my fashion teacher—OMG—she used to work for Carla Zampatti. And she knows Collette Dinnigan and Stella McCartney.'

'Wow.' Some of the tension Deb had been carrying all day eased. 'That's wonderful, but how did you pay for the food?'

'Oh, the girls shouted me. I said I'd pay them back, but they told me not to bother. Honestly, Mum, they're all loaded.'

Before Deb could remind her there were more important things in life than money, Ramona added, 'But obviously I can't let them shout me all the time. I was thinking … maybe I could get a part-time job?'

'When would you have time for that?' Deb didn't mean to dampen her spirits but now she was at school further away, she was going to be lucky if she got home before five, and Saturday mornings she had to play netball for school. Sundays were for homework and family time. Besides, she didn't like the idea of Ramona working—doing late shifts, not to mention meeting people that Deb wouldn't be able to veto.

Ramona shrugged. 'I'll fit it in somehow.'

'You should focus on your studies. I can give you a little more pocket money,' Deb offered, mentally already going through the budget trying to work out where she could cut back. Her Friday lunchtime dumplings with Quinn would have to be the first to go.

'Really? That'd be great, thanks, Mum.' Ramona leapt off the bed and threw her arms around Deb. 'You're the best.'

'I know.' She squeezed her back, endorphins at Ramona's happiness and the hug helping to allay her own fatigue. 'But right now, I'm starving. Even if you don't want to eat anything, you can keep me company while I do.'

'Okay, but I can't talk long. I've got *loads* of homework.'

'On the first day?'

'I'm in Year 10 now, you know. Things are getting serious.'

Deb stifled a smile as she and Ramona headed into the kitchen. She loaded some satay and rice into a bowl and then opened a bottle of pinot grigio. She rarely drank—and never on weeknights—but she'd bought the bottle on the weekend because she thought she might need a drink after Ramona's first day at school.

'So, I want to hear *everything*,' she said as they flopped onto the couch where they always ate dinner. But never with the TV on—she had *some* standards.

'Well, first up, I met three amazing girls who are also in Drysdale— that's my house—and two of them are in the fashion program.'

'That's great.' Deb herself had gone to a similar private school in Perth, where the rich girls had excluded anyone on a scholarship. She was ashamed to admit, she'd never stood up for any of the scholarship girls. 'What are their names?'

'Kenzie—short for Mackenzie—Sydney and Nyra. You'll never guess what, but Kenzie has read all the Ramona books. She said they were her favourite books growing up.'

'That's wonderful.' Deb smiled, thinking about how those stories and many more had kept her entertained as a child when her parents were too busy to make time for her. How she'd longed for a mum like Ramona Quimby had. 'And what are the others like?'

'Nyra is really cool, and funny. Like in a sarcastic way. Sydney is like the most popular girl in the school. She's gorgeous, fashionable, smart, and she's in the best rowing team. She told me if I stick with them, I'll be invited to all the cool parties.'

Parties? Deb's insides twisted a little as Ramona continued chattering about her new friends. Kenzie sounded like a lovely girl, but she wasn't sure about Sydney and Nyra. Sydney came across as a bit of a bossy know-it-all.

'I'm so glad you've made some friends,' she said, 'but it's early days; don't get locked into a friendship group before you've met a few more people.'

Ramona rolled her eyes as if Deb had no idea what she was talking about. 'Anyway, I better start my homework, but before I do, I wanted to ask you something.'

'Sounds ominous.'

'It's nothing really.' Ramona bit her lip, then, 'I was just wondering if I could get social media?'

Deb swallowed and put her glass down on the coffee table. Parties, make-up, and now this. 'Social media?'

Ramona nodded. 'Just a couple of apps. It's how everyone chats, and I don't want to be left out.'

She supposed she should feel lucky she'd managed to keep her daughter away from social media this long, but all she could feel was dread. Every parent knew the dangers online—sexual predators, bullying, screen addiction—and the rules that helped you protect kids. You had to know your child's password and they had to be friends with you on whatever platforms they used.

The problem was, Deb wasn't on any social media platforms, had no intention whatsoever of joining, and the usual concerns were the least of her worries. She'd spent the last sixteen years making sure she and Ramona couldn't be easily found; putting her photo and details online could destroy all of that in an instant.

'I don't know, sweetheart. Why can't you just message your friends?'

'You're so out of touch. No one uses text messages anymore.' Ramona threw her hands in the air. 'And isn't it better that I asked you rather than just go ahead and get it behind your back?'

'Behind my back?' Deb felt like someone had stolen the air from her lungs.

She knew mother–daughter relationships were supposed to be fraught during the teen years but she and Ramona had always been more like friends, and Ramona had never pushed boundaries or spoken to her in such a manner.

The moment stretched.

'I'm sorry, Mum … but *everyone* has social media—I'll be a reject without it. And it's not just to chat with my friends, it'll help with my homework as well.'

'Is that right?' Despite feeling as if someone was eating her insides, Deb laughed. 'Since when do teachers give assignments that require Facebook?'

'*Facebook?*' Ramona screwed up her nose. 'I don't want Facebook. That's for Boomers. And it's nothing to do with the teachers, but I can follow vintage fashion curators and keep up to date with the news and stuff too.'

Deb bit down on the impulse to tell Ramona she could always read a newspaper. Instead, she thought of what Quinn had said about what it was like to be a teenager. Although she wanted to keep Ramona safe, she didn't want her to be a 'reject'. 'What social media do you want?'

Ramona shrugged. 'Just Snapchat and Instagram. Maybe TikTok?'

Snapchat? TikTok? Deb had heard they were the work of the devil, but also, the more platforms she was on, the easier it would be for her to be found. 'How about you choose one?'

'Only one?!'

'One or none. Your choice?'

'Fine.'

'And … your account must be completely private. Only use your first name.' Despite a clamminess coming over her at what she'd just agreed to, Deb tried to keep her tone even, not wanting Romana to register her terror. 'I don't want you friending anyone you haven't met in person or accepting any requests from strangers.'

'As if, Mum. We've been learning about cyber-safety since we were in kindy and I'm not an idiot.'

'I know that.' She shuffled across the couch and pulled Ramona into a side hug. 'I'm so very proud of the young lady you're becoming. I couldn't have asked for a better daughter if I'd sent a checklist to God himself.'

Ramona gave a sort-of laugh. 'I didn't think you believed in God.'

'Touché. So, what's it to be? Instagram, Snapchat or TikTok?'

Ramona stood. 'Snapchat.'

'Where are you going?' Deb asked, desperate to hear more about her day.

'To start my homework.'

'You're supposed to do that out here.'

Ramona gestured to the table, which was covered in craft supplies and the half-constructed miniature model—a cute little bookshop— the two of them were currently working on. 'There's hardly any space.'

'I can make space.'

'Thanks, but I'm going to do it in my room from now on—less distractions. This way we don't have to clear up the craft and you can watch TV or whatever without worrying about me.'

But it's my job to worry about you!

Somehow, she withheld this sentiment. 'Fine, but don't waste too much time on Snapchat and don't send any naked selfies to boys!'

'*God*, Mum,' Ramona groaned. 'How am I supposed to do that when I go to an all-girls' school and you won't let me friend anyone I haven't met in person? Besides, you shouldn't make assumptions these days. Maybe it's girls I want to send boob shots to?'

'Is that supposed to make me feel better?' Deb called as Ramona flounced off to her bedroom.

Quinn

'Wow.' Quinn's brother Declan looked up from where he was cooking salmon on Wednesday night and wolf-whistled as she entered the kitchen. 'Look at you. Who's the lucky guy?'

'Is that Quinn?' came her mother's voice from Declan's phone lying flat on the kitchen bench.

Quinn's eyes went to the phone. 'Why didn't you tell me you were chatting to Mam?' she mouthed as Roisin barked further questions.

'Are you going on a date, darling? What's the young man's name? What's he do for a crust? Where are you meeting him? I hope it's a public place. How do you know he's not a serial killer?'

Quinn glared at Declan as she picked up his phone. 'Hi, Mam, how are you?'

'Never mind about me. You didn't mention a date when we spoke yesterday.'

'Sorry, must have slipped my mind. Actually,' she said as she plucked a bottle of cold water from the fridge, 'I'm meeting two guys.'

'What?' her mother and brother exclaimed at the same time.

She chuckled. 'Drinks with one at seven and then a late dinner with another.' After two weeks of messaging with Paul the Podiatrist and Bako from Bondi, both men had asked if she could meet midweek.

'I ... I ...' Roisin was clearly lost for words. 'I don't know what to say. Are you being careful, Quinn?'

'Oh, geez, Mam, I'm just meeting them. I'm not having their babies. Anyway, I've got to go; do you want to talk to Dec again?'

He shook his head violently, swiping his finger across his neck making cutting movements.

'No, love, tell him I'll speak to him soon. I'm off to Irish dancing.'

'Bye, Mam,' Quinn said. 'Love you.'

Declan raised an eyebrow as she ended the call. 'What if you really like the first guy and want to turn drinks into dinner with him?'

She shrugged. 'Then I'll message Bako and tell him I've come down with a nasty gastro and ask to reschedule for next week.'

Sometimes tiny white lies were necessary when hunting for Mr Right.

'I don't know how you keep doing this,' Declan said, flipping over his salmon. 'Maybe I'm just getting old, but I'm so glad I've got Darpan and don't have to worry about going on another date ever again.'

'Well, we can't all be as lucky as you,' she retorted.

They heard the front door open, keys falling into the expensive bowl on the expensive side table, and then dark-haired, ridiculously handsome Darpan entered the kitchen.

'Speak of the devil.' Declan closed the distance between them and planted his lips on his beloved's.

Theirs was the type of relationship Quinn yearned for. They were best friends, shared many interests, but also enjoyed separate pursuits with different friends, and had chemistry that could cause explosions. If she didn't adore them both, their PDAs would be nauseating.

'Don't wait up for me,' she said as she headed for the front door to put on her rollerskates.

The bar where she'd arranged to meet Paul was just around the corner in Darlinghurst and he was already there when she arrived. *Good sign.* She hated to be kept waiting. Even better, he stood as she entered, gave her a polite kiss on the cheek and then waited until she'd climbed onto her stool before sitting again himself.

Tick. Tick. Tick.

'What can I get you to drink?' he asked with a smile that reminded her of a choir boy, a little too eager to please. Or maybe he was just nervous.

Benefit of the doubt, Quinn, benefit of the doubt.

'I'll have a glass of prosecco, please?'

He nodded and went to order.

'Thanks so much,' she said as he handed her the glass. Their fingers brushed in the exchange and while she felt not so much as a flicker of a spark, she wasn't going to write him off yet.

'You're welcome. By the way, I should have told you when you arrived, but you look amazing.' He gestured to her rainbow-coloured, geometric-patterned jumpsuit and then up to her pale blue hair, which she'd done in two braids and decorated with a zillion sparkly clips. 'So happy-looking.'

'You can never have too much colour in your life, your hair or your wardrobe.'

He chuckled. 'Did you make it yourself?'

'No. I wish I had such talent. I bought it from a maker on Instagram. That's where I buy most of my clothes.'

'Wow. That's so cool. I get most of mine from Kmart.'

Quinn laughed as he took a sip of what looked like a schooner of water. 'You don't drink?'

'Not during the week, but I've really enjoyed our messages, and I couldn't wait till the weekend to meet you.'

A little presumptuous to think she'd give him the prime real estate of a Friday or Saturday night for a first date, but the poor guy did do feet for a living—she should cut him a little slack. She took a sip of her bubbly, not feeling one iota of guilt for drinking on a Wednesday. Life was short—she believed in having fun. 'So, how long have you been on Tinder?'

'Tinder?' His brow creased. 'Don't you mean Bumble?'

Whoops. 'Yep, sorry.'

'I only joined a couple of months ago, after I broke up with a long-term girlfriend. Felt a little weird at first, but it's how everyone meets their spouses these days, right?'

She nodded. 'So, you want to get married one day?' It was a big question for Date Numero Uno, but she no longer wanted to waste her time with little boys who simply wanted to sow their wild oats.

'Oh definitely. I want marriage, kids, a backyard with a Hills hoist and a trampoline. Probably not the thing to admit the first time we meet, but I'm thirty-five, I guess ...' He shrugged as his voice drifted off.

'No. It's cool.' *Another tick.* 'I'm the same. Well, I'm only twenty-seven but I don't want to be ancient when I'm popping out sprogs. My mother had five kids by my age.'

'You come from a big family then?'

'Yep. I have four older brothers. My mam's Irish Catholic and my dad's Italian, also Catholic. I'm surprised they stopped at five. What about your family?'

'I'm an only child. My parents wanted more, but it didn't work out for them. My house was very quiet growing up—not just because there was only three of us, but my mum was really sad about not being able to have any more.' He shook his head as if not wanting to get too solemn. 'I always wanted brothers, maybe even a sister. Are you close to your family?'

'Sometimes we're too close,' she said.

Paul grinned. 'So how long have you lived in Darlinghurst? Such an awesome suburb. Sadly, slightly out of my price range.'

'Oh, I couldn't even afford a shoebox here on my wage,' she admitted. 'I'm lucky my older brother and his husband took pity on me and offered me their spare room.'

'Your profile said you were from Adelaide? Do you miss it?'

'Um … I miss some of my friends, but the shopping's much better here and the fact I don't need a car to get around. And it's not bad having a bit of distance between Mam and I. If I were home in Adelaide, she'd be trying to matchmake me with all her friends' sons.'

'How's that different from Bumble?'

She gave him a look. 'Uh … *I* control my dating account.'

He nodded. 'Have you been playing this game long?'

'A couple of years.' Maybe a slight understatement.

'Wow. You must have been on a few dates in that time. Anything serious?'

'A few that had potential.'

'You might have to give me some tips.'

'Well, clearly I'm not having that much luck, so maybe I'm not the best person to ask for advice.'

'Or maybe,' he said, tilting his head and hitting her with a puppy-dog grin, 'your string of bad luck just ended.'

Quinn took another sip, slightly put off by what she thought was an attempt at flirting. 'So, tell me about your work. Don't think I've ever met a podiatrist before. Why'd you become one?'

'I didn't get a high enough score for medicine.' Paul looked down at his glass and gave a self-deprecating chuckle. 'Probably shouldn't be telling you that either. Might have sounded better if I told you I had a foot fetish.'

'Well, do you?' she said with a laugh. As much as she enjoyed her monthly pedicure, it was hard to understand why anyone would willingly choose to spend so much time scraping bunions and dealing with ingrown toenails.

'I think it's a little early in our relationship for such confessions, don't you?'

She nodded as her phone vibrated in her pocket. 'Will you excuse me for a minute? I need to pop to the restroom.'

'Of course … Can I get you another drink?'

'I'm good for now.'

It felt weird drinking alcohol while he sipped water; besides, she needed to pace herself. It wouldn't pay to turn up to her next date half-sloshed.

The bathroom door had barely closed behind her before Quinn had her phone in her hand. Notifications from her various dating apps, a message from her mother and another from Bako filled the screen. She ignored the one from her mother.

I've been thinking about you all day. Can't wait for our date. See you soon. Bako. XO

Quinn deliberated a moment before replying. It was too early to call it either way with Paul. The fact he'd admitted not getting a good enough score for medicine showed honesty, but maybe not ambition, which was disappointing because ambition was sexy.

Not long now. xx

Before heading back to the bar, she replied to messages from the other guys she was currently chatting with, answered a couple of newbies, and swiped left on someone who admitted their best friend was their mother.

'What exactly do you do for a living?' Paul asked when she climbed back onto her stool.

'I'm a digital marketer for The Energy Co. Basically I run social media campaigns for our products.'

'The sports drink?' When she nodded, he added, 'I can't believe checking Facebook and Instagram are actually jobs these days. Sounds a lot more fun than looking at feet.'

And that sounded like an insult concealed in an attempt at humour. 'There's actually a lot more to it than that.'

'I'm sorry. I didn't mean to offend you. I guess I'm just a bit old-fashioned—I only joined Facebook myself last year because my work wanted me to post before and after photos on their page.'

Quinn raised an eyebrow. Perhaps this guy would be better suited to Deb. And if she was even having those kinds of thoughts, she was wasting both their time.

She lifted her glass and downed the last few dregs. 'Look, Paul, it was nice to meet you, but I've got some place else I need to be. Thanks for the drink.'

He stood to join her. 'Do you want to have dinner next time?'

She gave him an apologetic smile. 'You seem like a great guy, but I just don't think it's going to work out between us. Good luck with everything though.'

Quinn picked up her bag and escaped quickly, walking around the corner in the direction of her next rendezvous before plonking herself down on a bench and retrieving her phone.

Another no-go.

Deb's response came only seconds later. *Paul or Bako?*

Paul. I'm meeting Bako in an hour.

She sent a quick message asking if he could meet earlier and while she waited for his response, checked out new options. Despite the disappointment of tonight's first date, she still got a rush of adrenaline every time she opened her dating apps. She bit her lip as her fingers swiped through the options. You never knew who would appear on the screen next.

By the time Bako replied—*Hell yeah, you've saved me from another episode of* Outback Truckers. *I can be there in fifteen*—she'd initiated two new connections.

The pub where they were meeting was a mere two-minute skate away, so she scrolled through the apps a little longer, before realising almost fifteen minutes had passed and she was going to be late.

'Shit!' She grabbed her rollerskates out of her bag and switched them with the pumps on her feet, then sped down the footpath and almost crashed into someone as she turned the corner.

The stranger caught her in his arms and recognition flashed in his near-black eyes. 'Quinn?'

'Bako?' OMG, this was *not* the entrance she'd hoped to make. 'Hi.'

'Hi indeed.' His amused tone washed through her body like hot chocolate.

Hope flickered in her heart.

They stayed like that for a few long moments, just staring into each other's eyes, before he finally broke the silence. 'Shall we go inside?'

'Yes. Good idea. Let me just switch to shoes,' Quinn said.

'Is this your only mode of transport?' Bako asked, as he patiently waited beside her.

'Yep. They're environmentally friendly, cheap and keep me fit. Do you skate?'

'I haven't since I was a teenager, but you make it look so fun. Maybe I'll have to give it a try again.'

'Maybe you will,' she said with a wink.

They found a table in the corner, not too far from the stage where a band was playing pop songs from the eighties. Bako offered her a drink and this time she went for a glass of rosé. She was pleased when he returned with a schooner of beer as well.

'So,' she said as they clinked glasses. 'Tell me about *Outback Truckers*.'

Debra

Deb stepped out of the elevator at level thirteen and almost crashed into Quinn.

'Happy Thursday,' her friend sang, holding out her latte.

'Thanks,' she said as she took it. 'You're in a good mood. Guess the second date went better than the first last night?'

'Understatement of the century.'

Deb glanced at her watch. Ten minutes until the workday officially started. 'Rendezvous?'

Quinn nodded and ushered Deb down the hallway, passing several people who looked like they should have stayed in bed, before they slipped into the copy room.

'Ramona still enjoying the new school?' Quinn asked, closing the door behind them.

'Yeah.'

'You don't sound so happy about that.'

'I am.' Deb sighed as she peeled the lid off the top of her drink. 'It's just … never mind, tell me about Bako from Bondi.'

Quinn's eyes sparkled as she settled in her usual spot on top of the copier. 'Where should I start?'

Deb drank and listened as Quinn told her how she'd crashed into him outside the pub.

'It was like hurling myself into a wall—he's *that* built. We ordered drinks and he asked me more about myself than he talked about himself. You don't know how rare that can be. But he's so smart—I *wanted* to know everything about him. He came up with the idea for his first app when he was only twenty-two. Sold it at twenty-four to Microsoft and bought his house overlooking the beach outright. Like, no mortgage.'

Quinn paused a moment as if to let that sink in.

'Wow.' Deb couldn't help thinking that someone who boasted about their finances on a first date sounded like a bit of a douche.

'But he's really nice too. And funny—I can't remember the last time I laughed so hard on a date. And he's socially conscious, which is probably the most appealing thing about him. He came to Australia as a refugee when he was little, and he's never forgotten his roots. He only takes what he needs to live from his company and donates the rest to charity. Plus, he volunteers at the local homeless soup kitchen and has an electric car!'

'Sounds like a saint,' Deb joked—it was easy to be environmentally friendly when you could buy a Tesla from the loose change in your wallet.

'I know.' Quinn's excitement dimmed a little. 'There's gotta be something wrong with him, right? How else could he have got to the ripe old age of thirty-one without being snapped up?'

'Hey, thirty-one isn't old! It's a decade younger than me,' Deb pointed out, although she did feel particularly ancient this week.

Quinn grinned. 'You know what I mean. Anyway, I have a good feeling about this one. While I was with Paul, my phone was burning a hole in my pocket. Every time I felt it vibrate with a new notification, I died a little inside, but with Bako … I almost forgot it existed.'

Deb couldn't hide her scepticism. This was the girl who treated her phone like an extension of herself. She changed the cover almost as regularly as she changed her outfit and had a waterproof case so she could use it in the shower.

'As I gazed into his jet-black eyes, all I could think about was how adorable our babies would be. My Irish-Italian genes combined with his Nigerian ones—can you imagine?'

Deb didn't think she could make ugly babies no matter who she bred with. 'So, you think you'll see him again?'

'We're meeting to go for a skate on Saturday morning.'

'That's great.' Deb tried to sound enthusiastic, but this wasn't the first time Quinn had got her knickers in a knot after a first date, and today she simply didn't have the energy for it.

'You okay?'

A lump formed in Deb's throat. She *should* be okay—Ramona seemed to have settled well into her new school, and of course that's what she wanted for her, but ever since she'd let her download Snapchat, she'd been so busy chatting to her new friends that they'd barely spent any time together. While Deb looked forward to dinner so they could sit down together and talk, Ramona scoffed her food as fast as possible so she could escape to her room to do 'homework'.

'I'm fine. Just tired. Feels like it's been a long week.' If she told Quinn the truth, she might start crying, and this was the last place she wanted to fall apart. She picked up her now empty coffee cup. 'We better get to work. See you at lunch?'

'Of course,' Quinn said, sliding off the copier and following Deb to the door.

Deb headed to her desk. She'd been all over the place this week and her emails were out of control. Still, as she tried to focus, all she could think about was that tomorrow night Ramona would be staying with strangers on the other side of the city.

What on earth was she supposed to do with herself?

Then she had an idea. She opened an email to Quinn.

Ramona's going to stay at her new friend's place tomorrow and I'll be home by myself. What do you say to a girls' night? I'll make some pizza and we can watch movies like we're in high school too. You can sleep in Ramona's bed.

Quinn's reply was speedy:

Oh, that sounds awesome, babe, but I've got a second date with Johan the Tennis Coach. Raincheck?

Deb's heart sank:

You're still meeting Johan? What about Bako?

Johan was so sweet, I don't want to cancel on him. Besides, I've only had one date with Bako—gotta keep my options open, right?

Deb sighed, her short-lived excitement deflated.

Of course Quinn would already have plans for Friday night.

Ramona

'Party time!' Nyra sang on Friday afternoon.

When Ramona saw Nyra and Kenzie pull massive designer bags out of their lockers, her nerves churned with excitement. Her Kmart bag contained everything she could possibly imagine she'd need, but it was tiny compared to theirs. As they headed for the school's exit, she went through a mental checklist: PJs, toiletries, a change of clothes for tomorrow and her cozzies because Sydney promised they'd spend most of the night by the pool. Ramona had spent ages trying to work out what to wear, not wanting to draw too much attention to herself. Most of her wardrobe she'd designed and made herself or found lurking in the back of op shops. She bet none of these girls had ever worn anything second hand or even stepped into such a place.

In the end, she'd gone with denim shorts and a T-shirt her mum's friend Quinn had passed down to her, but quite aside from clothes, what if she'd missed something important?

Although Sydney lived close enough to walk in Bellevue Hill, she ordered an Uber to collect them and five minutes later they were heading towards her place in a shiny black Jeep. When the driver pulled up in front of two foreboding gates and Ramona spied the house, her mouth fell open.

She knew her new friends were loaded but this looked like somewhere the prime minister would live.

'You coming?' Kenzie asked, and Ramona realised Sydney and Nyra were already at the gates, which had automatically opened.

'Yeah ... Sorry.'

'It's pretty impressive, isn't it,' Kenzie whispered as they followed the others inside. 'I always feel like a pleb when I visit.'

'What do Sydney's parents do for a living?'

Kenzie snorted. 'Mr Jamison is some big shot in commercial real estate and Mrs Jamison supposedly works for a charity, but I don't know how she finds the time—she always seems to be at the day spa or out shopping.'

'What do your parents do?'

'They're both surgeons—Mum does brains and Dad's an ENT.'

Thank God Kenzie didn't ask Ramona what her mother did!

Sydney let them into a vast and shiny, mostly marble entrance hall and Ramona tried to stay cool. It reminded her of a house on that show Mum liked watching—*Grand Designs*. Although too modern for her liking, you couldn't help being impressed.

She'd only taken a fraction of it in when Sydney announced, 'Let's get changed.'

Ramona followed the others two flights up the marble staircase and then down a hallway with the plushest cream carpet she'd ever walked on.

'Should we have taken off our shoes?' she asked, glancing behind her. 'We're leaving footprints.'

'No.' Sydney gave her a strange look. 'Maya takes care of all that.'

Ramona couldn't even imagine being so rich you didn't have to worry about making a mess. She wondered if Sydney had ever done the washing up in her life. At the end of the corridor, they came to her bedroom with a private bathroom and walk-in robe as well.

Like Ramona's own room, Sydney's was cluttered, a teenage haven. The similarities stopped there. Whereas Ramona's walls boasted framed posters of her idols—Coco Chanel, Jeanne Lanvin, Claire McCardell and Irene Lentze, all female designers who'd paved the way for women in an industry stupidly dominated by men—and retro fifties wallpaper she'd saved up an entire year to buy, Sydney's looked like it was designed for a princess. The walls were glossy ice-pink and plastered with selfies with glamorous people, many of whom were vaguely recognisable and Ramona thought might be famous. One looked the spitting image of Taylor Swift.

Sydney had a king-size bed and matching shiny furniture. All the furniture in Ramona's room—her bed, dresser, art-deco mirror and two fringed lamps—were from op shops. The dresser had been in bad condition when they'd found it, but she and her mum had restored it together and now her room looked like something out of *Teen Magazine*, of which she had a massive collection. Her most favourite piece in the entire room was an exquisite iron birdcage that was far too pretty to ever put an actual bird in, but she wasn't sure any of her new friends would see the appeal.

Then again, they wouldn't ever see it because hell would freeze over before she ever invited Sydney, Kenzie and Nyra to their tiny rented flat. Her mum would be a nightmare if she did—trying to become besties with them and getting in their business.

As if they'd want to trek all the way out to Granville anyway!

After changing into their cozzies—Ramona praying none of her new friends noticed hers were last season ones she'd picked up from

Vinnies—they headed downstairs and out to the resort-style pool area, which had an actual view of the harbour. Although the water glistened and she was itching to go for a swim, the others appeared content to lie in the late afternoon sun, drinking Diet Cokes and taking selfies on the loungers in front of the pool house that was, like everything else, massive. It was probably bigger than her whole flat.

'What's in there?' she asked.

'Oh, a pool table, couches, TV, fridge, you know, that kind of thing. It hardly ever gets used.'

'Didn't you run away and move in there for a weekend once?' Kenzie asked.

Sydney nodded. 'Until London decided to join me.'

'What was it like going to a co-ed school?' Nyra asked Ramona out of the blue.

'Must have been like an all-you-can-eat buffet,' Kenzie joked, reaching for an olive from the fancy platter the infamous Maya had brought out a few minutes ago.

'Um …'

'Did you have a boyfriend?' asked Sydney.

Ramona didn't want to lie, but she also didn't want to admit she'd never so much as kissed a boy. She was fifteen, for crying out loud, but none of the boys at her old school would have looked twice at her.

'Or are girls more your thing? Everyone in London's class are lesbians and Nyra reckons she's still deciding.'

'I'm not still deciding,' Nyra snapped. 'I told you, I'm bi. I'm more interested in what's inside a person than the package they come in.'

'Who's London?' Ramona asked.

'Sydney's little sister,' Kenzie informed her. 'It's all the rage to be a lesbian in Year 7, but who can blame them? Boys are pretty icky at that age.'

'Your sister is called *London*?' Ramona said, before realising that might sound rude. 'I mean, it's cool.'

Sydney snorted. 'I think you mean cringe. Like we need to be reminded where our parents were when they conceived us.' She visibly shuddered and Ramona blushed.

She wondered where London was, but then again, this house was so huge you could probably live here for a year without bumping into anyone else. She looked across to Sydney who was now back to taking photos in her gold bikini and sending them to her boyfriend. 'So where'd you meet Blake?'

Sydney held up her phone. 'Tinder for teens, of course.'

'What?'

Nyra laughed. 'She means Snapchat.'

'Oh right.' Ramona tried to pretend she'd just had a mind blank for a moment. *Tinder for teens?* Her mother would die if she heard any such thing.

'Is it just you and your mum then?' Nyra asked after a while. 'No siblings?'

Ramona nodded.

'Half your luck,' Sydney said, and the others agreed. 'I'd give anything to be an only child.'

'It's not all it's cracked up to be.'

Ramona had spent a lot of her childhood longing for a little brother or sister, and the older she got the more she wished she had someone else around to soak up some of her mum's attention. If Deb had another child to fuss over, maybe she wouldn't have been so reluctant to let Ramona come tonight and maybe Ramona wouldn't feel so guilty about leaving her alone. She knew her mum loved her, but sometimes her love felt claustrophobic. How was she supposed to make new friends, become her own person, if Deb was always hovering?

As if on cue, her phone beeped, and she looked down to see a text message from her mum: *Hope you got to Sydney's safely. How was your day? Let me know what you're up to and don't forget your manners. Call me if there are ANY problems. Love you.*

'Yeah, I guess all the pressure's on you,' Nyra said.

'Huh?' Ramona asked, glaring at her phone before turning it over. She bet Nyra and Kenzie's parents weren't checking up on them.

'The pressure. At least my parents divide all their nagging between me and my older brothers,' Nyra continued, then paused a moment. 'You know, you probably have more siblings than all of us.'

Kenzie frowned. 'What do you mean?'

'Because of her being a donor baby,' Nyra clarified. 'Hell, you could have brothers and sisters all over Sydney.'

'All over Australia,' added Sydney, glancing up from her phone.

This wasn't news to Ramona, but she wasn't about to admit that sometimes she played a game when she was out where she scrutinised people, trying to see if she could spot any similarities to herself. It had started a few years back, when she and her mum were at the movies and the girl sitting a couple of rows in front of her looked familiar. It was only when the lights came on and they were leaving the cinema that she realised why—it was almost like looking in a mirror.

Ramona had blurted out her theory, that maybe the girl was also a donor baby, possibly even her sister. She'd been so excited, she'd begged Deb for the chance to run after her and ask the question, but her mum wouldn't allow it.

Even if you were related, that girl might have no idea about her origins and it's not our place to tell her.

'What if you meet someone and don't know you're related and ... *Ew.*' Kenzie screwed up her nose. 'Sorry, you probably don't want to think about that.'

Ramona forced a laugh, despite the thought horrifying her.

'What about your mum?' Nyra asked. 'She still single? Does she have a boyfriend?'

'Or do you have lots of "uncles" like Kenzie?' Sydney teased.

Kenzie gave her the finger. 'Shut up.'

'No, no boyfriend,' Ramona said.

'What? *Ever?*' Sydney looked at her as if she'd told them her mum had no limbs.

Ramona couldn't remember her mum ever mentioning a man—aside from the old blokes she worked with who were all married. She shook her head. 'I don't think so.'

'Maybe she's ACE,' suggested Nyra.

'What?' Ramona said, forgetting she wanted to look all knowledgeable in front of them.

'You know, asexual?' Nyra looked excited by the prospect. 'Doesn't wanna have sex with any gender.'

Kenzie cocked her head to the side. 'Could be, but not all ACE people don't wanna have sex, some just don't get the hots for *any*one.'

'You think that's your mum's issue?' Sydney asked.

'It's not an *issue*,' snapped Nyra. 'Just cos *you're* straight as, doesn't mean *everyone* is.'

'I don't know,' Ramona admitted. 'Maybe?'

The others barely heard her—they were now bickering about who was the most woke—but their conversation got her thinking.

Debra

An eerie silence greeted Deb when she got home. There were no shoes strewn across the floor and no mess in the kitchen left over from Ramona making herself an after-school snack.

When was the last time she'd been here without her daughter?

She'd been dreading this evening since Ramona first asked about the sleepover. Deb had insisted she call Sydney's parents and Ramona freaked out at the mere idea.

'I'm not just dropping you off at some stranger's house,' she'd tried to reason. 'They could be axe murderers or members of the mafia.'

Ramona had rolled her eyes, something she was getting very good at. 'You won't be dropping me off. You can meet her parents on Saturday morning when you pick me up.'

Somehow, Deb had found herself railroaded into agreeing, and now she only hoped it wouldn't be a decision she'd live to regret. She might have been joking about the axe murderers, but there were bad people in the world. No one knew this better than she did.

Dumping her things on the coffee table, she snatched up the remote and turned on the TV for company, then forced herself into the kitchen to make dinner. As she heated up leftover spaghetti, she glanced at the *one* text message she'd received from Ramona in response to her multiple ones that afternoon.

Stop stressing.

As if. That was like telling a child to stop growing or a dog to stop sniffing crotches. What else was she supposed to do all night? They usually spent Friday nights working on their latest miniature model, but she couldn't do that without Ramona.

Taking her bowl into the living room, she began flicking through the channels. Maybe she could distract herself with a movie. Her hand stilled on the remote when a preview for *You've Got Mail* flashed up in front of her.

Her heart clenched and she put her barely touched dinner on the coffee table. The rom-com was released the year she turned eighteen and had rapidly become her favourite. She must have watched it at least fifty times and had dreamed of one day visiting New York and finding the love of her life in such a romantic way. At the time *Sex and the City* was in its second season and Deb also fantasised about living such an exciting life as the ones she watched Carrie, Samantha, Charlotte and Miranda play out on screen. Years later, when the opportunity presented itself to further her studies in psychology in the Big Apple, she couldn't resist.

She'd settled into her new life well, got herself a casual job at Starbucks, hung out with fellow graduate students and enjoyed living in such a vibrant city. When a friend invited her to tag along to an Aussies in New York speed-dating night, she thought, why the hell not?

Despite the warm summer evening, Deb shivered at the memory. What would her life be like now if she'd stayed home that night?

She didn't usually let herself fantasise about that because it would mean she wouldn't have Ramona, and a life without her girl wasn't worth thinking about. But tonight, alone in their rented apartment, she couldn't help wondering.

Would she be living her dream, practising psychology? Would she have her own clinic? Would she be married with a couple of kids and an actual house with an actual mortgage she shared with her husband? Would they have a dog? Maybe even a couple of chickens on a quarter acre block. That was the life she'd craved growing up, but instead she'd got herself pregnant to a psycho.

She switched the TV off, snatched up the bowl and stood.

As she scraped her barely touched dinner into the bin, she eyed the time on the microwave. Not even 7 pm. What would Ramona be up to now? Would she be eating dinner? What would they have? Even if Deb sent her another text message, it was highly unlikely she'd respond. For the first time in her life, she wished she had social media so she could check out her daughter's Snapchat account, but even with the highest privacy settings, she didn't trust having her name or face anywhere on the internet. Allowing Ramona was terrifying enough, but putting herself out there would be way too risky. These days even normal people stalked their exes on Facebook, but the person she was worried about was anything but normal. That kind of access in the hands of the wrong person could put everything she'd done to protect herself and Ramona in jeopardy.

Deb sighed and glanced around the apartment, looking for something to distract her.

She went across to the bookshelf and plucked out an old copy of *Pride and Prejudice*, one of her comfort reads. These days she didn't have much time for books, but she hoped Jane Austen would work her magic.

Tonight, however, even her favourite novel couldn't take her mind off Ramona. She missed her. She missed her laughter and her anecdotes from the day. She missed her smile. She missed the way she stuck her tongue out when she was concentrating hard while gluing something together for one of their miniatures. She missed hearing the excitement in her voice as she talked about fashion and history. She missed Ramona's head resting against her shoulder as they sat together on the couch watching a movie. She even missed the scent of her strawberry shampoo.

God, she was pathetic.

Here she was home alone on a Friday night and instead of making the most of her freedom like most parents would be doing, she was a snivelling mess.

Feeling desperate, she was contemplating ringing her father when there was a knock at the door.

Quinn

Quinn thanked her Uber driver, then started up the path towards Deb's rather ugly red-brick apartment building. What had the architects in the sixties been thinking? A short, stocky old man who didn't seem to give a thought to security came out of the lobby as she was staring at the intercom trying to remember the apartment number.

'You heading in?' he asked, holding the door open.

'Yeah, thanks.'

On the second floor, she knocked on a door she felt almost certain belonged to her friend. It peeled open a fraction and Deb peered out.

'Hey there.' Quinn yanked a bottle of prosecco out of her bag. 'Does the offer for a girls' night still stand?'

'Oh my goodness!' Deb pulled the door wide open and burst into tears.

Quinn raised her eyebrows—'Looks like I'm here not a moment too soon'—as she stepped inside and wrapped an arm around her.

'I was this close to calling my dad,' Deb sobbed.

'Geez, things must be bad.'

Deb didn't speak much about her family, but a few months into their friendship, over their first dumplings lunch and, yes, a glass of wine, she'd told Quinn her mother left when she was ten and she wasn't close with her father. These days he lived overseas in Dubai and the way she spoke, their conversations were more obligatory than enjoyable. He hadn't been supportive of Deb's decision to have Ramona, which had caused a bit of a rift between them.

'Let's crack this and you can tell me all about it,' Quinn said.

Deb swiped the back of her hand over her eyes. 'There's nothing to tell really. I thought you were on a date?'

'Johan's not The One.' Quinn stepped past and headed into the kitchen in search of wineglasses.

'What happened?'

'He started telling me about this kid he's been coaching in tennis. He spoke with such passion, and it should have been cute, but I didn't feel a thing—not one tiny tinkle of chemistry. I looked him in the eyes, and I just knew he was not my Ride or Die. And I thought, why am I wasting my Friday night with this nice but boring, tennis-obsessed man, when I could be with my work wife? So here I am.'

'You just left him there in the restaurant? Alone?'

Quinn shrugged as she opened and closed yet another cupboard. 'I know. I'm a beast, but he'll get over it—plenty more girls online. Now, where the hell are your glasses?'

Deb reached for the cupboard above the fridge. 'I've only got one, but you can have it. I probably shouldn't drink in case Ramona needs me.'

'Why would she need you?'

'Um … maybe she'll decide she doesn't feel comfortable staying the night at a strange house and I'll have to go get her?'

'Okay. But that doesn't mean you can't have fun.' Quinn popped the cork. 'Ramona needs us, we'll call an Uber.'

'You've got an answer for everything, don't you?'

'You better believe it, girlfriend.' She handed Deb the proper glass and took a tumbler from the same cupboard, filling it almost to the brim.

'Thank you,' Deb said as they headed over to the couch.

'No worries. Now at least I know what to buy you for your birthday. So, why were you about to call your father?'

Deb took a long sip of her drink and then sighed. 'I was bored. And lonely. I'm pathetic, aren't I?'

'*No*. You're anything but pathetic.'

'I guess I'm just not used to being alone. It's always been me and Ramona against the world. I look forward to our Friday nights all week.' She gestured behind them to the small dining table that was covered in all sorts of craft paraphernalia. 'It's when we work on our models together.'

'But isn't it great she's making new friends?' Quinn said. 'It's tough at her age starting at a new school, and didn't she have some issues making connections at her old school?'

'Yeah.' Deb sighed. 'I know I should be happy for her, and I am, but I just don't know what to do or even who I am without her.'

As much as Quinn adored her friend—in many ways she'd become like the big sister Quinn never had—listening to her now, all she could think was that Deb seriously needed something in her life other than her daughter.

'How long has it been since you last spoke to your dad?'

'Um ...' Deb thought a moment. 'I left a message on his birthday last September, but he didn't call back and ... Oh, that's right, he called at Christmas to make sure I got the money he'd sent for Ramona. I could hear his other kids in the background, and we only spoke for a minute before his wife called him for lunch.'

'The wife that's the same age as you?'

Deb grimaced. 'That's the one. Actually, she's six months younger than me. How are *your* parents?'

'They're good. Dad's joined some local community garden and Mam's taken up Irish dancing again. She keeps sending me links for clubs over here, but I'm like, hell no, that was torturous enough when I was a kid. No way I'll voluntarily do it now.'

'I don't know ...' Deb grinned over the top of her glass. 'I think you'd look pretty good in those cute costumes.'

'The costumes are the only good part. Anyway, I thought they'd be bored out of their brains when they sold the restaurant, but they seem to be keeping busy. Although they do keep threatening to come for a visit. I made the mistake of telling Mam how much I love Forster and now she wants us to go on a holiday there. Together.'

Deb laughed at the expression on Quinn's face. 'Speaking of restaurants ... did you eat before you abandoned poor Johan? I think I need to have something else, or this wine is going straight to my head.'

'Maybe we should order in?'

'No, that'll take too long. I'll see what I can scrape together.'

As Deb headed into the kitchen, Quinn picked up an old magazine from a neat stack on the coffee table. She guessed it belonged to Ramona—she loved how Deb's daughter was obsessed with all things vintage. She flipped through the pages, shaking her head at the images of women in aprons, pearls and pretty dresses advertising kitchen appliances alongside slogans like 'wifesaver' and 'my washdays are now holidays'. As if these ads weren't preposterous enough, an article about romance made her laugh so hard she almost spilt her drink.

'What's so funny?' Deb asked, returning with a plate of cheese, crackers, dip and carrot sticks.

'Have you seen this? It's an article about how to get a husband. Seriously, no wonder I haven't found Mr Right yet. Turns out I've been doing it all wrong.'

'What should you have been doing?'

As Deb sat, Quinn began to read. 'Number one—get a dog and walk it. Number two—have your car break down at strategic places.'

'What happens if you don't have a car? Could you make one of your rollerskate wheels fall off on purpose?'

Quinn snorted and continued. Other suggestions included reading the obituaries—apparently that's where eligible widowers were to be found—taking up golf, sitting on a park bench and feeding pigeons, becoming a nurse or air 'stewardess', volunteering for jury duty and befriending ugly men.

'"Handsome is as handsome does",' Quinn read. 'What exactly does that mean?'

'I think it means you shouldn't judge someone by their looks. That what's inside is more important.' Deb gestured towards the magazine. 'Go on, this is hilarious.'

Quinn grinned, happy to have distracted Deb from Ramona. 'Apparently I should get a job demonstrating fishing tackle in a sporting goods store but *not* take a job in a company run largely by women.'

'I guess that's because so many people meet their partners at work.'

Quinn nodded.

'Well, you're on the right track there, then,' Deb said. 'Plenty of men at The Energy Co.'

'Tell me about it,' she scowled.

The two of them often complained about the demographics at The Energy Co. The sports drink industry tended to attract more men than women, and the senior positions were filled almost entirely by middle-aged white men. Not long after they'd first met in the copy room, Shaun had brought in someone to run diversity and inclusion training for all employees, but they were fairly sure it was all about ticking boxes as they were yet to see any evidence of change.

'Next time one of the directors quit, if they don't hire a woman, I'm out of there. And I'll set fire to the building on my way out.'

'I'm surprised that's not on the list.'

'What? Arson?'

'Yeah—set something on fire and wait for all the handsome firefighters to come and rescue you.'

The list continued to crack them up as it got more and more ridiculous.

Wear a bandaid—apparently men would stop and ask what happened.

Buy a convertible—'What if you're not rolling in cash?'

Deb suggested robbing a bank. 'If you get caught, maybe the arresting police officer will be single?'

If you dye your hair, pick a shade and stick to it.

'That's where you're going wrong,' Deb laughed as Quinn ran a hand through her currently magenta-coloured hair. Last month it had been green, the month before streaked purple and black.

Dress differently from other girls in the office.

'You're definitely doing that one. You always look amazing. I feel like a right frump next to you.'

'You're not a frump,' Quinn said emphatically, 'but you sure do a good job of hiding your assets.'

'What assets? I'm a forty-two-year-old woman who still hasn't managed to lose my baby weight fifteen years after giving birth.'

'You have curves I'd die for. And you're very pretty. Don't underestimate yourself. But I don't dress for men—I dress to make myself feel good. Honestly, you should try something other than black one day—you'll be amazed at the effect.'

'What's next on the list?' Deb asked.

Quinn focused back on the article. '"Get a sunburn". What the actual? Who wrote this crap? I might be desperate to meet the love of my life but even I draw the line at courting cancer for him. "Watch your vocabulary". Do you think that means I need to curb my swearing?'

'Probably.'

'Fuck it.'

They both laughed.

'"Double date with a gay, happily married couple". Ooh, do you think I should ask Dec and Darpan to come to dinner with me and Bako? Assuming tomorrow's date goes well, that is.'

'I'm pretty sure that wasn't what they meant by *gay* all those years ago,' Deb said, reaching for a carrot stick.

'Oh, *of course*. I forget gay used to mean something else entirely.' She sighed and continued reading. '"Don't be too fussy".'

'I hate to ask,' Deb said, 'but do you think maybe that's your issue? Since we've met you've dated, how many guys? And some seem to have real potential, but the moment it looks like things might be getting serious, you pull back. It's like you're scared if you commit to one, someone better might be just around the corner?'

'I'm not fussy, I just have high standards.'

Accidentally have your handbag fly open, scattering all its contents on the street—any man would run a mile if her bag spilled out in front of them.

'"Rent a billboard and post your picture and phone number on it"—wonder how much that'd cost?'

'You could always try going on a reality TV show?' Deb suggested.

'Been there, done that.'

'What?' Deb sat up straight. 'How do I not know about this?'

'Oh, it was before our time. I applied to go on *Farmer Wants a Wife* and *The Bachelor* but I didn't even get close, then I watched a couple of those shows and decided it was a lucky escape. For certs, I'd have been the one they made out to be the villain.'

By the time they'd finished going through the list, the bottle of wine was empty, and Deb produced another almost full one. 'Sorry,' she said, 'it's been open since Monday night, so I'm not sure it'll taste very good anymore.'

Neither of them cared. It was Friday night and wine was wine. Their tastebuds had already been numbed by the first bottle.

'Do you think you'll ever date again?' Quinn asked.

Deb stared long and hard into her glass. 'I doubt it. From my limited experience before I had Ramona, relationships are more trouble than they're worth. Men are more trouble than they're worth.'

Quinn had only heard bits and pieces about the boyfriends Deb had had before she decided to give up on love and have a baby on her own, but she'd heard enough to sense that her friend had dated some right wankers.

'I might not have found The One yet,' Quinn said, 'and sure, I've met some creeps that I never want to run into again as long as I live, but I've also met some really awesome men. Men like my dad, my brothers and Darpan, who are kind and genuine and wouldn't hurt a fly.'

'Hmm …' Deb smiled but didn't sound convinced. 'Pity your brothers are all taken—maybe I'd consider one of them. Then again, I've got Ramona to think about. It's been just us for so long, I'm not sure she'd cope with an intruder. Honestly, I'm fine. I know I was a bit tender tonight when you first arrived, but I'm happy with my lot. I love my life. And I definitely don't need a man to complicate it.'

'Okay, fine. I get it.' Quinn gulped the rest of her drink and reached for the bottle. She knew when she was flogging a dead horse.

'Anyway,' Deb said, 'now that we've got the talking about boys part of our girls' night out of the way, shall we watch a movie?'

'Excellent plan. But only if I get to pick. What are you in the mood for?'

Deb reached for the remote and handed it to her. 'Anything but a romance. I've had enough talking love and men for one night.'

Ramona

Ramona reached for her phone the moment she woke up and couldn't believe it was almost four in the afternoon. Then again, she'd got barely a wink of sleep last night at Sydney's place. She pulled herself out of bed and zombie-walked towards the kitchen, her stomach rumbling loud enough to wake the dead.

'Sleeping Beauty finally rises,' said her mum as she passed her ironing school uniforms in the lounge room.

'Haha.' Ramona stifled a yawn as she yanked open the fridge. 'Did you go shopping today? If I don't eat in the next thirty seconds, I'll die!'

Deb chuckled. 'Do you want me to make you a toastie?'

Slumping against the bench, Ramona nodded. 'Thanks. Just cheese, please?' She filled a glass of water and took a sip. Her throat was parched—likely from the vodka she'd tried last night—but she didn't want to gulp it down and make her mum suspicious.

'I take it you had a good night?' Deb said as she pulled a couple of slices from a loaf of bread.

'It was awesome.'

'What did you do?'

She'd asked her the same question on their way home, but Ramona had been half asleep, too out of it for conversation. It wasn't just the late night, but as much as she liked her new friends, she couldn't relax around them. They were all so cool—they knew everything about the latest music, TV shows and fashion trends— whereas Ramona could only pretend to be interested in that stuff. And that was exhausting. She'd tried to keep up but felt terrified they'd catch her out, discover she was truly a weirdo and kick her out of their group.

'Oh, you know, the usual sleepover stuff. We spent most of the evening in Sydney's pool and then we watched a couple of movies. She has a massive TV in her bedroom.'

'Lucky girl.' Deb slapped the sandwich in the toaster machine. 'What did you watch?'

'*House of Gucci* and *Gunpowder Milkshake*.'

'*Gunpowder Milkshake*? What kind of movie is that?'

'It's a thriller, but it wasn't bad or anything,' she added, cursing herself for not saying they watched *The Sound of Music*. Deb had always been overprotective and still didn't like Ramona watching MA-rated movies even though she was almost sixteen.

'And what did you have for dinner?'

Ramona couldn't help being annoyed by the inquisition, but if she snapped, it would only make things worse. 'We ordered in from this fancy sushi place nearby.'

'I didn't think you liked sushi?'

'I was a guest so I couldn't exactly be fussy, besides, it wasn't that bad.' She'd swallowed it down with Diet Coke laced with vodka.

Deb removed the toastie, cut it in half and put it onto a plate. 'I'm glad you had fun.'

Ramona really wanted to take it into her bedroom, but eating there wasn't allowed—heaven forbid she get crumbs on the carpet. Instead, she flopped onto the couch and soon started to feel human again.

'Thanks for the food,' she said, standing to take her empty plate to the sink.

'Want to work on our bookshop?' Deb gestured to the model on the table. 'Or do you have homework?'

'I'm going to do it tomorrow.'

The last thing Ramona wanted to do right now was craft with her mother. Making miniatures had been their thing since she'd been little and desperate for a doll house. Instead of buying one, Deb bought supplies to make it. They'd enjoyed the project so much they'd been creating tiny models ever since. Their latest was a bookshop and they were in the process of making all the bookshelves and covering tiny books with tiny paper jackets.

Deb loved it so much that Ramona couldn't bring herself to tell her she was losing interest. Maybe she could spare an hour, but if her mum thought she was going to be sharing more about last night, she had another think coming.

'Yeah, we can do some,' she said. 'Just let me get my phone.'

By the time she returned, Deb had brought a bowl of M&Ms to the table and was sorting wooden pieces for yet another bookshelf. She passed a ziplock bag containing more tiny pieces to Ramona. 'Why don't you start on the ladder?'

Ramona took the bag and began to sort pieces. 'So, what did *you* get up to last night?'

'Oh.' Deb's face lit up. 'I had a lovely evening actually. Quinn came over.'

'Really?' Ramona couldn't hide her surprise. She'd met her mum's work friend a couple of times and Deb talked about her a lot, but they didn't really hang out outside of office hours.

'Yeah. We watched a movie too, although unlike *some*,' Deb winked, 'I was in bed by midnight.'

'What movie?' Ramona asked, not really caring about the answer.

'Ramona! Are you listening to a word I'm saying?' Deb asked after a bit.

'Sorry.' She blinked. She'd been thinking about the conversation she'd had with her friends last night. 'I was just wondering … could I ask you a question?'

Deb's smirk changed into a full-blown smile. 'Of course. Anything. Anytime.'

'Why did you decide to have me?'

Her hands stilled on the two pieces of wood she'd been gluing. 'I had you because I desperately wanted you.'

'But you were pretty young, right? Didn't you think you might meet someone you *could* have a baby with?' After hearing about Kenzie's mum's string of never-ending boyfriends, Ramona realised how weird it was that her own mother had never shown any interest in dating. She wasn't ancient—she'd only been twenty-seven when she had Ramona. If Deb had a boyfriend maybe he'd take some of the pressure off her—she'd be busy with him instead of worrying about what Ramona was up to. 'Was it because you're not attracted to men?'

'What?! Why would you think that?'

'Well, it seems a pretty big decision to decide to have a baby on your own so young, so I thought maybe it was because you didn't think you'd ever find a man you wanted to have a family with.'

'I'm not a lesbian, if that's what you're asking.'

'I'm not. I was actually wondering if you're … if you're asexual.' Ramona's cheeks burned—this was not the kind of conversation she'd ever thought she'd have with her mum.

'A-what?'

'Asexual. It means you're not attracted—you know, in *that* kind of way—to others.'

'I know what it means, but what's brought this on?' Deb reached across and took hold of Ramona's hand. 'Sweetheart, are you worried about *your* sexuality? You're only fifteen. There's plenty of time to have those kinds of feelings.'

Ramona snatched her hand back. 'I'm almost *sixteen*, but no, this isn't about me. I'm asking about you! As far as I know you've never had a boyfriend and I was just wondering … why?'

'I've been attracted to men before.' Deb looked slightly affronted. 'I had plenty of boyfriends in my late teens and through my twenties—I just didn't feel the desire to settle down with anyone. And I don't know why people feel the need to label everything these days. I'm sure you'll find someone you like one day, but there's no rush. Whatever you do you must *never* feel pressured to do something with someone that you're not one hundred per cent—'

Oh geez, Ramona could feel a lecture coming on about respect and consent, and that had not been her intention at all when she started this conversation. Deb had totally missed the point. 'I *know*, Mum. I'm not stupid. But if you *are* attracted to men,' she persisted, 'then why have you never even gone out with anyone since having me?'

'Well, I guess there are a few reasons,' Deb began. 'I don't meet many new people and going on dates would have been impossible when you were little, because I didn't have any family nearby who I could leave you with.'

'Haven't you heard of babysitters?'

'Babysitters are expensive, and I didn't trust anyone with my precious daughter. There are dodgy people out there. I didn't want to expose you to that. Besides, you always said you didn't want to share me with anyone else.'

'I did?'

'Sure, when you were little, you came home from school one day and announced that one of your friends' mums was getting married, that she was going to have a stepdad. You were distraught—you made me promise I'd never do such a thing, that it would always just be the two of us.'

Ramona vaguely remembered that conversation. 'But I was only … what? Five?'

'Six, I think.'

'Well, that was an unfair thing to ask.'

'It was never an issue. I never needed anyone but you.'

But Ramona only felt stifled by this confession. It wasn't natural. 'You know, I don't need a babysitter anymore and I promise I'm not going to chuck a tanty if you decide you want to go on a date. In fact, I think you should.'

'What's brought this on?' Deb grabbed a handful of M&Ms and shoved them in her mouth. Usually, she limited herself to only a few over their whole crafting session.

'Nothing. I just don't want you to end up lonely, you know … when I leave home.'

'Planning on doing that shortly, are you?'

'No,' Ramona said, exasperated, 'but I might not be around as much anymore now I've got new friends. I don't want to feel guilty thinking about you here all alone.'

'Guilty? You've got nothing to feel guilty about. I certainly don't want to be a burden on you.'

'That's not what I mean.' This was not going at all how Ramona had hoped. 'I just really think you should consider doing something for you.'

'You sound like Quinn.'

'How?'

'She's constantly on at me to sign up for one of those dating apps.'

'That's a great idea. I could help you.'

'What do you know about dating apps, young lady?'

'Well, nothing.' Her cheeks heated as she thought about 'Tinder for teens' and the messages she'd already had from random boys asking to hook up. 'But I know my way around a smartphone better than you.'

Deb offered a small smile of concession. 'That's true.'

'Oh my God, does that mean you're actually thinking of doing it?'

'Why are you so excited by this?'

'I just think you deserve some happiness, Mum.' *And I deserve some peace!* She pushed back her seat and stood. 'I'll go get your phone.'

'Hold your horses, Ramona Lee Fast. I haven't agreed to anything.'

Ramona's heart sank. 'Do you promise you'll give it some thought?'

Deb hesitated a moment and then nodded. 'Okay. I'll think about it.'

Debra

Deb hadn't meant it when she told Ramona she'd think about venturing into online dating, but, weirdly, since then, she hadn't been able to think about anything else.

While she washed up their dishes, finished the week's ironing and finally dropped onto the couch to watch some TV, Ramona's words haunted her.

I don't want to feel guilty thinking about you here all alone.

Alone. Is that how she saw her—as some lonely, pathetic, sad case? Worse, did she consider Deb a burden? *Her* burden.

All she'd ever wanted was a good relationship with Ramona—she wanted them to be friends, for her to feel like she could come to her with anything—and she thought she'd succeeded, but doubt began to gnaw at her heart. The last thing she wanted was for her daughter to feel guilty about having her own life. She'd only hesitated about letting her go to Sydney's place because she didn't know anything about her family. That was normal parental behaviour. Wasn't it?

Then again, what would *she* know about normal parental behaviour? Her parenting decisions were based on actively making sure she was nothing like her own mother and reading every parenting book she could get her hands on.

Still … she had to admit Ramona was right about one thing. She *had* felt lonely. Until Quinn showed up, Deb had wished her daughter was home. Desperately. And judging by Ramona's concern this afternoon, she'd suspected as much.

Oh God. Did she rely too much on her?

This thought made her sick to her gut. The last fifteen years had passed in a flash and Deb had never really thought about what she'd do once Ramona was an adult. But that should be *her* concern, not her daughter's, and she vowed to somehow show Ramona she had nothing to worry about.

As she tried to pay attention to Jamie Oliver stuffing fish on TV, her gaze kept drifting to her laptop. Could she risk signing up to the website Quinn mentioned?

Maybe she could do something else instead? Take some sort of night class or start a new exercise regime. Deb laughed to herself— that made it sound like she already had *some* kind of regime.

She tapped away at the keyboard, looking up local gyms and night school offerings, and while there were plenty of possibilities, none of them spoke to her. Before she could talk herself out of it, she typed 'eMatch' into her browser.

Surprisingly, the site seemed less daunting than what she'd seen of Quinn's dating apps—it promised to choose matches for her and only a certain number at a time, which sounded good. No way she could handle the pressure of swiping left or right, never mind juggling the number of men that Quinn did. If Deb was going to do this—and that was a massive *if*—then she wanted to make it as simple as possible.

To get a proper look at how it all worked, you had to sign up. She gulped, wishing she'd bought another bottle of wine. Right now, a little Dutch courage would go a long way, but all she had was a cup of herbal tea. Telling herself she could stop any time, she answered the registration questions—'I am a woman looking for a man'—and then, her heart thumping, clicked 'Join Now'.

A compatibility quiz appeared. The first few questions were straightforward, even the one asking why she was looking for a partner. There were lots of options but nothing about 'because her best friend and daughter were pestering her'. In the end she went with 'someone to spend free time with' and 'so she wasn't alone'.

Some of the questions were quite specific, like what she thought of cheating in a relationship. How do you feel about climate change? Which party did you vote for in the last election? What values matter to you the most? Having always liked quizzes, Deb enjoyed contemplating her answers to various situations and almost forgot the reason she was doing so until she got to the very end and had to fill in the final details for account activation.

Her heart sank. Even though it said only her first name would be visible to other members, they required her surname for their records. And that felt too risky.

That's the end of that then.

She was about to close her laptop, when a thought struck. Perhaps she could use an alias? Her middle name and her mother's surname—Lee Alexandra? That sounded quite good, much more exotic than Debra Fast, and it wouldn't exactly be a lie.

Oh, my goodness. She reached for her tea and took a gulp—was she really contemplating this?

Her insides thrummed as if they were being played like a guitar. She felt light-headed as she allowed herself to think about her own needs. What would it feel like to go out to dinner with a handsome man? Or even just a nice one. She wasn't picky. Although tall would be good. And broad-shouldered if possible. She closed her eyes and imagined holding someone's hand again, a man's hand. Having his arms wrapped around her. Feeling his lips pressing firmly but tenderly against her own.

She shivered.

Logically, Deb knew Quinn was right—there had to be some good men swimming among the sharks. Now she was older and wiser, she'd be more discerning.

Opening her eyes, she typed the name Lee Alexandra and began to fill in the rest of the personal details—her postcode, date of birth, religion (or lack thereof), email address. She paused, her fingers hovering over the question asking if she had children. On the one hand, she didn't want to bring Ramona into the equation at all, but ticking 'no kids' wouldn't simply be a white lie, it could drastically affect the kind of guy they matched her with. If she were to meet someone special, she wanted them to know that she and Ramona were a package deal.

Argh. This shouldn't be so hard. No wonder Quinn treated dating like a game—you could when you were young and had no baggage.

After another sip of tea, she ignored the guilt and ticked the box that said, 'No kids', clicking continue before she could think better of it.

'What? No way!' she shrieked as she came face to face with the biggest hurdle of all.

They wanted her to upload a photo. *Of course.*

She might be able to hide behind a fake name, but she could hardly get away with using someone else's picture. And the idea of posting her own gave her heart palpitations. What if, somehow, *he* saw her? It might have been years since she'd last seen Oscar, but his threats still haunted her dreams. *You'll never be able to leave me,*

Deb. You and me, we're meant for each other. I'll go to the end of the earth to find you and prove that to you.

'Mum? Are you okay?'

'Huh?' Deb startled and snapped her laptop shut as Ramona entered the living room.

'I heard a scream. I thought you'd hurt yourself.'

'No, nothing like that. I was just watching something and ... never mind.' Shaking her head and putting the laptop down on the coffee table, she stood and feigned a yawn. 'I'm going to call it a night. See you in the morning, okay?'

'Okay.' Ramona blinked as if confused that she hadn't told her to put down her phone and go to bed as well, but Deb felt too shaken by her near brush with online dating to think straight.

While getting ready for bed, she eyed herself in the mirror and shook her head at the face looking back at her. It looked every bit its forty-two years—there were dark shadows under her eyes, grey was showing at her roots, her eyebrows looked like two bushy caterpillars, and—to her great dismay—a thick, black whisker poked out of the bottom of her chin. Rinsing her toothbrush, she picked up the tweezers and yanked out the offending hair before promptly bursting into tears.

She was hardly recognisable as that girl who'd ventured off to New York, excited about having an adventure. Once upon a time she'd taken pride in her appearance, but at some stage she'd let things slide. She'd let her hair grow out and kind of just got used to tying it up in no-nonsense fashion off her face. There didn't seem much point paying for fancy waxing appointments, and she couldn't remember the last time she'd bothered changing her earrings or wearing a necklace.

Oh my God.

She hadn't only given up on men, she'd given up on herself!

Ramona

'Okay, ladies,' finished Ms Rose, after explaining what their major assessment of the semester would be, 'get yourself into pairs and discuss which era you'd like to choose as your focus. We're going from 1900 right through to the nineties, and I don't want any double ups. There are twenty of you, so one decade for each pair.'

And there was that dreaded word—pair.

Ramona shuddered, nausea swelling in her stomach as all around her, girls scrambled to grab a partner.

'Scuse me, Miss.' Nyra's hand shot into the air, and she spoke before being given permission. 'Can Sydney and I have a threesome with Ramona?'

Giggles erupted around them, but Ms Rose didn't so much as crack a smile. 'Ramona can work with Lucy.' She pointed towards the redhead loner who sat at the front of the room. Alone.

Despite them sharing a number of classes, the girl who wore glasses, had freckles *and* acne covering her face, and apparently spent every lunchtime in the library, had still never said a word to her. Lucy was one of the kids her friends warned her about avoiding. She remembered Sydney's exact words: *I reckon her dad must have slept with the headmistress to get her into the fashion program. A camel has better style than that stutterer.*

'Ramona, you move to the front next to Lucy. There's more space here.'

At Ms Rose's words, she reluctantly gathered her things. Sydney and Nyra shot her conciliatory looks.

'Hi,' Ramona said as she lowered herself into the seat next to Lucy.

'H-h … hello,' Lucy said, only meeting her gaze for a second.

'So, what's your favourite fashion decade?'

Lucy shrugged.

'First half or second half of the century?' Ramona asked, praying for the first.

Another shrug—this time only one shoulder as if she really couldn't be arsed. Ramona began to get annoyed as everyone around them started calling out like they were bidding on an auction.

Sydney and Nyra grabbed the sixties, the twenties were next to go—no surprises there, everyone loved flapper dresses—the eighties went next, then the nineties, the forties followed. The buzz of a new project filled the air.

'How about the fifties?' Ramona asked.

'I d-d … don't know. Y-you choose,' Lucy said, staring at her nails, which were bitten down practically to the cuticles.

If they didn't act fast, they were going to be stuck with the seventies, which had to be one of the most ridiculous eras in the history of fashion. How were you supposed to make psychedelic patterns look good on a red carpet?

Ramona shot her hand into the air. 'Miss, we'll take the fifties.'

With a nod, Ms Rose turned and scrawled 'Ramona and Lucy' on the whiteboard next to '1950'.

She bit down on a smile; she could work with just about anyone if she got to do a project featuring some of the best designers of all time. Although she loved all vintage fashion, the fifties held a special place in her heart. The assignment had two components—a theory and a practical. Each duo would have to do a presentation about the major new trends of that decade, including brief biographies of the most influential designers. And then they'd have to design their own ball gown, incorporating the most distinctive features of that decade into a dress that could be worn today.

'Think a gown for the red carpet of the Academy Awards,' Ms Rose said.

Ramona opened her laptop, her fingers already poised on the keyboard. 'So, how do you want to do this?'

'I … I'm not really good at essays and s-stuff, but I can d-draw okay.'

No way was this chick leaving Ramona to do all the hard work while she just did a few sketches.

'How about we take half a decade each,' she suggested, 'and make notes on the major trends and designers. I'll take 1950 to 1955.'

Lucy simply nodded and opened her laptop.

They spent the last ten minutes of class, heads down in silence. When the siren went for lunch, Lucy handed Ramona a tiny piece of paper and fled the room.

Here's my number and email address if you need to talk about anything before next class.

Ramona stuffed the note into her pocket and hurried back to Sydney and Nyra.

'It's so lame you have to work with the stutterer,' Sydney said as they joined the hordes in the corridors walking towards the cafeteria.

'She, like, barely speaks anyway, so how are you, like, supposed to make any progress?' Nyra asked.

Ramona grimaced. 'Guess I'll have to carry most of the load if I don't wanna fail.'

'So stupid,' Nyra said. 'We'd have made such an awesome threesome.'

'Who's having a threesome?' Kenzie came up behind them as they entered the cafeteria. From the scent of things, quesadillas were today's special. Ramona's stomach grumbled—she loved Mexican, but could only afford to buy lunch once a week.

'Poor Ramona got stuck with the stutterer in our semester-long fashion project,' Nyra explained. 'Ms Rose wouldn't let the three of us work together.'

'What's the assignment anyway?' asked Kenzie.

Nyra quickly explained.

'And what eras have you got?'

'We've got the sixties,' Sydney gloated. 'Our gown is gunna be to-die-for.'

'And Ramona has the fifties,' said Nyra.

Kenzie frowned. 'What's the fifties famous for again?'

Ramona opened her mouth, but Sydney got in first. 'Those awful poodle skirts they wore in *Grease*. It was all about being feminine and elegant, like Sandra Dee.'

'I don't mind a poodle skirt,' Nyra announced, 'but the sixties will be so much more fun.'

Ramona almost defended her favourite era, explaining there was a lot more to it than you saw in *Grease*, but thankfully, they arrived at the front of the queue and the others were distracted buying their food.

They walked back to Drysdale and as her friends dug into their quesadillas, Ramona unwrapped her usual—cheese and salad sandwich on wholegrain bread.

'Hey, Ny,' Sydney said. 'Do you wanna come over to my place after rowing on Saturday morning and work on our assignment?'

'Does anyone know where Lucy lives?' Ramona asked. They might have to work outside school hours as well.

They all sniggered again, and she waited for them to fill her in on the joke.

'Behind some church,' Nyra said eventually. 'Her dad's a priest.'

Ramona's hand froze with her sandwich halfway to her mouth. 'But ... I thought priests couldn't have kids? I didn't think they could even get married. Aren't they supposed to be, you *know* ...'

'Yep.' Sydney snickered. 'But he had her before he signed up. Her mum was an addict or something. She's not around anymore.'

'Jesus.' Ramona let out a long breath. 'Why doesn't she go to a Catholic school?'

'Eff knows,' Kenzie said. 'Guess now that you're gunna be spending a lot of time with her, you'll be able to find out.'

'But, if you have to go to her place, be careful,' Sydney added, wriggling her perfectly waxed eyebrows. 'We all know what priests are like.'

Nyra shook her head and laughed. 'Nah, Ramona will be fine— she's not a little boy!'

Debra

Mid Monday morning in the thick of a professional development day about ransomware and how the finance and IT departments could protect themselves against what was becoming a real threat to big corporations, an email notification from Quinn appeared in the top corner of Deb's laptop. She read it surreptitiously.

Can you do lunch today? I have something BIG I want to discuss.

Deb inwardly groaned. Lunch with Quinn would be far more enjoyable than sharing stale sandwiches brought in from the café downstairs while listening to her colleagues talk about their golf handicap and the size of the fish they caught on the weekend, but all those attending today's training were expected to partake in the group lunch.

Sorry, I'm in training all day. Is this about Bako? He didn't propose, did he?

The last she'd heard from Quinn was a message on Saturday arvo saying they were going back to Bako's place, but then radio silence. Quinn had a rule about never sleeping with a guy until at least the third date, which meant although she went on lots of dates, she rarely took that leap. Bako must be something special for her to have made an exception.

'Something funny, Denise?' asked Steve from IT who was running today's seminar.

Deb blinked up at his smarmy face, with his gelled-back hair and creepy moustache that he twirled whenever he was making snide remarks.

'No, Steve.' She was tempted to call him Stuart. He'd known her how long and still didn't remember her name? 'There's definitely nothing funny about cyber pirates.'

'Good.' He nodded and turned back to his PowerPoint.

She waited until it was safe again, then read Quinn's reply.

Yeah, in a way it is. I did a lot of soul-searching this weekend and I've come to a decision. I know it's a school night, but don't suppose you have time for a quick drink after work?

Deb's curiosity was well and truly piqued. Normally she aimed to get home as soon as possible, but a drink would be a welcome reward after sitting in this stuffy room listening to Steve drone on for the better part of eight hours. Besides, going out with Quinn would show Ramona that she wasn't a lonely middle-aged woman with no social life.

That sounds great. Meet in the lobby just after 5?

*

'I thought that day would never end,' Deb said as she approached Quinn who was already waiting downstairs. She looked slightly different, and it took a moment for Deb to realise it was because she didn't have her phone in her hand.

Quinn half-chuckled. 'I don't know … weren't you learning about pirates? That sounds like fun to me. And kinda sexy.'

'Trust me, there's nothing sexy about these types of pirates. Or Steve, who was doing the presenting.'

Quinn visibly shuddered.

'I don't know if he really doesn't remember my name or he gets it wrong on purpose, to make me feel as if I'm not important enough to remember.'

'Either way, he's a jackass,' Quinn said.

Deb nodded. 'Anyway, enough about work, let's go get that drink. I can't wait to hear about your soul-searching.'

They headed to the pub just around the corner and Quinn grabbed a table while Deb bought the drinks. Wine at a bar on a weeknight was not in her budget but her friend looked like she needed a little TLC.

'So, what's going on?' she asked as she delivered two glasses of rosé to the table.

'I'm going on a digital detox,' Quinn said.

'What?' Deb's hand paused with her glass midway to her mouth. This could only mean one thing. 'Is this because of Bako?'

Quinn nodded, but she didn't look happy.

'I'm confused.'

'Well,' Quinn began, 'we were having such a fabulous day—skating in the morning, then an early lunch at the Opera Bar, basking in the sun and feeding each other rock oysters. He's an excellent skater, a great conversationalist, and I was super attracted to him, so when he asked if I wanted to see his place, I jumped at the chance.'

Deb nodded.

'Anyway, his house was … wow. It almost had better views than the restaurant. And his bed. It's the comfiest one I've ever slept in. Not that there was much sleeping.'

'But?' Deb prompted when Quinn went quiet.

'I stuffed it up. After we did the deed, he went to dispose of the condom, and I took the chance to check the apps. My fingers were twitching because I hadn't so much as looked at my phone for a couple of hours. I was checking out the new options on Tinder when—'

Deb gasped. 'He caught you.'

'Yep.' Quinn looked like she'd kicked a puppy. 'He got really upset. Said he couldn't believe I was searching for my next fuck while still in his bed. He called me a liar because I'd told him I was looking for serious, and said if he knew I was only after cheap hook-ups he'd never have invited me home.'

'Oh, honey.'

She sniffed. 'I told him I wasn't like that, that I desperately wanted to find Mr Right, but the evidence in my hand said otherwise. He asked me to leave and then he blocked me.'

'Hey.' Deb reached across and squeezed Quinn's hand. It was the first time she'd seen her looking truly glum. 'You stuffed up, but he sounds slightly controlling. It was only your second date, it's not like you were exclusive or anything.'

In fact, he reminded her of someone she once knew—all charm when they were trying to get you into bed, but with a temper that could flare up at the least thing.

'I guess you're right. And if he was The One, then we'd be able to work through this or I wouldn't have messed up in the first place. Although maybe he had a point. Sure, I want serious and commitment, but …' Quinn let out a long sigh as she fiddled with her earring. 'It felt so good when I was swiping in his bed. Like the time Mam made me give up chocolate for Lent but I stole some from the corner deli and scoffed it before I got home. When I was skating home with my tail between my legs, it clicked. I have an addiction to dating apps that's sabotaging my chances of ever finding any real connection with anyone.'

'So what are you going to do about it?'

Quinn sat up straight. 'I'm throwing in the towel. I'm done with the apps. I've been using them for years with no luck whatsoever. They consume my every waking hour and many hours when I *should* be sleeping. You were right on Friday night.'

'I was?' Deb had drunk way more alcohol than usual that evening and struggled to remember any words of wisdom she may have uttered.

'Yes. You said I'm scared to commit to anyone in case someone better is just around the corner. I think you hit the nail on the head. After what happened with Bako, I did a little research and dating app addiction is a real thing. The only way to cure me is to go cold turkey.'

Deb's hand halted—her glass hanging in mid-air—in surprise. 'So, you're giving up your pursuit of Mr Right?'

'No. I still believe there's someone out there for me, but it's time to try a different approach. I've been thinking about that article—The Husband List? I think maybe there's some merit in it, so I've decided to try to find a man the way my granny probably found hers.'

Deb laughed so hard she snorted, a trait she tried her utmost never to do because the noise mortified her.

'I know most of the list is ridiculous,' Quinn said, 'but—'

'That wasn't why I laughed.' Deb inhaled sharply and wiped the tears from her eyes. 'You weren't the only one doing some soul-searching over the weekend.'

'Oh?'

'Ramona told me she's worried about me being alone. She thinks I should start dating. I almost signed up to eMatch.'

Quinn's eyes went wide. 'You *what*?'

'How hilarious that when you decided to give up, I almost began.'

'Hang on.' Quinn held up a hand. 'I really want to hear this story, but I think we're going to need another drink and I'm famished. Do you have time for dinner?'

Deb thought of her bank balance. Two glasses of wine had already blown her weekly budget.

'My shout,' Quinn said as if reading her thoughts. 'Come on … live a little.'

'Okay. You've twisted my arm, but let me just call Ramona and tell her I'll be late.'

'I'll go get us some menus and another drink.'

Despite being Monday, the pub had filled with after work revellers and Deb struggled to hear Ramona, but two seconds after she hung up, her daughter sent a thumbs-up emoji followed by: *Have a good night, Mum. Say hi to Quinn for me.*

'Ramona says hi,' Deb said when Quinn returned with a whole bottle of bubbly, two glasses and two menus.

'Tell that sweet child "Hi" back.'

'Why the change in drink?' Deb asked, taking hers from Quinn.

'Because we're celebrating you finally deciding to start dating again.'

'I think you misheard; I said I *almost* joined eMatch but luckily I saw sense before publishing my profile.'

'You do know I'm going to change your mind on that.' Quinn frowned as she checked the menu. 'I'm thinking the creamy spinach, pine nut and cheese ravioli. You?'

'That sounds good, but I wouldn't be able to eat for the rest of the week if I had that. I'll have the green salad with chicken and avocado.'

Quinn grimaced but skipped off to place their orders anyway. In her twenties, Deb had also been able to eat pretty much whatever she wanted, but her metabolism slowed the moment she had Ramona.

'Okay.' Quinn sounded like she meant business when she sat down again. 'Take me right back to the beginning. You said Ramona thinks you should start dating?'

Deb relayed the conversation they'd had Saturday afternoon. She was embarrassed to admit her daughter viewed her as a pathetic spinster, but as usual, Quinn showed no judgement as she sipped her prosecco. 'I only intended to look, see how the site worked, but you had to sign up to get proper access and before I knew it, I was answering all sorts of questions.'

Quinn nodded with enthusiasm. 'Although I prefer the apps—or rather I *did*—I tried eMatch for a while and they go deep on their questionnaire.'

'Yeah, it was actually pretty fun, but then I got to the part where I had to upload a photo and I chickened out.'

'Most people want to see what the person they're messaging looks like before they take the next step.'

'So shallow,' Deb said with a shake of her head. 'Besides, as if anyone would pick me from my photo. I've let myself go. *That* was my weekend epiphany. I've downloaded this app called Couch to 5K and I'm going to start running, and I've booked in for a face and leg wax on my lunchbreak tomorrow. But this isn't for a man, it's for me. I want to feel good about myself again.'

'That's awesome.' Quinn lifted her glass so they could clink again. 'But … if it wasn't for the photo, do you think you might have followed through?'

'Maybe.' This answer surprised even Deb. 'But I probably wasn't thinking straight after our drinking session the night before. I might still have been drunk.'

Quinn scoffed. 'We barely had a bottle of wine each.'

A waiter arrived with their dinners, and they paused their conversation long enough to thank him.

'Personally, I think you look perfect as you are,' Quinn said, stabbing her fork into a delicious-looking piece of ravioli, 'but if you're really worried about uploading a photo, I could come over and do your hair and—'

'No, no, no, no, no!' Deb picked up her own fork. 'Why would I start online dating when you've just declared how addictive and unfulfilling it can be?'

'Because we're two totally different people and our situations are totally different as well. It's terrible for me, but you're *much* wiser and more sensible than I am and—'

'You mean older,' Deb said wryly.

Quinn winked. 'With age comes wisdom, girlfriend. Besides, eMatch is different to dating apps. It's the swiping left and right that's addictive—it causes the same chemical reaction in the brain as poker machines.'

'You have done your research. If eMatch is so good, why'd you give it up?' Deb lifted her glass—the prosecco was infinitely better than the salad.

'Most of the guys were far too old for my liking—everyone they matched me with were all, like, in their forties or fifties. The perfect age for you.'

'From what I've heard those men want women *your* age. I'd probably have to date someone in their sixties or seventies.'

'Total myth,' Quinn said with a smile. 'One of my neighbours met her second husband on eMatch and she just turned fifty. He's only forty-eight. Oh my God, this pasta's good. How's your salad?'

'It's a salad. Anyway, enough about my brief dalliance with online dating. Are you seriously going to follow the advice in that old magazine?'

'Not exactly.' Quinn chuckled again. 'I mean, I'm not going to walk around with a fucking hatbox—what was that about?—and some of those suggestions were so misogynistic. I'm not looking to be a 1950s housewife, but there were a few ideas that weren't too crazy. Like walking a dog, going to your high school reunion or signing up for a night class ... doing things and going places that widen your social circle. Let's just say it got me thinking.'

'So are you going to get a dog then?' Deb joked.

'Dec won't let me because Darpan's allergic, but I've asked Mrs Dagliesh, the old woman next door, if I can walk hers. Her husband died of a heart attack last year and she's got a bad hip, so the poor dog has been a bit neglected. It's been barking something chronic and driving all the neighbours wild. I'm taking him out for the first time this Saturday.' Quinn frowned. 'What time of day do you think single men walk their dogs—morning or early evening after work?'

'I wouldn't know.' Deb snort-laughed again, but the prosecco had gone to her head and she no longer cared.

'Oh my God!' Quinn put down her fork. 'I've got the best idea.'

'Why do I get the feeling I'm not going to like this?'

'We'll do a swap—I'll give up the apps for a few months and see what happens if you promise to finish your registration on eMatch and go on at least five dates.'

Deb shook her head in bemusement. 'You already told me you're going on a digital detox; don't drag me into your craziness.'

'Come on ... it'll be fun. And it'll help me stay on the straight and narrow if I can hear about your sexcapades instead.'

Deb shuddered. 'I told you, I don't want to put my photo online.'

'Ah, don't worry about that. I'll give you a makeover, so you'll hardly recognise yourself—not that I think you need it, but a bit of make-up will give you confidence. You'll feel like a new woman.'

But that wasn't the issue. Could a bit of make-up transform her enough that Oscar wouldn't recognise her if, somehow, he stumbled across her pic?

Again, she thought of his threats, but they *had* been a long time ago. Would he even recognise her anymore? She looked a lot different from sixteen years ago—an extra ten kilos and a few more wrinkles did that. Besides, her photo would only be on one website. What were the chances he'd be on the same one or matched with her? And hadn't she decided she was going to use a fake name?

For all she knew Oscar was still in America.

Oh my goodness. Was she actually considering this?

'Shouldn't the photo look at least a bit like me, so if I actually meet a man, he recognises me and isn't disappointed? Hypothetically.'

Quinn grinned victoriously. 'Oh, it'll look like you—just the very best version of you. Go on,' she pleaded, 'let me help. I can't wait to dye over those greys and put some make-up on you, but if you truly don't like the photos or decide you don't want to follow through, I'll back off. Promise.'

'Okay,' Deb sighed. She couldn't tell if it was her or the prosecco speaking. 'You can come over on the weekend and we'll take some photos.'

Quinn

One hand firmly gripping Snoodle's leash, Quinn stood in the tiny front courtyard of Mrs Dagliesh's terrace house and rang the doorbell. Due to her 'bung hip' as she called it, her next-door neighbour took an eternity to answer.

'Hello, dear,' she said when the door eventually swung open.

Quinn wasn't sure whether she was talking to her or the Newfoundland, but she smiled nevertheless.

'Was he good for you?' Mrs Dagliesh asked, her brow furrowing.

'He was an angel,' Quinn lied.

'That's wonderful, I'm so pleased. I've been feeling so guilty since Eddie passed—he used to take him out every day, and with my daughters living overseas, well ...' She blinked as her voice drifted off. 'The sensible thing to do would be to rehome him, but that would break my heart.'

Please don't cry. Please don't cry.

Quinn glanced next door, willing Dec to appear. He had a knack for comforting people in a way that made them feel better, whereas her remedy of humour didn't always have the right effect.

'I'll walk him whenever you need,' she gushed. 'As I said, I need the exercise.'

Not that she'd got much because the dog stopped to sniff disgusting things every few seconds. He *had* attracted the attention of others though, she had to give him that. Just not the right kind of attention.

Mrs Dagliesh reached to take Snoodle's leash. 'Do you have time for a cup of tea?'

'Just a quick one. I'm going to a friend's place for lunch and she lives way out west.'

Mrs Dagliesh unclipped Snoodle's leash and as the dog bounded inside, she shuffled back to let Quinn into her immaculately kept house.

'Wow, this place is gorgeous,' she said, unable to keep the surprise from her voice. She was ashamed to admit she'd expected the décor to be stuck in the last century with crochet rugs on floral sofas and orange macrame owls hanging on the wall, but it was almost as stylish as Dec and Darpan's next door. Abstract art dominated, massive canvases hanging on the walls.

'Thank you. The art is all Eddie's—he was a curator—but I'm proud to say the rest is me. I went back to university and studied interior design when Crystal and Michelle left home, but it was always a passion of mine,' Mrs Dagliesh said as she slowly led Quinn down the hallway into the kitchen. 'What do you do, dear?'

'Me? Oh, I'm in digital marketing at The Energy Co. Creative in its own way, I guess.'

'Digital marketing, indeed. That's to do with the internet and apps and things, isn't it?' When Quinn nodded, Mrs Dalgeish added,

'Sounds fascinating. There are so many jobs now that didn't even exist when I was a girl. Do you enjoy it?'

'Mostly.' She wouldn't say it was a passion the way Mrs Dagliesh spoke about interior design. 'Although my line manager is a bit of an arse and, between you and me,' she leaned close in a conspiratorial manner, 'I can't stand the taste of sports drinks. Plus, they're so full of sugar. If I'm going to have something bad for me, I want to enjoy it.'

'Well, I tend to agree with you there,' Mrs Dagliesh said, glancing towards the dog who was now sprawled on the floor snoring and taking up half the kitchen. 'Although it looks like Snoodles could do with one of your energy drinks.'

Quinn smiled as her neighbour reached for the kettle and started to fill it up.

'English Breakfast or green tea? Sorry, I don't have any fancy herbal stuff.'

'English Breakfast is fine, thanks. How did you and Mr Dagliesh meet?' Quinn asked, noticing a photo of the couple pinned to the fridge.

'I had a summer job working in a fishing tackle shop off George Street—I knew nothing about fishing, but my father was friends with the owner and when he heard I wanted work, he offered me a few days a week, working at the cash register. One day Eddie came in with a mate of his who wanted to buy a rod for his father. While Luke selected the present, Eddie and I got talking. He asked if I'd take a walk with him the following day and the rest, as they say, is history. We were married six months later and together sixty-two years.' She sniffed. 'Come on, let's take our tea into the dining room.'

'Aw, that's the best meet-cute I've ever heard,' Quinn said, finding herself a little teary as well. *Fishing tackle!* Wasn't that one of the suggestions in the list?

'What's a meet-cute, dear?'

They went into the dining room and sat down at a table—far too big for someone who lived alone—to drink their tea. Mrs Dagliesh offered Quinn some homemade gingernuts which she couldn't resist. 'It's that scene in movies, or novels, where the romantic leads meet for the first time. It's usually funny or cute in some way.'

'You mean like Hugh Grant throwing orange juice over Julia Roberts in *Notting Hill*?'

'Yep, exactly.'

They spent the next few minutes sharing their faves—*When Harry Met Sally*, the Prime Minister with the hired help in *Love Actually*, *Sleepless in Seattle*. Mrs Dagliesh hadn't seen *50 First Dates* and was horrified to learn Quinn had never watched *Singing in the Rain*. They decided they should have a movie night to educate each other.

Three little beeps sounded from the kitchen where Quinn had left her phone in her bag.

'I don't mind if you get that.'

'Thanks.' Quinn went to stand but stopped at the last moment. 'You know what? It can wait.' She reached for another biscuit instead.

Mrs Dagliesh smiled. 'You live with your brother and his husband, don't you? Lovely gentlemen.' When Quinn nodded, she added, 'They're much quieter than the young people who lived there before. Parties every weekend. Went till at least three in the morning.'

'Have you lived here a long time?' Quinn asked.

'Since I got married. We thought we were oh so hip living among the bohemians and artists. Eddie and I bought this place for a song and did it up ourselves. So much love in these walls.' She glanced around and smiled wistfully. 'Do I remember Declan saying you are from Adelaide?'

'Yeah, that's where we grew up. Dec's a few years older than me and I was so jealous when he moved here. He raved about the city and after visiting a few times, I knew I wanted to move too. Plus, it has the bonus of being in a different state to my mother.'

'You don't get along?'

'Oh, we get along just fine,' Quinn said, 'when she's not telling me how to live my life, what to eat and what to wear. She thinks my style is too loud, too flamboyant, which is saying something coming from an Irish woman.'

'I'm sure she means well. Perhaps that's how my girls feel about me,' Mrs Dagliesh mused, and Quinn metaphorically kicked herself.

'I doubt that,' she said, trying to save the situation. 'It's just my mam's way. She lives for meddling in other people's business. She enjoys gossip even if she doesn't know the person it's about.'

Mrs D laughed. 'She sounds like a hoot. I've never met an Irish person I didn't like.'

'You said you had daughters? How many?'

'I've got two, Michelle and Crystal. They both live in London. Michelle went there for a gap year after school and never left, and then Crystal went to visit her a few years later and fell in love.'

'You must miss them,' Quinn said.

'I do. When Eddie was alive, we used to visit regularly, but I don't like travelling on my own these days, and the girls have such busy lives they don't get here much either.'

When her phone beeped again, Quinn remembered her date with Deb. She was having so much fun chatting with Mrs D that she'd lost track of time.

'Thank you so much for the tea,' she said as she made plans to walk Snoodles again in a few days. She meant it when she told the older woman she was looking forward to seeing her again.

As she headed next door to change, she checked her phone, ignored the messages from her mother and clicked on the one from Deb.

I'm doing my weekly shopping. Anything I should grab for this afternoon?

No, I'm bringing everything. But I'm running a little late. Got stuck talking to Mrs. D

No worries. Any luck with the dog-walking?

Absolutely none. See you soon. xx

Debra

By the time Quinn arrived, Deb was a bloody mess. Even Ramona—who'd turned into a self-obsessed teen hermit since starting at SLC—had tried to calm her down.

'Thank God you're here,' Ramona said as she stepped into the apartment.

'What's going on?' Quinn asked.

'Mum told me about your plan, and I think it's brilliant, but she's about to tell you she's chickening out.'

'I'm not chickening out. I'm reassessing my decision after—'

'I'll deal with this.' Quinn stepped into the apartment, kicking the door shut with her foot. 'I've got all sorts of goodies to help in this bag.'

Deb eyed the giant bag, feeling like the kids in *Mary Poppins*. 'What on earth is in there?'

'Good luck.' Ramona lifted the can of soft drink she'd just swiped from the fridge. 'I'm gunna leave you to it.'

If Deb was a different kind of person, she'd have given her daughter the finger, but her insides were trembling so much she couldn't even stick out her tongue.

Quinn pulled a bottle of wine from the bag. 'Sounds like you need a glass of this.'

'It's barely one o'clock.'

'And?' Quinn shrugged as she proceeded into the even more immaculate than usual kitchen because anxiety turned Deb into a cleaning maniac. 'It's always five o'clock somewhere.'

'You getting me drunk was what got me into this predicament in the first place.'

In reply, Quinn heaved the bag onto the kitchen bench, dug around inside and conjured a box of wineglasses. 'I decided not to wait for your birthday. These are a Happy New Deb gift.'

'Thanks. I think?'

Quinn took two glasses from the box, rinsed them and poured the wine. 'Let's take this one step at a time,' she said, speaking to Deb as if she were a five-year-old not wanting to go to kindergarten.

'Okay.' Deb took a large sip. She could see she was fighting a losing battle.

Quinn upended the bag's contents on the table, set up a portable Bluetooth speaker and tapped her phone a couple of times. Shania Twain's 'Man! I Feel Like a Woman!' blasted into the room.

'I didn't know you were a country music fan.'

'Everyone's a country music fan,' Quinn said, flicking her pale blue hair over her shoulders. 'Just not everyone's prepared to admit it. Right, first things first—hair dye.'

'What colour did you get?'

Quinn grinned. 'Don't worry, you're not going green or anything like that, I'm just going to fix your roots and add some depth to your natural colour with a few highlights.'

Deb's natural colour was mousy brown. 'You can do that?'

'I can do a lot of things, girlfriend, and I can definitely update your do. In high school I used to colour and cut all my friends' hair. Even did our family dog once. Got grounded for a month.'

Deb laughed, already relaxing a little. 'Why didn't you become a hairdresser?'

'Mam and Dad wanted me to go to university. They loved their restaurant, but it was hard work. They thought us kids would be better off using our brains than our hands in a career.'

'So, is the fact you change your hair colour almost as much as you change your outfit because you regret not becoming a hairdresser?'

Quinn shrugged. 'I guess maybe a bit, but it also makes me feel good. Bright colours make me happy. Life's boring enough without having a dull …' She stopped mid-sentence as if realising who she was talking to, but Deb finished it herself.

'Without having a dull wardrobe.'

Quinn shrugged, then opened a box to begin the proceedings. While she painted a potent-smelling potion onto Deb's hair, they chatted about work. There were rumours that Samira from customer service and Mikael from legal were indulging in a torrid affair.

'I know they both adamantly deny it,' Deb said, 'but I read this book about body language at uni and theirs tells me two things. One, they're sleeping together and two, they're lying when they say they're not.'

'Aren't they married?'

'Ah huh,' Deb said.

'I guess they could be in open marriages?'

'Hmm ...' Deb mused. 'I wouldn't be surprised about Samira and her husband, but no way Mikael and Faith are. They go to church every Sunday and I'm pretty sure God still disapproves of that kind of thing.'

Quinn laughed as she set a timer on her phone. 'You're done for half an hour. Now it's your turn to do me.'

'What?!'

'I'm sick of blue. I think I'm in the mood to be a redhead for a few weeks.' Quinn thrust a box of dye at her.

Deb eyed it like it might grow teeth and bite her. 'Can't you do your own?'

'It's much easier if someone else does it.'

'Maybe we should get Ramona.'

'Don't be ridiculous. Let the poor girl do her homework and stop being a wuss. Come on, swap seats.'

Deb stood. 'Anyone ever tell you you're very bossy?'

'Yep, all the time. But it's a requirement when you have four older brothers.'

'This is actually quite therapeutic,' Deb said ten minutes later as she massaged bright red dye into Quinn's previously pale blue hair, the plastic gloves she wore crackling as she worked.

'You haven't told me how the dog-walking went this morning?'

'God,' Quinn groaned. 'Snoodles was a nightmare. It was like trying to walk an octopus—he kept pulling me in all different directions in the park. He's a magnet for little kids. Their mothers all flocked over after them; where the hell were all the single dads, that's what I want to know?'

Deb chuckled.

'The only men who stopped to talk to me were two guys jogging—clearly gay—and a man in his fifties or sixties who growled at me when Snoodles accidentally got away and started *harassing* his chihuahua.'

When she'd finished, Quinn ordered Deb to go take a shower and when she returned with her wet hair wrapped in a towel turban, she found her friend and daughter laughing at something on Ramona's phone.

'What's so funny?'

'Nothing,' Ramona snapped at Deb and then stalked back into her bedroom.

'I swear she hates me these days, and I don't know what I've done wrong.'

Quinn gave her a sympathetic smile. 'I keep telling you, you've done nothing. She's fifteen and you're her parent. You breathing annoys her. It'll pass.'

Deb slumped into a seat. 'What were you laughing at?'

'It was just a meme about cats and teachers. Let me see your colour?' Quinn pulled the towel from Deb's head. 'Ooh, that's looking awesome.'

She grabbed the fancy pink hair dryer she'd brought with her and plugged it into the closest socket. 'Oh my God, I haven't told you about Mrs D. She met her husband doing something from the list.'

'The Husband List?' Deb shouted. It was hard to hear over the noise of the dryer. 'Did she read the article in the magazine when it came out?'

Quinn shook her head and explained how her neighbour had met the love of her life while working in a fishing tackle shop. 'It was fate, and they were happy for almost sixty years before he died.'

Finally, she switched off the hair dryer and Deb stood to go look in the mirror, but Quinn pushed her back down.

'Not so fast.' She grabbed a pair of scissors. 'Trust me.' And then she snipped off a chunk of hair before Deb could say anything else.

'I hope you know what you're doing,' she said, and downed another glass of bubbles while Quinn worked.

She refused to let Deb go check her new do in the mirror even after she'd finished. 'I'm going to do your make-up first.'

Deb rarely swore but she did now as Quinn picked up a smaller bag. She always wore bright colours—sparkly magenta eyeshadow, blue mascara, deep purple lipstick, stuff like that—and on her they looked fabulous, but Deb would look like a clown.

'It's okay,' Quinn said, reading her mind. 'I've got some lovely soft neutral colours in here as well. You'll barely look like you're wearing make-up, I promise.'

They were silent the next little while, except for the occasional instruction.

Look up. Suck in your cheeks. Purse your lips.

'*Now*, can I look in the mirror?' Deb asked when Quinn put the lid back on a glossy, pale pink lipstick.

She grinned and nodded as if pleased with her handiwork.

Holding her breath, Deb fled to the bathroom and gasped as she saw herself. 'Oh, goodness. I look ...'

Quinn came up behind her, beaming. 'Like a MILF.'

'A what?'

'A mother I'd like to ... *you know what*?'

'Shh!' Deb brought her finger up to her lips, but couldn't stop grinning. She did *not* look like a clown, but she also looked nothing like she did fifteen years ago either. She looked a lot more sophisticated. Close to tears, she ran her hand through her silky soft locks, which now fell in layers just above her shoulders. Golden highlights shone beneath the bathroom lights and her make-up looked flawless.

Quinn didn't give her long to admire herself, before nudging her away from the mirror to blow-dry her own hair. Deb sat on the toilet seat, sipping more prosecco, and smiling every time she saw her reflection.

'You need to teach me how to do that,' she said when Quinn was done and looked like she'd just stepped out of a salon.

'The things we do for love, hey?'

Until then, Deb had almost forgotten why they were going to all this trouble. Quinn grabbed her hand and led her to Ramona's bedroom, where she banged on the door. 'Ramona! We need your help out here.'

Seconds later the door opened, and Ramona grinned at Quinn. 'What's up?'

If Deb had pounded like that, she'd have got an earful.

'Oh my God, Mum.' Ramona's mouth dropped open. 'I can hardly recognise you.'

'I'll take that as a compliment.'

'Doesn't she look amazing?' Quinn said. 'And now we need your help choosing an outfit for the photos.'

They all headed into Deb's bedroom and she flopped down onto her bed, watching as Quinn and Ramona went through her clothes, scrutinising them. It would have been amusing if it wasn't *her* wardrobe they were talking about.

'Pity you two are different sizes,' Quinn mused, smiling at Ramona. 'You have such great taste. Where'd you get that skirt?'

'Thanks.' Ramona grinned and did a little pirouette in her red polka-dot swing skirt. 'I made it myself. Found the material at Lifeline round the corner. Only two bucks.'

'You are amazing.' Quinn high-fived her and then dug around a little more, eventually pulling out a short-sleeved black floaty blouse and a pair of black skinny jeans. 'This might work.'

She threw the items at Deb. 'Put these on.'

While Deb changed, Quinn asked Ramona how school was going and she told her about the teachers and her new friends—apparently Sydney had a boyfriend, her little sister was a lesbian and Nyra might be bisexual—and chatted excitedly about being assigned the 1950s for a fashion assignment. First Deb had heard of any of it.

'Only probs is, Ms Rose wouldn't let me work with Sydney and Nyra.' Ramona pouted. 'I'm stuck with this girl nobody likes and every time I ask her a question, she gives a monosyllabic answer. It's infuriating.'

'I hope you're being kind to her,' Deb said.

Quinn looked Deb up and down and then turned to Ramona. 'What d'ya think?'

She pursed her lips. 'Would be better with some colour.'

'Agreed. Do you have a bright scarf or a brooch?' Quinn asked Ramona.

'You know,' Deb said, 'I actually have some jewellery of my own.'

Quinn gave her an exasperated look. 'Why didn't you say so?'

Deb crossed to her dresser and opened a wooden treasure chest that sat on top.

'Wowsers.' Quinn gazed down at the assortment of earrings, brooches and chunky necklaces. 'Why don't you ever wear any of this?'

'I got out of the habit of wearing earrings when Ramona was little and kept pulling at them, and I'm always in such a rush in the mornings that accessories are the last thing on my mind.'

'This is cool,' Ramona said, lifting a rainbow brooch.

'I made that,' Deb admitted.

'What?' they said in unison.

She laughed—'It was a hobby'—and pointed to some of the other items. 'Those as well.'

Quinn picked up a pair of sparkly drop earrings. 'These are fantastic. You know you could sell them. I follow lots of makers on Insta who sell things only half as good as these.'

'Don't be silly,' Deb scoffed. 'Who'd want to buy my stuff? Anyway, is there anything here you think will do the trick?'

After a quick consultation, Quinn and Ramona decided on a long, purple and pink beaded necklace and the glitter drop earrings. They felt heavy and alien, but Deb had to admit, she looked good.

Quinn clapped her hands in excitement. 'Time for photos.'

Deb assumed Ramona would retreat to her cave, but she hung around, acting like Quinn's assistant as they snapped what felt like a million photos inside the apartment and then outside on the footpath.

'Enough!' Deb said, when an elderly couple walking past paused to stare at them and she heard them mutter something about her maybe being famous. 'Surely you've got something we can use by now.'

They went back inside, and Ramona made tea for everyone as Deb and Quinn sat down to select a photo. Quinn had suggested Deb change her outfit a few times so they could upload a few different images, but she'd put her foot down. One photo of herself on the internet was more than enough.

Finally, they agreed on a shot of Deb sitting at the kitchen table, sipping her bubbly. 'Makes you look easygoing and approachable, but also fun,' Quinn said.

And then it was time to log back into the website and upload it.

'I thought you had homework to do,' Deb said as Ramona hovered behind the couch, looking over their shoulders at the screen.

Deb's nerves returned with a vengeance as Quinn sent the photo to her laptop and then took it upon herself to finalise registration. 'Just in case you chicken out.'

Moments after she pressed 'Go Live', the first eight matches appeared on the screen.

'Ta dah,' Quinn said. 'A veritable smorgasbord of men.'

Ramona giggled and pointed to a dark-haired man on the screen. 'Ooh, he looks nice. You should message him, Mum.'

Deb felt like she was about to faint and snapped the laptop shut before either of them could say anything else.

Ramona

'I can't believe you're *actually* going to her house!' Nyra exclaimed as they headed back to Drysdale.

It had been two weeks since Ramona and Lucy were paired together; they'd finished their research components and they needed to start putting together their presentation and drawing concepts for their ball gown. During that time, Lucy couldn't have spoken more than a hundred words, but they'd been text messaging regularly. Some of her messages were quite amusing and Ramona was almost warming to her partner.

When Lucy asked if she wanted to come over so they could 'really get our teeth into things', she'd felt torn. On the one hand she didn't want the others thinking she *wanted* to hang out with the stutterer outside school hours, but she also didn't want to fail their assignment.

However, when she'd mentioned the invitation to Sydney, Nyra and Kenzie, they'd encouraged her to go.

'You've got to take one for the team.'

'Yeah, I've never been inside a priest's house before.'

'You can report everything back to us. I bet her place is even weirder than she is.'

Feeling slightly uneasy, Ramona forced a smile and promised she would.

She met Lucy at the school gates and they walked to the bus stop in silence. There were other girls from SLC already there who gawked at Ramona as they approached. She could tell what they were thinking—*What's the new girl doing with the stutterer?*

'So have you had any more thoughts about our project?' she asked loudly, hoping the other students would realise their relationship was purely professional.

Lucy gave her a look that said she knew exactly what Ramona was doing. A pinprick of guilt stabbed her in the heart, but at least *she* was making an effort to fit in.

The bus arrived and they slid into the seat right behind the driver. Down the back, the other SLC students were yelling and screaming, not at all the kind of behaviour you'd expect from private school girls. Her mother would be horrified.

Ramona got out her phone. There were already a dozen Snapchats from her friends. She didn't dare open them while sitting next to Lucy, but a pleasurable tingle skated down her spine at the fact she had friends. And they were popular!

After a couple of stops, Lucy stood. 'M-my house is just a sh-short walk this way,' she said once they got off and the bus pulled away from the kerb.

'Cool,' Ramona replied.

'So, w-what school did you … g-go to before SLC?'

Ramona blinked, shocked that Lucy had said something that wasn't to do with logistics or their project.

Their eyes met and Lucy smiled as if she could read Ramona's mind, before dropping her gaze back to her feet. It was the first time Ramona had ever seen her so much as quirk her lips.

'You have such a pretty smile,' was what she wanted to say, but instead she named her old school, the local Catholic high.

'Are you C-c-catholic?'

'No. Mum's an atheist and … I guess I am too,' she said.

'And … w-why'd you leave?'

'Because I heard about the fashion program and got a scholarship.' Silence followed for a few moments, then Ramona said, 'I heard your dad's a priest?'

She kind of expected Lucy to laugh and deny such ridiculousness but she nodded. 'He's a minister. Weird, hey?'

'I've heard of weirder things.' Not that she could think of any in that moment. 'Why don't you go to a Catholic school?'

Lucy smirked. 'We're Anglican. But Mum went to SLC as well. It's a tradition in her family.'

'Where's your mum now?' Ramona asked, wondering if maybe her father was married after all and Sydney and co had got the wrong end of the stick.

'Dead.'

Oh, shit. 'I'm sorry.'

Lucy shrugged and didn't say another word. Ramona had heard of comfortable silence but the two minutes it took to reach the house were anything but.

Lucy lived in this little cottage set off to the side of a church—*Anglican*—with an old cemetery in the garden between. Ramona shuddered at the sight.

'This is nice.' She gestured to the garden as Lucy unlocked the door.

They went inside and down a narrow hallway to the back of the house, where Lucy dumped her bag on the kitchen bench, picked up a remote and aimed it at the air conditioner on the wall.

'S-sorry,' she said, fanning her face. 'Dad never puts it on.'

'My mum's the same. Always on about it being a luxury we can't afford, unless it's like, over forty degrees.' Ramona rolled her eyes and saw another glimmer of a smile from Lucy.

'Do you ... w-want s-s-something to drink and a-a snack? We have b-b-bickies, and I could ... make milkshakes?'

'That'd be great.'

While Lucy peered into the pantry, Ramona looked around. From here she could see into the dining room. Aside from the fancy cross hanging on one wall, it looked like a normal home. Warm and welcoming. Kinda similar to her own.

She jumped as the back door opened and in walked a tall, thin but strong-looking man. His head was shaved, and he wore all black except for the glimpse of white at his collar.

'Hello, hello,' he said, grinning widely as he offered his elbow for a bump. 'You must be Ramona. What a pleasure to meet you.'

'You too, sir ... I mean, father.'

'Call me Jake.'

Jake? Jake was too cool for a minister—they should have names like Matthew, Mark, Luke and John.

'I hear you girls have a project to get on with. Lucy's so excited to be in the special fashion program.' He shook his head with a chuckle and gestured to his outfit. 'I never have to worry too much about what to wear, but Luce here loves that stuff.'

Luce-here looked like she wanted the floor to open and swallow her.

'Dad,' she pleaded, 'I'm going to make us a milkshake but then we really do have a lot to do.'

'Message received loud and clear.' He saluted them and then retreated.

'S-sorry about him,' Lucy said as she grabbed the milk and ice-cream. 'You ... want vanilla or ch-chocolate?'

Ramona noticed Lucy didn't stutter when talking to her father and she wanted to ask why, but didn't want to appear rude.

'Chocolate please, and he seems great.' Much more normal than she'd expected. He only looked about thirty-five and if you added a leather jacket, he'd almost look like a biker.

Ramona tried to make small talk as Lucy scooped chocolate ice-cream into a blender, but it was like having a conversation with a pet rock.

'Do you get creeped out living next door to a cemetery? I'd be terrified,' she tried after the weather and TV shows reaped no reward.

'N-no. I'm not ... s-scared of ghosts.' She handed Ramona a tall glass almost filled to the top. 'I'm ... fascinated by them.'

'You *believe* in them?'

'Don't you?'

'I'm not sure. I don't think so,' Ramona replied, taking her first sip of milkshake.

Lucy laughed, and Ramona realised it was the first time she'd ever heard her do that, despite having worked closely with her for the last two weeks.

'If you don't ... believe in them, then why are you scared of them?'

'You know what? That's a really good point!'

They smiled at each other and then went into the dining room with their milkshakes and a tin of choc-chip cookies to start their work.

'This milkshake is so good,' Ramona said, 'and these biscuits. Did you make them as well?'

'N-no, my ... dad did.'

'I might have to ask him for the recipe—my mum only cooks boring healthy stuff.'

'D-does your dad cook at all?'

'Oh, didn't I mention?' Ramona shrugged. 'I haven't got a dad. My mum used donor sperm. You don't have the monopoly on weird parental situations, you know.'

They spent the next half hour looking at each other's notes. Ms Rose had said they could write an essay, make a poster, create a PowerPoint, or do something else entirely. 'The more creative the better' had been her exact words.

'It's ... p-probably stupid, but I do have ... one idea,' Lucy said.

'Shoot.'

Lucy inhaled sharply, then her words came out in a rush. 'We could display each year of the decade like pages from a magazine.'

'Oh my God. That's genius. I collect vintage magazines,' Ramona said.

'Really? Y-you like it?'

'Like it? I love it! But we have to keep this idea to ourselves, because it's totally gunna be better than everyone else's.'

'It's n-not like I have anyone to tell.' Lucy leaned down to grab something out of her school bag. 'I've also ... s-started to draft some ideas for our g-gown.' She put the sketchbook down on the table and opened it.

'Holy moly,' Ramona breathed as she looked at the first sketch. 'Why didn't you tell me you could draw like this?'

The sleeveless design that pinched in at the waist with a full skirt didn't look like any kind of draft.

Lucy's cheeks went so red her freckles almost disappeared. 'I-I-I ... did tell you I was okay at it.'

'Did you get this super talent from your dad?'

'No. He struggles to d-draw stick figures, but ... M-m-mum was an artist.'

Hoping she didn't sound too nosey, Ramona said, 'How old were you when she died?'

'Almost two. I-I-I ... don't remember her, but I've got th-this weird aversion to ... d-disinfectant Dad reckons m-must have come from spending so much ... t-t-time on the ... oncology ward when I was a baby.'

'Your mum died of cancer?' Ramona couldn't keep the shock out of her voice. The way the others spoke, she'd have guessed a drug overdose or something.

'Yeah. She was diagnosed when she w-was ... pregnant with me.'

'That sucks.' Ramona paused a moment. 'So your dad became a minister ... after?'

Lucy nodded. 'Yeah, he and Mum were both ... C-Christians, but just Christmas and Easter. He says it was the local minister who ... v-visited us weekly that helped him survive it. After Mum died, he-he wanted to do the same for others.'

Ramona reckoned if she lost the love of her life, the last thing she'd do was turn to religion. Wouldn't you wonder why God had to give your partner cancer?

'Must be tough not having a mum.' As much as hers sometimes smothered her, Ramona couldn't imagine getting through life without her.

'It's m-mostly okay,' Lucy said, 'except when I first got my ... p-period and Dad had to take me to buy sanitary p-products. Neither of us had any idea what to get.'

'Oh my God.' Ramona cracked up. 'Did he also go with you to buy your first bra? My mum was like, so embarrassing when I had to get one. She made it like this big occasion where we went out to high tea afterwards to celebrate.'

Lucy laughed and then gestured to the sketchbook. 'Anyway, you should ... p-probably know I'm not as good at sewing as drawing.'

'Well, I can sew with my eyes closed.'

Ramona flicked through the next few pages and couldn't believe her eyes. Who would have known Lucy was hiding such talent? Maybe being partnered with her hadn't been the worst thing after all. She pointed to a black gown that had almost a train in the form of a crimson sash that wrapped around the waist and fell in two dark slashes to the floor.

'The ... r-red bit's supposed to be ... chiffon,' Lucy explained.

'That would work perfectly. Lucy,' Ramona said genuinely, 'I think we're gunna make an awesome team. The only problem is going to be choosing which design to make.'

Quinn

'Earth to Quinn?'

She startled at the voice and looked up from her computer screen to see Deb peering over the cubicle. 'How long have you been standing there?'

'Oh, only about half an hour. Are you coming to lunch or do I have to go get dumplings on my own?'

Quinn looked to her watch. 'Is it that time already?'

'Yes, and I'm starving.'

As they escaped the building a few minutes later, they breathed in the warm midday air. It might not technically be fresh with all the traffic fumes, but it always *felt* fresher than the artificial air in the office.

'How's the latest campaign going?' Deb asked as they headed across the road in the direction of their regular dumpling place across the other side of Hyde Park.

'Don't ask,' Quinn replied before ranting and raving about how Mr-Carrot-Up-His-Arse—her line manager, Travis—had made them sit through an hour meeting that could have been an email because he liked the sound of his own voice. 'And then he has the audacity to wonder why we're behind on our work.'

Deb laughed as she dug into her purse and tossed a few coins to a busker playing the didgeridoo. She was such a good soul; ever since Ramona had started at that fancy-schmancy school she'd been stressing about money. They'd had to cut their weekly dumplings down to once a month, yet here she was giving her spare change to a stranger. Quinn felt guilty she didn't carry cash, so she took a Picnic from the chocolate stash in her bag and threw it in the hat with all the coins.

'Hey.' Deb nudged Quinn and whispered, 'Check out her.'

A woman about her own age, dressed in a grey business suit that looked straight out of the nineties, sat on a park bench tossing seed to ibises and pigeons.

'What about her?' Quinn asked.

'Wasn't that on the husband-catching list?'

'Oh my God, yes! Do you think she's trying to catch a man?'

'Who knows? But, if that *is* her intention, it doesn't seem to be working,' Deb said as two men striding purposefully, earbuds in their ears, gave her and the birds a wide berth.

Quinn sighed. 'Honestly, sometimes I think it's a miracle anyone ever ends up meeting anyone. I've been off the apps for almost a week now—I've walked Snoodles almost daily and haven't had so much as a hello from an eligible bachelor.'

'You're not thinking of downloading them again, are you?' Deb sounded almost hopeful.

'No way.' Quinn saw right through her—if she threw in the towel, Deb would have an excuse not to follow through on her part of the deal. 'I'm no quitter and neither are you. I'm thinking maybe I should try some of the other suggestions on the list, sign up to a woodworking class or something.'

At the restaurant, Sami, their fave waiter, welcomed them.

'Oh, my goodness.' He looked as if he wanted to throw his arms around them. 'I've been worried sick about the two of you. Three Fridays in a row I kept your table and you didn't come. I considered sending out a search party.'

Both women smiled and gave an awkward chuckle.

'I was worried we did something to offend you. Or did you find better dumplings somewhere else?'

'No,' Quinn assured him. 'That would be impossible.'

'It's my fault,' apologised Deb. 'I've had to cut back on my spending.'

'Say no more—my electricity bill last month almost bankrupted me—I'm just glad to see you again.' He led them to their favourite table by the window. 'Same as usual, ladies?'

'Yes, please,' they said in unison.

For almost as long as they'd been coming here, Quinn had ordered steamed vegetable buns. She still remembered the first time she tasted them and knew she'd never find anything as perfect again. She imagined that was exactly how she'd feel when she finally found The One.

'So,' Quinn said once Sami had gone, 'progress report time.'

'There's really not much to report. The first few men who messaged me were no-goes. Despite eMatch's supposedly perfect algorithm, we found little in common to talk about.'

'Have you arranged to meet anyone yet?'

'No! If I can't get a conversation going online, how awkward would it be face to face?' Deb went pale. 'Or rather, even more awkward than it's going to be anyway.'

'You're sure you're not making excuses? Remember, you have to go on at least five dates.'

Sami arrived with a bottle of sparkling water and two glasses of wine.

Deb waved her hand at him. Only on special occasions did they allow themselves alcohol with Friday dumplings, otherwise Deb found herself falling asleep at her desk in the afternoon. 'No wine today.'

'My treat,' Sami said, putting the drinks on the table and then pouring them each some water. 'Have to keep my favourite customers sweet.'

Quinn picked up a glass and raised it to him. 'Well, thank you, kind sir. You know I can't say no to free booze.'

He winked and retreated again.

'I wonder if *he's* single?' Quinn mused.

'Pretty sure he's gay. So, how's Mrs D and Snoodles?'

'Mrs D's great.' Making friends with her was a perk Quinn hadn't expected when she'd offered to walk the dog. 'And Snoodles is still the devil in a canine body. But we're not talking about me right now. If you've ruled out the first few guys, what about the other matches? They can't all be duds.'

'Can't they?' Deb reached for her wine. 'How many men did you connect with who you eventually decided were duds?'

Ignoring her friend's pessimism, Quinn said, 'Let me take another look.'

'I haven't got my laptop.'

Quinn was having none of it. She grabbed Deb's phone off the table, held it up to Deb's face to unlock it and then typed in eMatch to the browser. 'What's your username and password?'

'I'm not telling you that. You'll probably log in and start chatting to men on my behalf.'

Quinn didn't deny it. 'Then you do it,' she said, handing back the phone.

The food arrived while Deb reluctantly entered her details.

Sami saw what she was doing over her shoulder. 'Ooh, you're on eMatch? I met my partner on Zoosk. So much easier to meet people in this day and age, isn't it? Good luck.'

And then he was off again.

Quinn devoured a few mouthfuls—'Oh, how I've missed you, little buns of perfection'—then started scrolling Deb's current matches.

'Okay. What about this guy? Tristan.' She turned the phone to show Deb. It was the man Ramona had first pointed out last Saturday, so at least he had her daughter's seal of approval. Not at all Quinn's type, but he was cute in a Bradley Cooper kinda way, and he had warm eyes and a slightly serious expression that made her think he'd be perfect for quiet, reserved, cautious Deb.

'He's a vet,' Deb said as if that put him up there with used-car salesmen and tax collectors.

'You got something against vets? Maybe he can give me some advice on how to get Snoodles to stop eating other dogs' poo.'

'No, although I can't help thinking about where he must put his hands sometimes,' Deb said as she got stuck into her pot stickers. 'If that doesn't turn you off, maybe *you* should find out where he works and take Snoodles to visit him yourself?'

'Tempting, but this one's more your vintage. And look, it says his favourite idea of a good date is a night on the couch, drinking wine, eating cheese and playing Scrabble. Isn't Scrabble your favourite board game?'

'Yes, but—'

'No buts. He sounds dreamy. And he's got grown-up kids, so you wouldn't need to worry about blending families—'

'I think you're jumping ahead of yourself a bit. I haven't even messaged him.'

'Only a matter of time, girlfriend, only a matter of time. We could send him a quick line now?'

'Absolutely not.' She tried to grab her phone, but Quinn held it out of her reach.

'Seriously, his profession speaks volumes. Have you ever heard of a nasty vet? Only good humans choose such a career. Animal lovers are always—'

'There must be *something* wrong with him if he's still single at forty-nine.'

'I guess there's only one way to find out.'

Then, before Deb could stop her, Quinn clicked on the heart to like Tristan's profile.

'I can't believe you just did that,' Deb said.

She smiled smugly as she handed back the phone. 'You can thank me in your wedding speech. Ooh, can I be your bridesmaid?'

'If I haven't killed you by then.'

That was a risk Quinn was willing to take.

'You know.' Deb glanced at her phone. 'I think this is the first lunch we've ever had where *your* phone didn't make an appearance.'

'Was I really that bad?'

Deb gave her a look.

'You're right—don't answer that.' The truth was she'd had major withdrawal symptoms when she'd first deleted the apps. It was worst when she was waiting for their coffees in the morning, taking a shower, or at nights when she was lying in bed watching Netflix or reading—times she'd usually multitask and surf the apps. She'd considered reneging on her decision—maybe cold turkey had been too much? Maybe she could just drop down to one app?

However, somehow, she'd stayed strong and although she hadn't had any luck on the man front, she had to admit she'd found more time in her day—she'd finished two books this past week whereas usually it took her a couple of months to get through one. And it was paying off at work also. She'd thought she was doing a good job before, but not checking her phone every five minutes had meant she'd managed to achieve so much more in a shorter period. Even Mr Carrot-Up-His-Arse had commended her yesterday.

Deb moaned, her eyes rolling backwards, as she swallowed another mouthful. 'God, I've missed this.'

'Me too.'

After more gushing about how good the food was, conversation turned to other things.

'You ladies enjoy your meals?' Sami asked, appearing the second their plates were clear.

'What do you think?' Quinn retorted, patting her now contented stomach. 'I've eaten so much I'll have to crawl back to the office.'

They promised Sami they'd see him next month and then walked back through the park. The woman feeding the pigeons had gone but the didgeridoo busker was still livening up the afternoon with his low-pitched, soulful music.

'What are you up to this weekend?' Deb asked.

'Tonight, Mrs D and I are having a movie night, then tomorrow I'm going to a whiskey tasting thing with a friend from Spin.'

'The movie night sounds fun.'

'What about you and Ramona?'

'I'm guessing she'll be in her room talking to her new friends and I'll spend it alone on the couch watching TV while doing a jigsaw puzzle.'

'What happened to your Friday night crafting?'

Deb snorted. 'Ramona has more important things to do apparently.'

'You know, you could always come to Mrs D's with me? I'll shout you an Uber home so you don't have to catch the train with all the drunk drongos.'

'Tempting.' Deb sighed. 'But I can't afford a babysitter and I don't really want to leave Ramona alone late at night.'

'Maybe another time then,' Quinn said.

She was pretty sure that Deb had never left Ramona with a babysitter in her life. At fifteen, Quinn had been babysitting other kids herself, but she knew better than to comment on Deb's parenting decisions.

Ramona

The intercom buzzed at 9.30 am Saturday morning and Ramona rushed to greet Lucy and her dad. He was wearing the same shirt as the day she met him, except today he wore jeans.

'Good morning, Ramona,' he boomed.

Lucy smiled shyly.

'Good morning, father … I mean, Mr Campbell,' Ramona replied.

He smiled warmly. 'Please, call me Jake. Is your mum in? I'd love to meet her.'

'I'm sorry, Jake, but Mum's just popped out. She won't be back for another half an hour, but you can wait if you want?'

Jake looked at his watch and then scratched his stubble-covered chin. 'I'd love to, but I have an appointment in an hour—meeting a young couple who I'm going to marry next month. Maybe I'll meet her when I pick Lucy up?'

'Dad, I told you I can get the train. Ramona does it every day.'

'And then how will I meet Ramona's lovely mother?'

'Fine.' Lucy rolled her eyes. 'I'll text you when we're almost ready.'

'Or my mum can drive her back? I'm sure she'll be happy to.'

'Sorry,' Lucy said as her father headed back down the steps, and they went into the apartment. 'He's a little … over-protective.'

'No need to apologise to me. I bet my mum gives him a run for his money. She only just started letting me stay home alone—during the day!'

Ramona led her into the open plan lounge/dining area and gestured to the table. 'It's probably best if we work here—my room is smaller than Harry Potter's cupboard.'

'You a Harry … P-potter fan?'

'Yeah,' she said, and then realised that perhaps Jake hadn't let Lucy read the books or watch the movie because of the witchcraft. There'd been people at her old school who'd been forbidden for that reason.

'M-me too.'

Phew. 'Do you read a lot of books?' Ramona asked, thinking of how Lucy spent every lunchtime in the library.

She nodded. 'Helps p-pass the time and makes me … forget the real world.'

Unease swept through Ramona—she remembered all too well what it felt like to have no one to hang out with at lunch and recess. 'Should we get started? I grabbed some of my magazines and thought we could look through them for inspiration.'

'That's only *some* of your magazines?' Lucy eyed the pile of *Teen Magazine*, *Vogue*, *Home Journal*, *The Women's Mirror* and of course, the *Women's Weekly*.

'I may have a little obsession,' Ramona confessed.

'Cool,' Lucy breathed as she reached for the top magazine and held it with the care of a museum curator. 'I only collect stamps.'

Oh God, no wonder Lucy was so unpopular—quite aside from the stutter, the freckles, the acne, and the whole dad-priest thing, she was even more geeky than Ramona.

They were so engrossed in the magazines and brainstorming ideas for their project that they didn't even hear Deb return from her run.

'Hello, girls,' she said, panting slightly as she appeared as if from nowhere.

'Mum,' Ramona shouted as she and Lucy jumped. 'You shouldn't creep up on people like that.'

Ignoring her, Deb smiled at Lucy. 'Hi, I'm Deb. So lovely to meet you.'

'S-s-same … I-I'm Lucy.'

'I'm sorry I'm all sweaty.' She beamed as she wiped her shiny brow. 'I'm just back from my run. *So* invigorating. Best way to start the day.'

Now it was Ramona's turn to roll her eyes. Deb made it sound like she'd been running for years, when in reality she'd only taken it up a couple of weeks ago. In that short time she'd become a running maniac, constantly going on about the physical and mental benefits of her new passion. At least it got her out of the house.

'Is Lucy one of the girls you've been chatting to for hours every night?'

Lucy turned back to an autumn edition of *Vogue* from 1957 as her freckles once again disappeared in a swathe of red.

'We're doing that huge fashion project together. I told you, remember?'

'Ah, that's right. Sorry, Lucy, I'd lose my head if it wasn't screwed on.' So not true, she was the most organised person on the planet but she liked to pretend she was chill. 'Well, I'll leave you to your homework while I take a shower.'

'Wow … you and your mum … d-don't exactly look alike but you sound like twins,' Lucy said as Deb disappeared into the bathroom.

'Heard that before. Once I answered her phone and before I could say who I was, the guy—someone from her office—started asking all these questions.'

Lucy giggled. 'You could … h-have some fun with that.'

'Maybe,' Ramona said. 'By the way, do you want a drink?'

'What have you got?'

Ramona listed off a number of drinks that were supposed to be sports drinks but may as well be soft drinks.

'Wowsers,' Lucy breathed.

Ramona laughed. 'My mum works for The Energy Co. She gets all these for free.'

Lucy grabbed a blue bottle. 'Thanks. This is so cool. The only perks that come with Dad's job is he has the keys to the communion wine cupboard if I ever feel like a drink.'

Ramona couldn't hide her shock. 'Do you sneak it?' Maybe the others would change their opinion on Lucy if they knew she wasn't always a goody-two-shoes.

'No,' she scoffed. 'He's a great dad but there are certain things he has a hard line on. The one time I took the Lord's name in vain, he washed my mouth out with soap. All these years later, I can still taste it. If I got drunk on church wine, he'd kill me. And then, I'd not only have a minister for a dad but also one who was in prison for murder. That would be too much drama, even for me.'

Ramona laughed. 'You're really funny, you know that?'

Lucy blushed again, but Ramona saw the hint of a smile as she realised Lucy had said three whole sentences without stuttering once.

'Have you ever thought about … finding your d-dad?'

Lucy's question came out of the blue when they'd been working quietly for a few moments, but maybe she was a mind-reader, because for the last few weeks, Ramona had been giving this very thing some thought. 'Why?'

'It's just … like I said, you don't look much like your m-mum, so you probably take after him. And, although I don't really remember my mum, Dad t-talks about her all the time and we have lots of photos … I-I can't imagine not knowing anything.'

'I am curious,' Ramona admitted. 'But I can't do anything about it at least for a few years.'

'What do you mean?'

'There's this register,' she explained, having researched it herself. 'All donors since 2010 have to agree to going on it, so that any children conceived using their sperm can find out stuff about their origins, maybe even meet the donor if they're agreeable.'

'But you were born before 2010.'

Ramona nodded. 'I can still apply, but I'll only be connected with my donor if they've also registered. So, it's basically a crapshoot; I might never find out and I can't register until I'm eighteen anyway.'

'That's so unfair. Did your m-mum choose the donor from … like, a menu? Has she given you any idea what … y-your dad might be like?'

Ramona had never spoken about this to anyone, but she thought about it more and more as she got older. Lucy might understand better than anyone because of not really remembering her own mum. She glanced towards the closed bathroom door.

'S-sorry.' Lucy gave an apologetic smile. 'I shouldn't have said anything. Dad says I have a bad habit of asking too … m-many questions.'

'It's fine,' Ramona said. 'It's actually good to talk about it.' And she could hear the water running in the shower, so it was safe to talk. 'Mum's never said much at all. The few times I've asked her, she gets kinda … edgy.'

'Why?'

'She doesn't really have a good relationship with either of her parents—I've never even met her mum—and so she's always said that we're enough, you know, just the two of us.'

Deb would probably freak out if she knew Ramona was even thinking about finding her dad.

'But she knows who both her parents are, right?' said Lucy.

'Yeah.'

'I get why she might think that though. It's just me and Dad too. It makes you close in a way I don't think people with two parents ever really can be.'

Ramona nodded. 'I agree, but don't you sometimes find it stifling?'

'Not really. Dad's busy with church a lot of the time, his ... congregation and stuff. He also volunteers at the hospital. He's always saying he feels g-guilty about not spending enough time with me.' Lucy paused. 'Maybe your mum's right, maybe it's best you don't know who your father is. I m-mean ... w-what kind of guy could just hand over their sperm and not care about never seeing their own kids?'

'I dunno,' Ramona said, feeling a little defensive on behalf of her biological father, despite the fact she'd also wondered about his motivation. It couldn't have been money, because you couldn't buy or sell sperm in Australia. Was it some kind of power play? He wanted to be the patriarch of lots of future generations? But then, wouldn't someone like that want to know his children? 'I guess maybe they see it as doing a good deed or something? Almost like giving money to someone in need.'

Before Lucy could answer, the door to the bathroom opened and Deb emerged wrapped in a towel. Ramona shot Lucy a look telling her that this conversation was over and, even after her mum had disappeared into her bedroom, neither of them raised the topic again.

Debra

Deb's phone rang the moment she closed her bedroom door.

'Hey there,' she answered, putting Quinn on speaker so she could get dressed. 'Aren't you supposed to be at some whiskey thing?'

'It's not till this afternoon. I'm doing my laundry and thinking about you. Has Tristan responded to your like yet?'

'You mean *your* like,' Deb chided, grabbing underwear from her drawer. 'And no, he hasn't.' Or rather … she hadn't checked.

'Ah well, maybe he will today.'

'Maybe.' Deb tugged a black T-shirt dress over her head. 'How'd your date with Mrs D go last night?'

'Best date ever. She's a crack-up. We had this delicious berry cake and tomorrow she's going to teach me how to bake one myself so I can wow everyone in the office at the next Bake-Off.'

Deb groaned. 'Dammit, is it that time again?'

Once a year The Energy Co had a Bake-Off—everyone had to bring a cake or dessert to share for morning tea. Deb usually found cooking therapeutic but didn't like feeling obliged to do it and hated the competitive nature of her male colleagues.

'Still a few weeks away, but this time I'm going to steal Steve's crown. I swear he gets his wife to cook for him. Anyway, I'm off to walk the devil-dog. Make sure you message me the moment Tristan replies.'

Quinn was gone before Deb had the chance to say goodbye.

She applied the new serum she'd bought 'to reduce the appearance of fine lines'—it was only a cheap one from the supermarket but hopefully it would do the trick—then covered it with tinted moisturiser before heading back out to the living area. Lucy seemed like a sweet kid and she and Ramona sounded as if they were making great progress on their project, so Deb set to writing up her weekly shopping list.

It wasn't long before curiosity got the better of her and she opened eMatch to check if Tristan had responded to *her* 'like'. It had been almost twenty-four hours—if he was interested you'd think there'd be some kind of reply waiting in her account. Deb held her breath as she clicked open the app.

And there it was. Her stomach turned inside out. He *had* sent her a message.

Dear Lee

For a second, she thought it must be meant for someone else, but then remembered her alias.

Thanks for connecting. I must admit I'm very new to this whole online dating thing. Have no idea what I'm doing.

Kind regards, Tristan.

'Kind regards?' She read that bit out loud, already imagining what Quinn would say about such formality, but Deb kinda liked it. The way Quinn spoke about dating these days, it sounded as though you were more likely to get a dick pic than a 'kind regards' in a first message.

Glancing over at the girls, Deb carried the laptop into her bedroom, closed the door, climbed onto her bed and took about fifteen minutes to draft a response, typing and deleting multiple times before she finally went with:

Hi Tristan

I too am a novice at this. My friend from work encouraged me to give online dating a go. It's kind of terrifying.

Cheers, Lee.

Assuming he wouldn't reply immediately, Deb opened Maggie Beer's website and clicked on the baking and desserts section. She'd barely started scrolling before her computer pinged with a new message.

This wasn't exactly my idea either, but I've always been a try anything once kind of bloke.

She smiled at the screen as another message appeared.

I think we're supposed to start by asking each other some getting to know you questions. Tell me if I'm being presumptuous, but I'll go first. What do you do in your downtime?

Deb laughed—downtime wasn't really a thing when you worked full-time, had a long-ish commute and were a single mother, but she didn't want to mention Ramona.

I craft. I make miniature models and sometimes earrings and jewellery.

That last bit was a stretch because she hadn't made anything like that for years, but she'd been thinking about dabbling again ever since Quinn had put the idea into her head.

That sounds fun. I used to make model trains when I was a kid but never thought about doing it as an adult. Maybe I'll have to give it another go.

Maybe. So, what about you? Any current hobbies?

I'm a bit of a gardener myself, although my roses might disagree. Maybe it'd be more honest to say I enjoy trying to get things to grow in the patch of dirt at the back of my house.

Deb laughed and typed something she always berated Quinn and Ramona for overusing.

LOL—I like gardening too but live in a flat so a few indoor pot plants are my limit.

The messages continued back and forth until the bedroom door flew open and Ramona barged in. 'Mum, we're *starving* and there's nothing in the house for lunch. When are you going shopping?'

Deb glanced at the time and couldn't believe she'd been chatting to Tristan for almost an hour. She snapped the laptop shut as if she were a teenage boy caught watching porn.

'Sorry, got distracted. I'll head out now. What do you guys feel like?'

'Can we order a pizza?'

Bamboozled by her more than pleasant message exchange with Tristan, she nodded—'Sure, go for it'—completely forgetting that the treat would be totally stretching the weekly budget.

Ramona

On Monday morning as Ramona was getting off the train, her phone beeped with a text. Busy watching Nyra's hilarious videos on TikTok and assuming it would be from her mum anyway, she was swiping it off screen, when she registered Lucy's name.

I've had an idea. Can you meet me in the library before the bell?

Is it urgent?

Surely it could wait till fashion class that arvo. Ramona was itching to get to Drysdale and see her friends.

It's about your dad!

My dad? Ramona's heart skipped a beat, her hand tightening on her phone as she checked the time. Even after the walk from the station to school, there'd still be twenty minutes till she had to be in class.

Okay. Be there in five.

She picked up her pace as she headed towards the school and then straight to the library. The door groaned as Ramona pushed it open. Ms Woo, the librarian, welcomed her with a smile as she passed on

136

her way to Lucy, who was sitting on a stripy, multicoloured couch in the far corner.

'Hey.' Lucy's eyes lit up as Ramona approached. She snapped her book shut.

'What's this about my dad?' Ramona asked, sinking down onto the couch next to her.

'Well ... I-I've been thinking about what we were ... t-talking about on the weekend. You ... know about how you c-can't apply to find your father until you're eighteen ...?'

'And?' Ramona wished Lucy would just spit it out. What if someone saw them together?

Lucy tapped the book she'd been reading. 'This is about this w-woman who does a DNA test. And the result tells her that her ... d-dad isn't who she thought he was. It got me thinking that—'

'That *I* could do a DNA test and maybe it would help me find my dad?'

Lucy nodded. 'Well, it's an idea, but it might be a long shot.'

'What do you mean?'

'The woman in this book found out about her dad because his ... s-sister had done a DNA test and so the link appeared. To find your father, he or s-someone related to him will also have to have done the test and ... I-I did a bit of research and there a few ... c-companies that do it, so ...'

'So, if my dad or someone in his family hasn't taken a test with the same company, we wouldn't find each other?'

'Yeah. Of course, they show ... m-more distant connections too. You might find a ... c-cousin and that could help you start to track your dad down.'

Ramona's heart leapt. That was more hope than she'd had before. Imagine having a cousin!

'Lucy,' she beamed, feeling as if she had just been given a present she hadn't even known she'd wanted. 'Have I told you lately you are a freaking genius? I could honestly kiss you.'

Lucy grinned as her cheeks turned tomato. 'That could make things awkward.'

'Does the book tell you how I get one of those tests?'

'You have to order it online. I-I've found a list of places that do it. This one ...' She lifted her phone and pointed to the screen. 'Seems to be the most reliable and most ... p-popular, which means you're more likely to get a m-match through them.'

Ramona's heart deflated as if it were a balloon popped by a pin. 'I'd need a credit card for that, and no way Mum will allow me to use hers.' Not only was it for emergencies only, but she'd tell Ramona there was a reason the register didn't allow you to sign up until you were eighteen, and that rules weren't made to be broken. She'd probably be hurt as well.

But it was Ramona's life. *Her* dad. Shouldn't she be the one to decide if and when she wanted to find out about him? 'Thanks for the idea. I'll give it some thought. Better get to parade.'

They headed out of the library together and Lucy turned in the opposite direction. Lost in thought, Ramona jumped when Sydney came up behind her.

'Boo! Were you in the library with the stutterer?' Sydney made it sound like she'd seen Ramona coming out of a sex shop.

'We were talking about our project,' Ramona said defensively as they headed towards Drysdale.

'Well, of course. As if you'd *choose* to h-h-hang out w-with h-h-h-h-*her*.'

'She's not that bad. And she's really good at drawing.'

Ramona was about to add that they were wrong about her mum and dad too, but Sydney had stopped and was giving her a look that made her blood go cold.

'You know, if she's so fantastic, maybe you should hang out with her more often. Maybe next sleepover, you'll be too busy going to midnight mass with the stutterer instead.'

'What? Don't be ridiculous,' Ramona scoffed, her heart beating fast. If Sydney decided to stop hanging out with her, she'd lose Nyra and probably Kenzie as well. 'I'm just happy she can draw because God knows she's not much good at anything else.'

Sydney sniggered and opened her mouth as if to say something, but Ramona got in first, hoping to distract her. 'I'm thinking about looking for my father.'

'Wow. That's … How are you going to do that?'

Ramona told her about the registry and how she wouldn't be able to join it until her eighteenth birthday.

'That sucks. It's not like you're a baby or anything. If you wanna find your dad, you should be able to.'

'But Lu—*I* just realised that maybe there's another way. I can do a DNA test that might give me some answers. Well, I *would* be able to if I could actually order one, but you need a credit card for that.'

'I could order one for you.'

'What?' Ramona blinked. 'You have a credit card?'

'No, but I know my dad's numbers. I get stuff on his Amex all the time. He never notices.'

'Wow. Are you serious? I mean, I could give you the cash.' She'd have to get it out of her savings account, but she could do that one arvo before her mum came home from work.

'For certs. And don't worry about the money, he won't miss it.' Sydney shoved her phone in Ramona's face. 'Just give me the address and we'll do it now.'

Ramona hesitated—did she really want to do this? What if it was a waste of time and she discovered nothing? Or worse, what if she found her dad and he wanted nothing to do with her?

Then again, how boring would life be if you never took any risks?

'Okay, I'll have to google to find out where to order from, but …' She bounced up and down on her toes. 'Let's do this.'

Debra

'I'm going to be sick.' Deb pressed a hand against her roiling stomach as she stared into the bathroom mirror on Wednesday night, Quinn and Ramona standing on either side.

She could *not* do this.

'No, you're not,' Quinn assured her, 'because you haven't eaten anything all day.'

It was true; aside from three coffees that had possibly only amplified her jitters, she'd been unable to stomach anything. She hadn't been on a date in over sixteen years. What should she wear? How should she greet Tristan? What if he was a serial killer masquerading as a seemingly safe middle-aged vet? Or another evil narcissist who charmed the pants off her and then made her life a living hell?

Quinn had been in back-to-back meetings all day and by the time she'd emerged Deb had been close to cancelling.

'I shouldn't leave Ramona,' she'd argued. Even though she trusted Quinn, it wasn't entirely an excuse. She'd never left her daughter with anyone before.

'Absolutely not,' Quinn had said. 'There is no way in hell you're backing out. We had a deal, remember? Five dates.'

'That deal is ridiculous. And you're not having any luck either. Maybe we should both admit defeat?'

'No way. I'll come over to your place and hang with Ramona if it makes you feel better.'

'Relax, Mum, you look great,' Ramona said now, 'and it's not like you're going off to marry the guy.'

In the end, it was because of her that Deb somehow managed to follow through. Ramona had been so much nicer to her since she'd agreed to try dating, and she wanted to show her daughter she could be courageous and do something without her.

'Don't do anything I wouldn't do,' Quinn teased as they waved her off.

Her heart thumped in time to the tap of her shoes on the path as she headed for her car and her hands were shaking so badly that it took a few attempts to get the key in the ignition. Sweat pooled under her bra as she reversed out of the car park. Tristan would probably smell her before he saw her.

Oh God, what if she did stink?

She drove just far enough that she could be certain Quinn and Ramona could no longer see her and then pulled over and sniffed under her arms. Not too bad.

You're just looking for excuses.

The voices in her head were right. She contemplated staying right here on the side of the road for an hour and then going home and announcing it had been a fizzer. Quinn and Ramona would be none the wiser.

But *she'd* know.

And as terrifying as this was, Deb was tired of letting fear rule her life. Even if nothing came of this, it would feel good to have stepped out of her comfort zone and done something she'd never imagined she'd be able to do. Although she'd never allow herself to play the victim again, she had to turn on the radio to try and drown out the noise in her head as she drove towards the café in Parramatta where she'd agreed to meet Tristan. He lived in Castle Hill, so not too far away if things went well, but also not so close that if they didn't hit it off, they might accidentally run into each other at the local supermarket.

Her phone beeped with a message as she arrived in the car park.

I've got us a table by the window. In case you don't recognise me, I'm the one wearing an orange shirt with cats all over it.

Imagining poor Tristan sitting all alone in the café waiting for her to show up, she checked her lipstick in the visor mirror, locked her car and walked right on inside.

'Hi, you meeting someone?' asked the bubbly waitress at the entrance.

'Yep. Him.' Deb pointed to a man sitting exactly where Tristan had said he would be, wearing the loudest shirt she'd ever seen. Quinn and Ramona would very much approve.

He looked up, met her gaze with a smile and stood as he lifted his hand in an awkward wave.

Something inside her unwound. Not only was he even more handsome, tall and broad-shouldered than his photo gave him credit for, he looked as nervous as she felt. With only a quick inhale, she made her way over to him.

'Well, hello. I guess you're Lee?' His voice had the deep, dulcet tones of the didgeridoo she and Quinn had heard last week in the park.

She nodded, ignoring the guilt at the tiny white lie. 'Tristan?'

'The one and only.' He grimaced. 'Sorry—I knew I'd say something cheesy. Can we start this again?' He leaned forward and brushed a kiss against her cheek. 'Hi, Lee, it's lovely to meet you. I'm Tristan.'

'You too,' she managed as his stubble grazed against her face, sending shivers down her spine. She couldn't tell if they were good or bad shivers, yet the scent of something sweet but tart gave the alluring aromas from the kitchen a run for their money.

When he pulled out her chair for her, Deb tried to ignore the alarm bells going off in her head. Even the worst of men could be charming in the beginning.

'Thank you,' she managed as he slipped into the seat opposite her. 'I like your shirt.'

'Thanks. My daughter gave it to me as a joke—she didn't think I'd wear it. Don't tell her, but I kind of like it.'

'Me too,' she said, and then a semi-awkward silence followed.

'Shall I order us a drink?' Tristan asked eventually.

'Yes. Good idea. I'll have a hot chocolate, please. If I drink coffee now, I'll never sleep.'

His chair scraped loudly against the floor as he pushed it back to stand. 'Would you like something to eat as well? The cakes look great.'

Deb followed his gaze to the glass cabinet. Her instinct was to say no, but the cakes did look amazing and at least it would give her something to do with her hands. 'Actually yes. I've hardly eaten all day.'

She decided on a slice of raspberry and white chocolate cheesecake and then dug her phone out of her bag to text Quinn while Tristan went to order.

I'm here.

And?

And I'm undecided about whether he's a serial killer.

144

Never mind that? Does he look like his profile picture? Better? Worse?

Deb risked a glance over to where Tristan stood at the counter. His hair—the colour of dark chocolate—was what you might call slightly scruffy, but the way it curled at the ends suited him.

Better. I guess. It felt quite a miracle for a man in his late forties to still have all his hair and not be going grey. *But looks aren't everything.* Oscar had been one of the best-looking men she'd ever seen.

She slipped her phone back into her bag as he approached.

'They're going to bring it over to us.'

She nodded as he sat back down, and they smiled awkwardly at each other again. While Deb tried again to think of something to say, she couldn't help noting he had lovely espresso-brown eyes and lines around them that indicated he'd had a lot to smile about in his life.

They both spoke at once.

'So, you're a payroll manager?'

'What made you decide to become a vet?'

Deb snort-laughed and then covered her mouth, only to realise that Tristan had just done the same. 'Oh my goodness, you sound like a pig when you laugh as well.'

'Geez, thanks.' He snorted again. 'Usually, people don't tell me that until they've known me at least a few weeks.'

She smiled, immediately relaxing. 'Did you get picked on because of it when you were little?'

'Relentlessly. This one kid, Joshua Wheeler, used to tell jokes so I'd laugh, and everyone could take the micky out of me.'

'Kids can be so cruel.'

He grinned. 'Ain't that the truth? Even as adults, my two still taunt me on an almost daily basis.'

Resting one elbow against the table, Deb leaned forward a little. 'Tell me about them.'

'Well, Tara is twenty-one and the life of every party. She's just started her third year of law at Sydney Uni, which I think she'll do very well at as she's never lost an argument in her life. I feel sorry for her boyfriend.' His dark eyes sparkled as he spoke. 'Then there's Tom, he's much quieter. He's twenty-three going on fifty-five. He's always been an old soul.'

'And what does he do?' Deb asked as a waiter delivered their drinks and two pieces of cheesecake. Tristan had gone for the triple chocolate.

'He's almost finished his dentistry degree. He also does triathlons. He's won a few medals of late.'

'Sounds like both your kids are terrible underachievers,' she said, digging her fork into the cheesecake. 'You must be so disappointed.'

Tristan snort-laughed again, which made Deb do the same—not a good idea when she'd just taken a mouthful of deliciousness. He handed her a serviette.

'Thanks.' She wiped her mouth and composed herself again. 'Do Tom and Tara still live with you?'

He nodded as he lifted his mug. 'But they're both so busy, we're like ships in the night. They're worried I'm going to end up a lonely old man and they'll come around one day and find me half-eaten by Alsatians. That's why they've been on at me to start dating.'

She almost mentioned Ramona then—about how she had similar worries—but remembered herself just in time. 'How many Alsatians do you have?'

'None.' He grinned. 'But it's always Alsatians you read about doing such things. Poor babies—they get a bad rap. They're actually very loyal, loving and protective animals.'

'Do you have any pets?' It seemed as if a vet would.

'Yep. Two cats and a golden retriever. You?'

She shook her head as she dug her fork into her cake again.

'How is it?' he asked.

'Delicious. Yours?'

'Same. So who convinced you to start online dating?'

'My friend Quinn. We met at The Energy Co, but she's become a very important part of my life, both at work and outside of it. She keeps me from turning into an old stick-in-the-mud and I try to keep her from doing anything too crazy.'

'Does Quinn work in payroll too?'

Deb shook her head. 'No, she's in digital marketing, which is exactly where she should be. She's colourful and creative. We're as different as *Schitt's Creek* and *Downton Abbey* but our friendship just works. She's the yang to my yin.'

'Are you *Schitt's Creek* or *Downton Abbey*?'

'I'm surprised you have to ask!'

They shared a smile as they both sipped their drinks again.

'Who started at The Energy Co first?' Tristan asked.

'Me. I've been there three years, and Quinn started a few months after me. She jammed the photocopier in her first week and I found her in the copy room in a tizz and helped her fix it. She bought me a coffee the next morning to say thanks, and it kind of became a thing. Now we take turns.'

'So why and how did Quinn get you into this situation with me?'

'Well, she's only twenty-seven and desperate to find the love of her life. She refuses to believe I'm happily single.'

'And are you?'

'Yeah, most of the time. Although I'm enjoying this more than I thought I would.'

'Me too.' He smiled and held out his mug so they could clink. 'Did you get into payroll because you liked maths at school and you're good with numbers?'

'Yes and no. I am good with numbers, but I actually studied psychology at uni.'

'Really?'

She nodded.

'And what happened? Didn't you enjoy it?'

Deb took a long sip of her drink to bide time; she couldn't tell him the truth. 'Loads more people do the degree than there are jobs. I kinda fell into payroll and,' she shrugged, 'I enjoy it. It's not too taxing, but there's more to it than most people think.'

'Yeah, I understand. When I had my own practice, I had to do my own payroll. I'm glad I just work with the animals now.' She laughed and he hit her with another question. 'When was your last serious relationship?'

It was a reasonable query for a first date, but Deb's temperature shot to boiling. 'A very long time ago,' she said eventually. 'It wasn't a good experience, and if I'm honest, it's made me very wary about getting involved with anyone ever again.'

He looked chagrined. 'I'm sorry. You don't have to talk about it if you don't want to.'

'Thanks.' She smiled, appreciating his discernment. 'So, what made you become a vet?'

'I've wanted to be one almost as long as I can remember. My parents have a small holding in the Blue Mountains and we had a menagerie of animals growing up. My brother and sister used to complain about having to clean out the rabbit cages and walk the dogs, but I loved it all. One day, our goat—that we'd raised from a kid—got sick, and I was terrified. I thought she was going to die. But we took her to the vet and he diagnosed her with indigestion, gave her some pills, and she lived a long and happy life eating underwear off the washing line. I decided then and there that I wanted to do the same—spend my life saving animals.'

'I don't think I've ever known anyone who had a pet goat.'

He chuckled. 'They're actually having a moment. You'd be surprised by how many miniature goats I see.'

'Sounds like an idyllic place to grow up though.'

He swallowed a mouthful of cake. 'Yeah, it was. I get back there as often as I can to visit Mum and Dad, or at least that's what I tell them, but it's really because she makes the best damn chocolate cake in the Southern Hemisphere.'

Deb smiled, thinking his parents and his childhood sounded the exact opposite of hers.

'What about you?' he asked. 'Did you grow up in Sydney?'

'No, I was raised in Perth. I didn't move to Sydney until I was an adult.'

'And are your parents still together? Are you close?'

She scoffed.

'I'm sorry,' Tristan said. 'I tend to ask a lot of questions when I'm nervous but tell me if I'm being too nosy.'

'No, not at all. It's just … close is the last word I'd use to describe the relationship I have with my parents.' She took a sip of her drink, then, 'They're divorced. When I was ten, Mum simply decided she no longer wanted to be a wife or mother. One day she packed her bags and left while I was at school and Dad was at work. I came home to a note tacked to the fridge telling us she needed to be true to herself and her current situation wasn't working for her.'

'Wow. Her current situation being wife and mother?' When Deb nodded, Tristan shook his head in disbelief. 'How did your dad take it?'

'To be honest, I think he was relieved. Although he probably wished she took me with her, so he could get on with his life as well.' Deb chuckled, despite still not finding her childhood amusing. 'He tried his best. He sent me to an expensive private high school, gave me everything money could buy but ...'

'You just wanted your parents?' Tristan finished.

She nodded and water welled in her eyes. The last thing she wanted to do was cry in front of this man, but his sympathetic understanding almost unravelled her.

'What happened to your mum? Did she stay gone? Are you in touch with her now?'

'No.' Deb swallowed. 'Dad tracked her down to get a divorce and once in a blue moon she'd send me a postcard, but she never left a number for me to call her, and I decided long ago, I wasn't going to chase her. Last I heard she was living off the grid in some commune in Tasmania, but sticking to one thing isn't her forte, so she could be anywhere by now.'

'Geez. I can't even imagine thinking about leaving my kids.'

'I know.'

'Sorry, I didn't mean—'

'It's fine.' Deb shook her head and, not wanting to waste breath talking about her mum, returned to their previous topic. 'Anyway, your job must be tough sometimes. Like when you have to put an animal down?'

He didn't blink at the change of subject. 'Yeah, it can be, but mostly I know I'm doing the right thing for my patient. Watching their owners have to make such a heart-wrenching decision and then say goodbye though ... that never gets easier.'

'I can imagine. I had a dog that I had to put down and it was just horrendous.'

'I'm sorry to hear that,' he said. 'Did you have it a long time?'

She nodded. 'My dad got him for my tenth birthday. Just after Mum left.' The adorable puppy had been a guilt-gift, someone to keep her company at home when he was working late and on the weekends. Which was always.

'What breed was he?'

'A beagle. His name was Doogie and I adored him.'

His eyebrows squished together. 'Doogie?'

'Yes. As in Doogie Howser, from the TV show.'

'You *liked* that show?'

She smiled at his teasing tone. 'Hey, I was ten years old. Sue me.'

Their eyes met and her stomach flipped. It had been so long since she'd experienced any kind of attraction that she almost put it down to eating her cheesecake too fast after practically starving herself all day.

'Doogie got sick—kidney disease—and eventually … It broke my heart, and I haven't been able to bring myself to get another one since.'

'Grief for a pet is a terrible thing and not given enough gravitas in our society. These days I recommend a lot of people see a therapist after the loss of a pet.'

'It's not the worst thing that can happen to you though,' Deb said, suddenly feeling stupid when the poor man had lost so much more in comparison. 'It can't be as bad as losing your wife?' Tristan had mentioned he was a widower in one of his messages.

His expression grew serious. 'Loss isn't a competition.'

'True.' But still. 'Do you mind me asking how she died?'

'Marie had ovarian cancer. One day her periods stopped, and she thought it was early menopause. We were super busy at the clinic and by the time she went to see a doctor … she was stage four. Her body was riddled with it. She was gone within six months.'

'I'm so sorry,' Deb said, not at all feeling like those three little words were enough. 'How old were Tom and Tara?'

'Twenty and eighteen. Tara was in the middle of her HSC. She was sitting her English exam when Marie took her last breath.'

'Oh God. Poor girl.'

'She was amazing. So was Tom. I was a mess. If it wasn't for them ...' His voice drifted off.

'Was Marie a vet too?'

'Yeah. We met at university—first lecture. I'd forgotten my pens and so she lent me one of hers. She had black and pink ones, but she refused to give me a black one. Said that maybe if I had to write everything in pink ink, I'd remember to bring my own next time.'

Deb smiled at the affection in his voice. 'And did you?'

'Yep. But we spent almost every waking hour together after that. We studied together, graduated together, went to London and worked together in a big practice there, then came back and bought our own clinic.' He smiled sadly. 'Tara is the spitting image of her and sometimes when she walks into the kitchen, for a moment, I forget ...'

Heavy silence hung between them for a few long moments.

'You're still in love with her, aren't you?' Deb said.

He looked down into his now empty mug, nodding. 'I'll always be in love with her.'

'Oh, Tristan.' Deb's heart broke at the anguish in his voice.

He looked up and his eyes swum with unshed tears. 'I'm sorry ... we're on a date and I'm about to start blubbering about my dead wife.'

'It's okay,' she said, but it wasn't.

Her chest felt hollow with sadness at his admission. Even though Marie was dead, she'd been loved by this kind, gentle, smart, good-looking man and Deb didn't think she'd ever know what such love felt like.

Quinn

'I thought she was going to chicken out,' Ramona exclaimed as Deb's old Corolla disappeared down the road.

Me too, Quinn thought but didn't let on. 'Your mum's braver than you think. Now, shall we go inside? Have you got homework to do or do you want to watch *MAFS* with me?'

'I'm not allowed to watch *MAFS*, but you don't need to stay anyway. I don't need a babysitter.'

That's not what your mother said.

'Babysitter?' Quinn pretended to scoff. 'That's not why I'm sticking around. This is the first time my best friend has gone on a date in over fifteen years. I want to hear the goss the moment she walks in the door.'

Ramona giggled, seemingly buying the story. It wasn't all lies—Quinn couldn't wait to hear about Deb's night.

'Are you really not allowed to watch *MAFS*?' she asked, once they were inside and Ramona was making them each a Milo.

'No.'

'What are you allowed to watch?'

'*The Wiggles. Bluey. Playschool.*'

Quinn snorted. 'Please tell me you're joking.'

Ramona grinned. 'Yeah. She's not *that* bad. I've watched *Outer Banks* and *Ginny and Georgia*, but my faves are reruns of *Bewitched*, *Golden Girls* and *I Love Lucy*.'

Quinn loved that Ramona had such a passion for old things. 'Well, if you don't have homework, I'm happy to put on any of those.'

Ramona handed a mug to Quinn. 'I'll do my homework out here. Mum prefers me to do it at the table. But feel free to watch something you want to watch.'

Quinn glanced at said table, which was clear at one end and covered in little packets of polymer clay and jewellery-making tools at the other. It was good to see Deb was getting back into making. 'Are you sure the TV won't distract you?'

'Nah. I've done most of it already. Just got to highlight some stuff in my science textbook, but I'm good at multitasking.'

As an expert multitasker herself, Quinn couldn't argue with that, so she took her Milo to the coffee table, picked up the remote and flopped onto the couch.

The way Deb spoke, it was almost impossible to get a word out of Ramona these days, but she was chatty from the moment she sat down next to Quinn, textbook in her lap, phone in her hand. So much for working at the table. While running a highlighter over the occasional sentence in her book, Ramona talked about her new school, the project she was doing in fashion class, her new friends and their love lives. This Sydney girl sounded like she had a more successful love life than Quinn. Listening to Ramona made her feel like she was back in high school again, although even in the decade since she left so much had changed.

'I wish they'd had programs like you're doing when I was at school.' Quinn gestured to the violet high-waisted pants Ramona was wearing with a white blouse with cute ruffled short sleeves. 'Are all your new friends into vintage fashion as much as you?'

Ramona's expression dimmed. 'Don't think so. They're much more interested in what's current. Hey, do you have a boyfriend?'

Wondering if the change of subject meant anything, Quinn shook her head.

'But you're on the apps, right?'

'I was but I'm taking a break for a bit.'

Ramona nodded. 'Why do you think Mum's never had a boyfriend?'

'Um ...' Quinn hadn't been expecting that question. 'She's been busy raising you.'

'That's a bullshit—sorry.' Ramona gave a sheepish smile. 'That's a crap excuse. I have friends with single mums and they manage to have a social life and date as well as working and doing the kid thing.'

Quinn shrugged. 'I'm guessing most of those friends also have a father around, grandparents who can babysit. Childcare is expensive, you know.'

Ramona rolled her eyes in that way only teenagers can, once again making Quinn feel ancient. 'That's what Mum said, but I've been old enough to stay home alone for years now and she still never goes out. She's suffocating sometimes! I just hope this date works out and she chills out a little.'

Quinn had to admit, she'd sometimes wondered if something terrible had happened to Deb to turn her off men altogether. Going out of her way to have a baby alone in her twenties seemed a rather drastic decision, but whenever she raised the topic of old boyfriends, Deb always managed to quickly change the subject, and would not be comfortable with her talking to her daughter about this.

Thankfully she was saved by the bell. Or rather her phone. 'Speaking of mothers,' she said, answering the call. 'Hi, Mam. What's up?'

'That's no way to talk to your mother. The proper way to answer the phone is, "Hello, Quinn speaking, how may I help you?"'

Now it was her turn to roll her eyes. 'Maybe if you don't know who it is. Maybe if you're not related. And maybe I don't expect that you're calling to ask me for something? Forgive me for thinking you might simply be calling to see how *I* am.'

'No need to take that tone with me. I have good news.'

'Don't tell me—Rowan and Mia are pregnant again?'

'Guess again!' Mam sang, clearly over her irritation.

'You've won an award for your Irish dancing.'

'Oh, don't be silly, Quinn. They don't give awards at my age. I'm doing it for the fitness and the fun. But, I'm going to have to miss dancing in a few weeks.'

'Why?' Quinn asked.

'Because Daddy and I are coming to visit you and Dec. And, that's not even the best part,' she added before Quinn could get a word in. 'You know how you're always telling me how gorgeous Forster is. Well, we've booked a fancy apartment for you, Declan, Darpan and us for a week.'

'When?'

She named a date about a month away.

'I'll have to see if I can get time off work—that's pretty short notice,' Quinn said, half-excited at the prospect of a family holiday in one of her fave beachside towns, half-dreading it. Roisin Paladino was fabulous in small doses, but it never took long for her overbearing and interfering to get on Quinn's nerves, and she also didn't relish the prospect of being the fifth wheel.

'Will you be bringing anyone with you? The apartment has four bedrooms, so if you've got a gentleman friend you'd like to introduce to us, he can have the fourth room?' Roisin suggested hopefully.

'It's fine. I'll be coming alone.' Then, before her mother could pry into her dating life, she added, 'Really sorry, Mam, but I've got to go. I'm at Deb's place.'

'Oh, say hello from me. Maybe I can meet some of your friends this visit?'

'Maybe. Talk soon.'

'Was that your mother?' Ramona looked up from her phone. She'd discarded the textbook a while ago and was now switching between Snapchat, Instagram and TikTok, giggling every few moments.

Quinn nodded.

'She sounds almost as annoying and controlling as mine. You have my sympathies.'

'Your mum is awesome,' she said with a reprimanding smile. 'Everything she does is because she adores you. Cut her a bit of slack, okay?'

Ramona shrugged and went back to chatting with her friends on her phone, while Quinn surreptitiously checked her own for *MAFS* spoilers.

Debra

'How was it?' Quinn and Ramona demanded the moment Deb stepped through the door.

They were sitting on the sofa—Quinn holding the TV remote and Ramona her phone. At least she appeared to be being semi-social rather than holing herself away in her bedroom.

Deb kicked off her shoes and flopped into an armchair. 'He's the frog's clogs,' she told them, then sighed.

Ramona looked to Quinn. 'I take it the frog's clogs is a good thing?'

'I think so.' She muted the TV and then looked to Deb. 'So why do you look like your dog just died?'

She couldn't possibly look that sad, although she had to admit she was disappointed. Her hopes had not been high, but Tristan had exceeded them. If only she'd met him a couple of decades earlier. 'Because he's totally and utterly in love with his dead wife.'

'Ew, that's gross,' Ramona said, screwing up her nose as she leapt off the couch. 'Catch ya later, Quinn.'

'So you're not going to see him again?' Quinn asked as Ramona escaped to the confines of her bedroom.

'No. I don't think so, it got kind of awkward at the end. Anyway …' She forced Tristan from her mind. 'How was your night with Ramona? Was she out here with you long?'

'All the time you've been gone.'

'Really?' Jealousy squeezed Deb's heart for the second time that night. 'What did you guys do?'

'Well, Ramona did some homework, then mostly I was watching old episodes of *Friends* while she scrolled Insta and stuff. But never mind that, let's check eMatch and find your next victim.'

Deb blinked. 'Don't you mean Snapchat? Ramona isn't on Instagram.'

'Um …' Quinn looked torn. 'She was definitely on Instagram. *And* Snapchat. I think I saw her giggling at a TikTok video as well.'

'Oh. My. God.' Deb's head began to pound. No wonder Ramona was spending so much time in her bedroom.

She shot to her feet.

Quinn did the same. 'Deb, chill. It's not like she was looking at porn.'

'Who knows? She's probably doing that as well. I'm going to kill her.'

Quinn grabbed her arm as she turned to go. 'Maybe you should wait until you've calmed down a little.'

'Don't tell me how to parent,' Deb snapped, shaking her arm free. 'You can see yourself out.'

She charged down the hallway and flung open Ramona's bedroom door.

'Mum! What the—'

'Don't you "what the" me!' She snatched the phone out of her hand and glared at the screen. There was a message from Kenzie—or rather a selfie with some kind of weird unicorn filter on it. It seemed benign, but still. She looked Ramona dead in the eye as she turned the phone towards her. 'What's this?'

'It's a Snap from my friend and that's a total invasion of my privacy,' she yelled, reaching for the phone.

Deb held it high above her head. 'How many social media platforms are you on?'

'One,' Ramona answered immediately but didn't meet Deb's gaze.

'Don't lie to me. Quinn saw you on Instagram and TikTok. If there's one thing we don't do it's *lie* to each other.'

Ramona's bottom lip quivered. 'Okay. I'm on Snapchat, Instagram and TikTok, but only—'

'What about Facebook?' She racked her mind for any others she'd heard of.

'I told you, Facebook's for Boomers.'

'So that's a "no"?'

Ramona nodded and Deb sighed, clutching the phone against her chest as she tried to work out how to handle this. This was the first time, as far as Deb knew, that Ramona had ever blatantly disobeyed her and she wanted to make sure it never happened again. Should she ground her? Take away her phone? But then they wouldn't be able to contact each other if there was an emergency. However angry, hurt and worried Deb was, the punishment could not put her daughter at possible risk.

She glanced down at the phone again and saw the screen had locked. 'What's your password?'

'I don't have to tell you that. It's my phone.'

'Actually, I paid for it, and I pay for the bills. Password?'

'You didn't pay for it,' Ramona retorted, her arms now crossed fiercely across her chest. 'Kenzie gave me her mum's old one cos it's better than the crappy one you got me.'

Deb turned the phone over in her hand and realised it did look different—larger and shinier. An iPhone! How had she not noticed before? Her anger, combined with the irritation that she couldn't afford to buy Ramona a better phone herself, grew to downright rage. She could barely speak.

'Okay,' she said after a few deep breaths. 'Here's what's going to happen. You are going to give this phone back to Kenzie tomorrow and you're going to get your old one out right now. You are going to delete *all* your social media apps in front of me, change your password to the same as mine *and* I'm going to set up that thing so that you can't download anything without my permission.'

'As if you know how to do that,' scoffed Ramona.

'You'd be surprised what I know! Would you rather I just take your phone altogether, young lady?'

'Mum, please, no. I'm really sorry,' Ramona pleaded, clearly close to tears. 'I shouldn't have lied to you, but you don't understand. I *need* social media—it's the way everyone connects these days and if I don't have it, well, Sydney, Nyra and Kenzie will probably talk about me behind my back.'

'They're not very nice friends if they do that then, are they?'

Ramona opened her mouth but seemed to think better about whatever she was going to say. She sighed, then opened her bedside drawer and pulled out her old, apparently insufficient, phone.

'It's dead,' she said, thrusting it at Deb.

'Well, we can charge it overnight in my room and I'll look after this phone too until you have the chance to give it back tomorrow. Don't even think about keeping it and hiding it or there'll be hell to pay. And from now on, no phones in the bedroom and you can go back to doing your homework at the kitchen table where I can watch you.'

Ramona shook her head. 'You don't understand. I'll take any other punishment. I'll delete everything else; I'll give you my phone at night, but puh-*lease* can I at least keep Snapchat. Just Snapchat.'

Deb felt herself wavering, but she didn't want Ramona to think she'd got away with lying.

'The punishment stands,' she said. 'For two weeks. If your behaviour is impeccable during that time, then we'll discuss reinstalling Snapchat. Just Snapchat.'

'Two weeks? You're just being a total cow because your date sucked!'

'Excuse me? Did you just call me a cow?'

'If the shoe fits!'

Deb's fury ignited again. She shoved her hands into her pockets to stop from slapping her daughter, something which she'd never done and would never forgive herself for.

'Go to bed,' she said, turning to leave. 'We'll talk more about this in the morning.'

'What's the point?' screamed Ramona. 'It's not like you're going to listen.'

This time it was Deb who slammed the door behind her, and then promptly burst into tears.

Quinn

Quinn tried to keep positive as she readied herself for her blind date on Friday night. Declan and Darpan had been over the moon when she'd asked them to set her up with an eligible guy from their office and she wanted to give it her best shot.

She eyed her phone on the vanity as she applied her make-up. If things tonight didn't go well with the investment banker, she might not be able to resist downloading the apps again. So far, the dog-walking had proved fruitless. Maybe Deb was right, maybe they should forget their deal and go back to how things were.

Poor Deb, after her disappointing date with Tristan, she'd had a mammoth fallout with Ramona. She'd looked terrible yesterday when she'd handed Quinn a cupcake with her morning coffee and apologised for snapping the night before. Quinn had followed with an apology of her own—Deb was right, she couldn't even keep a boyfriend, what did she know about parenting teenagers?

'Wowsers,' Declan said when she appeared, ready to go meet his colleague. 'Garth isn't going to know what hit him when he sees you. You look smokin', little sis.'

She looked to Darpan who sat next to Dec on the couch, nursing a glass of red wine. 'Tell him a brother should not say things like that about his little sister.'

Darpan shrugged and grinned. 'He's absolutely right. Garth's a great guy; I think you'll both have a fab night.'

'Thanks.' She gave each of them a peck on the cheek. 'If not, you two will have a lot to answer for.'

Mrs D was in her front courtyard watering her pot plants when Quinn emerged.

'Where are you off to looking so glammed up?' said the older woman, smiling her approval as she put down her watering can. Snoodles appeared to be devouring a potted geranium.

'I've got a blind date,' Quinn explained as she stooped to put on her skates.

'Ooh, splendid. Hope the gentleman knows how lucky he is.'

'Thanks. I'm a bit nervous to be honest, which is silly because it's not like I've never met a strange guy before. That's what online dating is all about. But Declan and Darpan set me up with this guy from their office—I've never even messaged him before, so I'm literally going in blind.'

'That was the only kind of blind date in my day,' said Mrs D with a chuckle.

'That's why I'm doing this,' Quinn blurted.

'What do you mean?'

'You know how I offered to start walking Snoodles? Well, it wasn't just my kind and generous heart that made me do it.'

'I know.' Mrs D smiled kindly. 'You want to get exercise as well, although between you and me, you don't really look like you need much of it.'

'Please, don't be upset,' Quinn said, because she genuinely liked her now and wanted them to be friends. Last Friday night watching movies together had been so fun—she'd almost rather be doing the same again than going on a date. 'But I found this article in an old magazine from the 1950s. It was called "129 Ways to Get a Husband" and one of them was getting a dog and walking it.'

Mrs D seemed torn between amusement and confusion. 'How is that supposed to help you get a husband?'

'Fuck knows,' Quinn said, then immediately apologised for her language.

'Don't worry about that—I love a good F-bomb as much as the next person. What else is on this list?'

She laughed as Quinn recalled some of the others. 'Read the obituaries. Get lost at football games. Make and sell toupees—apparently bald men are easy catches.'

'And are you working your way through this list?' asked Mrs D, looking slightly concerned.

'Hell no! No way I'm turning my hair a boring colour for some guy, nor am I going to stand in a corner and sob so he'll come over and see if I need rescuing, but I've decided to try some of the more reasonable options. Hence the blind date, which was number eighteen or something.' Quinn glanced at her watch. 'Speaking of which, I'm going to be late.'

'Oh dear, I'm sorry for keeping you. Have fun and let me know how you go later.'

'Will do,' Quinn called over her shoulder as she skated down the path towards the strip of cafés and restaurants just around the corner. She and Garth were supposed to be meeting at a tapas bar ten minutes ago.

She was weaving in and out of pedestrians who all seemed to be going in the opposite direction, when a blasted wheel caught on a crack and she went flying.

'Shit,' she yelled, coming face to face with the dirty pavement, her handbag upending in the process and spilling its contents all over the ground.

'Watch where you're going,' grumbled a jogger as he stepped over her. 'I could've tripped.'

Quinn gave him the finger as she snatched up her purse and phone first, then pushed herself into a sitting position, trying to ignore the sting on her hands and knees as pedestrians continued around her.

'Are you okay?' a deep voice asked.

She looked up to see a man dropping down to his haunches beside her.

'That was quite a nasty fall.' He smiled warmly at her, and all the pain disappeared as she took him in—sun-kissed caramel-blond hair, heavy stubble beard and striking eyes in a unique aqua colour, only enhanced by his in-vogue black glasses. He looked exactly like Alexander Skarsgard.

She swallowed as a gentle tingling spread from her heart to her belly.

'Here, let me help you,' he said, and she snapped out of her trance as he started to collect the items scattered around them. Her favourite hot-pink lipstick, pens galore, business cards, a packet of painkillers, loose coins, chocolate, her change of shoes, and much, much more.

Her knight in dark jeans and casual white shirt pushed up to his elbows and proffered her a tampon and her birth control pills. 'I think this is the last of it. Can I help you with anything else? Go buy some bandaids?'

'No.' Her cheeks burning, she snatched the items from him, shoved them back into her bag and hurried to stand. 'I'm fine, really. Thank you for your help.'

'Not at all,' he said, sliding his hands into his pockets. 'You have a lovely evening.'

'You too,' she whispered, but he was already sauntering away.

'Shit,' Quinn hissed again, glancing at her watch. Not only was she now rudely late but also probably looked like she'd gone a couple of rounds with Mike Tyson. Well, maybe not that bad and, if Garth *was* The One, a few grazes wouldn't put him off.

She skated cautiously for another block and finally arrived at the tapas bar, quickly swapping to the ballet flats in her bag before going inside.

'Garth? I'm so sorry I'm late,' she said by way of introduction as she made her way to the only lone guy in the place. Dec and Darpan had given her a good description, but he was even hotter than they'd made out.

He stood and gave her a sweet smile. 'No worries. At least you're here now.'

They hugged awkwardly and he frowned as she pulled back. 'You've got something in your hair.' He leaned forward to pluck it out.

Quinn cringed as he held out a dirty cigarette butt. 'Gross. That must have stuck to me when I fell just now.'

'Oh no. I guess that accounts for the cut on your cheek and ...' He glanced down. 'The grazes on your knees. Are you okay?'

She nodded. 'But do you mind if I go and clean myself up a bit?'

'Of course not. Shall I order you a drink?'

'Yes, please. Anything alcoholic.'

At that moment, she didn't care what she'd be drinking as long as it contained booze. She put her skates on the floor by the table and hurried to the restroom, where she took a long, hard look at herself in the mirror. She felt worse than she looked, and it wouldn't take much to clean her face up and wipe the dirt from her knees.

As she pulled her powder compact out of her bag, a thought struck. Her hand froze mid-air. Wasn't one of the items on the list 'accidentally have your handbag spill open' or something?

'Oh my God!' She dropped the compact and palmed her hands against her cheeks. Any number of people could have stopped to help just now, but only one person had. And that person was possibly the best-looking man she'd seen in her life. He'd been kind and gentle too. Not to mention that voice—it sounded like hot chocolate would if it could talk.

Oh God, what had she done?

She remembered Mrs D's words about fate being the thing that brought her and Mr Dagliesh together. What if fate had caused her to trip and she'd been too dumb to recognise The One when he was staring her in the face? What if she was supposed to say yes to the bandaids and then offer to buy him a drink to say thank you?

What if right now she was supposed to be sitting in some bar getting to know her future husband and instead she was about to have dinner with some guy her brother and brother-in-law had picked out for her? Since when did Dec and Darpan know the type of man who'd suit her?

Argh.

There was only one thing for it. She had to go after the Alexander Skarsgard lookalike. She should hunt him down and …

And then what? Tell him you've changed your mind about the bandaids? Offer to buy him a drink?

'Don't be stupid,' she told her reflection. 'You'd look like a psycho.'

And wasn't she supposed to stop doing this? She hadn't even given Garth a chance yet—a man who'd already waited *twenty* minutes for her—and here she was thinking about walking the streets, hunting for someone she knew sweet F-all about.

'Are you Quinn?' asked a waitress who'd just come into the bathroom.

She turned and nodded. 'Yes, why?'

'Your friend or boyfriend or whoever he is out there—the good-looking redhead—is worried about you. He asked if I'd come and make sure you were okay.'

'Oh, how sweet.' Chastised, Quinn picked up her compact. 'I'll be back out in a second.'

The waitress retreated and Quinn tidied herself up, vowing to put Handbag Dude out of her mind while she enjoyed a nice night with Garth.

If it *was* fate, then surely they'd run into each other again.

Debra

'You're looking for *him*, aren't you?' Deb stopped in her tracks and glared at Quinn.

She looked sheepish. 'I can't help myself.'

It was rare for Deb to feel anything but affection for Quinn, but she did have a lot on her mind right now—most importantly how to get her daughter talking to her again—and she was hoping Quinn would listen to her vent, if not have some ideas for reconciliation. Yet, instead of sitting at their usual bench in the park for lunch, Quinn had suggested a walk as they ate their sandwiches and she'd seemed distracted from the moment they left the office.

'Have you even been listening to a word I've been saying?' Deb asked.

'Yes, I promise I have. You know I'm good at multitasking.' As if to prove her point she took a bite from her apple.

The *him* in question was a guy Quinn had met while she'd been rushing to a blind date last Friday. She'd called Deb the moment she'd got home.

'You won't believe what happened!'

'You hit it off with Garth?'

'Oh, he was fine. He's a very nice man, we got along well and had a nice dinner, but there wasn't any chemistry. I did find out what an investment banker is, besides someone who wears a suit and carries an expensive leather laptop bag though, so not an entirely wasted evening.'

'Your brother is an investment banker,' Deb had reminded her.

'I know, but I always switch off when he starts talking about work. Anyway, I was running late and my wheel caught on a crack and I face-planted and everything spilled out of my bag.'

'Ouch. Are you okay?'

'A couple of scratches, bruises on my knees, but never mind about that. This guy ... he stopped to help me and oh. My. God. He was divine. Like an angel—but a hot one from TV or something. Remember on The Husband List there was one on there about spilling your handbag and hooking up with the guy who stopped to pick it up.'

Deb laughed. 'I don't remember the words "hooking up" *anywhere* on that list.'

'Anyway, I tried my best to focus on Garth, but I couldn't get this guy out of my head. I know it sounds ridiculous, but I have this crazy feeling that he's The One. My Ride or Die. The person I've been waiting for my entire life. We didn't even touch, but I felt it Deb. I felt *The Buzz*.'

'The Buzz?' Deb had tried not to sound sceptical.

'It was nothing like anything I've ever experienced before.'

'Have you any idea who this dream man is?'

'No. But if I see him again, I'll know. He's permanently imprinted in my mind. He's mid-to-late thirties, six feet, maybe a little taller. His hair's a caramel blond and mussed in a way that makes you want to run your fingers through it. He had about a ten-day-old beard on his perfect jawline, and his eyes—'

'You sound like you're writing a romance novel,' Deb had interrupted with another chuckle. 'If this guy was so fantastic, why didn't you ask his name?'

Quinn had sighed dramatically. 'I was in pain. I wasn't thinking straight. I should have accepted his offer of a bandaid, I should have gone after him. *Oh God.* Now I just have to hope against hope that fate will lead me to him again.'

'I thought you were leaving things up to fate?' Deb asked now as she leaned against a nearby post, her feet starting to ache.

'Sometimes fate needs a nudge in the right direction.'

Deb didn't know whether to laugh or suggest Quinn go see someone about her obsessive personality. 'Maybe you should go back on the apps,' she suggested instead. 'You've proven you can go without for a couple of weeks. And if this guy is single and lives in Sydney, then there's every chance he's on Tinder or Bumble as well.'

'Oh my God. Why didn't I think of that?' Quinn was already digging her phone out of her pocket. 'You're absolutely right.'

Deb smiled. Maybe now they could talk about *her* problem.

'Hang on …' Quinn's fingers froze as she frowned. 'Are you only suggesting that because it'll get you out of online dating?'

'No, but I'm not sure I'm going to follow through anyway,' she admitted. 'The date with Tristan was a disaster. I'm too old for this kind of stress.'

'You're only forty-two. That's hardly over the hill and I'd hardly call your date a disaster either. You had a nice night, and didn't you say you're still messaging each other?'

'No, just playing Words with Friends.'

'Girlfriend, in the dating world, that's foreplay.'

'Maybe in *your* dating world.'

'Have you messaged anyone else?' Quinn asked, still glancing around.

Deb shook her head. 'I've had a couple of likes from men, but I haven't replied. I think I'm going to delete my profile. I've got enough to worry about with Ramona at the moment.'

'She's still not talking to you?'

Deb *knew* she hadn't been listening. She swallowed her irritation. With her daughter giving her the silent treatment, the last thing she wanted was to fall out with her best friend as well.

'Nope. Well, unless you count "Have you washed my sports T-shirt?" or "Can you pass the salt?" as conversation.' Fifteen years ago, when she'd been suffering sleepless nights with a colicky baby, she'd never imagined anything could be harder than that, but the growing distance between her and Ramona was breaking her heart *and* keeping her up at night again. How long could this go on before one of them backed down and admitted defeat? 'Do you think I was too harsh on her?'

Quinn bit her lip, then, 'I don't know. Maybe a little. Two weeks with no social media probably feels like the death penalty to a fifteen-year-old. Then again, she could be sulking because she knows she was in the wrong but doesn't want to admit it. There was nothing I hated worse than saying sorry at her age.'

'I just don't want her to think she can get away with lying to me.'

Oscar had been an expert liar, skilled in the art of deception, and Deb always freaked whenever she saw flashes of his personality coming through in Ramona.

'I think you're overreacting slightly,' Quinn said. 'What Ramona did is normal teenage deception. I told more lies than not to my mother when I was growing up. She's a good kid and you're an awesome parent, but even fabulous people make mistakes.'

'You're right.' Deb sighed. 'I'll talk to her tonight. See if we can't come to some sort of compromise.'

Lord knew she couldn't stand even another day of Ramona's very cold shoulder.

'Good idea.' Quinn smiled as they entered the building and headed to the elevators, their shoes click-clacking on the tiles.

'What are you up to this evening?'

'Mrs D and I are continuing our film education—tonight is *The Sweetest Thing* and *Pillow Talk*.'

'You two are spending a lot of time together,' Deb said, trying to ignore the squeeze of jealousy.

'Mrs D is a hoot. Hey, why don't you join us? Ramona can come too, that way you don't have to worry about a babysitter.'

'You know what?' Deb felt chastised by her ridiculous jealousy of an octogenarian and perhaps getting Ramona out of the house would help defuse the tension between them. 'That would be lovely.'

Ramona

It was raining when Ramona got off the train at Granville and she didn't have an umbrella because it had been sunny when she left home that morning. But that wasn't the main reason she was walking more briskly than usual towards her apartment building.

There was a ticking bomb inside her school bag.

She hadn't expected the DNA test kit to arrive so quickly and had been shocked when Sydney handed it to her just before parade that morning.

'We should do it at recess,' Kenzie said excitedly.

Nyra nodded. 'Good idea. And then you can post it back straight after school.'

'Apparently, the result can take up to six weeks,' Sydney added, 'but the sooner you send it, the sooner we can find out the truth.'

While her friends were so enthralled by this mystery, it was all just a bit of fun for them, whereas for Ramona, it was real life. She'd have to deal with the consequences of her decision. Although she'd been thinking lots about her father since ordering the test, the moment she'd held the unassuming cardboard box in her hands, she wasn't sure she wanted to follow through.

Once she did it, there'd be no turning back.

If she managed to track down her father, her curiosity would get the better of her and she'd have to try to meet him, and then she'd have to tell her mum what she'd done. As they weren't currently on speaking terms, this was both appealing and terrifying. It would be good to get back at Deb for her ridiculous overreaction, but it could also make things worse. The way her mum was acting lately, Ramona wouldn't be surprised if she flushed her phone down the toilet and banned her from social media for life!

Then again, if she found her father, everything could change. It had been sixteen years since he'd given away his sperm. Maybe he too wanted to meet the results of his donation and was counting down the days until she might contact him. Maybe he was rich and would buy her a new phone when she told him what a monster her mother was.

Maybe she could even go live with him.

'I'd rather do it at home,' Ramona had said as she shoved the box into her bag.

The girls were disappointed, but by the time the siren rang, they'd moved on to more pressing issues, like whether Sydney should sleep with Blake or make him hold out a little longer.

Ramona, on the other hand, hadn't been able to think about anything but the little box in her bag all day. She'd told Lucy in fashion class that it had arrived and whispered about her second thoughts.

Lucy agreed there was no rush. 'You've gone almost sixteen years in the dark, what will a few more days or even weeks matter?'

She'd managed to get through the afternoon and had all but decided not to do the test at all, when she grabbed her phone from her locker after the final siren and a message from her mother changed her mind again.

Hello darling

Ramona rolled her eyes—did Deb think that sucking up was going to make her forget how unreasonable she'd been?

We're going to Quinn's neighbour's house this evening for a girly movie night, so we'll have an early dinner as soon as I get home and head out. See you soon. Love Mum.

'You've got to be kidding me!' Ramona stared in disbelief at her screen.

'What's wrong?' asked Kenzie, who was grabbing her things from her own locker nearby.

'My mother.' She flashed the message at Kenzie. 'It's like she thinks I'd be excited to spend the evening with her and her stupid friends.' The fact she liked Quinn wasn't the point—she'd never even met the neighbour. 'And who actually types "love" in a message? Hasn't she heard of emojis?'

'You expect too much of grown-ups,' Kenzie said, then pulled her in for a hug. 'Have a good night. We'll miss you.'

Until that moment, Ramona had been so consumed with the DNA test she'd forgotten she was missing a sleepover at Nyra's. Apparently her social media ban wasn't enough—her mum had also grounded her, like they were living in some stupid American TV show.

She was tired of Deb acting like a dictator—it was time to take back some control.

The rain was really pelting by the time she got to their building and if she hadn't had to pause to find her key, she might have missed the pale purple budgie perched on the windowsill of grumpy Mr Bergman's ground-floor apartment. At least she thought it was a budgie, but she'd never seen a budgie this colour before. It was beautiful, but its feathers were all ruffled and it was shivering.

'Hey, cutie pie,' she said, taking a step towards it.

It didn't fly off so she slowly reached out and squeaked with glee when the darling little thing allowed her to run her finger down its soft feathery chest.

'Hello.'

'Oh my God, you speak.' Delighted, Ramona giggled. 'Hello to you too. What are you doing out here all alone?'

'You're a pretty boy,' said the bird in reply as it stepped onto her finger.

She glanced around, looking for someone who might be able to tell her who he belonged to but there was not a soul in sight. 'What's your name?'

'Hello, gorgeous.'

She laughed. 'Are you talking to me or is that *your* name?'

'You're a pretty boy,' it said again.

'Okay, I can see I'm not going to get any sense out of you,' she said as the budgie dipped its head and nuzzled its beak against the end of her finger. She could hardly leave it out here in the summer storm—what if that big orange cat from across the road saw it? 'Do you want to come inside?'

'Inside, gorgeous.'

'I'll take that as a yes.' Carefully, she dug her key out of her bag and slipped it into the lock, the bird still perched on her other hand.

Once inside their apartment, she took it into her bedroom and showed it the vintage birdcage that was only ever supposed to be for show. 'Do you have a cage like this somewhere?'

It jumped onto the top and winked at her. She didn't know if it was on purpose or not.

'Water. I should get you some water. And something to eat.' She didn't have any seed so after grabbing a tiny bowl of water from the kitchen and placing it next to the bird on the cage, she opened her laptop. While googling what else she could feed it, she put her favourite fifties playlist on Spotify.

Within seconds of Perry Como's 'Hot Diggity' starting, the budgie began chirping and bopping up and down.

She laughed. 'Glad to see you have good taste in music. Maybe I should call you Perry? Or do you prefer Diggity?'

In reply the bird turned around and shook its tail feathers at her. Joy filled her heart. This little guy might even be worth missing the sleepover for.

By the time Deb arrived home an hour later, Ramona was besotted with her new friend and had all but forgotten the DNA test and her animosity towards her mother.

'Mum, come see what I found this arvo?' she called from her bedroom, keeping a careful eye on Perry who was still dancing atop the cage—right now to 'Diamonds Are A Girl's Best Friend'.

Deb appeared in the doorway and her eyes widened.

'Isn't he adorable?'

As if knowing Ramona was talking about him, Perry paused his funky moves and looked over. 'You're a pretty boy.'

'He's also a confused charmer,' Ramona said as she put her finger out for him to hop onto.

'Where did you get him?'

'He was sitting on Mr Bergman's windowsill when I came home.' She stroked his chest again. 'Can I keep him, Mum? He won't be any trouble. I'll look after him and buy his seed with my pocket money. I've already got a cage. Puh-lease?'

'Puh-lease,' echoed Perry.

Debra

'That cage is not suitable for a real bird,' Deb said, remembering the day they'd found it in an op shop. Ramona had fallen in love with it on sight and Deb had gone back the next day and bought it as a surprise for her thirteenth birthday. Back when things felt so much simpler and her relationship with her daughter wasn't on rocky ground.

'Does that mean I can keep him if we buy another one?' Ramona asked, her eyes widening.

Deb had to admit the budgie was adorable and the fact it had given Ramona a reason to talk to her again made her heart sing.

'I didn't say that,' she said gently. 'The fact he's so tame makes me think he's a pet, which means someone is probably beside themselves with worry right now.'

'If they cared about him that much, they shouldn't have let him escape during a storm. Anything could have happened to him,' Ramona pouted.

'He's lucky you found him, but he might have escaped by accident.'

'And how are we supposed to find his owner? He's a bird, who knows how far he flew?'

Deb sighed—she'd been looking forward to a nice night out and now she had a budgie drama on her hands. 'How far did you fly, little guy?' she asked, buying herself some time.

'You can touch him,' Ramona said, pushing her finger towards Deb. 'He likes it when you rub his belly.'

'Pretty boy, pretty boy,' said the bird as Deb did. She smiled, but then noticed his feathers were a little matted above his foot. 'Is that blood?'

Ramona leaned closer to look. 'Oh no, how'd I miss that? What should we do? Do you think he needs antiseptic?'

'He seems happy enough, so it can't be too bad, but maybe we should take him to the vet, just in case. Hopefully they can help us work out who he belongs to.'

Ramona looked torn between wanting to do the best for the budgie and the possibility that doing so might mean she lost him anyway, but Deb was firm. They didn't have time to waste as the local vet would likely be closing shortly and having to pay for after-hours attention would no doubt cost a fortune.

Despite its impracticality, they put the bird into the vintage cage and Ramona held it on her lap as Deb drove.

'The vet's just finishing up with his last patient,' said the smiley receptionist when they arrived. 'Can I get your details?'

Deb glanced at Ramona who'd plonked herself down on a plastic chair and was now hugging the cage as if *it* might fly off if she let go. 'It's not actually our bird.'

The receptionist gestured to the computer in front of her. 'It's just for our records.'

'Right, of course.' Deb gave her address and phone number and then took a seat next to her daughter. 'How was school today?'

Ramona hesitated as if contemplating whether or not to continue their war. 'It was okay. Ms Rose told Lucy and me that in all her years of teaching fashion, she's never had anyone make their own magazine and she's excited to see the final product.'

'Wow. That's great.' Deb smiled, happy because it was the most she'd said to her in days. 'Can I see your progress so far?'

Before Ramona could answer, a door off to the side opened and out walked an elderly woman cradling a rat-sized dog. Beside her was a tall, broad-shouldered, handsome man, his navy-blue scrubs clearly identifying him as the vet.

Oh God. Deb's stomach turned inside out. This could not be happening! What was *he* doing here? He'd told her he worked at a clinic in Castle Hill. If she'd known he was going to be here, she'd have made more of an effort with her appearance. At least reapplied her lipstick.

Then again, if she'd known he'd be here, she'd have driven to another vet.

Tristan patted the elderly woman on the arm, then said something to the receptionist that Deb was too befuddled to hear, before glancing down at a sheet on the desk. 'Debra Fast?'

His gaze landed on her, and his eyebrows drew together in obvious confusion.

Ramona jumped to her feet. 'I found this bird this afternoon, and he's got blood near his foot. Can you check he's okay?'

With a final glance at Deb, Tristan turned his attention to her daughter. 'Of course, bring him in,' he said warmly, gesturing for her to go ahead of him.

Ramona started into the consulting room but then looked back. 'Mum? Are you coming?'

'Of course. Sorry.' Deb blinked and somehow managed to follow, but she couldn't bring herself to meet Tristan's eyes as he closed the door behind them.

What must he think of her? Not only had she lied about her name, but also about having children. He'd been so gut-wrenchingly honest about his wife and she hadn't even been able to bring herself to tell him the most basic things about herself.

'Hey, little buddy.' Tristan slowly reached inside the cage. 'What have you done to yourself?'

'I'm calling him Perry, and he's really friendly,' Ramona said.

'Fuck off,' the bird chirped as he leaned forward and pecked Tristan's finger.

'Well, he was,' Ramona exclaimed, as she slapped her hand across her mouth to cover a laugh.

Tristan chuckled. 'Don't worry—his bark's worse than his bite.'

While her daughter and the man she'd gone on one date with chatted like old friends and he coaxed the budgie into letting him examine him, Deb struggled to control her breathing. The four walls of the tiny room felt as if they were closing in, and the overpowering scent of disinfectant made her stomach turn.

Wait till Quinn heard about this—she'd find it hilarious but right now it felt anything but.

'Is he going to be okay?' Ramona asked.

'Yeah, it's just a little scratch. I've cleaned up the blood and there doesn't appear to be any infection.'

'Hear that, Mum? So, can I keep him?'

'Um ... I don't know.' Deb forced herself out of her head and looked properly at Tristan for the first time since they'd entered the room. God, he was gorgeous—even better looking in scrubs than he'd been in that silly shirt. 'Is there any way to tell if he belongs to someone else?'

'I was just about to suggest we check for a microchip. Not many people do their budgies though, so if nothing comes up, we can put up a sign on our noticeboard, but your best bet is to post to some groups on Facebook.'

'Mum's not on Facebook,' Ramona said with a roll of her eyes. 'She believes social media is the devil's work.'

'I do n—' Realising she was shrieking, Deb sighed. 'Let's check for the microchip and go from there.'

Much to Ramona's disappointment, Perry was accounted for.

'Ah, he's actually one of the patients here,' Tristan told them. 'My colleague did the microchip. I'll call the owner and see if they can come pick him up. I'm sure he'll be very grateful to you both for bringing Frodo in.'

'The bird's name is Frodo?' Ramona's face crumpled in disgust and disappointment.

Forgetting her own discomfort, Deb put an arm around her as she said her goodbyes to the budgie.

'I'll never forget you,' Ramona sniffed, stroking her finger down his feathered chest.

'You're a pretty boy,' chirped Frodo, bouncing up and down on the top of the cage.

With a sob, Ramona turned, yanked open the door and fled.

Deb pulled her purse out of her handbag. 'How much do I owe you?'

Tristan shook his head. 'Nothing. He's not your pet, so it's fine. Thanks for bringing him in.'

'Okay. Thank you,' Deb managed.

'Lee?' Tristan said as she got to the door.

Her heart thumped and she turned back to face him. 'Yes?'

'I hope your daughter's okay. And it was nice to see you again.'

'Thank you. And you too,' she lied. Seeing him again had been excruciating. Her cheeks burned and she felt torn between explaining herself and going after Ramona.

In the end, she offered an apologetic smile and then hurried to the car where Ramona was already waiting, the unrelenting summer rain bucketing down upon her.

'Oh, sweetheart,' Deb said, pulling her into another hug when they were both safely inside.

She half-expected to be pushed away, but Ramona clung to her and her heart broke. Her beautiful daughter was so grown up in some ways, yet still a child in so many others, which was why Deb desperately wanted to keep her safe.

'We did the right thing, sweetheart,' she said, stroking Ramona's silky soft hair. 'If you're this upset after only having the bird a couple of hours, imagine how his owner must have felt?'

Ramona sniffed, then pulled back. 'Do you mind if I don't come with you tonight? I'm really not in the mood to be sociable.'

Deb had almost forgotten they were supposed to be going to Quinn's neighbour's.

'Let's both stay home,' she said, and then, not even thinking about the budget, added, 'Why don't we order pizza and watch a movie ourselves? Unless you'd rather stay in your bedroom messaging your friends?'

'Bit hard when I'm banned from social media.'

'About that,' Deb said as she started the car, 'I think after the sacrifice and maturity you showed tonight, perhaps we can come to a compromise. You can download the apps you want again, on one condition?'

Ramona eyed her suspiciously. 'What?'

'You adhere to a time limit each night and you let me know your password.'

'That's two conditions!'

'Take it or leave it. Your choice?'

'Fine.' Ramona grinned as Deb turned out of the car park and onto the main road. 'I'll take it. But I want extra pineapple on the pizza, *and* I get to choose the movie.'

'Deal.'

Deb wasn't a fan of fruit on dinner herself and she and Ramona didn't always see eye to eye on movies, but right now, she was simply happy to have her daughter talking to her again.

Quinn

Turned out dating apps weren't as fun when you were looking for one particular person. Since Quinn had downloaded the apps again, her thumb already had RSI from swiping left. She no longer wanted to meet just anyone, she wanted to find Handbag Dude. It was easy to rule out most guys—they had the wrong colour hair, no beard, or their skin was too pale.

But then again, what if he was using an old photo? She updated her profile shot every time she changed her hair colour but plenty of people didn't. Especially men. So maybe his beard was a recent thing.

But those eyes. No way she'd miss those eyes if she saw them again!

A shiver ran down her spine, her insides fizzing as she recalled the intense way they'd stared into hers when he'd leaned down to help her. He could have a whole conversation with those beautiful aqua eyes.

Dammit, if only she could go back in time and have a do-over.

Her phone beeped and she flicked apps to see a message from Deb.

Really sorry but it's been a bit of an afternoon, so I'm going to have to cancel. Have fun with Mrs D and tell her I'm looking forward to meeting her one of these days.

Quinn frowned, her own woes forgotten for a moment.

Is everything okay? Is Ramona okay? xo

Yeah, she's fine. I'll call you tomorrow and tell you all about it. xx

Noticing the time, Quinn put down her phone and switched from her work clothes into comfy leggings and an oversized T-shirt. She and Mrs D were already such good friends that neither of them felt the need to dress up when hanging out.

A knock sounded on her door. 'Can we come in?' called Dec.

She opened the door to her brother and brother-in-law standing on the other side, both dressed in black-tie, and could almost hear the hearts of straight women all over Sydney cracking at the unfairness of life.

'Where are you two off to looking so fancy?'

'The Heart Foundation Gala dinner,' Darpan said. 'We just came to say bye.'

'Ah, right.' She offered him a compassionate smile. His younger sister had died five years ago from a heart condition, and they donated heavily to the charity and attended all their fundraisers. 'Must be nice to have someone to take to such things.'

Dec raised an eyebrow. 'It is. And you could be off on a second date with Garth tonight if you'd given him half a chance. Anyway, we better go.'

'Enjoy yourselves,' she said begrudgingly.

Switching off her bedroom light, she headed out, snatching a bottle of real champagne from Dec and Darpan's collection on her way.

'Evening, Mrs Dagliesh.' She leaned forward to kiss her cheek the moment she opened her door.

'I told you to call me Muriel,' Mrs D said as Snoodles jumped up, excited to see Quinn.

She removed his paws from her shoulders and ruffled his head. 'Sorry, no walkies tonight, but I promise I'll take you in the morning.'

Snoodles slunk off to the lounge room with the humans in pursuit.

'What time are your friends arriving?'

'Oh, I'm sorry.' Quinn eyed the spread of cheese, crackers and other goodies that were laid out on the coffee table. 'They're not anymore.'

'I hope everything's okay?'

'I think so. I'm guessing Deb's having dramas with her daughter. Ramona's fifteen and pushing her buttons a bit.' She held up the bottle of bubbly. 'Shall we crack this? I'm in dire need of a drink.'

Mrs D gestured to the crystal champagne flutes on one side of the coffee table. 'You don't have to ask me twice.'

Quinn did the honours, then they clinked glasses and assumed their positions—Mrs D in her comfy leather recliner and Quinn in the one that had belonged to Mr D but which she was rapidly coming to think of as her own. 'How was your day?'

'Well, let's see … I had an argument with the lady who brings me my meals-on-wheels because she keeps telling me I should get rid of Snoodles because he's too much for me, and then my doctor tried to convince me to join some exercise group for people with one foot in the grave, but I also Zoomed with my daughters, which was lovely, and now you're here and we're drinking champagne so I can't complain.'

Quinn grinned, her heart blooming at Mrs D's words—she may not have found what she'd hoped for when she offered to walk Snoodles, but she'd got something equally as good.

'Amen to that!' She leaned across so they could clink glasses again.

'What about you, hun? How was your day?'

'It was okay—got some ideas on this new campaign I'm working on, and my narky boss actually approved it.'

'What's the campaign?'

Quinn told her a little about their mission to make their latest energy drink more appealing to the health conscious—it sounded boring even to her ears. 'I'm sorry,' she said after a while, 'you don't want to hear all about this. Besides, it's the weekend. I'm off the clock.'

'Do you like your job, dear?' asked Mrs D.

'It's okay. I'm good at it. Mr Carrot-Up-His-Arse—sorry, I mean Travis. He's my boss, and he's been dangling the promise of promotion under my nose for a while. And that'd be good—it'd mean a pay rise and maybe then I could move out, get a small apartment of my own. I love Dec and Darpan, but sometimes I feel like I'm overstaying my welcome.'

'I'm sure that's not the case. From what I've seen, those boys adore you, but—and I hope you don't mind me saying this—you don't seem very passionate about your job.'

'Hah,' Quinn said. 'My mam would say you sound like a millennial, that people my age have too much of an obsession with happiness over practicalities.'

Mrs D shook her head. 'Your mother and I clearly disagree on this. You're young, you should be doing something that lights a fire in your heart. I spent too many years doing what I thought I should be doing and my only regret in life is not becoming an interior designer earlier. If you could do anything you wanted, would it be digital marketing for energy drinks?'

Quinn took a moment to think. 'I guess not. I don't even like energy drinks. But it was the job I got when I moved to Sydney and as I said, I'm good at it.'

'Hmm … well, that's something, but you feel to me like someone who should be in a more creative job. Even your leggings are bright and colourful,' she said, gesturing to Quinn's outfit. 'You dress like a piece of art, and it just makes me wonder if you do that because you're not reaching the full potential of your creativity in other areas. Did you draw or craft at school?'

'Marketing's actually quite creative, you know? I have to come up with lots of new and innovative ideas for our social media campaigns,' Quinn said, feeling slightly defensive. 'Besides, Deb's at The Energy Co, and I'd miss her like crazy if I left.'

'I'm disappointed I didn't get the chance to meet her. I take it she's no longer married to her daughter's father?'

'No. They never were. She hasn't even met him.'

Mrs D leaned forward. 'Oh?'

'Ramona is a donor baby,' Quinn explained. 'She did IVF on her own. She was only my age at the time.'

'That seems very young to make such a decision.' There was no judgement, only curiosity in Mrs D's tone.

'I guess, but Deb's such an organised, planner-type person. She knew that she wanted to have kids by a certain age so she did what she had to do to achieve that.'

'No such options were available in my day. Sometimes I think that was a good thing and other times I'm glad that women have more choice and opportunity these days. I'm sure your friend Deb doesn't regret her decision.'

'Oh no, definitely not. She's such a good mum, sometimes I think a little too good, but that's cos she didn't have a great childhood herself. I think she's trying to be the mum she didn't have.'

'We all try and right the wrongs from our past,' said Mrs D. 'Do you want to have children, Quinn?'

She took a sip of her wine. 'Yep. Definitely. But I couldn't do what Deb did. Maybe I'm old-fashioned but I don't just want kids, I want the whole shebang. I want the kind of love my parents have and the kind of love it sounds like you and Mr D had.'

Was that really too much to ask?

'I don't think that's old-fashioned at all; just because there are so many options for women these days doesn't mean you can't want love as well, but you have to remember nothing is ever perfect. I was very lucky to have Eddie, but like all marriages, we had our ups and downs. There were many times over the years I contemplated leaving him …' She smiled fondly. 'But in the end, the ups outnumbered the downs and I miss him very much. I don't think you should give up hope just yet though. You're only, what … twenty-five?'

'Twenty-seven. I'll be twenty-eight in June.'

'Well, there you go—you're a spring chicken. There's still plenty of time to meet someone special and have a baby.'

'That's the thing. I *have* found him,' Quinn said, aware she probably sounded like a crazy person.

'I thought you said you were single …' Mrs D frowned as she twirled her champagne flute. 'Oh, is it a case of unrequited love? He's not married, is he?'

Quinn shook her head. 'No, at least I hope not. This is going to sound a bit bonkers, but you know how I told you about that magazine article?'

When Mrs D nodded, Quinn spilled the whole story of meeting Handbag Dude and how she'd kind of been on the lookout ever since.

'I hate to be a Debbie Downer,' Mrs D said when Quinn had finished, 'but maybe he doesn't even live in Sydney? Maybe he was here for work?'

Quinn hated to admit that this had crossed her mind as well but each time it did, something stronger told her not to worry.

'I'm *sure* he lives in Sydney. I can't explain it, but I just feel it in my gut. Now I just have to find him again.'

If she heard anyone else saying the words that were coming out of her mouth, she'd be struggling to keep a straight face, but she felt strongly that she and Handbag Dude were supposed to be together.

Mrs D looked contemplative for a moment. 'Maybe you will meet him again and maybe he is The One, but don't shut your heart off to other possibilities. You should have fun while you can—while your bones don't groan when you move, and you don't have anything tying you down. Think about whether you're truly in the right job and if not, pursue it. Drink too much, dance all night, sleep with the wrong people ... because one day you'll be old like me and wishing you could have that time again.'

Yet Quinn had been doing most of those things already and as much as she wished they still fulfilled her, they weren't cutting the mustard anymore. 'Logically I know you're right, but I'm lonely. I want someone I can come home to and binge-watch TV with. I want someone to go to Bunnings with on the weekend and choose paint colours for our house. I want someone to wake up to, who's more than just a one-night stand, someone I can rely on to be there when I'm sick or grumpy as well.'

'Ah, honey, I know exactly what you mean. Since Eddie died, I've often felt lost and alone. When I'm asleep I sometimes forget he's gone and then when I wake up and he's not there, the hurt starts all over again. My daughters want me to move to the UK to be closer to them, but I'm too old to uproot my life. I've got my U3A meetings and my book club and my friends here, although sometimes it is easy to get downhearted. For a while after Eddie's funeral, after Crystal and Michelle went home, I started buying tinned food and eating that because making food for just one felt too much of an effort.'

'Oh, Mrs D.' Quinn was suddenly close to tears. 'I wish I'd known you better back then; I would have come over and shared a meal with you.'

'Thank you, dear.' Her eyes looked glassy too but then she cleared her throat. 'Maybe we should start one of these films before we get too maudlin.'

Quinn laughed. 'Good idea,' she said, and grabbed a cracker with brie before refilling both their glasses.

Debra

Absorbed in a podcast about raising teenage girls, Deb didn't hear the footsteps behind her as she did her post-run stretches outside her building. It was a beautiful sunny Saturday morning, she'd managed to jog for almost fifteen minutes without stopping, and she was still on a high after a lovely evening with Ramona.

'Hello,' said a deep voice as a shadow fell over her.

She turned, expecting to see one of her neighbours, and almost swallowed her tongue at the sight of Tristan standing only a few feet away holding Ramona's birdcage. He wore Hawaiian-type board shorts, a bright T-shirt that clashed, and his hair looked slightly damp as if he wasn't long out of the shower.

Oh God, why did he have to choose now to turn up when she was sweaty and red-faced, wearing daggy shorts and a T-shirt that might be older than her daughter?

'What are you doing here?'

'I thought I should bring this back.' He lifted the birdcage, making her feel like even more of an idiot. In the emotion of last night, neither she nor Ramona had realised they'd forgotten it.

'How did you know where I live?'

'You gave your contact details to the receptionist.'

'Oh, right.' Relief flooded her, and she finally remembered her manners. 'Thank you. But you could have called—I would have collected it from the clinic.'

'To be honest …' He gave her a sheepish smile. 'I was glad of the excuse to come see you.'

Her stomach somersaulted, but it was more confusion than joy. 'Really?'

He nodded. 'I feel like I owe you an apology.'

He owed *her* an apology!

'Do you want to come in for a coffee?'

'Yeah, that'd be great. If you're sure it's no hassle?'

'Of course not.' Deb sounded way more confident than she felt as she unlocked the door and led Tristan into the building. 'Do you want me to take the birdcage?'

'I think I can manage,' he said, bemused.

'Did the owner come pick up the budgie?' she asked as they started up the stairs.

'Yes, that's another reason why I popped by. He belongs to a sixteen-year-old boy who lives only a few houses down. He was so grateful when I called to let him know Frodo had been found safe and sound that he asked if he could have your address so he could send your daughter a thankyou note. Thought I'd better ask you first.'

Her heart hitched at the mention of Ramona, but that wasn't a conversation to have on the stairs. 'What kind of sixteen-year-old boy thinks of such things? I didn't think teenagers even knew letters existed.'

Tristan chuckled. 'I know, right, but I don't think he's your average sixteen-year-old boy. He lives with his grandmother and seems rather old-fashioned.'

'In that case, I'm sure Ramona would be delighted to receive a thankyou card,' Deb said as they came to her apartment.

She unlocked the door and held it open for Tristan. 'What were you doing at the Granville clinic? I thought you worked in Castle Hill.' She hoped she didn't sound too accusing—she couldn't throw stones when it came to fabricating the truth.

'I was filling in for a friend. I don't usually work Fridays, and his wife went into labour early yesterday morning, so ...' He shrugged as if that explained everything.

Which it did—he was a nice guy who helped his friends, and she was the only one who'd deceived anyone.

'That's lovely. What did they have?'

'Twin girls, and he's already sent me at least a dozen photos.'

Deb smiled. 'That's sweet, and kind of you to help out.'

He looked a little awkward as he indicated the birdcage. 'Where should I put this?'

'Just on the table there, please.' She pointed to the dining table and then glanced down the hallway to Ramona's bedroom door, which was still closed. Ramona had always been an early riser, but the last few months she'd taken to sleeping until at least noon on the weekends. 'Sorry, I've only got instant, or would you prefer tea?'

'Tea would be great.' Tristan shoved his hands in his pockets and glanced around. 'This is a nice place.'

'Thanks. It does the trick.' She gestured to her couch. 'Take a seat. I'll go put the kettle on and then I'm just going to freshen up quickly if you don't mind.'

'Not at all.'

Deb needed a shower—she could feel the sweat dripping down her back—but didn't want to leave him alone so made do with spraying herself liberally with deodorant, changing into a clean T-shirt and brushing her hair. She contemplated lipstick but didn't want to look like she'd gone to too much effort. This was weird enough as it was.

She glanced at her phone, desperate to call Quinn and ask her how the hell she should handle this, but she could hear the kettle whistling already.

'Sorry, I thought I'd better switch it off,' Tristan said when she found him in the kitchen.

'Thanks.'

She made the tea, and they carried their cups into the living room and sat at opposite ends of the couch. Deb took a sip, hoping he didn't notice her hands were shaking. She was unaccustomed to having men in her home. Never mind the smart, sweet, and rather sexy variety.

Or maybe it was the elephant on the couch between them. The big fat lies she'd told on her online dating profile.

'So, is it just you and your daughter living here?' he asked, looking around at the photos and paintings of Ramona's that hung on the wall.

Her heart shot to her throat and she glanced down the hallway to make sure Ramona's door was still firmly shut. 'Look, I'm really sorry I lied to you about having a child, it's just—'

'Hey, I'm sure you had your reasons. Apparently, a lot of people use false names on their profiles, and I don't blame you being cautious—you hear a lot of horror stories. But I didn't come here to grill you.'

'That's generous of you.' But she felt compelled to say *something*. 'It's just ... Ramona's father ...' She dropped her voice and again looked down the hallway. 'He wasn't a good person—he's why I used a fake name in my profile. I've avoided being on social media for so long in case he found me and venturing into online dating was a massive step. I just thought it was safer to take precautions.'

Oh my goodness, the moment the words were out she regretted them. What kind of temporary insanity had compelled her to tell a practical stranger something she hadn't even told her daughter or closest friend?

'Shit, Lee,' Tristan said as she started to shake. He put his tea down on the coffee table and inched closer to her. 'Sorry, I mean Debra. Is that what I should call you?'

His confusion brought a glimmer of lightness to the situation. 'How about Deb? That's what everyone calls me. Although Lee *is* my middle name.'

'They both suit you, but we'll go with Deb.' Tristan paused. 'I take it you and Ramona don't see her father anymore?'

'No.' Her chest cramped at the mere thought. 'I know I shouldn't have lied, and I almost did mention Ramona on our date, but ...'

When her voice drifted off, he placed his hand gently on hers. Deb felt a spark of something she hadn't felt in over sixteen years.

'It's okay,' he said. 'I understand. There's nothing I wouldn't do to protect my children.'

'Thank you.'

'Well, good morning, Mr Vet.'

'Where did you come from?' Deb shrieked as she looked up to see Ramona standing mere feet away, smirking as she eyed their joined hands. Deb yanked hers away and sprung from the couch as if Ramona had just found them getting down and dirty. How long had she been standing there? How much had she heard?

'Uh, I came from my bedroom?' Ramona said. 'Where I *sleep*.'

'Tristan's here to return the birdcage,' Deb managed, trying to compose herself.

'I see. Thanks heaps. Mum, I'm starving—can I make pancakes?'

'Sure. Go … ahead.' She could barely get the words out as relief flowed over her like hot fudge on ice-cream. No way Ramona could act so normal if she'd overheard their conversation.

'Do you want some, Mr Vet?' Ramona asked with a cheeky smile.

Please God, let him say no. Deb wasn't sure if her heart was thudding because of their conversation or how it had felt to hold his hand, but either way, sitting through brunch with him and her daughter might cause her to go into cardiac arrest!

'Thanks for the offer, but I'm meeting my kids for lunch, so I better take a raincheck.'

'No worries.' Ramona all but skipped into the kitchen as Tristan stood.

Deb followed him to the door. 'I'll see you out.'

'Ramona seems a great kid,' he said as they headed downstairs.

'Thank you, she is. Although things have been a bit strained between us lately. Sometimes I feel like I can't do anything right.'

Tristan grinned. 'Ah, the teenage years. Don't worry, they don't last forever.'

'Part of me is happy to hear that but it also makes me sad. It only seems like yesterday she was a toddler.'

They stopped in the lobby, and she thanked him for returning the cage.

'As I mentioned, I did have an ulterior motive.'

'Oh?' Her mouth went dry.

He nodded. 'I really enjoyed our date and I've been kicking myself for stuffing it up ever since.'

'Oh?' she said again, wondering where her vocabulary had suddenly absconded to.

'Yes, and I feel like fate gave me a second chance in the guise of a budgie. Or more like a shove. I was thinking about asking if you'd like to try again when I walked out to the waiting room and saw you there.'

Deb blinked. 'You want to try again? Even after I lied?'

He nodded. 'You had good reason, and although I believe in honesty in relationships, you hardly know me. Trust takes time to build.'

Trust. *Could* she grow to trust him? She didn't know if that was something she was capable of.

'What about your ... about Marie?'

'I will always love her, and because of that, I know how rich a life with love in it can be. I'd like to experience it again. I'm only forty-seven. Hopefully I've still got a lot of life left and I don't want to spend it alone. Marie was a fiercely protective mother as well and I think she'd have liked you very much. I feel like she's probably looking down at me right now, angry that I let her come between us.'

Despite the crazy hum in her heart, Deb said, 'But there is no us?'

'Not yet,' he conceded with a bashful smile, 'but maybe there could be. However, it sounds like we've both still got a fair bit of healing to do though, so, what say we start as friends and see where that takes us?'

Friends?

Aside from Ramona and Quinn, Deb didn't really have any friends and that option sounded far more appealing, much less daunting, than what she'd originally signed up for.

'What do you say?' he prompted.

She smiled. If he wanted to see her again even after she'd lied to him, then she'd be stupid not to take him up on the offer. 'I'd like that.'

Tristan beamed back. 'Well, I better be off, but ...' He made a phone sign with his hand to his ear. 'I'll call you.'

Deb felt like she floated back up to the apartment.

'So,' Ramona said when she entered, 'either Mr Vet is a fast mover or you two have met before?'

'He was the date I went on,' she confessed, crossing to the fridge to grab herself some much-needed cold water.

Ramona's eyes widened. 'The one who's still in love with his dead wife?'

'That's the one.'

'But … why was he holding your hand?'

'Ah …' Deb racked her mind for a suitable reply but couldn't think of any reason—aside from the truth—why Tristan would have been comforting her. 'Because he was asking if I'd like to go out with him again.'

'Wow. That's awesome. He seems great.' Ramona abandoned the pancakes a moment and crossed the tiny kitchen to give Deb a hug. 'I'm happy for you, Mum.'

'Thanks,' Deb squeaked, surprised by the sudden display of affection. 'Although don't get too excited. It's not officially a date—we've decided on friends.'

'Whatever. I saw the way he looked at you. That vet has a serious case of lust.'

'Oh my God.' Deb laughed as she shook her head, but Ramona's observation gave her a massive boost and she couldn't help hoping her daughter was right.

Ramona

As Ramona turned into her street Monday afternoon, she wished that Perry was there to welcome her. She might feel better if she knew that when she went into her bedroom, he'd be sitting in her cage ready to offer her a cheeky word. Or maybe even a swear word—she giggled at the memory of him swearing at the vet. She'd told Lucy about that in fashion today and she'd thought it hilarious.

'I wonder what other ... naughty words he has in his v-vocabulary,' Lucy had asked and then they'd started amusing each other with crazier and crazier possibilities.

'What on earth were you and the stutterer laughing about?' Nyra asked afterwards.

'Just stuff,' Ramona said, and then changed the subject.

She was starting to tire of the way her other friends hated on Lucy. It reminded her of the sniggers that had once upon a time been aimed at her, but she didn't have the guts to stand up to them and risk being alienated, even if sometimes she thought she had more in common with Lucy than she did with Sydney and Nyra. Neither of them had a real passion for learning about fashion; they mainly seemed to be in the program because they liked shopping and taking selfies in expensive clothes. Lucy, like Ramona, lived and breathed it.

Thankfully, by the end of the next period Sydney and Nyra had moved on to planning day trips for the upcoming school holidays. Ramona wouldn't be able to afford to go on more than one unless she robbed a bank. *How depressing!*

As she approached their apartment block, she frowned at the sight of a tall, lanky boy lurking around the letterboxes. He didn't look like he was delivering junk mail and she was certain he didn't live in the building either. She'd remember if one of her neighbours was a boy around her age.

As if sensing her presence, he turned. 'Are you Ramona?'

He had dark, straight hair that fell just below his shoulders, tanned skin, dark green eyes and, if he wasn't wearing a *Lord of the Rings* T-shirt, might even get the Sydney seal of approval. 'How do you know my name?'

'I'm Elijah,' he said with a goofy grin. 'Frodo's owner.'

Ah, so that accounted for the T-shirt. But what was he doing here?

As if he was a mind reader, he said, 'I wanted to say thank you for taking such good care of Frodo, so I brought you a card and a present but it didn't fit in your letterbox so I was about to leave it on the doorstep.'

'How did you know where I live?'

'I asked the vet if I could have your address.' His smile dimmed. 'He said he'd got your permission.'

'Tristan.' Ramona nodded. 'He must have asked Mum.'

He thrust out the gift, which felt like a box of chocolates. 'Anyway. Thank you.'

'It was my pleasure. Perry—I mean Frodo—he's really cute. Or is *he a she*?'

Elijah chuckled, making some of his hair fall over his face. He pushed it out of his eyes as if it were something he did a thousand times a day. 'No, he's male. You can tell by his ceres.'

'His what?'

'The little bit above their beaks,' he said, running his finger over the bridge of his own nose. 'Once the budgie is mature, you can tell their gender by the colour. Blue for cocks, brown for hens.'

Ramona tried not to giggle when he said 'cocks'. He had to be the first boy she'd ever met who could say that word with a straight face.

'However, there are a few exceptions to the rule,' he added. 'You can get Albinos, Lutinos and mottled birds that can have all different shades of ceres, but mostly the blue/brown rule applies.'

'You seem to know a lot about budgies?'

'I breed them.'

'That's so dope.'

He beamed. 'Well, actually it was my grandfather who bred them, but he died a few years ago and I took over.'

'I'm sorry. Were you close?'

'Very.' He paused a moment. 'Do you have a pet?'

'Nah, my mum won't let me. She reckons it would get lonely cos we're not here most of the time. I'm not even sure building regulations would allow it.'

'Budgies would be great for you then—especially if you get a pair. They can keep themselves amused and they don't generally bother neighbours. Hey, if you're not busy, don't suppose you want to come and visit Frodo and meet his other friends?'

'What?' She blinked. 'Now?'

He nodded. 'Unless you've got something better to do?'

Her mum would tell her not to go with this boy as he could be a rapist or an axe murderer—she was super paranoid about stuff like that—but Elijah seemed friendly enough and although he was taller than her, she reckoned she could take him on if need be. When she was younger, she'd done two years of karate because Deb believed girls should know how to look after themselves. Her mum had wanted her to continue but Ramona had hated it and had finally convinced Deb to let her stop.

'Only homework,' she replied, some of the stress of the day lifting at the thought of seeing Perry again. 'And that can wait. Lead the way.'

'Would you like me to carry your bag?' he asked as they headed down the footpath.

Wow—a gentleman, she'd heard of them but thought they were extinct! 'It's fine, it's not that heavy, but thanks for asking. So, what school do you go to?'

'The local high.'

She made a face. 'I've heard it's pretty rough?'

'It can be. What about you? I don't recognise your uniform.'

'I go to Smythes Ladies College in the eastern suburbs.'

He whistled. 'Doesn't that school cost a bomb?'

She nodded. 'I'm on a scholarship.'

'You must be pretty clever then?'

'I do okay, but I really only wanted to go there because they have this awesome fashion program.' She didn't think that would be something Elijah would be very interested in, but he surprised her.

'Really? That sounds unreal.'

As they walked the short distance to his place, she explained that it was a selective program for girls who wanted to work in the fashion industry.

'Do you want to be a fashion designer or something?'

'No. I do like making my own clothes, but I actually want to be a curator at a museum. I'm really interested in the history of fashion.'

'That sounds awesome. Most people I know want to be boring things like doctors or engineers.'

Ramona laughed. 'What about you?'

'I'm going to be an ornithologist.'

'Should I know what that is?'

It was Elijah's turn to laugh and he had such a lovely, throaty chuckle. 'It's a type of zoologist, but with a focus on birds.'

He stopped in front of a picket fence with peeling white paint—'This is me'—unlatched the gate and held it open for her, then led her round the back. 'I'd take you through the front, but Gran's had a migraine all day and she's sleeping it off in her bedroom at the front.'

'Your grandmother lives with you?' Ramona had always been fascinated by other people's grandparents, especially grandmas. They were always the relatives cheering the loudest at school assemblies, baking over-the-top birthday cakes, spoiling the kids in a way parents didn't. Until recently, she'd kind of longed for a granny more than she had a dad.

'No. I live with her,' he said as they emerged into a beautiful backyard, filled with cottage flowers, cast-iron furniture, and pebbled pathways lined with aviaries.

'Oh my God. When you said you bred birds, you meant it!' He must have a hundred different budgies. Elijah probably wouldn't have realised Perry was even missing if her mum hadn't insisted on taking him to the vet.

'Did you think I was lying?' he asked with a wry smile.

She shook her head as they stopped in front of the first aviary, and she tried to see if she could find Perry. 'Do you have names for all of them?'

'Most of them. These guys are the youngest and they're all named after characters from *Harry Potter*, those ones'—he pointed to another cage—'are from *The Hunger Games* and the last ones are all from *Discworld*.'

'Terry Pratchett,' she said, then frowned. 'Where are your *Lord of the Rings* ones?'

'They're my really special ones and they live on the back verandah. I can't get too attached to these ones as they're all for sale.'

'How much do they cost?' Ramona asked, glancing at the closed-in verandah.

'They're thirty dollars each. Fifty for a pair, but if you want one, I'll give you a special deal. What say a hundred per cent off?'

She smiled. 'Maybe I'll ask Mum.'

'Let's go see Frodo.'

She followed Elijah up the few steps to the verandah. There were rows of square cages at one end, an old but comfy looking couch at the other, and the walls between were hung with fancy silk ribbons, presumably prizes for the budgies.

'You've got a visitor, Frodo,' Elijah said, opening the door of his cage.

Immediately, the little violet-coloured budgie flew out and landed on Ramona's shoulder. She shrieked with glee.

'Hello, gorgeous. Who's a pretty boy?'

'Perry!' she exclaimed. She stroked his stomach and his feathers fluttered.

Elijah opened the other cages one by one. Within seconds there were ten budgies flying around them, clearly excited to have escaped for a while. Perry flew up to join his friends on a fancy looking, multi-levelled perch to bask in the afternoon sun.

'Why'd you call him Perry?' Elijah asked.

'I named him after a singer.' Weirdly, she didn't feel embarrassed admitting her love of old music to him. 'When I got him home, I put some music on, and he started dancing to "Hot Diggity" by Perry Como.'

'He's such an exhibitionist.'

'He's a character,' Ramona agreed. 'Did you teach him to swear?'

'Oh God, what did he say to you?'

'Not me.' She laughed at his expression of horror. 'The vet.'

'Frodo!' Elijah put his palm against his forehead and shook his head. 'It's the neighbours. They're always shouting and swearing at each other and some of the birds have picked up bad habits. Gran sprays them with water whenever she hears them.'

'She sprays the neighbours?'

'No.' He laughed. 'The birds, but they're not cats so they don't care.'

'That's hilarious.'

'Would you like a drink or something to eat?'

'Nah, I'm okay, and I don't want to disturb your grandma. But thanks. I should probably be getting home anyway. You know, homework and everything.'

He nodded.

She kinda hoped he'd ask her to stay longer anyway, but he didn't.

'Thanks so much for letting me come visit Pe—I mean Frodo,' she said, as Elijah put his hands on her shoulders and manoeuvred her out the door so as not to let any of the budgies escape. A wobbly sensation whooshed through her at his touch.

'You're welcome. Come visit him whenever you like.'

'Thanks. I might just take you up on that offer.'

'And …' He hesitated, shuffling slightly on his feet. 'Maybe you'd like to go see a movie in the holidays?'

Her heart thumped. Was he asking her on a date? Her insides twisted with something she'd never felt before, but she told herself he probably just meant as friends. 'Yeah, that'd be great.'

Elijah smiled and nodded towards the front. 'Come on, I'll see you to the gate.'

'So why d'you live with your grandma?' Ramona asked as they walked round the front. 'Do your parents live here too?'

'No. My mum died when I was eighteen months—drug overdose.'

'Oh my God. I'm so sorry.'

'She hadn't told Gran and Gramps who my dad was.' He cleared his throat and stared down at his feet. 'They don't think she even knew herself.'

'That sucks.' Ramona's heart ached for him.

'Yep,' he said. 'Lucky I had awesome grandparents.'

'I don't know my dad either,' she blurted.

'What? Not at all?'

She shook her head and gave him a brief run-down of her situation. 'Does it bother you not knowing who yours is?'

She hoped he didn't think her nosy, but she was fascinated to find someone in a similar situation to her. She'd met plenty of kids in single-parent families but most of them, like Lucy, at least knew both their parents in *some* capacity.

'I think about it occasionally. But then I realise it's likely my father was as messed up as Mum. I do wonder if I've got a whole other family sometimes.'

'I know what you mean. I wonder about that too. Once I had to do this family tree for school. Mum said we should just make one whole side up. We bought massive sheets of coloured cardboard from Officeworks and came up with outrageous relatives—royalty, celebrities, famous inventors … No one could have possibly believed any of it.'

Elijah groaned. 'Oh yeah, those projects are hell. And Father's Day breakfasts and assemblies in primary school. Although I was lucky my granddad went to those with me and my grandma to the mum ones. What about you? Do you have a grandfather you take?'

'No. He lives overseas. I don't know him well, definitely not well enough to ask him to Father's Day events, and I've never even met my grandma. She left when Mum was a kid and hasn't seen her since.'

'What do you mean left?'

Ramona shrugged. 'Exactly that. One day, Mum came home from school and there was a note saying she'd gone to find herself. She joined some cult or something.'

'Wow.' Elijah looked impressed.

'Yeah, she sounds way more interesting than Mum,' said Ramona before remembering she was supposed to be leaving. 'Well, I guess I'll see you soon?'

He nodded. 'Can't wait.'

The moment she got home, Ramona rushed over to her wardrobe where she'd buried the DNA testing kit and peeled off the plastic protection. She hadn't been able to do it on the weekend because Deb was always buzzing about and also, the guilt of going behind her back after their semi-truce had got to Ramona, but her conversation with Elijah had made up her mind. She didn't want *her* kids to have the same problem as her—unable to answer questions about who she really was, living their lives never knowing if the person sitting across from them in the train or in front of them in line at the supermarket was related.

After reading the instructions, her hands shaking with a combination of trepidation and excitement, she swiped the inside of her cheek and then slipped the test stick back inside its protective cover. She scribbled her details on the attached form and then ran down the street to the post office, hoping she'd make it before it closed.

And before she chickened out and changed her mind.

Debra

'Have fun, Mum, and don't do anything I wouldn't do,' Ramona teased as Deb picked up her phone and keys, ready to head out to meet Tristan.

'Hardi-hah.' As it was the first weekend of the school holidays, she was surprised her daughter was even out of bed yet. 'We're going to do the Duck River walk and we might stop for a coffee after, but I'll be home by lunch and then it's cleaning time.'

'You said I could go to the movies with Elijah this afternoon.'

'I did?'

Ramona and this mystery boy had been hanging out an awful lot this week, but it had all been at his house down the road, so Deb hadn't met him.

'Yes, you did. Honestly, I think you're getting Alzheimer's sometimes. Can't I do my jobs tomorrow?'

'Why can't you do them this morning?'

'Because I'm helping Elijah clean out his aviaries,' Ramona said, her tone exasperated.

'You won't clean your own bedroom, but you're prepared to scrub *bird poo* from cages for a boy? He must be something.' Surely a boy this devoted to his birds couldn't be a bad egg. *Could he?* Still, it wouldn't hurt to be sure. 'When do I get to meet him?'

'We're *just* friends,' Ramona glowered. 'Why do you need to meet him?'

'Because I'm interested in your *friends*.' Deb leaned down and kissed her forehead. 'And because Elijah sounds interesting. I like interesting people.'

'He is, and the birds are so funny. They each have their own unique personalities, and did you know that budgies have three thousand feathers? Three thousand! On such a tiny animal.'

'I did not,' Deb said. 'That's impressive.'

'And, they have more vertebrae in their necks than humans do, so they can turn their heads like 180 degrees and look backwards. How cool is that?'

'Very cool. And you said he lives with his grandmother?'

Ramona nodded. 'His mum died when he was young.'

'Okay,' Deb relented, 'cleaning can wait until tomorrow, but please be careful. Make sure you keep your phone on you at all times, and if you ever feel uncomfortable—'

'Mum! You're acting like Elijah's a creepy old man.'

'Well, I've never met him, so how the heck am I supposed to know?' Deb glanced at her watch, not wanting to keep Tristan waiting. 'Anyway, have fun. If I'm not back before you go out, don't forget to lock the door and I want you to come straight home after the movies. Actually, why don't you ask Elijah and his grandmother if they want to come for dinner?' Meeting them might help allay some of her anxiety. 'It's about time we met some neighbours.'

Ramona looked torn. 'Maybe, although you have to promise not to be embarrassing.'

'As if.' Deb rolled her eyes in the way Ramona had perfected lately.

'You better go—don't wanna keep lover boy waiting.'

'We're just friends as well,' Deb said, shaking her head as she left the apartment.

Tristan was already at Mona Park—a golden retriever standing patiently by his side—when she arrived seven minutes later.

'Hi there.' He waved as she hurried over to him.

'Sorry to keep you waiting, I got distracted talking to Ramona,' she said as she dropped to greet the dog.

'All good, we're just enjoying the beautiful morning.'

'You must be Hammer?' Deb let him sniff her hand before ruffling the soft, golden fur at his neck, then looked up to Tristan. 'He's gorgeous.'

'He likes to think so.' But she could tell from the warmth in his voice that he agreed. 'Thanks for meeting us.'

'Thanks for asking me.' They'd been messaging a lot, but this was the first time they'd seen each other in person since agreeing to be friends and she thought she'd feel more nervous than she did.

'Shall we?' Tristan gestured to the trail ahead that would take them through bushland along the river.

'Yes, let's. How old is Hammer?' Deb asked as they started at a gentle pace.

'Three years and finally starting to calm down a little. The kids bought him for me not long after Marie died. Our cats were always hers, so they felt I needed a pet for me.'

'That's sweet,' she said as they moved out of the way of a couple of hikers coming in the opposite direction, looking very much as if they meant business.

'Sorry …' Tristan said when they'd gone. 'I swore I wasn't going to mention Marie today.'

'It's fine,' Deb reassured him; she didn't want him to censor himself around her. 'I'd love to hear more about her.'

'Thank you. But right now, I'd rather talk about you.'

'There's not much to talk about. Ramona will tell you I'm incredibly boring and she's probably right.'

'I'll reserve judgement on that,' he said as Hammer paused to relieve himself against a tree. 'Your profile said you enjoy going to the theatre. Have you got a favourite show?'

'Ooh, tough question.' Taking Ramona to the theatre was one of her greatest joys and she tried to plan tickets into their budget at least once a year. One of the best things about her time in New York had been easy access to Broadway. 'It's a toss-up between *Chitty Chitty Bang Bang* and *Wicked*, although *Mary Poppins* was fabulous. Ramona squealed so loudly when Mary flew above the audience.'

Tristan chuckled. 'I saw all three of those with my kids too. They tried to say they were too old when *Chitty Chitty Bang Bang* came around, but they loved it almost as much as me.'

'And Marie? What was her favourite?'

'Musicals weren't her thing. I always took the kids by myself because she didn't like crowded places.'

They walked a little further, admiring their surrounds, holding Hammer back as a blue-tongue lizard scuttled across the trail.

'What's Ramona up to today?' he asked.

'She's hanging out with that boy who owned the budgie she found. Elijah. They seem to have hit it off. I'm just waiting for her to ask me if she can have a budgie of her own.'

'And will you say yes?'

'I don't know. She's wanted a pet for a long time. When she was little, she was constantly pestering me for a puppy or a kitten, but

I didn't think it would be fair on them being home alone while we were at work and school.'

He nodded. 'I get that, but budgies are pretty easy to take care of, they can be a lot of fun and even if you only have one, they're pretty happy with their own company when you're not there. As long as you give them a couple of mirrors to admire themselves in.'

'I guess. Until the last few years, we moved around a lot, and it's hard enough to find good rentals as it is, never mind ones that allow pets.'

'True, although I reckon most would allow a bird or a fish.' He paused a moment. 'Does the fact you've moved around a lot have something to do with your ex?'

She swallowed. The first twelve years of Ramona's life they'd moved every eighteen months or so, because Deb feared that putting down roots would make it easier for Oscar to find her. He'd sworn to her when she'd tried to escape him that he would never let her go. He wasn't the type of man who liked to be rejected. And his actions made her believe him. If he'd known about their baby, she could only imagine the lengths he might have gone to in order to find them.

After New York, she'd considered going back to Perth but figured that would be the first place he'd check, so they'd moved around rural New South Wales before coming to Granville in Sydney's outer suburbs.

'Yes,' she finally admitted. 'I can't ever allow him to find us. Not staying in one place too long felt like a good strategy. It might sound over the top but there's nothing I wouldn't do to protect Ramona.'

'What did he do to you?' Tristan asked, his voice barely more than a whisper. When she didn't reply immediately, he added, 'I'm sorry, you don't need to tell me if you don't want to, but have you ever spoken to a therapist about what you went through?'

Deb shook her head. There hadn't been any money for one when she'd been pregnant, or since. Therapists were a luxury she couldn't afford when there were nappies, childcare, then school fees and uniforms to pay for. Her father had offered her money for an abortion, but after refusing, she'd wanted to prove she could handle her choice and therefore hadn't wanted to ask him for anything else.

'Have you spoken to *anyone*?' asked Tristan.

A lump formed in her throat. There were so many times she'd almost told Quinn, but she hadn't wanted to see any further pity in her friend's eyes. She loved their friendship—it felt like one of the few pure and uncomplicated things in her life—and unloading all this would have tainted that. Never mind the fact that she still felt so stupid to have fallen victim to him.

Deb meant simply to say 'no', but other words fell from her lips instead.

'When I was twenty-six, I moved to New York to do a masters in psychology. I got a casual job at Starbucks and another Aussie I met who worked there asked me to a speed-dating event.'

When she paused, Tristan said, 'Speed dating, hey? Haven't heard of that in years.'

'I wasn't really looking to settle down or even get into a committed relationship, but I met a man there—Oscar—and fell head over heels. He was extremely attractive, but it wasn't just his looks, it was everything about him. He had this passion for life that was contagious, and he made me feel like I was the only woman in the room. There were at least twenty other girls at the event, and he told me almost all of them wanted his phone number, but that he only had eyes for me.'

Within days of meeting, they were spending almost every hour of every day together. He told her he loved her before the first week was out and said he couldn't imagine living his life without her. He showered her with presents and sweet nothings, brought her breakfast in bed and rubbed her feet when they sat on the couch watching TV together. After years of having boyfriends who sometimes didn't return her call for days, a mother who was incapable of loving her in the way all mothers should and a father who cared more for his career than he did for his daughter, his attention had been like a powerful drug.

'I couldn't get enough of him. I spent all my time with him and started to neglect the few other friendships I'd begun to form. At first things were wonderful ...'

At first, he'd worshipped her like a goddess, but after a while he started becoming more aggressive in bed, wanting more from her, and giving much less. And he also became controlling and jealous.

'Anyway, things started to turn sour. We'd go out to dinner, and Oscar would accuse me of flirting with the waiters. I tried to tell him I only had eyes for him but—'

'Did he hit you?' Tristan growled. Hammer looked up from where he'd been sniffing.

'No.' She reached out to soothe the dog as she continued. 'He punished me in other ways.' Like refusing to have sex with her or making her do things she wasn't comfortable with in the bedroom. 'Then things would be good for a while. Better than good—*amazing*, so that all my doubts faded, and I'd start to think I'd overreacted. But it was like a cycle—just when I was beginning to feel safe and secure again, he'd stonewall me. He'd stop coming around, would take days to return my messages and refuse to tell me what I'd done wrong.

'He was a sales manager for this big pharmaceutical company. When we first met, he didn't travel much but then all these business trips came up that had him flying back and forth across America, schmoozing clients, as he called it. He'd be out of town for days, sometimes a week at a time and he wouldn't message or answer my calls. I started to wonder if he was cheating on me, but when I questioned Oscar, he told me *I* was crazy, that he was just busy working, that he couldn't handle my neediness.'

Subconsciously, she ran her fingers through Hammer's soft, warm fur. At some stage they must have stopped walking because they were now sitting side by side on a wooden bench right in front of the shimmering water. Its gentle lapping sounds were in direct opposition to the way she felt inside.

'I'm sorry, I don't know why I'm telling you all this,' she said, blinking up at Tristan. They were supposed to be having a relaxing morning stroll and she'd made it anything *but* relaxing.

'Because I asked you to,' he replied, touching her cheek with his thumb to brush away a tear she hadn't even realised she'd shed. 'And because we're friends, remember?'

Perhaps it was because his gentle touch unbalanced her, perhaps it was because he was a virtual stranger and talking to him was almost like talking to a therapist, or maybe it was simply because now the floodgates had opened, she couldn't stop. But whatever the reason, she kept talking, and it felt good to be finally getting it off her chest.

'About four months into our relationship, we went to my work Christmas party. He seemed on edge all night and was drinking a lot. I told him maybe he should slow down a little, but that only made him angry. And then, while he went to get yet another drink, this guy I kinda knew, a barista I worked with, told me a joke. I laughed, Oscar saw, and he … he lost the plot.'

'What did he do?'

'He accused me of cheating on him and walked out. I ran after him, desperate to make him see sense—I told him he was drunk and being unreasonable and that I didn't feel anything for the other man.

We got back to my place and ...' She sucked in a breath. 'We had pretty intense sex. I thought he'd forgiven me but when we were ... finished, he called me a whore, tied me to my bed and left me there.'

'What do you mean? All night?'

'No.' Tears filled her eyes again. 'For two whole days.'

'Oh my God. What the fuck!' It was the first time she'd heard Tristan swear. 'Did he leave you food? Water?'

She shook her head. She was starving, thirsty and smelling of her own urine by the end of it. 'I couldn't reach the phone. I honestly thought I was going to die.'

Tristan looked horrified. 'What happened?'

'Eventually Oscar came back. He untied me and begged my forgiveness. He was crying, telling me he didn't know what had come over him. He promised he'd get help. That he couldn't live without me. He said he got so jealous because he couldn't bear the thought of another man touching me.'

'You didn't take him back, did you?'

'No.' She was glad to say she hadn't. 'I told him it was over and that I was going to report him, and he stopped sobbing immediately. It was like a switch had been flicked. He said the police would never believe me. That there wasn't any evidence so it would be my word against his and that he had the money to get a better lawyer. He told me he couldn't allow me to ruin his life and if I tried to get him into trouble, he'd make my life a living hell. I was terrified.' She sucked in a breath. 'I promised I wouldn't report him if he just left me alone.'

'And did he?'

She shook her head. 'Almost immediately I felt as if I was being followed, and I started getting flowers and notes delivered to my flat, saying things like we were meant to be together, and he was going to prove it to me. I did go to the police then, but he was right, they weren't helpful at all. By that time my bruises were gone and he'd been careful not to write anything directly threatening, but I *knew* ... I could read between the lines. The police told me to come back if he actually did something I could prove.'

'That's terrible.'

'Yep. They almost made me feel like I was overreacting, but things were different back then. I hope they'd be more receptive now. Anyway, not long after ... I found a tiny camera in my bathroom. I knew it had to have been planted by him and realised he must have come into my apartment when I wasn't there.' Even now, saying these words made the hairs on the back of her head prickle. 'I'd made him give me my key back, but I guess he must have made a copy, or he'd been filming me all along.'

'Finally, the evidence you needed. What did the cops do?'

'Nothing,' she admitted. 'I would have taken it to them but just before I found the camera, I'd taken a pregnancy test. It was positive and I'd freaked out. I didn't want to believe it. I knew I didn't want him to be a part of my life, but how could I possibly have a baby on my own? When I found the camera, I realised he'd have footage of me taking the test.'

'Shit.'

'Yeah.' Tears came into her eyes as she relived the terror she'd felt. 'I knew I'd never escape him if he knew I was having his baby and I didn't want any child of mine growing up with a father like him.'

'You never thought about ... you know ...' He paused and gave her an apologetic shrug. 'Not following through?'

She nodded. 'I considered it. I immediately went to see a doctor to discuss my options, but when she confirmed I was pregnant, I felt this bond unlike anything I'd ever felt before. I knew with absolute certainty that I wanted the baby and I'd do anything in my power to protect it from ever being hurt by its father.'

'I'm so sorry he put you through that,' Tristan said.

'Thank you.' Deb let out a deep sigh—unloading all this had been exhausting. 'I'll never regret Ramona but at the same time I'll never be able to forgive myself for falling for such a psycho.'

'Hey, don't beat yourself up. How could you possibly have known what he was like? The important thing is that you got away. I think you're amazing to have been through all that and be able to hold down a job, live a normal life and raise a wonderful daughter.'

'That's sweet but because of Oscar, I'm not sure I'll ever be much of a ...' Her voice trailed off; she'd almost said girlfriend. 'What I meant was I wouldn't blame you if you wanted to run a mile. I want to get to know you better. I want to see where our friendship might lead but ... I'm pretty damaged. I don't know if I can give myself over to someone completely again.'

He looked right into her eyes, then took her hand and squeezed it. 'It's okay. I understand and I'm not going anywhere. Unless you want me to?'

Heat flowed through Deb's body from her hand up to her cheeks. She beamed. 'No, I'd like you to stay right here. With me.'

'Good,' he said, 'because I'd like that too.'

Could it be her luck had finally changed?

Ramona

During the school holidays, Ramona and Elijah caught the train into the city to meet Lucy at the Powerhouse Museum. She couldn't believe it when she'd said they were going to see a Barbie fashion exhibition and he'd asked to tag along.

'Not so much for the Barbies,' he'd clarified with the grin Ramona was becoming rather fond of, 'but I love the Powerhouse. Last time I went there was this awesome taxidermy exhibit with some really cool birds of prey.'

'You're such a geek,' Ramona had teased him.

'As if you can talk,' he'd retorted.

'Touché. And yeah, of course you can come. Lucy won't mind. I reckon you two will get on like a house on fire.'

Lucy was curious about meeting the infamous Elijah—the owner of the foul-mouthed budgie—although very nervous to start with. She didn't say much when Ramona introduced them, but Elijah had a way of putting her at ease and before they'd seen even half of the exhibition they were acting like old friends.

Ramona thought Elijah might explore other parts of the museum while they lingered over each Barbie, scrutinising the way her outfits and general appearance had changed over the years, but he stuck by them, seemingly equally as interested.

'Barbie Millicent Roberts,' he said aloud as he read a sign about the iconic doll's full name. 'Wow. I thought she was like Cher and Madonna and just had a first name?'

The girls laughed, but admitted they'd thought the same.

'And I can't believe she began with a blonde and a brunette option—I've never seen a brown-haired Barbie—or that she didn't smile until 1971!' He shook his head as if astounded by these facts.

'I think you're enjoying this more than we are,' Ramona mocked.

Elijah merely wriggled his eyebrows at her. Her heart fluttered.

'Such a pity Barbie didn't … de-debut until 1959,' Lucy mused, 'because including her outfits in our magazine would have been fun.'

'Yes,' Ramona agreed, 'but maybe we can do an intro to Barbie in the final pages? We can feature her black and white swimsuit and that navy pencil skirt with the fabulous red coat.'

'You two get very passionate about school projects,' Elijah said with a chuckle.

'Only ones we're invested in. I bet if you did an assignment on birds, you'd be just the same.'

'You already know me so well.'

Ramona glowed at his words, and saw Lucy raise her eyebrows.

'Do you want to be a fashion curator too?' Elijah asked Lucy as they continued through the exhibit.

She shook her head. 'I want to be a fashion … illustrator.'

'You should see her drawings,' Ramona said. 'They're out of this world.'

Lucy blushed and smiled down at the ground.

'It's true and you know it.'

'Excuse my ignorance, but is a fashion illustrator the same as a fashion designer?'

'Oh, Elijah.' Ramona linked her arm through his. 'You have so much to learn. Luckily we are exactly the people to educate you.'

Once they'd finished the Barbie exhibition and Elijah understood that fashion designers create garments and sketch out ideas, but their focus is on the product, whereas a fashion illustrator is an artist that focuses on fashion and creating designs for clients, they moved through the rest of the museum, chatting and laughing as they went.

At the exit, Lucy needed to go to the bathroom and Ramona went with her and checked her email on her phone while she waited. Although it hadn't been long since she'd sent back the DNA test, she couldn't stop thinking about it or checking her email constantly.

'He's dreamy,' Lucy said as she emerged from a cubicle.

'Who?' For a second Ramona thought she was talking about her dad.

Lucy gave her a 'duh' look. 'Um, Elijah. Don't tell me you're not crushing on him, because if you do, I swear I'll go for him myself.'

'I *think* I like him, but I'm not sure. I've never had a crush on anyone before.'

'Seriously?'

Ramona shrugged. 'Yeah. I've never met a boy I could get remotely excited about. I thought maybe I didn't have those kind of feelings.'

'Or maybe he's just the first one you've ever met who's actually worth thinking about that way. Boys our age are pretty gross.'

'That's true,' Ramona said, thinking about the guys at her last school who were always telling crude jokes and scratching their crotches in class. 'There's one other issue.'

'What? Don't tell me he's gay?'

'No. At least I don't think so, but how do I know if he likes me or if he's just nice to everyone?'

'Well, I don't pretend to be an expert on boys,' Lucy said with a grin, 'but I'd say the feeling's mutual. I keep catching him staring at you.'

'Really?' Ramona felt as if she were melting like cheese under a grill.

'Yes.' Lucy squeezed her hand. 'But we better get back to Mr Handsome before he thinks we've done a runner on him. Come on.'

'Anyone else starving?' Elijah asked as they emerged. 'Why don't we head over to Paddy's Markets and see what we can find?'

They were soon digging into boxes of cheap but amazingly delicious noodles as they sat at a rickety plastic table, listening to a busker playing a ukulele and watching the world go by. After lunch, they strolled around, trying on silly hats and sniffing smelly candles until they started to get headaches from the cocktail of powerful aromas.

'I'm just gunna go to the loo,' Elijah said.

'No worries. We'll just wait over there.' Ramona pointed to a stall bursting with handmade earrings, kinda like the ones her mum had started making.

She was admiring a pair of blue budgie earrings when a familiar voice pierced the air. 'Well, well, well, what have we here?'

Ramona froze. What the hell was Sydney doing at Paddy's Markets? She seemed much more likely to be hanging out in Pitt Street Westfield with all its luxury labels.

Lucy's smile faded as they turned to face the coolest girl in the school. Sydney was hand in hand with the guy Ramona recognised as Blake from all her social media. He had a sun-kissed mullet—one of the few trends Ramona didn't appreciate from the past.

'What are you doing here?' Sydney asked, directing the question to Ramona, before give Lucy a quick once-over and curling her lips into a sneer.

'W-w-we …' Suddenly *Ramona* had turned into a stutterer. What would Sydney say if she knew she'd *chosen* to hang out with Lucy?

Sydney stared at her expectantly.

'W-we were at the … m-museum getting inspiration for our … f-fashion assignment,' Lucy explained.

Ramona nodded, relief flooding through her. 'Yeah, we've just had something to eat, and were both about to head home.'

'Right. Well.' Sydney sounded as if she wasn't quite sure she believed this story but had decided to give Ramona the benefit of the doubt. 'Blake and I are off to see a movie …'

He looked up from his phone and gave them a cool nod in greeting.

'Not that we'll probably end up seeing much of it.' She winked. 'I'll see you next Friday night for back-to-school sleepover.' It was more of a statement than a question and Ramona felt a wave of guilt when Sydney looked directly at her, clearly not extending the invitation to Lucy.

'Sure. Can't wait,' she chirped.

'Well, chat soon,' Sydney said, before turning on her brand-sparkly-new pink Off-White sneakers and sashaying away like she was a Kardashian and Blake her latest rock-star boyfriend.

'Did you see those shoes?' Ramona said when they were out of earshot. 'How much do you reckon they cost?'

Lucy shrugged. 'Don't know. Don't care.'

'You're right. I think they're pretty ugly actually.'

Ramona expected Lucy to laugh but instead she said, 'I d-don't know why you hang out with her and her cling-ons. She reminds me of Malfoy, and those other two are just better-looking versions of Crabbe and Goyle.'

'I …' Ramona didn't know what to say to that.

'Never mind, I'm going home. Say bye to Elijah for me.'

And before Ramona could say anything Lucy was gone, leaving her watching as she disappeared into the sea of people.

A gloom descended upon her, putting a dampener on what until that moment had been an awesome day. Should she have played things differently? Lucy had given her the 'assignment' out and she'd run with it, making it sound like they were eating together purely for logistical reasons. If only Sydney and co could get to know Lucy, Ramona knew they'd like her.

But Sydney, Kenzie and Nyra weren't as bad as Lucy thought either. They'd made Ramona feel welcome when she'd first arrived at SLC and were generous too—Kenzie had given her a near-new phone and Sydney was kind enough to order the DNA kit for her, which had to be a risk even if she said her dad never checked his credit card statements.

When Ramona had wished for friends, she'd never imagined how complicated they could be.

'Sorry I took so long,' Elijah said when he returned. 'Apparently the ladies' loos were out of order and so a bunch of girls snuck into the men's. I had to wait a while.'

'It's fine.'

He frowned and looked around. 'What have you done with Lucy?'

'Um …' Ramona couldn't bring herself to tell him the truth, that she was a coward and had made Lucy feel like she was embarrassed to be seen with her, so she'd left, upset. 'She got a message from her dad and had to go. She said to say bye.'

He nodded. 'Do you want to head back too, or should we walk down to the harbour for a bit? There are some amazing birds that live near the bridge. If we're lucky we might see a peregrine falcon or a yellow-faced honeyeater.'

Ramona had no idea what either of those birds were, but she knew that Elijah would make them interesting. However, much as she wanted to roam the city with him a little longer, she was no longer in the mood to hang out.

'I think we'd better head home. I told Mum I'd organise dinner, so I don't want to be too late.'

'That's cool. There's always another day.'

She nodded and tried to summon a smile when inside she felt anything but happy. What was she going to do about the conflict between her school friends? Surely there was something she could do to bring them all together.

Quinn

Darpan held the front door open for Quinn. 'Are you sure you should be skating to work with that?'

'Trust me, I'm better on wheels than I am in heels or even sneakers.' She gazed down at the massive container she'd borrowed from Mrs D. 'No way in hell I'm letting anything happen to this masterpiece.'

'Okay, have a great day and good luck. Hope you beat whatshisname!'

'I don't need any luck,' she called as she started down the garden path. 'No one else stands a chance today.'

She heard her brother-in-law chuckle as he shut the door behind her, but he could scoff all he wanted. Under Mrs D's guidance, she'd baked a berry dream cake that would make Steve from IT's efforts look like supermarket mud cake. She couldn't wait to wipe the smarmy smile from his face when she unveiled her pink and white marbled base with its light and fluffy cream cheese icing, topped with chopped fresh strawberries. Mrs D had taught her that impressive and delicious didn't have to mean hours in the kitchen. This creation had only six ingredients and required less than half an hour actual labour time all up, yet Quinn was confident that the 'simple elegance, melt-in-your mouth texture, and classic flavours' described in the recipe would win her the title of this year's Baking Champ.

Skating through Hyde Park, much slower than usual so as not to ruin her precious cargo, her heart leapt as she registered a head poking out above the people in front of her. Not just any old head but the head she saw every night when she closed her eyes to go to sleep. Although she might only have seen it once before, the distinctive caramel colour of the guy's perfectly mussed hair would be imprinted in her memory forever.

She could hardly believe it!

'It's him,' she shrieked, causing the people on either side of her to glare and then take a wide berth.

''Scuse me,' she urged, picking up her pace as she weaved through the pedestrians up ahead, never letting her eyes stray from Handbag Dude.

Quinn didn't know what she'd say when she caught up with him, but that was the least of her worries. She could talk to anyone. Years of dating apps had at least given her that skill.

'Got any spare change?' asked a homeless man as she tried to dodge around him.

Quinn felt terrible; the poor guy clearly needed much more than spare change.

'Here.' She bestowed upon him the cake. There'd always be next year to put smug Steve in his place. 'Enjoy.'

The man looked confused, but there wasn't time to explain.

Handbag Dude was getting further ahead but now she didn't have the cake, she could move a lot faster. Due to his height his strides were wide. Thank God for her rollerskates.

As the distance closed between them, excitement compounded in her heart, but then someone called her name. 'Quinn Paladino? Is that you?'

She slowed automatically to look in the direction of the voice.

'Oh my God. It *is* you. I knew it!' As Quinn came to a standstill the woman threw her arms around her and squeezed tightly. 'How the hell are you?'

Quinn pulled back and resisted the urge to spit, *Who the hell are you?* 'Um … good.'

The woman giggled. 'You don't recognise me, do you? It's Naomi, from school. I look a lot different now—finally cut my hair and stopped trying to be a skinny person.' Her eyes skated over Quinn's red and white strawberry-print dress, which she'd chosen specifically to match her cake. 'I see you're still looking fabulous.'

'Thanks,' Quinn said distractedly.

'Do you live in Sydney?'

Quinn nodded, her heart sinking as she glanced ahead to see Handbag Dude getting further away, but she didn't want to be rude to Naomi, who she finally remembered. They'd been partners in Food Technology class; Naomi had never eaten anything they made because she was constantly on a diet. 'You too?'

'Yep.' Naomi flashed the sparkly diamond on her ring finger. 'My fiancé lives here. We met online, you know how it is, and I can do my job anywhere; besides, the shopping is better here than in Adelaide.'

Quinn should probably ask what that job was or perhaps more about the fiancé, but she couldn't afford to linger. 'I'm sorry, but I'm running late for a meeting. Great seeing you again.'

'Oh yeah, you too. Find me on Facebook and we can catch up.'

'Okay!'

Quinn scoured the surrounding streets, but her guy was no longer anywhere in sight.

'Dammit.' She could have cried, not to mention killed bloody Naomi. She'd lost her cake and Mrs D's container for nothing.

*

'Which one's yours?' Deb asked as they crowded into the foyer for the annual Bake-Off later that morning.

Three long trestle tables had been set up in the reception foyer and Lexi had laid out the entries upon them and placed a number in front of each cake or slice ready for the big vote.

But Quinn couldn't care less about the cake. 'You'll never guess who I saw this morning,' she blurted excitedly.

Deb frowned. 'Who?'

'Handbag Dude!'

'Really?' Deb turned her attention away from the cakes. 'Where?'

'Not far from the office.' She relayed her unfortunate meeting with Naomi.

'Are you sure it was him? I'm not sure I'd recognise someone I'd only seen once by the back of their head.'

'It was definitely him!' Quinn snapped. Why couldn't her friend share her excitement?

'I'm sorry.' Deb reached out and touched her arm. 'That's great. I guess it means he does live in Sydney, so maybe you'll see him again?'

'There's no maybe about it. I know you think I'm crazy but ... we're meant to be.'

'I don't think you're crazy, it's just ...'

'Anyway, I had to abandon my cake during the chase, so you'll just have to imagine how good it looked and how delicious it was. That is until next year.' She glanced at the rows of sweet treats. 'What did you end up baking?'

'Nothing flash—just an apple and cinnamon teacake.'

'Good morning, everyone,' boomed Shaun from in front of the floor-to-ceiling windows. 'And welcome to our famous Bake-Off. I can't wait to see what everyone has whipped up, but before we get to the tasting, I have some news to share while we're all together.'

Larry Larson, the director of sales, stepped up beside Shaun.

'It is with deep sadness I have to inform you all of Larry's resignation. I'd like to congratulate Larry on accepting a position at Apple and wish him the best in his exciting new role.'

Mutterings of all sorts filled the foyer. Some congratulations, some whispers of glee—Larry wasn't the most beloved of employees—and some people were already sampling the cakes.

'Thanks, Shaun.' Larry beamed at his colleagues. 'This will be a hard place to leave, but after much deliberation I feel this is the right move for me.'

'Larry will be with us for a few more weeks,' Shaun said, 'but I've already started the hunt for a new director of sales. Right, happy eating, everyone, and don't forget to cast your votes before heading back to work.'

As usual there was a rush to the tables, but Quinn and Deb held back, happy to chat until the crowd thinned.

'Do you think Sally's applied for Larry's job?' Deb asked, referring to one of the few women in the massive sales team.

'I hope so. She's been here for almost ten years and, the way I hear it, she carries a lot of Larry's load already.'

Deb nodded. Neither of them knew Sally very well—she worked hard but kept to herself. Quinn couldn't remember her contributing to Bake-Off or even attending the Christmas party and hoped these things didn't work to her disadvantage. Shaun was all about The Energy Co being one big happy family and placed a lot of importance on what he called 'team bonding opportunities'.

As gaps appeared around the table, Quinn and Deb selected a couple of pieces from what was left over. Along with what looked like a red velvet cupcake, Quinn took a slice of Deb's apple teacake. Deb picked up a mango framington, which Steve from IT told her was 'a cross between a friand and a lamington with the summery taste of mango. I reckon it's another winner, Denise,' he finished with a wink.

'You do know it's autumn, right?' Quinn asked, annoyed he didn't know Deb's name. If it weren't for her, he wouldn't get paid.

Steve glared at her. 'It was a figure of speech.' Then he slunk off to try and cajole others into voting for him.

'*Framington?* Really?' Quinn scoffed. 'I've never heard of anything so wanky.'

'But he's not wrong, they are delicious,' Deb said apologetically as she popped the last bit into her mouth.

'One of these days,' Quinn whispered with a scowl, 'I'm going to go to his house the night before Bake-Off, peek inside his kitchen window and catch his poor wife in the act. I swear.'

Deb chuckled. 'So, tell me more about Handbag Dude. Any idea where he was headed?'

'Well, since he was wearing a suit, I'm guessing an office somewhere around here. If only I knew his name. If only I'd not rushed off that night we met.'

Deb gave her a sympathetic smile as she grabbed a pink macaron from the leftovers. 'Do you have any exciting plans for the weekend?' It was clearly an attempt to take Quinn's mind off her disappointment.

'I've got a hen's night for a friend from spin tomorrow. She's a bit of a party animal, so it might be messy. Sunday will likely be spent recovering.' She lifted a hand to her hair and ran her fingers through. 'Might have a bit of a pamper day. Give myself a new colour. What about you and Ramona?'

Deb's cheeks flushed. 'I'm seeing Tristan again.'

'Ooh, what are you guys doing?' Quinn asked; it was weird that Deb was the one who had plans with a man, whereas she'd probably be spending any downtime with Snoodles and Mrs D or doing something mundane like rearranging her wardrobe.

'Don't laugh,' Deb began, 'but we're going to Luna Park.'

Quinn loved Luna Park but couldn't help smirking at the image of Deb on the Sledgehammer or the Hair Raiser. 'Was that your idea or his?'

'His. Our two dates so far—'

'Hang on, I thought you said you weren't "dating"?'

Deb's cheeks went so red you could probably fry an egg on them. 'We're not. What I meant was, our "outings" so far have been pretty heavy conversation-wise and so Tristan thought it would be good to do something fun and frivolous together.'

Quinn guessed she was referring to discussions about his dead wife. 'Sounds like a good idea. Are you taking Ramona?'

'No.'

'Definitely a date then,' Quinn teased. 'I can't wait to hear about it. Maybe he'll kiss you on the Ferris wheel?'

The colour drained from Deb's face. 'I'm not even sure I remember how to kiss.'

But she didn't say she didn't want to, and Quinn considered that progress. 'Don't stress, it's like riding a bike. You never forget.'

'Anyway ...' Deb wiped a crumb off the side of her mouth. 'Guess we'd better cast our votes and head back to work.'

Quinn nodded, swallowing her final mouthful of teacake. 'But I'm warning you, if you vote for Steve, I'm never speaking to you again!'

Debra

When Tristan suggested going to Luna Park, Deb thought he was joking but now as they approached the famous face and the carnival music from inside grew louder, she couldn't help smiling. Perhaps he was onto something. It would be impossible to feel too serious here.

They didn't talk much as they waited in the queue, but it was a comfortable silence. In such a short time, she'd told Tristan so much about herself and discovered so much about him that she didn't feel the need to make small talk. Until recently, she could count the number of other people she felt this relaxed with on two fingers and the addition of another gave her a pleasant feeling.

'Just two adults?' the teenage girl behind the counter asked, peering to the ground as if searching for their offspring. 'No kids?'

Tristan smirked, clearly as bemused as Deb. 'That's right. Just us old farts.'

She snort-laughed and the girl looked at them like they were aliens. 'That will be eighty-eight dollars, thanks.'

She opened her purse to pay for her ticket, but Tristan waved his hand. 'No, no, this is my treat,' he insisted as he handed over his credit card.

'Okay,' she relented, 'but I'm buying lunch.'

This wasn't supposed to be a date, after all.

'We'll see.' He grinned as he slipped his wallet into his pocket and gestured for her to go ahead through the gate.

She glanced around at the brightly coloured rides and bedraggled-looking parents clutching onto the hands of little kids. 'Where to first?'

'Why don't we have a wander and see what takes our fancy?'

'Sounds like a plan.'

They strolled past the Ferris wheel and the carousel opposite, past the showbags and food and sideshow alley, where tiny kids demanded treats. As a toddler threw himself onto the ground and slammed his fists on the pavement, wailing something about fairy floss, she and Tristan shared a knowing glance. They'd both been there but today they were footloose and fancy-free. She couldn't remember the last time she'd done something frivolous for herself. It had to be before Ramona was born. Sure, they'd been to circuses and other fun things, but those days were all about her daughter.

This was different and it felt a little naughty. *Good* naughty.

'Dodgem cars or Coney Island?' Tristan asked, interrupting her thoughts as he pointed ahead to Dodgem City.

'Hmm …' She considered a moment. 'Coney Island. I need to work up to the bumper cars.'

They chuckled their way through the mirror maze, and Deb almost lost her footing on the wonky walk, but Tristan reached out and grabbed her before she could fall.

'You all right?'

She nodded, a warm, gentle buzz flowing up her arm at the brief connection. 'There's a reason why everyone else in here is at least thirty years younger than us.'

But that didn't stop them going on the Devil's Drop or spinning themselves near sick in the Barrels of Fun. They snort-laughed so hard that when they got out Deb had to sit down for a few minutes.

'*Now* I'm ready for the dodgem cars,' Deb said. 'Although I should warn you. I'm very competitive.'

Tristan raised his eyebrows. 'That sounds like a challenge.'

They had to wait in the queue but unlike the little people surrounding them, they didn't mind the breather. Tristan told her about a cranky ferret he'd treated the day before and then chuckled as she told him about Quinn giving away her Bake-Off cake as she scrounged the city looking for Handbag Dude.

'*Handbag Dude?*'

'Oh, now that is a long story,' Deb said. 'Remind me to tell you over lunch.'

'I can't wait,' he replied as the park employee called them forward for their turn.

Deb commandeered a red car and Tristan climbed into the yellow one beside her. AC/DC's 'Thunderstruck' played at a deafening pitch and children screamed all around them as they chased one another around the track, pretending to be annoyed when they bumped into each other. She felt like a teenager but reckoned they were having even more fun than the kids.

After the dodgem cars, they took in sideshow alley and Deb spotted a massive rainbow unicorn. 'That would look great on my bed,' she joked.

Tristan spent an exorbitant amount of money before finally winning her one on the Test Tube Toss.

'Thank you.' She struggled to wrap her arms around it. 'Are you hungry? Because after that impressive performance I'm definitely buying lunch.'

On their way to Helter Skelter café, they were ambushed by a park mascot—someone dressed like a circus ringmaster with the actual Luna Park face covering their whole head—and its minder.

'Want a photo with Luna?' asked the smiley young man.

It felt rude to say no, so Tristan handed over his phone and they posed on either side, their hands brushing against each other as they wrapped an arm around Mr Luna Park.

'I'll send you the photo so you can show Ramona,' he said as Luna and his minder went off to find another victim. 'My kids are going to get a kick out of seeing this. They always said they thought I took them to fun parks more for me than I did for them and, between you and me, they were right.'

Deb laughed, remembering what he'd said about his wife's aversion to crowds. 'I'm guessing this kind of place wasn't Marie's cup of tea?'

He shook his head. 'The only time I ever got her into a theme park was on our honeymoon in New York. We went to Coney Island.'

Deb shivered. Any mention of the city where she'd been left tied up and alone for two days always left her cold.

Tristan misread her discomfort as not wanting to hear about Marie. 'I'm sorry. You probably don't want to hear about my honeymoon.'

'It's not that. I told you, I'm happy to listen to your memories and I meant it. I know Marie will always hold a special place in your heart.'

'Oh,' he said, his face falling as realisation dawned. 'I guess you might not have such fond memories of New York?'

'Yeah, but it's silly. It's a wonderful place and I should remember the good times I had there.'

They arrived at the café and joined the long line of people waiting to order. This gave them time to work out what they wanted and also talk more about the city that never sleeps. They shared memories of Broadway plays, favourite restaurants, and some of the places she'd discovered that only people who'd lived in the city knew about.

'What can I get for you?' asked a flustered-looking woman behind the counter as they finally got to the front.

'Two hot dogs with extra mustard on one,' Deb said, 'a basket of hot chips, and two Cokes, please.'

She tried not to think about the calories as Tristan carried their lunch over to a table. She didn't want anything to spoil this day, besides, now she was a runner, surely it meant she could indulge a little more.

'Can I ask you something?' Tristan said once they were seated and digging into their food.

Although Deb's chest tightened at the tone of his voice, she nodded.

'Why aren't you a psychologist?'

'What do you mean?' She popped a crunchy chip into her mouth, surprised by his question.

'You have a degree in psychology and mentioned you were doing your masters in New York. Why aren't you practising now? What happened?'

'Ramona happened,' she said with a nervous chuckle. 'I had to quit my masters to make money to support us. I did whatever I could, bookkeeping for a few small businesses where I settled after coming back to Australia. The next time we moved, I chose to take a bookkeeping job because a regular salary was more reliable. It was a small company and part of my role included payroll. I guess I kind of fell into it.'

'Have you ever thought of returning to psychology?' he asked, his brow creasing.

'No,' she scoffed. 'I'd have to do a whole load of study again and I don't have the time with work and motherhood.'

He looked at her in a way that made her feel as if he could see right through her. 'Are you sure that's what it is? That it isn't more because of Ramona's father?'

She swallowed. 'How do you do that?' she whispered, her vulnerability making her shiver.

'Do what?'

'Peel me open.' She sighed—what happened to enjoying a meal and easy conversation? 'I realised I'd have made a terrible psychologist. Falling for Ramona's father made me realise I am too clueless for such an important job. At least in payroll, any mistakes I might make aren't likely to destroy someone.'

'Oh, Deb.'

She blinked back tears at the pity in his voice. Their conversation had turned way too serious when today was supposed to be all about the fun.

'Ooh, I promised to tell you about Handbag Dude!'

'You did.' Tristan leaned back in his seat to listen, going along with her obvious effort to talk about something else.

While they finished their lunch, she talked about The Husband List and Quinn's decision to go off dating apps and try more old-fashioned methods. He laughed when she mentioned Quinn considering taking up woodworking.

'Aren't there any eligible young men at The Energy Co?' he asked. 'So many people meet their partners at work, and I'd have thought a company selling sports drinks would have plenty of them.'

'And you'd be right, but Quinn's rather picky and not one of them has piqued her interest.' Deb popped another chip into her mouth. 'Anyway, one of the things on the list is about spilling your handbag contents all over the ground so that men will stop and help.'

'Don't tell me she did that?'

'Not on purpose,' Deb said, then told him the story.

'And that's why she's coined him Handbag Dude.'

'Yep. And now she won't talk about anything else.'

'Quinn sounds like a hoot,' Tristan said with a grin. 'I hope I get to meet her one day.'

Deb's stomach twisted—him meeting Quinn would be her equivalent to meeting the parents; aside from Ramona, Quinn had become Deb's family. That felt like a mammoth step.

'Does she really think this mystery man is the one?' he asked.

She nodded.

'And what happens if she never sees him again?'

'I don't know.' Deb twisted the paper straw in her Coke and shrugged. 'Do you believe in fate?'

He frowned a moment. 'I like the idea of it, but I also believe that there's more than one person out there you can have a good relationship with. If you're prepared to put in the effort.'

She was about to ask him what kind of effort he and Marie had to put into their marriage, when his eyes lit up and he pointed. 'Hey, look over there.'

Deb looked up to see a bride and groom right at the top of the Ferris wheel. They were both waving at a photographer below. Although she'd long been a sceptic about romance and marriage, it was impossible not to grin at the sight.

'Shall we have a go?' he said.

'What? On the Ferris wheel?'

'Yeah, why not? One last ride before I take you back to Ramona. And how about a gelato on the way?'

'Sounds good to me.'

As they joined the line for the Ferris wheel, Deb felt Tristan's hand slip into hers. 'Is this okay?'

'Yes.' She smiled. It was more than okay.

Deb barely remembered getting onto the passenger car, but all of a sudden, they were at the top, looking down all over Sydney—she and Tristan seated on one side and the enormous unicorn taking up much of the other one.

Her heart hitched as he shifted even closer to her.

Looking directly into her eyes, he gently cupped her cheek, leaning forward so their mouths were almost touching, his warm breath tickling her skin. 'Can I kiss you?'

'Yes.'

She wasn't sure any sound came out of her mouth, but he must have got the message, because the next moment his lips brushed hers. And it was the most wonderful feeling ever. She thought she might have forgotten how to kiss but either that wasn't the case or Tristan was good enough for both of them. She didn't even care if Quinn had predicted this as long as he didn't stop. He tasted like the cookies and cream ice-cream he'd just eaten, and Deb knew she'd never be able to taste it again without remembering this perfect moment.

Sadly, eventually they needed air, and also there was a gangly teenage boy clearing his throat at them, indicating they were now at the bottom of the wheel.

Grinning so hard her cheeks ached, Deb climbed out as Tristan grabbed her unicorn. Hand in hand again, they walked back towards the entrance.

'Thank you,' she said when he dropped her off at her apartment almost an hour later. 'I had a wonderful day.'

'Me too.' Then he dipped his head and kissed her again.

Liquid heat rolled through her body, and she missed his lips when they broke apart.

'Goodbye,' she said reluctantly before turning to go inside.

Still smiling, she checked on Ramona who was listening to music in her room, and then messaged Quinn.

He kissed me.

And? came her near instant reply.

And I kissed him back.

And?

And it was amazing. I think I'm smitten.

OMG. I'm so bloody happy for you.

Me too.

Deb grinned as she pressed send on that last message. For once she didn't feel like a forty-two-year-old woman but like a teenage girl who'd just kissed her first crush.

Ramona

First day back of her second term at SLC, Ramona felt far more confident than when she'd arrived twelve weeks ago. Her commute had become a daily ritual as familiar as brushing her teeth; she knew the layout of the school, which teachers were strict and which bathrooms to avoid, but best of all, she had what she'd longed for since she first started kindy.

Friends.

There was only one problem—they didn't like each other. If someone had told her at the beginning of the year she might have to choose between two lots of friends, she'd have thought they were taking the piss. For her to have even one good friend would be a freaking miracle.

Therefore, her mission for this term was to bring her friends together. She'd started to sow seeds at the sleepover last Friday when the girls were in Sydney's theatre room, munching on popcorn, sipping Diet Coke laced with stolen vodka and watching Yuya and other make-up and fashion influencers on YouTube on the big screen. To be honest, Ramona had been starting to get bored.

'Is there any reason you guys hate Lucy so much?' she'd asked.

Sydney snatched up the remote and muted the TV. 'Why d'you ask?'

'I've just got to know her a bit because of our project and … you know, she doesn't seem that bad.'

'Doesn't seem that *bad*?' Sydney's pitch rose and she looked to the others for back-up.

Nyra grimaced as if she'd just tasted something sour. 'She's so basic.'

'Have you actually ever spent any time with her?' Ramona asked.

'Why would we?' Sydney spat. 'Have you seen her skin, her hair, the way she speaks and how she sucks up to the teachers? Do you need me to go on? It's like God took all the awful things he didn't want to use for anyone special and lumped them on her.'

Nyra snorted, but Kenzie didn't look quite as comfortable with the Lucy bashing as the others.

'So, she never did anything to offend or upset you?' Ramona prodded.

Sydney scoffed. 'As if that mole could offend us! Her and her religious father are so weird even her mum left them.'

'That's actually not true,' Ramona said, surprised at her own courage. 'Her mum didn't abandon them. She died.'

'Really?' Kenzie looked sympathetic. 'How?'

'Cancer,' Ramona said, hoping they might take pity on her.

'That's so sad,' said Kenzie.

Ramona nodded. 'I think if she had a mum, like we do, maybe she wouldn't be so awkward, but if you can look past her appearance—'

'And her g-g-g-godawful stutter,' exclaimed Sydney, looking to the others to reaffirm her.

Nyra rewarded her with a cackle.

'She actually doesn't stutter around me anymore,' Ramona said. 'I think she just gets nervous when she's in a group.'

Nyra frowned. 'Why do you care so much about her? Do you have a crush on her?'

Sydney snorted as if that was the funniest thing she'd ever heard. Kenzie shovelled a handful of popcorn into her mouth.

'No!' Heat rushed to Ramona's cheeks.

'Oh my God. You do, don't you? You must be some kind of freak as well.' Sydney narrowed her eyes at Ramona and she felt her pulse quicken.

Suddenly, she had a very clear vision of a future where both she and Lucy were outcasts, with no role at school but to provide entertainment for the popular kids. She'd been there once before and nothing—*no one*—was going to bring her down again.

'No, of course I don't.' When Sydney didn't look convinced, she added, 'I've actually got a *boyfriend* now.'

The others exchanged a look as if they didn't know whether to believe her.

'Why didn't you tell us?' This from Sydney.

Ramona attempted a coy smile. 'It's just early days. I didn't want to jinx it.'

'OMG have you kissed him yet?'

'What does he look like?'

'Where'd you meet?'

'Which school does he go to?'

The questions came fast and furious.

'Show us a photo!' ordered Nyra.

Thankfully, she and Elijah had taken some silly selfies when they went to the movies. She held her breath while the three of them huddled in to stare at her screen.

'Ooh, he's dreamy,' said Nyra, pretending to fan her face. 'I love long hair on a guy.'

'Would look better if he put it up in a man bun,' Sydney mused. 'What's his Snapchat? You, me, Elijah and Blake could double date.'

Ramona almost laughed out loud. She couldn't imagine bookish Elijah and jock Blake having anything in common. And while Elijah did have Snapchat, the last thing Ramona wanted was Sydney messaging him.

She scrambled to make up an excuse. 'He's banned from socials at the moment. His parents are really strict, and they didn't think his results from last term were good enough. They want him to focus on schoolwork.'

Sydney scowled. 'Parents are such dictators. Is he still allowed to see you?'

'Not really, but he lives a few houses down the street and sometimes he sneaks out late at night and knocks on my window.' The lies were just falling from her mouth, and she couldn't help basking in their reaction.

'Wow.' Kenzie placed a hand against her heart. 'That's so romantic. Like a movie or something.'

Although Ramona felt slightly bad lying to *her*, at least they'd forgotten about Lucy.

But she hadn't.

The moment the siren rang at lunchtime, she said she needed the bathroom and snuck off to the library instead. She found Lucy in her usual spot, reading a book on the couch, sneaking bites of a Vegemite sandwich whenever Miss Woo wasn't looking.

'What are you doing here?' Lucy said icily.

They didn't have fashion class today and this was the first time they'd seen each other since the markets. Ramona had messaged

Lucy a few times, but she'd only responded if it was about their project. And even those replies had been short.

Ramona got it. Lucy was hurt. But she was here to make up to her.

'I came to see you. What are you reading?' she asked, sitting on the couch beside her.

'A crime novel.'

'Any good?'

'It's all right.' Lucy closed the book and looked pointedly at Ramona. 'Do you need to talk about our project or is this a social visit?'

'I wondered if you wanted to come shopping after school?'

Lucy looked at her as if she'd asked if she wanted to help blow up the school. 'Shopping?'

Ramona nodded, undeterred. 'I need to buy a new foundation, so I was going to head to Sephora.' Once there, she'd encourage Lucy to try on some make-up too and maybe even buy a colour to put through her hair. Tone down the orange a little.

'Do your *real* friends have other plans?'

Ramona sighed. Maybe she just needed to be straight with Lucy. 'Look, I know what it's like to spend your lunchtimes alone and be the butt of everyone's jokes,' she began. 'That was me at my old school. Nobody ever wanted to hang out with me, and they made fun of my obsession with vintage and thought it was weird I liked making my own clothes. Until I started at SLC, the only friend I had was my mum. I couldn't believe it when Sydney, Nyra and Kenzie welcomed me into their group, but I doubt they would have if I hadn't made a conscious decision to do a few things differently. When I came to SLC, I was determined not to be a victim again. Changing schools gave me the fresh start I needed.'

'What are you suggesting? I change schools and start fresh as well?' Lucy asked.

'No.' She didn't want Lucy to leave. 'But I didn't just change schools. I did a few simple things to make myself less of a target. Things that you could do too.'

'Like?'

'Well, for starters, it wouldn't hurt for you to wear a bit of make-up.'

'That's against the school rules.'

'Just some mascara, a bit of blush, maybe some lip gloss and foundation to help cover your acne.'

'I suppose you think I should get contacts and do something with my horrible hair as well?' Lucy sounded angry but looked like she was close to tears.

'Your hair isn't horrible, but—'

'Thanks for telling me your ugly duckling story and I get that you think you're helping, but I'm not a charity case and I meant what I said. I don't want to be friends with people like Sydney—people who are shallow and get their kicks belittling others. I certainly don't want to change myself to try and make them like me.' Lucy shoved her book in her bag and stood. 'And I don't want to be friends with people who do that either.'

'Well, that went well,' Ramona said to herself as Lucy stalked away.

How could she help Lucy if she wasn't willing to help herself?

Quinn

Quinn scowled when an email landed at 4.40 pm on Friday afternoon—a reminder that all employees were expected in the boardroom at 4.50 pm to 'meet and greet' the new director of sales. Today of all days! When her parents were arriving from Adelaide and she'd invited Mrs D over for dinner to meet them.

'This better not take long,' muttered Linc from the desk next to hers. 'I've got plans tonight.'

'What?' Toby laughed. 'Netflix without the chill?'

Linc gave him the finger.

Quinn rolled her eyes as she shut down her computer and grabbed her bag. She deserved a pay rise for having to put up with these clowns.

Leaving them to their bickering, she headed down the corridor towards the finance department. Deb's cubicle was quieter than a library, all her colleagues bent over their computers, their fingers punching numbers into spreadsheets like it was an Olympic event. She bet the old blokes Deb worked with never discussed their sex lives—existent or otherwise—around her. The benefit of working with actual grown-ups.

'Hey, girlfriend. It's time,' Quinn said, leaning over the top of her friend's cubicle and tapping her watch.

Deb groaned. 'Why couldn't this have waited until Monday?'

'That's one of the many mysteries of the world. Along with why Shaun has employed yet another man to fill the position, when Sally deserved the promotion. So much for gender quotas and smashing the glass ceiling.'

She could see that Deb was as eager as Quinn to knock off and head home, although for entirely different reasons—Deb had a date with her hot vet to prep for. No matter how much she professed that she and Tristan were taking things slow, Quinn could see right through her. The way her eyes lit up and she got this goofy grin on her face whenever she talked about him told her everything she needed to know.

She was happy for Deb; she just hoped she didn't have to wait till she was in her forties to find love.

'So you think the rumour's true?' Deb asked. She hadn't received the paperwork for the new employee yet, but that morning in the copy room Lexi had let slip to them that she'd overheard Shaun saying 'him' and 'he' when talking to his PA about the recruit. Nothing remained secret for long at The Energy Co.

'Of that I have no doubt.' Quinn threw her hands up in the air. She could only imagine how poor Sally must be feeling right now. 'But you know Shaun's a man's man. Powerful women terrify him. Come on, the sooner we get to the boardroom, the sooner it will be over.'

'I've just got to send one email and I'll be there. Save me a seat.'

'You got it, girlfriend.' Quinn gave Deb a thumbs-up, then hurried back the way she'd come.

Her colleagues were already streaming into the room by the time she got there, but she managed to nab two chairs. Much to Linc's annoyance, she plopped her bag on the one next to her and refused to let him or anyone else sit down. Soon there was standing room only and Quinn shot Sally a conciliatory glance as she retreated to a corner of the room, her arms folded across her chest and a glower on her face that said she'd rather be anywhere else.

Finally, when Quinn was beginning to think she wouldn't be able to save Deb's chair a moment longer, her work wife appeared in the doorway.

She waved to get her attention. 'You made it,' Quinn said as Deb sat down.

'Where's Shaun?' shouted someone from near the back. 'Does he think we have all night?'

There were murmurs of disgruntled agreement. A text message distracted Quinn, and she looked down at her phone to see a message from her mother.

'Mam and Dad have landed,' she told Deb. 'Hope this doesn't take long. I wanted to be home to meet them.'

Suddenly everyone went quiet, and Quinn looked up to see that the door at the front had opened. Shaun appeared first, followed by the new director of sales. Her heart thudded and for a moment she froze, unable to believe her eyes.

'Oh my God,' she gasped as she recognised the man standing alongside the CEO.

It was *him*! Handbag Dude. And he was a hundred times better-looking than she remembered. It wasn't just his beautifully chiselled face and sparkly eyes that made her weak at the knees—thank God she was sitting down—but also his smile. The kind of broad grin that made you forget the world could be a dark place, riddled with things like famine, terminal disease, climate change and war. His grin made you believe in the goodness of mankind.

Every cell in her body buzzed and all thoughts of poor Sally, all thoughts of her parents, all thoughts of anything but *him* evaporated.

'Good afternoon,' Shaun said into the mic. 'I'd like to thank you all for coming to welcome our newest member of The Energy Co family, Oscar Darke.' He paused as everyone clapped. 'Oscar comes to us with an impressive resume of experience and lots of innovative ideas. I've asked him to say a few words, tell us a bit about himself and his vision for the future of our sales department.'

'Thank you, thank you.' Handbag Dude—no, *Oscar*—stepped up to the podium, thumping Shaun good-naturedly on the shoulder as he did so.

Oscar.

It suited him like nothing else could. How could she ever have imagined names like Adam, Travis or Joshua, which now seemed far too lacklustre for someone like him.

'I have to say I'm a little overwhelmed by such a warm welcome.' His eyes scanned the crowd and Quinn sat up straight in her seat, desperate for him to notice her.

I'm here, she wanted to scream. *Remember me?*

'I know you're probably all itching to hit the pub for happy hour ...'

Laughter rippled around the room, but no one seemed in such a hurry to clock off anymore.

'... so I'll try to make this snappy.'

Oh Mary, that voice. His *voice.* His Aussie accent had an American twang that caused the blood to rush to Quinn's head. Had she ever heard anything so deep and melodic before? She swore she felt her ovaries quiver.

'I was born and bred in the inner east but headed to New York in the early naughties for work. Thought I'd only be there for a couple of years, but I fell in love with the Big Apple and, well, two years turned to almost twenty.'

Another chuckle from the crowd. Another flutter in Quinn's belly. She considered sneakily pressing record on her phone so she could replay his words later.

He pushed his glasses up his nose and continued. 'I've worked for a number of different companies in various positions from sales rep to my last position, which was national sales director at Johnson and Johnson. While I loved the work and my life in Manhattan, the last couple of years ...'

His voice drifted off and she swore he caught her gaze. Smiling, she gave a small nod of encouragement, and he cleared his throat and continued.

'It was hard being away from our ... from *family*. My parents aren't getting any younger and it felt like the right time to come home.'

Our. Did he say 'our'? Cold flooded her. Could 'our' mean a wife? A girlfriend? A partner? *No.* After living with Dec and Darpan her gaydar was fairly accurate and she'd bet her life savings on the fact Oscar Darke was straight. And he wasn't wearing a wedding ring.

That doesn't mean he isn't in a relationship.

Oh, shut up! She shook her head, refusing to listen to the cruel voice within. Shouldn't her conscience be on *her* side?

Besides, fate wouldn't be that callous. It was far more likely her ears had been playing tricks on her or Oscar was referring to a pet or something. He looked like an animal lover, and she could imagine him with a dog. A labrador or even something a little bit different like a Weimaraner. She'd met one of those in the park the other day with Snoodles.

Maybe one day soon they could walk the dogs together. Quinn didn't hear much of what he said about the sales department, but when Oscar wished everyone a great weekend, she grabbed Deb's hand.

'Holy smokes,' she hissed as their colleagues started to stand. 'It's him.'

'What?' Deb's newly shaped eyebrows squished together in obvious confusion.

'He's The One!' When she didn't say anything, Quinn gestured towards the front. 'I'm going to introduce myself. Coming?'

Deb shook her head.

'Are you okay?' Quinn noticed her friend looked a little pale.

'Actually ...' Deb put a hand on her stomach. 'I'm feeling a little queasy. I've got to get out of here.'

'Are you going to be sick? Do you want me to come with you?' Quinn asked but Deb shook her head.

'I'll be fine. I just need some fresh air.'

As Deb fled from the room, Quinn couldn't help feeling relieved she hadn't said 'yes'.

She couldn't believe she'd found Handbag Dude—or rather he'd found her—and, although she hoped Deb was okay, in that moment, *nothing* could dull that joy and relief. This must be what it felt like winning Lotto.

All the single women in the office and even a couple of gay guys had already formed a small crowd around Oscar. He was like a shining beacon to moths. Even Sally, usually a vision of cool, calm and collected, looked flustered as she stood beside him, and something told Quinn it wasn't because she wanted to castigate him for stealing her promotion.

Step aside, people.

She fought the urge to tell everyone else to bugger off, that they were wasting their time because Quinn and Oscar—*Quinn and*

Oscar, how good did that sound?—were written in the stars and it was time to work her magic. Although patience had never been her virtue, she restrained herself and eventually the others started to disperse.

With only Sally and Shaun still at his side, she stepped forward and flashed Oscar a smile. 'Hi. Welcome to The Energy Co. I'm Quinn Paladino.' The way her head swirled it was a miracle she managed to remember her own name.

Oscar's lovely thick eyebrows quirked as he returned her smile. 'Have we met before?'

The breath caught in her throat. He remembered!

'Um … yes …' she managed, her cheeks heating. 'I think so. About a month ago … I was rollerskating on Oxford Street and—'

His grin widened. 'And you dropped your bag.'

She nodded. 'My stuff went everywhere and—'

'I stopped to help you pick it up.'

She tried not to swoon; they were already finishing each other's sentences. 'Yes. That's right. I never really got the chance to thank you, so this is very … fortuitous.'

'No thanks necessary. I did what anyone would do. But it's wonderful to see you again.'

Quinn nodded. Wonderful was an understatement.

'And what's your role here?' he asked.

'Um … I'm … I work in digital marketing. The social media campaign for our new wellbeing drink was my brainchild.' She described the campaign in minute detail as if she were pitching it to a client.

Oh Lord, she was rambling—both Sally and Shaun were looking at her as if she'd lost the plot. She'd almost forgotten they weren't alone.

'It sounds awesome,' Oscar said, reaching out and patting her arm. 'I look forward to getting to know you better as I expect to work very closely with the marketing department.'

Despite the fabric of Quinn's sleeve between them, heat radiated from his touch all over her body, leaving tingles in its wake. She needed to get out of there before she melted into a puddle at his feet.

'Me too,' she managed. 'Well, have a great weekend, everyone. See you all next week.'

Normally, Quinn wanted her weekends to last forever, but already she couldn't wait for Monday morning. It was only as she approached Dec and Darpan's house and saw her parents getting out of a taxi that she remembered she'd taken the whole week off to spend time with them.

Dammit.

'Mam! Dad!' She forced enthusiasm into her voice as she threw her arms around her mother. 'So great to see you both. How was the flight?'

Debra

Deb made it as far as the food hall downstairs before dashing into the grotty public restrooms and hurling everything she'd eaten at lunch into the toilet. She hugged the bowl, uncaring of the stench or the wetness seeping into her tights from the tiles.

What the actual *fuck* had just happened?!

One minute she'd been happier than she had in years and the next she'd been dumped right into the middle of her worst ever nightmare. How the tables had turned—Quinn talking about Friday night with her family and Deb coyly sharing her growing feelings for Tristan as she anticipated their evening ahead. For the first time they were officially calling it a date and she'd thought her biggest problem today would be choosing an outfit for dinner. Now …

Oh God.

She lurched back over the toilet bowl, tears spilling from her eyes. The only thing she knew for sure right now was that she'd never be able to eat dumplings again. They would forever remind her of the day Oscar Darke reappeared in her life.

And if she'd never seen him again that would have been too soon.

Her whole body began to tremble at the thought that he was, right now, likely still schmoozing with her unsuspecting colleagues and charming them with his saccharine smile and charismatic personality. She knew from experience that he had the ability to make every person feel like they were the most interesting, most important, most special person in the world, and she couldn't blame them—she had fallen hard and fast under his spell and into his web of lies and deceit herself.

It wouldn't take long until the whole office was as besotted with him as Shaun clearly was. Not that he needed to win Quinn over— she was already a devout fan.

Until this afternoon her friend's preoccupation with the guy she called Handbag Dude had been amusing, but this new development was terrifying. It seemed the cruellest twist of fate that Handbag Dude was in fact Oscar. Ramona's father.

And she was the spitting image of him. It wasn't only their hair colour, but also the rare aqua colour of their eyes, the aristocratic shape of their noses and the disarming way they smiled, as if they could see your inner thoughts.

A door slammed and then someone turned on the tap, reminding Deb she needed to get up and go home. Standing, she flushed the toilet and went out to the sink to rinse her mouth. A glance in the mirror showed bloodshot eyes, mascara streaking down her cheeks and vomit on her shirt.

She wiped the latter off, imagining the way Oscar would look at her if he saw her now. One moment he could make her feel like the dirt on the bottom of his shoe and the next he'd say something so charming to make her think she'd misunderstood.

In hindsight, their whole relationship had been a confusing rollercoaster. When he was around she'd not only lost her sense of self but also her ability to think straight. Shame filled her and nausea rose once again in her stomach as she recalled how she'd *allowed* him to treat her like that. She hadn't been strong enough to walk away before it was too late. Staring into the mirror, her chest heaved as she struggled to breathe. She needed to get out of here, get out of the city, get as far away from *him* as fast as possible.

But what if he caught the train home as well?

She froze at the thought. She could run right into him at the station. She didn't think he'd seen her yet, but she'd been so busy trying to not make eye contact that she couldn't be certain he hadn't clocked her. Her pulse raced even faster. Was this what a panic attack felt like?

'Are you okay?'

She jumped at the sound of a voice, which came from a woman she hadn't even noticed come in.

'Um … I …' She honestly didn't know if she'd ever be okay again.

'Are you hurt? Is there anything I can do to help? Shall I call someone?'

At the woman's concern, Deb took a deep breath and shook her head again. 'I'm fine. Really. Thank you. I just had some bad news.'

The worst possible news ever.

'Okay.' The woman didn't look convinced but stepped into a cubicle, nonetheless.

Deb didn't want to be there when she emerged, so she dug into her bag for her sunglasses, put them on, kept her head down and made eye contact with absolutely no one as she walked briskly through the food hall to the neighbouring underground station. Blessedly, the train arrived at the platform as she did and she slipped inside, her head darting from side to side searching the carriage for Oscar.

Only when she was certain she couldn't see him did she collapse into a seat, telling herself that someone like him would never live way out in the western suburbs.

Yet, even as the train travelled further and further away from the city and the tall office buildings made way for urban sprawl, she couldn't relax. The journey was a blur as she replayed in her head what had happened in the boardroom, searching for an explanation, or rather an alternative. She couldn't imagine the Oscar she'd known ever growing a beard—he'd once said everyone with facial hair looked like hobos or paedophiles. Maybe the glass of wine she'd had with lunch had warped her sensibilities and she'd been mistaken.

But although Deb had lied to others about her daughter's father for the past fifteen and a half years, she was hopeless at lying to herself. Beard or not, it was Oscar. No one could have his name *and* look exactly like him.

Under normal circumstances she'd be unloading on Quinn right now—asking her if she had any idea what the hell she should do, but the moment Quinn had announced Oscar as The One, that possibility had evaporated. Suddenly Deb wasn't sure whether she could trust her best friend with the biggest secret of her life.

She didn't even remember getting off the train at Granville or stopping at the liquor store, but almost an hour after leaving the office, she found herself climbing the stairs to the apartment, two bottles of sav blanc in a brown paper bag tucked under her arm. The receipt inside informed her there'd been a two for one deal.

Only when she'd swallowed half a glass in one mouthful did she register the absence of Ramona.

For one split second she panicked and then remembered that Ramona was going to a meeting of the local Budgerigar Society with Elijah tonight. Deb had no idea what this involved but was grateful for a few hours alone to work out what the heck she was going to do. The thought of going back to The Energy Co made her feel as if the walls were closing in. She never wanted to step foot into that building again, never mind share the same recycled air as Oscar Darke.

She took another large gulp of wine. Her instinct was to take Ramona and run as far away as they could—perhaps the Northern Territory.

The intercom buzzed and she startled at the sound, wine splashing over her fingers and onto her clothes. Almost immediately, it buzzed again, but she ignored it. Only when her phone started ringing in her bag, which she'd left in the kitchen, did she realise it might be Ramona.

Deb dragged herself off the sofa to check. The phone stopped ringing as she dug it out of her bag. The missed call was from Tristan.

Oh shit. She'd totally forgotten their date. He must be downstairs waiting for her, but she was in no fit state to see him, never mind spend an evening together. She was still wearing her work clothes, which smelled like the floor of the public bathroom and now had wine on them as well as a vomit stain.

When the phone started ringing again, she jabbed her finger against it to reject the call—she couldn't allow him to see her like this—and sent a message instead:

Have to cancel. Sorry. I've got a migraine.

She'd never had such a thing in her life but she *was* currently in pain. It wasn't just her head. Her whole body throbbed with shock and terror.

His reply came almost instantly.

I'm sorry. That's awful. Is there anything I can do for you? Do you need me to get you some medication or bring dinner for Ramona?

She sighed. He was so sweet.

No, I'll be fine after a good night's sleep. But thank you.

You've got nothing to thank me for. Get some rest and call if you need anything.

Deb put her phone down and contemplated eating something but there were too many other thoughts whirling through her head. The way she saw it, she had two options.

Number one: murder Oscar Darke. As appealing as that possibility was, it could bring a whole host of other complications.

So that only left option two.

Ramona

The monthly meeting of the local Budgerigar Society was held at a community centre in Parramatta, so Ramona and Elijah took the bus. When he'd mentioned he was a member of the society and attended meetings once a month, she'd been hugely curious.

'What exactly is a Budgerigar Society?'

'It's a group that caters for the needs of budgerigar fanciers—people who breed and show the birds, but also those who just love them as pets.'

'Budgerigar fanciers? Is that what I should be officially calling you? You don't all dress up as budgies, do you?'

He laughed at her teasing and shook his head.

'What happens at a meeting? Are there actual budgies there too?'

Elijah grinned. 'Why don't you come with me and find out?'

She hadn't been fishing for an invitation, but his offer excited her, as much because it would mean spending Friday night with him as anything else. 'Are you sure?'

'Yeah, visitors are always welcome. And we can grab some dinner at Macca's after.'

After a tough week at school, she'd thought about cancelling and just vegging at home. Her mum was going out with Tristan, so she'd have the apartment to herself and could drown her sorrows eating ice-cream and listening to her favourite music. But if she was home when Deb arrived back from work, she'd want to know why. She'd probably cancel her date and insist on them spending the evening together.

So instead, Ramona had showered, put on make-up, dressed in a polka-dotted swing skirt that always lifted her mood, and left her worries about her friends behind. Now, as she sat next to Elijah on the bus, she already felt a hundred times lighter than she had when she'd left school.

The bus stopped almost in front of the community centre and he gestured for her to get off ahead of him. Perhaps it wasn't very feminist of her, but she loved the way he treated her with the chivalry she read about in her old magazines. There'd been an article in an issue of the *Weekly* called 'How to Spot a True Gentleman' and so far, Elijah ticked all the boxes.

'I'm nervous,' she whispered as they approached the building.

'Don't be. They're not a scary bunch.'

Yet, it wasn't his words but the way he took her hand so casually that eased her anxiety. Her insides tightened. It was impossible to think about anything but the nerve endings exploding all over her body.

Ramona had been in this hall once before to watch a pantomime just after they moved to Granville, but it looked different tonight. The stage was bare; there were a couple of rows of chairs set up in a large semicircle and an old-fashioned screen at the front. Off to one side stood a long table with about five smallish cages, different coloured budgies nattering inside.

She'd expected the other members to be ancient but there were a variety of ages and Elijah introduced her to everyone. He was one of the youngest but there were a couple of kids, people who looked to be in their twenties and thirties, right up to those with grey hair and wrinkles. Aside from teachers, she'd never had much to do with anyone older than her mum and felt slightly awkward talking to them, but they were all very welcoming and didn't mind at all when she admitted to not owning any birds herself.

'We're working on her mum,' Elijah said with a wink.

The others chuckled and Ramona glowed at the way he made them sound like a team.

When a tall woman with long purple hair the same shade as Frodo's feathers whistled and called everyone to attention, Ramona felt as if she'd been granted access to some secret society, and she listened with interest as they discussed club business. She could only imagine what Sydney, Nyra and Kenzie would think if she told them that she was considering joining the Budgerigar Society.

Once the 'boring stuff'—as the purple-haired president called it—was over, she introduced a guest speaker. 'Tonight, we're very lucky to have Yarran Dann from the Alice Springs Desert Park to talk about wild budgerigars. Please give him a warm welcome.'

A man who looked about her mum's age, wearing jeans and a khaki shirt, began to speak. Over the next half hour, he showed them magical photos and videos of massive flocks of budgies that lived in the very middle of the country, their vibrant yellow and green feathers contrasting beautifully against the earthy reds of the outback dirt and the clear blue skies.

'Wild budgies are lighter and smaller than those bred in captivity. As you know, there are millions of different colour combinations of exhibition birds, whereas the budgies you'll find in the wild are only predominantly green with streaks of yellow. This is because they need to blend into their surroundings.' He gestured to the pale blue, violet, white and even a pink budgie in the cages at the side. 'Those pretty colours would make them easy targets for predators.'

After his talk, Yarran answered questions about the wild budgerigars and then it was time for tea and biscuits, but Ramona and Elijah didn't stay, instead heading to the Macca's down the road.

'That was so much fun,' she said as they walked. 'Thanks for inviting me. I definitely want to get a budgie now—if Frodo hadn't already won me over, Yarran Dann definitely did.'

They arrived at McDonald's, ordered their food on the self-serve screens, and then stood off to one side while they waited.

'How's Lucy?' Elijah asked, and Ramona's good mood took a tumble. Throughout the meeting, she hadn't thought about school once.

'She's not really talking to me,' she confessed.

'What? Why?'

Ramona sighed, not wanting to look bad in front of him, but also needing to get it off her chest. 'Lucy and I didn't know each other until we were put together on our project, and … well, my other friends at school … they don't like her. In fact, they really dislike her.'

'Why? She seems great.'

'She is. It's just—' Ramona was cut off by a guy behind the counter calling their order.

Elijah grabbed their tray—laden with two Big Macs, two large fries and two chocolate milkshakes—and they found a table right in the back corner of the restaurant.

'So, you were saying?' he prompted once they were seated and unwrapping their burgers.

Ramona popped a fry into her mouth, psyching herself up to explain. 'Lucy is different from most of the girls at SLC and it kind of makes her a target for teasing.'

'What do you mean different?'

'Her dad's a priest and—'

'Hang on,' he interrupted. 'Her dad's a priest? I thought they couldn't have sex, so how's he have kids?'

'You're thinking of Catholic priests. Lucy's dad is Anglican, although he had her before he was ordained anyway. But the rumour at school is that her mum died of a drug overdose.'

'Rumour?'

'It's not true. She died of breast cancer when Lucy was a baby.'

Elijah frowned. 'Who started this rumour?'

Ramona shrugged like she had no idea, although she was beginning to have her suspicions. 'And you may have noticed she sometimes stutters?'

He nodded and took another bite of his burger.

'The girls who welcomed me when I first started school, they think Lucy is …' Whatever way she put it, this was going to sound bad. 'A freak because of her dad and her stutter, but also how she looks.'

'They bully her because of a speech impediment and her appearance?'

She swallowed—that made her feel terrible. 'Not really. At least not to her face—not that I've ever seen. But they don't ever invite her to things, and when I got paired with her, they all pitied me like it was the worst thing that could ever happen. Every time I try and say something nice about her, they start mocking me, saying I must have a crush on her and if I like her so much I should start going to church with her. I actually told them you were my boyfriend so they'd stop teasing me.'

His eyes widened.

'Sorry.' She looked down at her food.

'So they bully her by exclusion?' he asked, clearly not wanting to discuss the whole fake-boyfriend thing.

Ramona nodded glumly. 'I offered to help Lucy try and make herself less of a target ...' Her voice trailed off. Even as she said it, she knew how awful it sounded.

'And that's why she's not talking to you?'

'Yep.'

'Can I ask you something?' Elijah said. Although there was only a beat between this question and the next, her stomach turned rock solid. 'Why do you hang around with them?'

'Because they ... because being friends with them makes me special.' She sighed. 'At my last school, *I* was Lucy. Everyone thought I was weird because I liked vintage fashion and old music and I had really bad acne, which didn't help either. The teachers were the only ones who were nice to me and that got me the label of goody-two-shoes and much worse. When I got the scholarship to SLC, I decided to reinvent myself. I got Mum to take me to a doctor over summer and I started on medication that cleared my skin. I bought some make-up. I learned all about what music and TV shows were popular so I'd have things to talk about at school. I never imagined how well it'd work, I just hoped I'd stay under the radar, avoid being teased, maybe make a couple of friends. I couldn't believe my luck when the three most popular girls in the year invited me into their group.'

'So basically you're pretending to be someone you're not to fit in with people who, quite frankly, sound like a bunch of shallow bitches.'

'They're not. They've been really nice to me.'

Elijah quirked an eyebrow. 'Do you think they'd have been friends with the old Ramona? Or rather, the *real* Ramona?'

She sucked a mouthful of milkshake through her straw as she contemplated his question. She wanted to say yes, but the truth was, probably not. Kenzie might have liked her if she'd had the chance, but because of Sydney and Nyra that likely wouldn't have happened. 'You don't understand what it was like at my last school. I was a social leper.'

'Ramona, I'm a sixteen-year-old boy who likes budgies and David Attenborough documentaries more than I like playing Xbox and watching *Squid Game*.' He jabbed his finger at his chest. 'I'm Lucy at my school.'

'You don't have any friends either?'

He shrugged. 'There are a few other misfits I hang around with, but we're friends more through circumstance than anything else.'

'But you've got friends—they might not be at school, but I saw how you fit in with the other budgie fanciers. That's all I've ever wanted, to feel like I fit in somewhere, and Sydney, Nyra and Kenzie … they gave me that.'

Silence rang between them a few long moments and Ramona regretted ever starting this conversation. 'You probably hate me now.'

He shook his head and reached across the table to take her hand. 'I could never hate you. I know it's hard to stand up to bullies, but if you really care about Lucy—and I saw the two of you together, so I think you do—then you should. You're stronger than you think, Ramona. And you and Lucy shouldn't feel like you need to change for anyone. You're both perfect as you are. If anyone needs to change it's your other so-called friends. Saying that, I reckon this Sydney character isn't very happy in her own life and she's bullying others to make herself feel better. So maybe she needs to be cut a little slack as well.'

'How come you're so wise?' Ramona asked, still so very aware of his hand in hers.

He chuckled. 'It's the budgies … I talk to them about my problems all the time, and they always give the best advice. Guess it rubs off after a while.'

Quinn

When the doorbell rang just before seven o'clock that night, Quinn raced down the hallway and flung the door open. 'Hello, Mrs D. Aren't you looking smoking hot!'

The older woman chuckled as she stepped inside and kissed Quinn on the cheek. 'Why thank you, and doesn't it smell fabulous in here?'

Quinn nodded—having lived with Dec and Darpan for almost three years now, she'd become accustomed to the spicy aromas that permeated the house whenever Darpan got busy in the kitchen. 'I promise you dinner will *taste* even better.'

'That's good because I'm starving.' Mrs D scrutinised Quinn. 'You look like the cat that got the canary. I guess that means your parents arrived safe and sound? I can't wait to meet them. I brought these for your mother.' She held up a bunch of beautiful flowers that looked freshly picked from her garden.

'They're gorgeous, and Mam and Dad are looking forward to meeting you too, but ...' Quinn grinned as she lowered her voice to a theatrical whisper. 'I've got big news.'

'Oh?' Mrs D raised an eyebrow, but before Quinn could say anything, her mother appeared.

'Hello, hello,' she exclaimed, throwing her arms wide. 'You must be the famous Mrs Dagliesh? I'm Roisin. Quinn's told us so much about you, I feel like I already know you.'

'I feel the same, but please, it's Muriel,' Mrs D replied. 'I hope you had a pleasant flight. Welcome to Sydney.'

She handed over the flowers and Roisin gushed accordingly before shoving them at Quinn and linking her elbow through Mrs D's. 'Come on, let's go have a drink and get to know each other properly.'

Her mother led Mrs D through the house to the large patio out the back where Dec and Darpan were discussing the latest scandal in parliament with Joseph Paladino—Joe to all his friends. Probably a good time to interrupt because as much as her mam and dad adored the boys, they did not see eye to eye when it came to politics.

Quinn passed the flowers over to Dec—he'd berate her for choosing the wrong vase if she tried—and Roisin introduced Mrs D to Joe. They didn't waste any time getting stuck into sharing stories of their recent ailments.

'Anyone want a drink?' Quinn asked.

'Good idea.' Darpan crossed over to the outdoor wine fridge and conjured a bottle of Italian wine, clearly trying to impress his father-in-law.

'Lovely set-up you've got out here,' Mrs D remarked as he began to pour the drinks. She was right—the patio held two gas heaters, a full and shiny outdoor kitchen and a gorgeous, handcrafted table with matching chairs that was set with bold pottery plates and sparkling glassware.

'Thanks.' Darpan grinned. 'All Declan's doing I'm afraid. He has a flair for making things pretty, whereas I …'

'You're good at other things,' Dec said with a wink, returning from inside with the flowers in a vase just in time to hear the compliment.

The love birds made googly eyes at each other for a few long moments before Roisin cleared her throat. She was uncomfortable with too much affection—more because it wasted talking time—whereas Joe loved it and, in typical Italian fashion, often kissed and hugged people he'd only just met.

'I'll go get the nibbles,' Darpan announced.

Quinn followed him inside to help, unsurprised to see the 'nibbles' were an elaborate selection of Indian appetizers, including samosas, corn pakora, lentil fritters and onion bhajis, which were her personal favourite. Darpan was a fabulous cook—he'd learned from his grandmother when he was only a boy—but tonight she was too pumped to eat.

When everyone had finished gushing about Darpan's culinary expertise, Quinn tapped her glass with a spoon. 'So, you'll never guess what happened today?'

All eyes turned to look at her. She hadn't told her family about Oscar yet because it had been impossible to get a word in with her mother giving them a blow-by-blow account of the journey from Adelaide—you'd think it was a long-haul flight—and filling them in on the neighbourhood gossip. Neither Quinn nor Declan had lived with their parents since finishing school, but Roisin misguidedly thought they were interested in who in the street had a grandbaby, a heart attack, got married again or bought a ridiculously overpriced caravan.

'Good Lord. Do I need to sit down?' she asked.

'You're already sitting down,' said Darpan, smiling warmly across the table at his mother-in-law.

'You're not pregnant, are you?' This from her father.

'She'd have to have a bloke for that to happen,' quipped Dec.

Quinn would have given him the finger if they didn't have company. 'Not necessarily—Deb had Ramona on her own and they're doing just fine. But no, I'm not pregnant.'

'Thank goodness.' Roisin made the sign of the cross. 'I know you all think I'm old-fashioned, but babies should be born in wedlock.'

Dec rolled his eyes. 'I suppose you think they should have a male and female parent as well? That two men or two women can't love a child just as much?'

'Well … I …' Roisin blustered, and Quinn glared at him. As much as she adored her brother, he always got defensive about his relationship when their parents were around. She didn't blame him; Joe had been happy for Declan when he came out and even happier when he'd married Darpan, but Roisin had taken a while to come around.

Still, they were supposed to be having a nice evening and *dammit*, this was about her, not Dec.

'So, if you're not pregnant, what is it? Are you finally moving out?' Dec said this with the greatest affection, clearly trying to lighten the mood again.

'Not yet.' She paused a moment, ready to drop her joy-bomb, but Mrs D got there first.

'Oh my goodness!' She pressed a hand against her chest. 'Is this about Handbag Dude?'

'Bingo, Muriel.' Quinn beamed like she'd just been crowned Queen of the Universe.

'Ooh.' Mrs D clapped her hands in excitement.

Roisin frowned. 'Who on God's green earth is Handbag Dude?'

'He's the man Dec was telling us about on the phone last week, darling. Remember?' said Joe, patting her knee. 'The gentleman who helped Quinn when she dropped her bag on the pavement. The one she's become obsessed with.'

Once again Quinn glared at her brother, but she'd deal with *him* later. Right now she could barely contain her excitement. 'He's the new director of sales at work. I thought I was hallucinating when he walked in next to Shaun, but when I introduced myself, he remembered me too.'

She thought of the way Oscar's eyes had flashed with recognition. The way her whole body had tingled with the slightest brush of his hand against her arm.

'You talked to him?' Mrs D reached for another samosa.

'Briefly,' Quinn admitted, although she planned to rectify that as soon as possible. And now she had a name, she'd be able to stalk him online. That was one good thing about the modern world—what did her parents and Mrs D do in their day when they wanted to do a full background check on someone? 'He said he's been living in New York until recently, but came home because he wants to be closer to his parents.'

Joe nodded his approval. 'Sounds like a good family man.'

'Maybe he's come home to make sure his parents leave everything to him in their will?' Roisin took a large gulp of wine.

'Why do you always think the worst of people, Mam? I happen to be a very good judge of character and I've got a good vibe about him. He wouldn't have stopped to help me if he was an arsehole. And you should have seen him this afternoon—people were flocking to him, and he took the time to speak to everyone.'

'Personally, I'm wary of men who are too charming,' Roisin said. 'They're usually hiding a sinister secret. He's probably a weirdo, or even a criminal.'

Quinn's fingers clenched around her wineglass, but she took a sip, rather than throw it at her mother.

'How old is he?' asked Darpan with an encouraging smile.

'I'm not sure. I'd say late thirties. Maybe early forties?'

'He's probably married then. Or divorced.' Roisin visibly shuddered. In her opinion, divorce was a sin greater than murder or adultery.

'Bit old for you, isn't he, sis?'

'There's eleven years between Mam and Dad.'

'True,' he conceded.

'And Eddie was eight years my senior,' added Mrs D, a twinkle in her eyes.

Quinn could have kissed her.

'However, as much as I hate to agree with Mam,' said Dec, 'she's probably right—if he's got to that age and isn't currently in a serious relationship, he's probably got a lot of baggage. He might even have an ex-wife and kids. Do you really want to be a stepmum?'

Quinn sighed. 'I haven't thought that far yet, but yes, of course I'd happily be a stepmum with the right person.' She'd be a great stepmum. One of the cool ones. Oscar's kids would love her. 'And you gotta admit, it's crazy that the guy I've been unable to get out of my head for a month, suddenly turns up in my office. If that's not a sign, I don't know what is.'

Darpan nodded. 'Certainly sounds like fate to me. Can I refill anyone's drinks?'

All except Mrs D thrust out their glasses and a debate ensued about whether anything in life was predestined. The table was divided—Darpan and Mrs D were believers and Quinn thought her dad was too, but he was a peacekeeper and sat on the fence so as not to get his wife or daughter offside. It was okay for Roisin and Declan—they'd found the great loves of their lives and forgotten what it was like to be alone.

'Look, I'm really not trying to be a prophet of doom,' said Declan, 'but aren't work relationships between employees and senior management frowned upon anyway?'

'What?' Quinn blinked.

'Aren't they against the rules? They are in my office.'

'Mine too,' added Darpan, his shoulders slumping slightly.

Quinn's heart sank. How had she not thought of this already?

No one said anything for a few moments, then she had an epiphany. 'If that becomes an issue, I guess I'll just have to quit my job.'

'What?' her family said in unison. Even Mrs D looked a little shocked.

'You're absolutely bonkers,' Roisin exclaimed, her hands punctuating every word. 'You can't just up and quit your job for some man you have some silly notion about.'

'I think it's romantic,' said Darpan. 'I'm definitely a believer in love at first sight. I knew the moment I laid eyes on Declan that I'd marry him some day.'

Quinn shot him a grateful smile.

'Yeah, true,' Dec said, 'but—'

'But she's a grown-up,' Roisin exclaimed. 'She has bills to pay, rent to give to you boys. Never mind the fact Quinn knows nothing about this man. I've never heard anything more ridiculous in my life.'

'Oh, I've heard a lot,' Quinn spat. 'And most of it comes from your mouth.'

'That's enough,' Joe said, his tone unusually terse. 'Quinn, you're a grown woman and you know your heart, but that's no excuse for rudeness. Roisin, it's time to stop interfering in the kids' lives. We raised them the best we could, and they're not fools. You need to trust Quinn won't do anything crazy.'

He looked to Mrs D and smiled as if he hadn't just reprimanded his wife and daughter. 'Muriel, how long have you lived in Darlinghurst? You mentioned Eddie—was he your husband?'

'Yes. Eddie and I bought our house in 1966, just after we got married. And we were very happy here. It was a great place to raise kids.'

'How many children do you have?' asked Roisin.

'Two daughters. They both live overseas now.'

'You must miss them,' Joe said sympathetically.

'Any grandchildren?' Quinn could tell any second now her mother was going to pull out her phone and show Mrs D her digital brag book.

'Not yet, but I'm hopeful,' said Mrs D, explaining that her daughter and her partner were about to start IVF.

While her parents and Mrs D exchanged life stories, Quinn's thoughts kept wandering to Oscar. She wondered what he was doing now—was he at some family dinner right now? Maybe thinking about her and marvelling about the coincidence of them meeting again.

Between courses, Mrs D excused herself to go to the bathroom and Quinn helped Dec and Darpan clear the table. Roisin followed into the kitchen to tell them how to load the dishwasher properly.

'So does this lad of yours have a name?' she asked.

Lad of yours. However much she knew her mam disapproved, Quinn glowed at this phrase. 'Oscar Darke.' She loved the way his name rolled off her tongue. She'd been repeating it in her head ever since she'd left the boardroom. 'Isn't that just the sexiest name you've ever heard?'

Darpan laughed and Dec shook his head as he wrapped some leftover lentil patties in foil. 'You're seriously not right in the head. Mam, do you think we should have her committed?'

'Oh stop.' Roisin flicked him with a tea towel, despite the fact she probably agreed with him, and Quinn knew it was her attempt to clear the air between them.

Ramona

'You don't have to come in with me,' Ramona said as she and Elijah approached her building.

'Hey, I said I'd see you right to your door, and as far as I'm concerned, that means the door of your apartment.'

Part of her wanted to tell him she could take care of herself, but he was so sweet and she couldn't help wanting to prolong their time together.

'Come on then,' she said, trying to stifle her grin as she unlocked the door and let them into the lobby.

'You know how you told your friends I was your boyfriend?' Elijah said when they stopped on the landing in front of her door.

She nodded, silently cringing at how desperate that made her sound. Should she apologise? Make him understand she hadn't meant anything by it?

'Well ...' He cleared his throat. 'What if I really was?'

Her heart shivered. 'Are you asking me to go steady with you?' She knew no one said that anymore but she loved the term when she heard it in old movies and knew Elijah would understand.

'Yes. I think I am.' He grinned. 'No, I know I am.'

Oh my God. She tried to contain her excitement and reply in a calm cool manner, but failed dismally. 'In that case,' she shrieked, 'my answer is yes!'

He punched the air and she laughed, unable to remember a time when she'd felt so happy. She had a *boyfriend*! Then, suddenly his expression grew serious. He reached out and took both her hands in his and it felt as miraculous and breathtaking as the first time.

'Do you mind if I kiss you?'

Her heart pounded and her mouth went dry, his question both terrifying and thrilling. She wanted to know what it felt like to have a boy's lips on hers—no, not just any boy's—Elijah's. But what if she didn't know what to do?

To hell with her nerves. If she didn't say yes, she'd spend all night regretting it. 'I'd like that,' she whispered.

In reply, he tugged her towards him and put his mouth on hers.

Ramona froze—unable to tell if the warm wetness felt good or disgusting—and then he skated his tongue against the seam of her lips, and they opened of their own accord.

And. She. Was. A. Goner.

All her anxiety about kissing and all her anxiety about her friends evaporated. He felt so good. He *tasted* so good. She never wanted to stop doing this. Ever.

'Nerds aren't supposed to kiss like that,' she said breathlessly when they finally pulled apart.

'Hey! Who are you calling a nerd?' he asked, and then kissed her again.

This time was shorter but even more intense.

'Do you want to come inside?' she asked after they came apart for the second time. She was almost certain her mum wouldn't be home yet, and it wasn't like they were going to have sex or anything. But she wouldn't say no to another kiss.

Elijah looked torn. 'You think I should?'

'I doubt Mum will be home for hours, so you're probably safe for a while. If she arrives while you're still here, I'll say you had to use the bathroom. She can't begrudge you that after you saw me safely home.'

'I'd be pretty desperate if I couldn't wait the minute it would take me to get back to my house,' he said with a smirk.

'Do you want to come in or not?'

He leaned so close his face was mere millimetres from hers. 'What do you reckon?'

Grinning, she slipped her key into the lock and opened the door to a dark apartment. But when she turned on the lights, a groan came from the couch.

'What time is it?' At least that's what Ramona thought Deb said. Her voice was so slurred she couldn't quite tell.

Ramona widened her eyes at Elijah, who followed her over to her mother. 'It's eight forty-five. What are you doing home?'

Deb tried to stand but spewed instead. All over the coffee table.

'Ew, Mum! Gross!' Ramona's stomach revolted at the sight. It was then she noticed the two bottles of wine—one empty, one half gone. 'What's going on? How much have you had to drink?'

Deb was incapable of a coherent reply but managed a sip of water when Elijah fetched her some.

'Do you think we should call an ambulance?' Ramona asked.

He shook his head. 'Not yet. If she keeps vomiting or passes out, then maybe. Let's just let her sit a few minutes and then see if we can help her get cleaned up and into bed. You stay here and with her while I go get something to fix this mess.'

'Thanks,' Ramona whispered, too shocked to say much else as Elijah took charge.

With his help, Ramona got Deb out of her jacket and then into the bedroom. Her shirt didn't look comfortable to sleep in but at least it was clean, and she didn't think her mother would appreciate her taking anything else off with a boy present.

They watched her for another fifteen minutes and then Ramona told Elijah he could go.

'Are you sure?' He glanced at Deb from where they were huddled in the doorway. 'I could call Gran and tell her the situation, let her know I'm staying here tonight.'

'No.' Deb would be mortified if the dear old woman who'd come for dinner a couple of weeks ago heard about her in such a state. 'Thanks, but I can take care of her from here. And, please, don't tell your grandma about ...'

Ramona's voice trailed off, but Elijah shook his head. 'I won't. Promise. But if she gets worse or you need anything, call me. No matter what time it is.'

'Thanks. I will.'

He hugged her goodbye and saw himself out.

Reluctant to leave her mother, Ramona didn't bother to brush her teeth, wash her face or change out of her clothes, climbing into bed beside her instead. It had been at least a couple of years since they'd shared a bed and back then it was always because Ramona was scared of the dark or simply didn't want to be alone. It felt weird that this time Deb was the one who needed looking after.

She didn't remember falling asleep but the next thing she knew the rooster down the road was cock-a-doodle-doing, light was creeping in through the blinds and her mother was stirring.

'Mum?' she whispered. 'How you feeling?'

'Morning,' Deb said, a slight frown creasing her brow as she registered Ramona in her bed. 'Oh my goodness. I need water. And some Panadol.'

Ramona gestured to the bedside table where Elijah had put supplies the night before.

Deb shuffled up into a sitting position, then popped two painkillers out of their packet before downing them with water.

'You really scared me last night, Mum. I came home and found you so drunk you could barely talk and when you tried to get up off the couch, you threw up all over the coffee table.'

'Oh God, I'm so sorry, sweetheart.'

'What happened? Was it something to do with Tristan?' Ramona couldn't imagine any other reason why her sensible mother would drink that much. 'Did he do something to hurt you?'

'What? No, nothing like that.' Deb shook her head and then immediately pressed her fingers against her forehead. 'I didn't even end up seeing him last night.'

'Then what happened?'

Deb took her time replying as if she didn't want to worry Ramona, but it was too late for that.

'There's some restructuring going on at work,' she said eventually.

'What's that got to do with you?'

'Um ... well, a few people might lose their jobs. Look, it's probably nothing. I was stressed yesterday because I like working at The Energy Co and we obviously need an income, but if it happens, I'll get something else, I'm sure.'

'At least I'm on a scholarship, right?' Ramona joked.

'Hmm ...'

What did 'hmm' mean? And then it clicked. Her mum would have to get another job and that might mean … 'Oh God. Please don't tell me we might have to move again. You promised!'

Things might not be perfect at school right now, but they were better than they'd ever been before. No other school had a whole subject dedicated to fashion.

And then there was Elijah.

'Relax, honey.' Deb pulled her into a side hug. 'I don't want you to concern yourself with this.'

Ramona winced at the smell of her still wine-soaked breath. *Relax?* How could she relax at a time like this?

'I'm going to start looking for other jobs in Sydney today, just in case. I know you love it here, and in everything I do you are always my number one priority.'

'Okay.' She let out the breath she'd been holding. 'I'll help you look if you want. And like I said, I don't mind getting a casual job if money's a problem. I saw a sign last night at Macca's saying they're hiring.'

'Thanks, sweetheart, but let's just take things one step at a time. I'm sorry I scared you last night. Did you have a good evening with Elijah?'

Ramona nodded. 'It's okay—everyone's allowed to have a wobble now and again. And yes, I had the best night.'

Then she proceeded to tell her mother all about the Budgerigar Society meeting and the interesting people she'd met there. She didn't tell her about the kiss or about her mega crush on Elijah because she didn't want her to freak out and say she could only see him if they had a chaperone or something.

For now, it was safer if she thought they were just friends.

Debra

Monday morning, Deb felt like the walking dead. She'd barely slept all weekend. Every time she closed her eyes, she imagined running into Oscar at work and terror had her heart racing and her stomach churning all over again. The only way she could see to safeguard herself and Ramona was to quit her job, and she must have applied for at least twenty over the weekend. She felt confident she'd get an interview for at least a couple, but how was she supposed to cope in the meantime?

Knowing her meagre savings wouldn't last them long, she fought the urge to email Shaun her resignation and take her notice as holiday, but even if she did that, there were several things she needed to wrap up so as not to leave her colleagues in the lurch. Besides, she didn't have much annual leave saved up because she often took school holidays off, and what she did have would be best to take in a small lump sum when she left.

Despite all this, if today went badly, she'd take everything The Energy Co owed her and run.

There were a hundred people in the office—at least a thousand in the building—sometimes weeks could go by without her seeing anyone from another department, and she rarely had anything to do with the sales team who worked on the floor below. If she avoided communal areas, it might be possible to avoid Oscar while she found another job.

Unable to stomach breakfast, she dressed in her most unobtrusive outfit and wrapped a silk scarf around her head like she was one of Ramona's fashion icons from the 1950s. Paired with dark sunglasses, this would hopefully be enough of a disguise. Even so, she almost got off the train numerous times. By the time she disembarked at Museum station, her shirt was drenched with sweat. She held her breath as she crossed the lobby, then kept her head down as she waited for the elevator. Thankfully there was no sign of Oscar.

Finally, an elevator opened and everyone rushed to get in. She found herself squished right at the front, someone's elbow digging into her ribs and the aroma of takeaway coffee teasing her nostrils. It was her turn to buy morning drinks, but knowing Quinn wouldn't be at work, she'd forgone her usual latte. Everyone from The Energy Co frequented the café beneath the building and she couldn't risk running into Oscar there.

The lift stopped four times on other floors and each time Deb shuffled to the side to let people out, her heart thudded at the stupid possibility Oscar might appear from a random office. After what felt like an eternity, they came to level thirteen. Neither Toby nor Linc recognised her as the three of them stepped out and she hoped this meant her disguise was working.

She followed them briskly through reception, relieved to see Lexi busy on the phone, and didn't breathe properly until she arrived at her desk.

Thank the Lord. She'd made it into the office without running into Oscar Bloody Darke.

'Morning, Deb,' chorused her colleagues.

They were always here when she arrived and rarely went home before she did. Sometimes she wondered if they slept under their desks and their wives were figments of their imaginations. But today she was glad they were oblivious to anything happening outside their computers. None of them commented on the scarf covering her head or the fact she was wearing sunglasses inside on a day you didn't even need them outside.

She sat down, removed her accessories, took a deep breath, and guzzled half her bottle of water before remembering she didn't want to be making constant trips to the loo today. Uploading the timesheets and running the prelim pay reports took forever because every time a shadow passed by the finance cubicle she panicked and lost her train of thought. She kept telling herself Oscar would be busy on the floor below, getting to know his team, but it was impossible to ignore the dread that sat like a bad takeaway dinner in her stomach.

At ten o'clock, when her phone vibrated on the desk, she almost jumped out of her skin. Quinn had been messaging non-stop since Friday night, every message gushing with excitement about Oscar. Deb had offered only short replies, trying not to stoke the flames of her crazy crush, but she wasn't getting through to her.

Rendezvous. Now!!!!!!

Huh? Deb squeaked like a mouse as she read this new message. What was Quinn doing here? She was supposed to be on holidays.

On shaky legs, she slipped out of her cubicle, looking from side to side as she checked that the path to the copy room was clear. Inside she found her friend pacing back and forth, wearing dark jeans, a figure-hugging pale pink sweater with black hearts embroidered all over it and sparkly silver boots on her feet. Not office attire, even for Quinn.

'What's with the headscarf? And the sunglasses?' Quinn asked as Deb removed the glasses.

'What are you doing here? You're supposed to be on holiday.'

'And it's nice to see you too.' Quinn grinned. 'Mam and Mrs D are shopping in DJs. I snuck away to ask a favour because you refused to return my calls on the weekend.'

'Sorry, I went home with a migraine that lasted most of the weekend. Couldn't face anyone.'

'Oh, that sucks. Are you okay now?'

'Okay' was not the word Deb would use, but Quinn didn't wait for a reply.

'So, I need you to get Oscar's address for me and find out if he's in a relationship.'

'Why can't you just stalk him online like you do everyone else?'

Quinn sighed. 'I tried, but it's like he doesn't exist; he's either not on Facebook or has the highest privacy settings possible. The only Oscar Darke I could find was a tennis coach from England. Not the right age and nowhere near as good-looking as Handbag Dude, although I did accidentally like a video of him and some girl doing handstands on a beach in Ibiza.'

'What?' Deb shook her head, struggling to keep up.

'In the end, I found him on LinkedIn but that's as useless as tits on a bull. I thought *you* were the only person not online.'

But this news didn't surprise Deb in the slightest. Men like Oscar didn't like leaving a virtual footprint because it meant their lies were too easily caught out. Facebook had only been a baby when she and him were together and neither of them had accounts back then, but she imagined it would make having multiple girlfriends difficult.

'So, will you do it?' Quinn prompted.

'I could get fired for giving out an employee's personal details.' Not that this would really matter as she'd soon be handing in her notice anyway, but Quinn didn't know that yet. 'Don't you think Oscar's a bit old for you anyway?'

'Don't you start. I got enough of that from Mam and Dec, but age has no bearing when it comes to love.'

'Love?' Deb scoffed, her body temperature rising as panic took hold. 'You don't even know the guy. And what happened to your outrage over another man being hired as director?' She was throwing everything she could at trying to dissuade Quinn from this insanity.

'It's not Oscar's fault Shaun hired him rather than Sally. Who knows, maybe he really was the best person for the job? *Please*, Deb,' she pleaded, clasping her hands together. 'I'm not asking you to rob a bank, and you know I'd never dob you in.'

'What would you do with the info?'

'Well, I might just happen to find myself on an errand near his house. Maybe I'll *accidentally* run into him. But I'll be able to scope out his *domestic* situation, if you know what I mean.'

'Oh my God, you sound like an honest to God stalker. You're deranged. What if you find out he's married?'

'He wasn't wearing a wedding ring.'

'Not everyone wears a gold band,' Deb said, thinking that Oscar would be exactly the type not to. 'If he is married, will you give up then?'

Quinn pursed her lips together long and hard. 'I suppose so. Although … not all marriages are happy ones.'

Deb glared at her. 'And have you forgotten that office relationships are forbidden?'

'Why are you being so pessimistic?' she spat. 'It's like you don't want me to be happy.'

'That's not true, I just …' Deb sighed. 'I'm worried about you. I don't want you to get hurt or in trouble.'

Quinn's glower softened. 'That's sweet, but office romances aren't forbidden anyway, they're just frowned upon.'

'Maybe so, but relationships between directors and employees can be problematic, so even if Oscar *is* available, he's hardly going to jeopardise his new job for someone he's just met. I don't want you to get your hopes up.'

'I think you underestimate my feminine wiles and powers of persuasion. Besides, I have a plan.' Quinn grinned victoriously. 'I'm going to become friends with him first and then when we know each other well enough to stay in touch, I'll quit my job.'

'Are you *crazy*?'

Quinn ignored the question. 'It's not like I can't get another job like this one, or maybe I'll do something else entirely. Anyway, don't you think he looks like Alexander Skarsgard?'

Deb nodded, having to concede Quinn was right. She'd seen the actor in the TV series *Big Little Lies*. The irony was that Oscar had more in common with the character in that show than simply good looks.

'Have you seen him this morning?'

'No.' *Thank God.* This was getting out of hand. It was one thing Deb quitting her job because of Oscar, but could she allow her friend to ruin her life over him as well?

'You'll have to be my eyes this week,' Quinn went on, 'and make sure none of the other single girls are getting too close. I'd cancel my holidays, but Mam will kill me—we're heading up to Forster for a couple of days tomorrow and she's so excited. We're even—'

'Quinn!' Deb interrupted, unable to let her friend go on a second longer. 'You can't quit your job for Oscar.' She had to come clean before this went too far, because you only had to look at Quinn to know that Oscar would be flattered by her attention. Position of authority or not, he wouldn't be able to resist her youthful beauty and effervescent personality. It would be just the kind of ego boost he thrived on. 'There's something I have to tell you.'

Quinn's expression turned serious at the sombre tone of Deb's voice. 'What is it?'

Deb swallowed, trying to work out where the hell to start, but before she could summon the courage, the door opened and Lexi waddled in.

She halted when she saw Quinn. 'Aren't you on holidays this week? If I was on leave you wouldn't catch me anywhere near this place.'

'Um ... I left my fave mug in the kitchen. Didn't want the Mug Thief to steal it, so ...' Quinn's voice drifted off. Maybe she heard how ridiculous her excuse sounded.

'O-kay then. Must be some mug.' Lexi shrugged and approached the copier.

'What did you need to tell me?' Quinn asked.

'Nothing.' Deb shook her head. 'It doesn't matter. I'll tell you later.'

No way she was going to air her dirty laundry with Lexi in earshot. Besides, perhaps Lexi's interruption was fate's way of telling Deb she was about to make a huge mistake.

She loved Quinn dearly, but could she trust her with the truth?

'I'd better be getting back to work,' she said, deciding to bide her time a little longer. Quinn going to Forster would give her time to think things through.

Quinn nodded and pulled Deb into a quick hug. 'Message me what you find out,' she whispered, then let go, hitched her bag on her shoulder and left.

Deb let out a long, slow breath as she worked up the courage to make the trek back to her desk. When was she going to wake up from this nightmare?

'What's going on?' she asked as she returned to her cubicle to find her colleagues turned away from their computers, their three swivel chairs facing inwards as they shared around a box of very fancy-looking donuts.

Ian held out the box to her. 'Donut delivery. Here you are.'

'Thanks.' She snatched up a pink one, suddenly starving and in dire need of some sugar. 'Who are they from?'

'Oscar,' announced Brendan, a smudge of chocolate icing in his salt-and-pepper moustache. 'The new director of sales.'

Her hand froze halfway to her mouth, and she dropped the donut back into the box as if it were on fire. 'He was *here*?'

Garry nodded. 'Yeah, you just missed him.'

Oh God. Her stomach twisted into a sickening knot. What if he'd seen the photo of her and Ramona? What if he recognised her? Worse, what if he recognised himself in Ramona? Why hadn't she thought to hide it already?

'What was he doing here?' she demanded.

'Besides bringing donuts?' Brendan chuckled, his expression bemused. 'He just wanted to say hello, introduce himself properly and tell us his door was always open if we had any ideas for his department.'

'First time anyone in sales has ever given us the time of day,' said Ian, before plucking her discarded donut from the box and taking a large bite.

'Seems like a great guy,' Garry added. 'Said he was sorry to have missed you and hopes to catch up soon.'

Deb shuddered. 'What did you tell him about me?'

The three men frowned.

'Nothing,' Brendan said. 'We just told him our best-looking colleague was in the ladies and he said he'd catch you soon.'

'Fabulous.' Deb forced a smile as she sank into her seat. Clearly Oscar was already working his charm. He had to be liked by everyone, couldn't stand it if he wasn't.

She snatched up the photo and shoved it into her handbag, her pulse flying at how close she'd come to running into him. As she fought tears of relief, she snatched up a tissue and prayed the boys hadn't told Oscar her full name. Hopefully he hadn't noticed the photo and hopefully he'd be too busy settling into his role to come visiting the lowly folks in payroll again any time soon.

Hopefully by the time he did, she'd be long gone.

Quinn

How long will you be? Muriel's getting tired and we're thinking of an early lunch. Shall we meet you at Little Rome in The Strand? Muriel said it does the best pasta but I told her I'm married to an Italian chef, so I'd be the judge of that!

Quinn smiled at the message from her mother as she waited for the elevator to take her to the street.

'What's so funny?' said a baritone voice coming up beside her.

She startled. *OMG*—she'd recognise that voice anywhere. She'd been trying to work out an excuse to head down to sales and 'accidentally' bump into him but fate had worked its magic. Again.

'Sorry, I didn't mean to scare you.'

She flashed Oscar her best smile. 'It's fine.'

'It's Quinn, isn't it? Digital marketing?'

She nodded, thrilled he'd remembered her name and her role. There were a hundred people who worked here—surely he couldn't remember *everyone*. 'How's your first day going, Mr Darke?'

'Well, everyone's been very welcoming. Have you been here long?'

'Almost three years, and aside from a few loonies, there could be worse places. The free energy drinks are a perk,' she said, twisting her hair between her fingers before she realised what she was doing. Thank God she hadn't batted her eyelids—it wouldn't pay to come on too strong and scare him off. 'When people hear you get free stuff, no matter what it is, suddenly everyone wants to be your friend.'

'That's not necessarily a problem. I've been out of Sydney so long I've lost contact with most of the people I knew in my twenties.'

Quinn was about to tell him she'd happily be his friend when he gestured to the elevators. 'These things take some time, don't they?'

'Haven't you heard? They're the slowest on the planet.' Although right now, she didn't mind at all.

'Maybe I should have taken the stairs, but …' He leaned in close and lowered his voice. 'Between you and me, I haven't worked out where they are yet.'

Quinn laughed as his breath dusted the side of her face. It smelled as if he'd just brushed his teeth. *Tick. Tick. Tick.* She liked a guy with good dental hygiene. 'Hasn't anyone given you a proper office tour? That's terrible. Come on, I'll take you to the stairs.'

'I don't want to waste your time,' he said, already following as she headed down the corridor.

'Don't be silly. I'm on holiday this week anyway. Just popped in to get something.'

'Ah, so that's why you weren't in digital marketing when I dropped by with donuts.'

'Donuts?' she said, as they arrived at the innocuous door that opened into the stairwell.

Oscar manoeuvred himself so he could hold it open, their bodies almost touching as she slipped past. 'It's my sneaky plan to get all departments on side. Butter them up with baked goods.'

'Dammit. I love donuts.' The door thunked shut behind them and Quinn shivered at the delicious realisation they were all alone.

He grinned. 'Who doesn't love donuts?'

'No offence,' she said as they descended the stairs, 'but you don't seem like a typical sales guy. Most salespeople I've met don't give a damn about their colleagues and save their buttering up for clients.'

He raised an eyebrow. 'You're not the kind of person to buy into stereotypes, are you, Miss Paladino?'

Oh God, the way he said her name, the way he looked mischievously into her eyes as he spoke, gave her a hot flush. She fought the urge to launch herself at him right there and then.

'You wouldn't want me to assume that just because you work in digital marketing you're addicted to social media, would you?'

'Touché.' Dammit, they were almost at the next level.

'You're not going away for your vacation?' he asked, reaching for the door.

'Yes, actually. My parents are here from Adelaide and tomorrow we're heading up to Forster for a few days.'

Gesturing for her to go through ahead of him, he said, 'We used to go there when I was a kid. Loved it.'

'It's a special place. Mam and Dad have heard me raving about it so they wanted to check it out.'

'*Mam?* Do I detect the smidge of an Irish accent?'

'Yes.' She blushed. 'My mother is Irish and my dad Italian.'

They lingered just outside the stairwell.

'Wow—two very strong and lively nationalities. Bet you have a hundred siblings and family gatherings are a riot.'

'You're not making assumptions, are you now, Mr Darke?' Quinn couldn't help flirting.

'I wouldn't dare, Miss Paladino.'

The air fizzed between them, and she felt her body temperature skyrocketing again. If he wasn't attracted to her as well, she'd eat her rollerskates.

'You're right though. I have four older brothers, all married, five nieces and nephews with another one on the way, and most Christmases I end up hiding under the table with Uncle Mario and a bottle of stolen port.'

'You do *not* have an Uncle Mario,' he said with a chuckle.

'I most definitely do, and he makes the best pizza south of the equator. What about your family? Where are you guys from?'

'Ah, my folks are both fourth-generation Aussies—English before that.'

'And do you have any brothers or sisters?'

He hesitated a moment then shook his head. 'No. It's just me, Mum and Dad.'

'Wow, that must have been so peaceful growing up.'

'Yeah.' He cleared his throat and glanced down at his watch. 'Anyway, I'd better be getting to my office before I'm accused of slacking off.'

'Of course. I'm sorry ... I do tend to chatter.'

'That's the Irish and Italian in you,' he joked. 'Guess I'll see you next week.'

That felt like an eternity away, but she nodded. 'You will. See you then.'

'I'm already looking forward to it,' he added as she walked away.

Quinn waited until she was in the elevator and it was beginning to descend before letting loose like it was a dance floor. She didn't even care that the security guard downstairs might be watching on CCTV. Her whole body hummed from her run-in with Oscar Darke.

What. A. Man.

Sexy. Funny. Kind. Smart (or Shaun wouldn't have hired him). How the hell was she going to get through the rest of the week without seeing him?

*

Ten minutes later she slid into a seat beside her mother and Mrs D at Little Rome. 'Sorry, that took longer than I thought.' Still warm, she peeled off her sweater and put it into her bag at her feet.

'We took the liberty of ordering a bottle of wine,' Roisin said as she thrust a menu at Quinn.

'You're absolutely glowing,' remarked Mrs D, smiling up at her.

Quinn grinned at her neighbour. 'I ran into *him*.'

Even her mother looked delighted at this news and the two of them leaned forward as she gave them a blow-by-blow account of their conversation.

'He does sound rather pleasant,' Roisin conceded as a waiter arrived with their drinks.

Despite the fact Quinn felt like she'd left half her head back in the office with Oscar, she enjoyed lunch. Her mam and Mrs D were both quite tipsy after only one glass of rosé and started sharing stories from when they were 'courting' their husbands. Quinn had heard most of her mother's before, but listening still made her heart sing—it was because of her parents' enduring romance that she had such high hopes for one of her own.

Halfway through the meal, she snuck to the restroom and messaged Deb:

What did you find out?

No matter how much she protested that looking into his employee records would be a violation of privacy, Quinn knew her friend would come good.

The three little dots appeared almost immediately.

You didn't hear this from me but his next of kin is a Sarah Darke.

Quinn's heart sank, but she refused to give up yet. How could her gut instinct be that far wrong?

Could be his mother or maybe his sister? Doesn't it say what relationship they are?

She stared impatiently at her phone waiting for the three little dots to appear to say Deb was responding but after about two minutes she gave up, disheartened, and shoved her phone into her bag. As she headed back into the restaurant, she replayed her conversation with Oscar in the stairwell. Didn't he say he was in need of friends?

Was that the thing someone happily married said?

Her questions were forgotten the moment she got back to the table and saw Mrs D clutching her head, her eyes squeezed tightly shut.

'Oh my God. What's wrong?' she cried, sinking down into the seat beside her friend.

'Muriel seemed a little confused. She asked me who I was and where we were, and then …' Roisin gestured anxiously to the older woman. 'She seems to be in pain.'

Mrs D tried to reach for Quinn's hand. 'I probably just had a little too much to drink.'

But Quinn didn't like this at all. Mrs D had barely touched her second glass but she looked paler than usual, and her words were slurring a little. 'I think we should call an ambulance.'

'Is everything all right here?' interrupted the waiter who'd served them earlier.

'I'm not sure,' Quinn said. 'My friend doesn't appear to be well. Can you call triple zero?'

His phone was out of his pocket before she'd finished the sentence. If it were possible, Mrs D's face had turned an even whiter shade of pale. Quinn racked her mind for everything she knew about first aid.

'Muriel,' she said, trying not to panic, 'I think we should get you to lie down while we wait for the paramedics.'

Time seemed to stand still as another waiter came to assist. They cleared the floor around their table and, much to her mortification, assisted Mrs D onto the floor. Roisin held her hand and, under direction from the person on the end of the phone line, Quinn loosened the collar of her blouse and answered questions about whether she was breathing properly (not exactly) and if she could talk normally (no).

'How long till the ambulance is here?'

'They've just parked outside the arcade. Help will be there any minute,' replied the operator.

'Thank God.' Quinn threw Mrs D a hang-in-there smile and begged a God she only rarely spoke to, to save her friend.

Ramona

'Aren't you coming to the caf?' Kenzie asked as she, Sydney and Ramona spilled out of English, and Ramona turned in the opposite direction.

'Not today.' She swallowed and clutched her books against her chest. 'I'm going to have lunch with Lucy.'

Sydney—who'd been not very surreptitiously checking her phone, which was supposed to be in her locker during school hours—looked up. 'You're working on your project over *lunch*?'

This was it.

Ramona prepared to be mocked as she shook her head. 'No. I'm having lunch with Lucy because I like her and I want to hang out with her. You guys can come too, if you want.'

Kenzie merely looked at the ground, but Sydney erupted into laughter as if Ramona had just told the most hilarious joke. 'What exactly is there to like about her?'

Ramona took a quick breath. 'A lot actually. She's smart, and kind, and really funny.'

'Funny to look at.'

Anger flared inside Ramona—she couldn't believe she'd ever seen anything appealing in Sydney. Then she remembered what Elijah had said about bullies being deeply insecure themselves. 'Why are you so mean?'

Sydney blinked. '*Excuse* me?'

'As far as I can tell, Lucy has never done anything to hurt you, but you've singled her out because she's a little different to you and you've made hating her your hobby.'

'My hobby? Oh my God, the stutterer is not my hobby. But if you want to be friends with her ...' Sydney gave a quick shake of her head as if in shock. 'Your funeral. Maybe her creepy father can do the service.'

'You're a bully,' Ramona continued, her voice wobbling only a little as other students turned to watch the show, 'and usually bullies are being hurt by someone else or have major insecurities, so I'm wondering if that's the case with you?'

'*Me?* Insecure?' Sydney narrowed her eyes and leaned in close to Ramona. 'I've got nothing to be insecure about. I'm not here because I'm on a scholarship—*my* parents actually have the money to send me here. I get good grades without trying, I look freaking fantastic, I have a gorgeous boyfriend who can't get enough of me, and I'm one of the best rowers this school has seen in decades. Clearly, you have rocks in your head.'

'Okay,' Ramona said. 'Then that's even worse because you have no excuse for being so cruel.'

'I ... I ... I'm done with this conversation, and we're done with you.' Sydney flicked her hair over her shoulder. 'Come on, Kenzie. I don't have to stand around and listen to this ungrateful bitch trash-talk me. Let's go.'

Kenzie hesitated a moment.

'Kenzie?' Sydney warned. 'Are you coming or not?'

With an apologetic smile at Ramona, Kenzie hurried off with the Queen of Year 10.

She watched them swish down the corridor, the sea of other students parting as they went. She'd probably just committed social suicide, but she didn't have one regret.

Adrenaline whooshing through her veins, she charged towards the library, excited to see Lucy and start being true to herself again. It would be so good to not have to think about the ramifications of every word she spoke.

'Hey, Miss Woo.' She waved as she passed the librarian's desk.

'Ramona, if you keep coming in here, I might start to think you like reading.'

She grinned. 'I *love* reading.' And then she continued on to Lucy's corner.

Her friend looked up from the book she was buried in and scrunched up her face. 'W-what are you doing here?'

Deja vu, thought Ramona, only this time she wasn't going to make the same mistake. 'I came to have lunch with you, but most importantly, I've come to apologise.'

Lucy raised an eyebrow. 'What for?'

Ramona sat beside her and took out her sandwich, which she'd smuggled inside in her laptop bag. 'For letting my insecurities blind me.'

'What's that supposed to mean?'

Ramona sighed. She sucked at apologising. 'I'm sorry for how I treated you before when I was talking about make-up. I was only trying to help but I can see how it must have felt. And I'm sorry I didn't stand up for you sooner when I realised how nasty Sydney, Nyra and Kenzie are to you.'

'You don't know the half of it,' Lucy said, 'and it's not just them. *Because* of them, everyone is scared to even look at me. You know why I'm not on Snapchat?'

Ramona shook her head as dread formed in her gut.

Lucy snapped her book shut. 'When I first started at SLC, they sent me the most sick online messages and told the other girls terrible lies about me and my dad. When he found out, he gave me the option of changing schools, but I knew it might not be better anywhere else and that if I stuck it out, I might get into the fashion program this year and that would make it all worthwhile. I don't know what I ever did to Sydney, but it was like she hated me from orientation day.'

'That's awful,' Ramona interjected. 'I don't know how you put up with it.'

'Over time I learned to stay under the radar, and she'd all but stopped making my life a living hell, but everything ramped up again recently.'

'What do you mean?'

'I've been getting messages to my phone since she saw us at the markets, and last week I even got a letter slipped inside my locker. They're anonymous, but I know they're from *your* friends.'

Ramona felt sick. 'What do they say?'

'What don't they say, more like? They tell me I'm so ugly it hurts their eyes to look at me, that I …' She sucked in a breath and looked back down at her book. 'That I should do the world a favour and kill myself.'

'You need to go to the head and—'

'What good would that do? Sydney's mother is president of the P and F and Nyra's dad is chair of the school board. They won't get more than a slap on the wrist. Honestly, I've survived three years of

307

their bull. I can handle another three and then I'll never have to face them again. But one day they'll regret what they did to me, because I'll be a famous fashion illustrator and everyone in the fashion world will know who I am.'

Ramona smiled at the vehemence in Lucy's voice—she obviously bought into the success-is-the-best-revenge theory. 'With your talent, I have no doubt that's true. But you shouldn't have to suffer through another three years. Surely if Sydney's and Nyra's parents knew what they were doing they'd be horrified.'

'Don't you even think about reporting them,' Lucy warned. 'The best thing you can do for both of us is to leave me alone and to keep any interaction between us strictly about our project.'

'But I don't want to leave you alone. I like you, Lucy.'

'This is what *I* want. Now if you don't mind, I'm busy.'

'But …' Ramona's heart dropped. This was not how this conversation was supposed to go. 'You really don't want to be friends with me?'

Lucy shook her head and made a big show of reopening her book. *I guess that's it then.*

Ramona stood. What was she supposed to do now? She couldn't go running back to Sydney and co after what she'd said, and the truth was, she didn't want to.

Tears pooled in her eyes, but she didn't allow them to spill as she went back to Drysdale and sat alone in a corner. Even though they weren't supposed to use their phones at lunch, she dug hers out of her bag and texted Elijah: *You free this arvo?*

You betcha, came his speedy reply.

She brought up her Snapchat for something to do while she waited for the end of lunch siren. And—*oh my God!*—not only had Sydney, Nyra and Kenzie already blocked her but most of the rest of their year had too. Ramona could only imagine the message Sydney must have sent around to organise that so quickly. Her throat tightening, she checked Insta and TikTok and discovered the same result.

She bit her lip to stop from crying.

Here she was, exactly where she didn't want to be when she started afresh at SLC. Sitting on her own at lunch. *Billy No-mates.*

Debra

Late Wednesday afternoon, Deb switched off her computer and grabbed her running gear from under her desk.

The moment she'd recovered from the donut episode on Monday, she'd opened the employee database, her hands shaking as she typed in the name of her former boyfriend. In the years after she'd left New York, she'd occasionally allowed herself to search for Oscar online. The last she'd known he was still working at the same pharmaceutical company he'd been with when she left.

After a while it had been easier to pretend he no longer existed. It definitely hadn't been a walk in the park parenting alone, but she'd chosen to believe he'd stayed in New York and begun to breathe easier back in Australia.

Until his manifestation in the office last Friday turned all that upside down.

Within seconds she had everything Quinn wanted to know. His address and next of kin—one Sarah Darke, listed as his mother.

Sarah Darke. Anger burned inside Deb at this reminder of his lies and her foolishness.

He'd spoken about his beloved mother on their first official date, a date which had begun halfway through the speed-dating session when he'd urged her to leave with him there and then. They'd gone to a pizza parlour around the corner and told each other everything. He'd looked deep into her eyes as she relayed her lonely childhood and when she'd asked about his upbringing, he'd almost been apologetic as he explained the close relationship he'd had with his parents. Tragically, his mother had been killed in a hit-and-run accident right before his VCE.

'How on earth did you manage to sit your exams?' she'd asked.

Deb still remembered the lost look on his face as he replied, 'I did it for her. I wanted to make her proud.'

Her heart had broken for him—it seemed so cruel that a mother so devoted and caring had been taken so young. 'So it's just you and your dad now? Doesn't he miss you, living over here?'

That's when Oscar had delivered the final blow. 'Dad died of grief a couple of years after Mum. Well, it says heart attack on his death certificate, but … it should have said broken heart. I came here for a fresh start.'

She'd never slept with anyone on a first date, but she invited him back to her place that night and he'd had her clothes off before she could offer him a drink. It had been the most intense sex of her life. He'd told her that very night he wanted to marry her and dedicate his life to making her the happiest woman on earth. He said they'd be so blissfully happy together that it would erase the hurts of her childhood.

Now she cringed as she thought about how ludicrous that sounded. They'd only known each other five hours. Her only excuse was that she'd been young and naïve and starved of affection.

'Do you want kids?' he'd asked, as they lay in bed, their limbs entwined, their skin still slick from lovemaking.

'Yes. Definitely.' She wanted to create the family she'd longed for growing up. She wanted to prove that just because her mother had been selfish and neglectful didn't mean she couldn't be a good one. She would use her mum as an example of what *not* to do.

'Good. Me too. If we have a daughter, I want to call her Sarah, after my mum, and if we have a son, Richard, after my dad. Maybe Ricky for short.'

He'd painted such an enticing picture, but it had all been lies. Clearly, Sarah Darke hadn't died in a hit-and-run, and judging by what he'd said the afternoon Shaun introduced him to the office, his father was still kicking too. She didn't know why she was so surprised.

Then again, who was to say that hadn't been a lie as well? She wouldn't put it past him to lie on his employment forms. Maybe his parents *were* dead. Maybe he was married. Maybe he didn't even live where he said he did.

These thoughts had niggled Deb all night and through the next day, until she had to do something to stop them. This morning she'd told Ramona she had an interview after work and would be home late, when really, she intended to investigate Oscar's 'home' address.

She waited until her colleagues had finally clocked off for the day, then with a quick check of the corridor, headed into the bathroom and changed into her running gear. Then she put on the scarf and sunglasses as well, before venturing to the elevators.

Inside, she held her breath as the lift stopped on the floor below— Oscar's floor—but let it out again when only Sally entered.

'Hey, Deb.'

'Hi. How's things going with the new guy?' she found the balls to ask.

Sally's lips lifted into a rare smile. 'He's really great. Such a team player. Doesn't make any of us feel like he's above us.'

'That's great,' Deb lied. She felt the urge to tell Sally to be careful, not to trust her first impressions and to watch her back, but then Sally would want to know why. If she hadn't been able to bring herself to tell Quinn, she was hardly going to share her secret with a woman she hardly knew.

'You off to a fitness class?' Sally asked, glancing down at Deb's sneakers. 'I really need to start doing something. Ever since I hit forty my metabolism has slowed right down.'

'Tell me about it,' Deb replied. 'I only have to look at chocolate these days and I put on weight.'

Sally chuckled as the elevator opened on the ground floor. 'Have a good night.'

'You too.'

Instead of heading for the station, Deb walked across Hyde Park towards Darlinghurst. As she crossed busy College Street and headed down into East Sydney, she thought about how great it would be to live so close to work and Ramona's school, but even if she could afford it, the fact that Oscar lived here meant she never would. The closer she came to the address on his employee records, the more her nerves compounded. Many times she almost turned back, but something compelled her onwards. She had to feel like she was being proactive, like she was one step ahead of him, and right now, seeing where he lived, watching *him*, felt like the best way to do that.

When she came to the terrace house she believed to be his, she dropped down on the footpath opposite and pretended to be doing up her shoelace, glancing up surreptitiously to …

To what? What exactly did she expect to achieve coming here?

It was a nice place; most of the houses in the area had no front garden to speak of but Oscar's tiny courtyard was filled to the brim with roses. She was admiring the garden and thinking he must pay someone to look after them because there wasn't a chance in hell he got his hands dirty himself, when she felt something wet and firm on her butt.

She shrieked and sprang to her feet as she realised the firm and wet thing was a nose belonging to a ginormous fluffy dog.

'Snoodles, no! I'm so sorry.'

Snoodles? Deb registered the face attached to the leash attached to the dog. *Quinn.* Her stomach flipped.

'What are you doing here?' they asked each other at the same time.

'I live here,' Quinn responded with a lift of her perfectly waxed brow. 'This is my street.'

So that's why it sounded familiar—Deb had never actually been to Quinn's house before, but of course she knew she lived in Darlinghurst. This nightmare just got worse and worse. 'Aren't you supposed to be in Forster with your parents?'

Quinn glanced at the dog who'd now stopped trying to violate Deb and was sniffing something disgusting at the edge of the footpath. 'Mrs D had a stroke on Monday. She's still in hospital. I volunteered to stay at her place and look after this one.'

'Oh my goodness.' Deb momentarily forgot her own problem. 'Is she going to be okay?'

'I hope so. The doctors aren't sure how much permanent damage there's been, but she looked a little sprightlier when I visited today.'

'I'm so sorry.' Deb knew how much Mrs D had come to mean to Quinn over the last couple of months.

'Thanks. But you still haven't told me why *you're* here.'

Deb dared a glance across the road as she tried to come up with an excuse.

'I … I uh, have to pick Ramona up from her friend's because I didn't want her catching the train home at this time. She lives nearby, so I thought I'd get a run in while I wait. If I knew you hadn't gone away, I'd have dropped by.'

'Sorry, things have been a bit hectic with Mrs D.'

'It's okay. I understand,' Deb said as the door of the house she'd been watching opened and a tall figure stepped into the tiny front garden. Her heart froze. Was it too much to hope it wasn't him—that she'd written the address down wrong or he had a housemate? Although it had been her decision to come, now she wished she was anywhere but here.

What kind of stupid game was she playing?

'I've got to go,' she said to Quinn. 'I'll see you next week.'

As she turned to flee, Snoodles barked loudly at the sound of a hose starting across the road.

'OMG. I can't believe it! It's him,' Quinn hissed as her hand shot out and gripped Deb's arm. 'If this isn't fate, I don't know what is. How do I look?'

Deb swallowed. 'You always look adorable.' Desperate to escape asap, she tried to shake off her friend's grip.

Quinn, oblivious, was bouncing on the spot. 'I'm going to go say hi. Welcome him to the neighbourhood. You should come.'

'I really have to get Ramona.'

Deb shot off down the footpath before Quinn could reply, but her friend was already crossing the street anyway. She didn't believe in God, but right then—her legs burning as she ran as fast as she could to the train station—she prayed for divine intervention.

Quinn

Unable to believe Oscar lived just down the street, but taking it as another sign from the gods, Quinn yanked Snoodles over to say hi. As she approached, she drank in the sight of him—utterly edible in black trackpants and a grey T-shirt. In one hand he held a bottle of beer and in the other hose.

He looked lost in thought as he watered his garden but glanced up as she called from the other side of the low fence. 'Mr Darke?'

He frowned slightly and then immediately replaced it with a smile. 'Miss Paladino? Are you stalking me?'

'You wish,' she said with a grin. 'Looks like we're neighbours.'

'Really?'

'Yeah.' Quinn pointed down the road. 'I'm at number sixty-nine.'

'Wow.' He paused for a moment. 'Hang on, I thought you were away on vacation?'

'I'm supposed to be, but my neighbour had a stroke on Monday and she doesn't have anyone to look after her dog while she's in hospital.'

Snoodles started tugging on the leash.

'It's very sweet of you to step in. That pup looks like it could be quite the handful.'

'You have *no* idea.' Quinn gestured to the bright-coloured roses that bordered either side of the tiny courtyard. 'Gorgeous flower beds.'

'Thanks. They're my mum's handiwork. This is the house I grew up in. I'm renting it off my parents—they moved into one of those retirement villages a few years back,' he said. 'I'm not much of a green thumb myself, so I'm terrified I'm going to kill them.'

She laughed and yanked on the leash as Snoodles tried to make a dash for home. *Not yet, demon.* 'You don't have anyone to help?' she fished.

'Nope. Just me. I'd love a dog but would feel bad leaving it home all day while I was at work.'

Quinn had to bite her lip to stop from grinning. 'Well, I'm sure you could borrow Snoodles anytime you want.'

'What kind of a name is Snoodles?'

Quinn shrugged one shoulder. 'Don't ask me. Apparently it was an in-joke between my friend and her late husband. I think Typhoon or Wrecking Ball would be more fitting.'

'Aw, is she being cruel to you, baby?' Oscar cooed as he continued to rub Snoodles' neck. His head was lolling back, his tongue hanging out of his mouth. Quinn could swear she even heard him purring. As she watched Oscar's beautiful hands, his lovely long fingers, she couldn't help feeling a tad jealous as she imagined them on *her* neck instead.

'Want one?'

Lost in her fantasy, it took a few seconds to register that Oscar was offering her a beer. 'Maybe just a quick one,' she replied, silently whooping.

Oscar opened the gate and was about to unhook Snoodles from his leash, but she stopped him before disaster struck. 'I'd better keep a hold of him, or your non-green thumbs will be the least of your roses' problems.'

She hoped he'd invite her inside—you could tell a lot about a man from their home—but he told her to wait there and then went to retrieve another beer alone.

Damn Snoodles. Oscar was hardly going to risk his sweet home when she'd just warned him about his garden. She should have taken the blasted dog back to Mrs Dagliesh's place.

'Here you are,' he said and handed her an ice-cold bottle. He'd also brought out a bowl of water for Snoodles. *How considerate!*

They sat on the front step, the dog between them slobbering all over her sneakers.

'Do you live alone?' Oscar asked, taking a sip of his beer.

Oh my God! Was he *fishing?*

'No, I live with my brother and his husband. I keep thinking about getting my own place but Sydney rent doesn't come cheap, and Darpan—that's my brother-in-law—is such a good cook, I can't bring myself to leave.'

'You don't cook yourself?'

'I do okay. Wait till the next Bake-Off and you'll be able to taste for yourself.'

'The Bake-Off?'

'Oh, you haven't heard about that yet?'

Quinn told him about The Energy Co's annual contest and how competitive it got. She followed with a Who's Who of the office and he laughed as she told him the nicknames she and Deb had for some of their colleagues.

'I can't picture Deb,' Oscar said, his brow creasing slightly.

'Well, there are a hundred people at the office—not counting everyone in the factory. You can't be expected to remember them all immediately.'

He shook his head. 'I'm very good with names and faces.'

'She works in payroll.'

'Ah, that'll be why then. When I delivered donuts to their office, she wasn't there.'

While they talked, Snoodles rested his head on Oscar's knee. Every time he stopped stroking, the dog raised its massive paw, begging him to start again. She didn't blame him.

'How long have you been back in Australia?' Quinn asked.

'Since mid last year.'

'Oh, did you have another job before The Energy Co then?'

'No.' Oscar lifted his beer to his mouth and took another long sip, his Adam's apple slowly moving in and out as he did. 'I had a bit of a sabbatical and was also dealing with some family stuff, but I'm stoked to be back in the saddle, so to speak.'

Quinn badly wanted to ask more, but he pushed to his feet before she could. 'Anyway, this has been nice, but I've got some work I need to finish before hitting the sack.'

'No worries,' she said, trying not to show her disappointment. 'I should probably be getting home anyway. But you know what they say about all work and no play.'

He grinned as he reached out to take her now empty bottle. 'Thanks for the advice. I'll bear that in mind. I guess I'll see you at work on Monday?'

'You sure will,' she replied. *Or sooner.*

Now that Quinn knew where Oscar lived, she and Snoodles would be finding multiple excuses to walk past his house.

Debra

Deb went into work early on Thursday morning because she'd scored an interview from one of her job applications and would have to finish at 3 pm to make it.

Please God, let me get it.

Every day she had to go into The Energy Co another grey hair sprouted on her head.

As she stepped into the lobby, she did her now ritual scan of her surrounds to check for Oscar. At this time of the day there weren't many people here, so it was easy to see that none of them were him. She breathed a quick sigh of relief as she headed for the elevators.

So far so good.

Apart from yesterday afternoon when she'd checked out his house, she'd only seen him once since Friday and even then, only from a distance when she'd had to walk past the floor-to-ceiling glass of Shaun's office. The two men had been sitting on either side of Shaun's mammoth desk, Oscar leaning back in the leather seat as if they were mates not boss and employee. Thankfully, he'd been too absorbed in whatever they were laughing about to see her slink past, but even still it had taken a good half hour for her heart rate to return to normal.

The sooner she could hand her resignation in the better.

She pressed the up button and tapped her feet on the ground in frustration. Why did these pesky elevators always take so long? Standing here in the open lobby made her feel like a mouse in a bare field—at any moment an eagle might appear and swallow her whole.

'Morning, Denise.'

'Steve!' she shrieked. 'You shouldn't sneak up on people like that.'

He raised an eyebrow as the doors pinged open. 'After you.'

'Thanks.' She slipped inside, disappointed her disguise hadn't done the trick. If Steve had recognised her, anyone could.

'What's with the scarf and sunglasses?' he asked as the doors began to close.

She opened her mouth to say she had a migraine and was having a bad hair day when hurried footsteps sounded just outside. Steve's hand shot forward to the open-doors button and terror flooded Deb's whole body as the elevator opened again to reveal …

Oscar Darke.

Her vision blurred. If only her eyes were playing tricks on her.

'Thanks,' he said as he stepped into the space that could supposedly hold twelve people but suddenly felt way too small for three.

Steve's eyes lit up. 'Good morning, Oscar. Good to see I'm not the only early bird catching the worm.'

Oscar chuckled and glanced at Deb as the doors shut. 'Morning,' he said with the same smarmy smile he'd always had.

'Hey,' she somehow managed, before shrinking back into the corner and staring at the floor, praying Steve would keep chatting.

The lift started to rise and Deb stayed frozen, not wanting to do anything that would draw attention and cause Oscar to take a proper look at her. Her heart was beating so fast, she wouldn't be surprised if the men could hear it.

'Shit,' Oscar exclaimed.

Said heart thudded. He'd recognised her! Should she play dumb? Try and persuade him he was mistaken? *Oh God.*

It was only when Steve started jabbing his index finger at all the buttons that she realised the elevator had stopped between levels.

'What's going on?' she asked without thinking.

Steve looked at her as if she were stupid. 'This fucking elevator has finally carked it.'

No freaking way.

Were the gods having a laugh?

The blood rushed to her head, and she gripped the rail around the edge of the lift as dizziness almost caused her to faint.

'Are you okay?' Oscar asked, reaching out and gently touching her arm.

She flinched, jumping back and slamming herself into the rail. She'd thought she was already living her worst nightmare. Perhaps this was fate's way of reminding her that things could always get worse.

He held up his hands. 'Sorry. I didn't mean ...'

'It's fine.' Her chest heaved as she fought back tears. 'I'm just ... claustrophobic.'

'Maybe you should sit down, take some deep breaths.'

She nodded, sinking to the floor. Her legs wouldn't hold her much longer anyway.

'Steve, see if you can alert someone that we need help,' Oscar ordered and then turned back to Deb, dropping down to his haunches in front of her. 'Sorry, what was your name?'

'Um … Denise.' Thank God Steve had never got it right.

'Denise.' Oscar nodded. 'Which company do you work for?'

'Denise is one of us. She's our payroll manager,' Steve helpfully provided.

'Ah, right,' Oscar grinned, and she felt her insides twist into a tight knot. Was that a smile of recognition? 'Nice to meet you.'

'Um … you too.' She sounded as breathless as she felt, but … could her disguise be working after all?

'I'm sure we won't be here long,' Oscar said. 'This is a big building—they'll have someone on call. Maybe just try to take a few deep breaths.'

If Deb didn't know better, she'd think his concern genuine. But this man could never care for anyone but himself.

At that moment, a voice came through the speakers in response to Steve's SOS. 'Is there a problem?'

Steve snorted. 'Not unless you call being stuck in a bloody broken lift a problem.'

As if she wasn't already on edge, his sarcasm was seriously starting to get on her nerves, although he wasn't the person she had to worry about and thank God he was here. She shuddered to think what might have happened if she and Oscar were alone.

After asking Steve a few brief questions, the faceless voice promised help would be there asap.

'May as well get comfortable,' Oscar said, sliding down to join Deb on the floor, leaning back against the wall and stretching his long legs out in front of him.

He was so close she could see the weave in his navy trousers and smell his signature cologne. Once upon a time, his scent had made her mouth water and her insides quiver. Now it made her stomach turn. She pressed a firm hand against it to try and quell the feeling.

'Have you seen any good movies lately?' Oscar asked.

'Huh?' Was he talking to *her*? She couldn't for the life of her think of the last movie she'd watched and didn't want to say too much for fear he'd recognise her voice. 'Not really. You?'

This was so weird. Was she really sitting on the floor of an elevator making small talk with Oscar Darke?

'I'm actually going through a bit of an old movie phase thanks to Netflix. Last weekend I watched *The Breakfast Club* and *Ferris Bueller's Day Off*.' He chuckled as if this was slightly embarrassing and Deb had to admit, they were the last films she ever expected him to watch. When they'd been together, he'd been a thriller and horror type of guy.

'Geez, I haven't seen those for years,' Steve said as he paced back and forth in the tiny space.

Deb wanted to yell at him to sit the fuck down—she couldn't think straight with him doing that, and she really needed to think straight. She also needed some air and a glass of water. She tugged at her collar. Had the air conditioning stopped working in here as well?

While Oscar and Steve continued their eighties movie chit-chat, Deb tried to regulate her breathing, but it was no good. Her pulse raced and her lungs felt as if they were getting smaller by the second. As little beads of sweat formed on her forehead, she dug into her handbag, pulled out a pamphlet someone had handed her at the station that morning and started flapping it against her face.

'If you're feeling hot, maybe you should take off your scarf,' Oscar suggested, turning his attention back to her.

'Yeah, what's with the new look anyway?' Steve asked, his lip curling. 'You look like my grandmother, only she carries it off better.'

'I think you look lovely in the scarf,' Oscar said, ignoring Steve, 'but it's probably not helping your cabin fever.'

She blinked nervously behind her sunnies. Had he made this suggestion because he was worried about her or because he had suspicions and wanted to be sure? Either way, Deb was in a quandary. If she didn't take it off, she might faint, but if she did, all her efforts to stay under his radar these last few days would have been in vain. Both options terrified her, but she didn't feel she had much choice. Just because he recognised her didn't necessarily mean he would find out about Ramona.

Unlikely Steve would bring her up—if he couldn't even remember Deb's name, no way he'd remember she had a daughter. Once again, she commended herself for never allowing herself to get close to anyone at work, except Quinn.

Her hands trembled as she undid the knot at her neck and slowly pulled the scarf down over her shoulders, feeling as vulnerable as if she'd just stripped naked.

She wanted to get in first, to say something snarky like, *Well, fancy meeting you here*, and act like she wasn't scared, but angry that he'd come back into her life. She wanted to show him she was a strong independent woman now, one who would not be conned by his charms again. But here in the elevator she felt anything but strong and couldn't bring herself to say any of it.

She swallowed, her insides turning to ice as she waited for realisation to dawn.

Time seemed to stand still.

Finally, Oscar's lips curved into a seemingly warm smile. 'Feel any better?'

Huh?

Either he genuinely didn't recognise her, or he was doing a stellar job pretending.

But *why*?

Her mind raced as she searched for answers, trying to keep one step ahead of this awful situation. Could it be he was lulling her into a false sense of security so she'd let down her guard? Or was it possible Oscar had been with so many women he'd lost track? It *had* been almost sixteen years. Maybe he'd forgotten what he'd done to her all those years ago?

Or maybe she simply wasn't that memorable.

That would be the best-case scenario, but she couldn't allow herself to relax.

'A little,' she managed to whisper. 'Thank you.'

'No problem. I can't have a fellow employee fainting on me in my first week.'

And then he winked, sending another dart of terror through her. Was that just an innocent wink—the kind you'd give anyone—or was it a message? Specifically for her.

Ramona

'Ramona!'

She looked up at the sound of her name as she trundled along the platform towards the exit and her heart kicked over at the sight of Elijah.

'What are you doing here?'

He grinned. 'Aren't I allowed to meet my girlfriend at the train?'

'Yes.' She struggled not to burst into tears. After another shitty day, there was nothing she needed more right now than a friend. The fact he happened to be cute and into her was a bonus.

'How was your day?' he said as he reached out to take her backpack.

'Don't ask.' After burning her bridges with Sydney, Nyra and Kenzie—and her disastrous attempt to make up with Lucy—school was simply about getting through the day. If it wasn't for the fashion program, she'd have asked her mum to let her transfer to the local high school. At least there she'd have Elijah.

He took her hand. 'Sounds like you need some budgie therapy.'

She smiled. 'I mean it. I really don't want to talk about my day. Tell me about yours instead,' she asked as they headed for his place.

Apparently, someone in his science class had almost set the room on fire with a Bunsen burner, and they'd all had to evacuate. Ramona was giggling at his description of the drama by the time they got to Elijah's front gate. It creaked as they entered and then headed up the cobbled garden path into the house.

'Elijah, you should have told me you were almost here,' exclaimed Barbara, his grandma, when they stumbled upon her ironing while watching *The Bold and the Beautiful*. She gestured to the TV. 'You know I don't like anyone knowing my dirty secret.'

'Your secret's safe with me, Barbara,' said Ramona, dumping her school bag by the door. 'Don't tell my mum, but sometimes I watch it before she gets home from work.'

The wrinkles around Barbara's eyes crinkled as she chuckled. 'Well, you kids have fun. I'll just be in here with Eric and Brooke if you need anything.'

'Thanks, Gran,' Elijah said as they continued through the house. Ramona loved Elijah's place—there were knick-knacks everywhere, mismatched lamps and furniture that somehow worked together, and the walls were covered in so many photos and paintings you could barely see them. It was such a contrast to her place, which was devoid of almost all clutter. Elijah had told her that his grandparents had lived there since they got married, forty-five years ago. She guessed if you stayed in the same place for such a long time you would accumulate stuff.

As they neared the sunroom, he grabbed her hand. 'Close your eyes. I've got a surprise for you.'

'What is it?'

'I said, close your eyes.'

'This better be a good surprise,' she warned as she shut her eyes tightly.

'Of course it is. Now keep them shut,' he instructed as she heard him open the screen door that led out to the garden.

'But I want to see Frodo,' she said, wondering why they were going outside.

'You will. After.'

'After what?'

'Patience, Ramona, patience.' After a few more steps, he added, 'Okay, open them.'

She gasped. In a space between two of the aviaries stood what looked like a teepee made of white bed sheets, billowing slightly in the gentle breeze. Inside, she could see a red-checked picnic rug spread on the ground with cushions scattered upon it, as well as a basket of flowers and what looked like a picnic basket.

'Oh my God.'

'Do you like it?' Elijah asked.

'Like it?' This had to be the most romantic thing anyone had ever done. Tears sprung to her eyes and she lost the battle she'd been fighting all week.

'Hey, don't cry,' Elijah soothed, wiping her tears with his thumbs. 'It was supposed to make you happy.'

'I'm crying cos I love it,' she sobbed, smiling through watery eyes. 'Thank you.'

'You're welcome. And worth it.'

'It looks like something out of a magazine.'

'Well ...' Elijah gave her a sheepish smile. 'That could be because I saw the idea in Gran's *Better Homes and Gardens*. It was a feature about kids' birthday parties, so I went easy on the pink and fairy lights.'

She laughed and he tugged her hand again. 'Come on, let's sit and eat. Setting up all this has given me an appetite.'

It was even more magical inside the tepee. The wind caused the large eucalypt trees above to swish, and the shadow of the leaves painted a pretty pattern on the sheets above them. Elijah opened the picnic basket to reveal its contents.

'Lemonade and scones,' Ramona said as he set about putting it all on the rug between them. 'Did you make all this yourself?'

'Course I did.'

She giggled. 'You're like an old lady trapped in a very sexy young man's body.'

'I'm gunna focus on the sexy part of that and forget you ever likened me to an old lady. Guys can cook too, you know?'

She took a bite of a scone he'd just smothered in jam and cream. 'OMG. These are amazing.'

He beamed. 'Super simple too. Only three ingredients.'

'Which are?'

'Ah, if I told you that I wouldn't have anything to lure you over here with.'

'Aside from your gorgeous budgies,' she said, taking another delicious bite.

'And here I was thinking it was me you liked.'

'Think whatever you like, but we both know my heart belongs to Frodo.'

He grinned—'Looks like I'll just have to be content to be second best'—then reached over and wiped some cream off the side of her mouth, before licking his finger.

It was the sexiest thing Ramona had ever seen, and she couldn't resist leaning forward and kissing him. Afternoon tea was forgotten for a while but who needed food when you had access to lips like his?

'You're amazing,' Elijah said as he tore his mouth from hers. 'But I think we'd better stop.'

Although she respected that he wasn't going to try and pressure her into anything she wasn't ready for yet, she gave a buttery sigh. 'Time to go see Frodo.'

They took the baskets inside and then Elijah went back to pack up the rug and tepee while Ramona visited with the birds. Usually, Frodo gave her a quick hello and then danced and played on the large perches scattered around the sunroom with his feathered friends, but today, as if sensing she needed some TLC, he stayed on her shoulder and rubbed his little face against her neck.

'How's the budgie therapy going?' Elijah asked on his return.

'It's almost as good as Elijah therapy,' she said as he came and sat beside her on the floor. 'I don't know what I'd do without the two of you right now.'

He took her hand. 'That's good because you're stuck with us.'

'You're a pretty boy,' chirped Frodo, making them both laugh.

'I know you said you don't want to talk about it,' Elijah began, 'but I'm worried about you. You've lost the spark you had when we first met. Is Lucy still refusing to talk to you?'

She leaned her head on his shoulder. 'Unless it's about our project. But now we've done most of the planning work, we can easily do our own bits. Although we need to start working on the actual dress soon, so that will be interesting.'

'And what about the others?'

'They're still trying to make my life a living hell, but I'm hoping if I just ignore them, they'll get bored and give up.' So far, since she'd confronted Sydney about her bullying, not only had everyone started treating her like a leper, but she'd also been finding little notes inside her locker. They generally only had one word—today's said 'RIP'. And several times Sydney had accidentally bumped into her, making her drop whatever she was holding so it scattered all over the ground.

'You don't have to put up with that,' Elijah said fiercely. 'You should go to the principal. If you and Lucy both tell—'

'Lucy won't. And you forget she's not talking to me. Besides, I can't report them because …'

'Because what?'

'I owe Sydney—she stole her dad's credit card for me and bought me a DNA test.'

His eyes widened so much she worried they might fall out of their sockets. 'What? When?'

'Just before I met you. It arrived the arvo I found Frodo.'

'Have you done it?'

She nodded. 'The day we met.'

'Wow. Is this to find your father?'

'Yeah. Who knows if it will work?'

'Why didn't you tell me?'

'I wanted to surprise you when I got the results.' She reached up to stroke Frodo's stomach. 'I figured if I found my dad, maybe you could do the same to find yours.'

He shook his head. 'I don't want to find out.'

'Really? You're not curious?'

'I've got a good life here with Gran. Mum was in a bad place when she got pregnant with me—there's every possibility my dad is a deadbeat or worse, and I'd rather not know. I landed on my feet with my grandparents. They're all the family I need.' He squeezed her hand. 'But I hope you get the answers you're looking for. Why don't you just pay Sydney back? That way you won't owe her anything.'

'I'm going to. But Mum only gives me ten dollars a week and she won't let me access my savings account unless there's a good reason.'

'I'll give you the money. I've got plenty from selling the budgies.'

'Thanks, but I've almost got enough,' she lied. After what had happened with Sydney, she didn't want to be indebted to anyone. Not even Elijah.

'Okay.' He kissed her forehead. 'But promise you'll ask if you need it.'

'I will.' She took a quick breath. 'Now, do you want help cleaning cages?'

'You really are the girl of my dreams, you know that?'

She grinned and pointed to Frodo. 'Don't you mean *boy* of your dreams?'

He chuckled and offered his hand to help her up. They went outside and did a bit of work in the aviaries, Ramona getting sidetracked when Elijah showed her some eggs.

'Oh my God, you're having babies?'

'That's usually what breeding involves.'

'When will they be born?'

'These guys should hatch in a couple of weeks.'

'I'm having one, I don't care what my mother says.'

'Kids!' called Barbara from the back door. 'Dinner's almost ready. Do you want to stay, Ramona?'

Shit. Was that the time already? Her mum would kill her for not messaging.

'That'd be wonderful,' Ramona replied; the opportunity to prolong her time with Elijah was too good to pass up. 'But I'll have to ask Mum; she should be home by now.'

Barbara wiped her hands on the apron she'd put on to cook. 'Good idea. In fact, why don't you ask her if she wants to join us? We're having spaghetti.'

'Thanks. I'm sure she'd love that.' And it might mean she'd say yes to Ramona being out on a school night.

She grabbed her bag and hurried the short distance home to find Deb in the kitchen staring into the fridge.

'Hi, honey.' Her mother barely looked up and didn't even ask where she'd been. She was still dressed in her work clothes, except for her shoes which she'd kicked off in the middle of the floor. Whenever Ramona left her shoes anywhere but the shoe rack in her bedroom, Deb went ballistic.

She frowned. 'Are you okay, Mum?'

'Huh?' Deb straightened, closed the fridge and looked at Ramona as if she was only just noticing her.

'I asked if you're okay?'

'Yes. Fine. Why wouldn't I be? Just trying to work out what we should have for dinner.' Her manic tone told Ramona she wasn't fine, but at least she had a solution to the dinner issue.

'Elijah's gran has just invited us over for spaghetti.'

'Oh, no, honey, I'm not in the mood to socialise. It's been a long week. I had that interview this arvo and I'm stuffed. I need to relax on the couch.'

With a glass of wine, Ramona added silently. She knew her mother had been trying to hide her drinking since the episode on Friday night, but she'd also seen the empty bottles in the recycling bin.

'How'd it go?'

Deb shook her head slightly. 'How'd what go?'

'The interview.'

'Oh right. Sorry, it was okay, I think. They said they'd tell me by mid next week.'

'That's great. Do you mind if I go to dinner at Elijah's? I won't be late,' Ramona added, bracing herself for an argument.

'Yes, go ahead. Have fun, honey.'

Ramona blinked. Not only was her mother letting her out on a school night, but she hadn't specified a time to be home. Something was definitely going on with her. She guessed it had something to do with the restructuring at The Energy Co, or with Tristan—she hadn't heard her talking to him all week. Either way, Ramona didn't have the mental energy to worry about it on top of her own stuff.

'Thanks,' she said and then realised now could be the perfect time to catch Deb when her guard was down. 'Oh, and have you thought any more about me getting a budgie? Elijah's going to have chicks in a couple of weeks, and he can give me a cage, so we don't have to buy one.'

'Yeah, sure. Sounds good.'

Ramona didn't stick around for Deb to realise what she'd just agreed to. A promise was a promise, and no way she would be letting her back out of it.

Instead, she raced down the street to tell Elijah the good news.

Debra

Less than thirty seconds after Ramona headed off to have dinner with Elijah and his grandmother, a knock sounded on the door.

Deb frowned. She crossed the apartment tentatively and peered through the peephole, her chest squeezing as she registered Tristan on the other side. Ramona must have let him into the building as she was leaving.

He wore snug-fitted faded jeans and a navy polo shirt that accentuated his broad shoulders and muscly arms, and held a pretty pot plant in one hand. For a moment she forgot all her problems and just admired the view.

Was it possible he'd grown even better looking since she'd last seen him?

She startled as he rapped loudly again on the door.

Composing herself, she summoned a smile and opened it. 'Hello.'

Tristan looked her straight in the eye. 'Are you ghosting me?'

'What?'

'Ghosting. It's when you stop communicating with someone without telling them why and ignore any attempts for them to reach you.'

'I know what it is.' She couldn't spend so much time in the company of a millennial without having some understanding of current dating terms. 'And no, I'm not doing that at all.'

'I'm not sure what else to think. You cancelled our last date, you haven't answered my calls since, and your messages have been short and sporadic. Did I come on too strong at Luna Park? Please, I'll understand, just let me—'

'It's not you. I'm sorry. Something happened at work,' Deb said. 'And I've been trying to wrap my head around it. I haven't had the energy for anything else.'

'I see.' Tristan's expression looked torn between hurt and concern. 'Are you okay?'

'Not really. Do you want to come inside?' This was not a conversation she wanted to have out here on the landing. She didn't really want to have it at all, but she guessed she owed Tristan an explanation for her disappearing act.

He held out the plant. 'I bought this for you. Wanted you to have something to remember me by.'

She half-laughed, some of her tension easing as she reached out to take it. 'Thank you. That's sweet of you. It's beautiful.'

'Just like you,' he said, and her heart swelled. It was so good to see him.

They stepped inside, he closed the door behind them, and she put the pot plant down in the middle of the table.

'What happened at work?' Tristan asked, shoving his hands in his pockets.

'Oscar turned up.'

'What?' His eyebrows shot up in surprise. 'Oscar, as in your *ex*, Oscar? Ramona's father?'

Her bones chilled as she nodded. 'Yes. He works at The Energy Co now. He's the new director of sales.'

'But I thought he was American?'

'The speed-dating event where we met was for Aussies living in Manhattan. He told me he was from Melbourne, but I think that was just another one of his lies. Turns out his family is in Sydney.'

'Shit.' They'd had some fairly serious conversations in the short time they'd known each other but this was the most serious Deb had ever seen Tristan.

'That's putting it mildly.'

'Have you spoken to him?'

'I've been trying to avoid him, but today … this morning, we ended up in the same elevator and it broke down. I freaked out. Hyperventilated. He tried to help me and … the crazy thing is he didn't seem to recognise me.'

Tristan's eyes widened and he glanced towards the couch. 'This is a lot to take in. Do you mind if we sit down?'

'No of course not.' Where were her manners? 'Can I get you something to drink? Coffee? Tea? Wine?'

She hoped he'd say wine because she'd been about to crack one for herself.

'Wine sounds good.'

He followed her into the kitchen and grabbed the glasses while she took a bottle of sav blanc from the fridge. Deb was ashamed when she thought about how much she'd drunk this past week, but she could only shut off her thoughts at night if she'd had a few glasses of wine before bed. She didn't want Ramona to worry so had been careful not to drink as much as she had last Friday, but let's just say her budget had gone out the window.

She poured them each a glass and they took them into the adjacent living room.

'Talk me through exactly what happened,' Tristan said as they sat down on the couch.

After a large gulp, she told him everything, from Oscar's arrival last Friday, to her narrowly missing him when he delivered donuts to her team and, finally, the terrifying but confusing encounter in the elevator.

'Are you absolutely sure it's him?' Tristan asked, his grip so tight on his glass his knuckles were turning white.

'I'm not an idiot.' At least she didn't *think* she was. 'It's him. It would be too much of a coincidence if they had the same name, same mannerisms *and* the same damn birthday.'

'How do you know his birthday?'

'I checked his details on the employee register. His next of kin is his mother and she has the same name as well.'

Tristan let out a deep sigh. 'And you really don't think he recognises you?'

'He didn't appear to.'

He scratched his jawline, which had the light dusting of a five o'clock shadow. 'I'm sorry, Deb, but I'm not buying that. There's no way anyone would ever forget you.'

In other circumstances she'd be flattered, but instead it sent a shiver down her spine. 'In that case,' she whispered, her eyes filling with tears, 'why is he acting like he doesn't know me? He's either playing mind games to get to me, or maybe he'd rather pretend we don't know each other so that I don't expose him for who he truly is. Whatever the reason, it's driving me crazy. I'm terrified he's going to find out about Ramona. Oh, God, what if he already has?'

'Hey, it's going to be okay.' Tristan took her glass and put them both on the coffee table before pulling her into a hug. 'We'll think of something.'

His arms were so strong and tight around her, his chest so warm and firm against her, Deb didn't know how it was possible to feel so safe yet so bloody terrified at the same time.

'I've been looking for another job,' she told him. 'I have to leave The Energy Co.'

'You shouldn't be the one who has to leave,' he whispered into her hair.

She pulled back slightly to look at him. 'I don't see that I have any other choice. I can't exactly go to the CEO and tell him he should fire his new director because he hurt me sixteen years ago, but there's no way I can continue to work at the same company as him. It's too much of a risk.'

'That's why you *should* go to your boss. And the police. It's never too late to report abusive behaviour. I'm guessing you're not the only one who's fallen prey to Oscar's abuse. Maybe if you make a statement, others will come forward.'

'No.' She refused to allow herself to think about his possible other victims. Her only concern was their daughter. No, *her* daughter. Not Oscar's. Ramona wasn't his and she never would be, if Deb had anything to do with it. 'I'm not even sure that's possible when the offence happened in another country and I don't have any evidence. And, if I did go to the police now, Oscar would definitely find out about Ramona, and I can't let that happen.'

'What exactly *does* Ramona know about him?'

Deb swallowed, a guilty heat rushing to her cheeks. 'Nothing. She thinks I used donor sperm to conceive her.'

'I see.' He rubbed his chin.

'I know lying is bad but—'

'I understand why you did it, Deb, but what are you planning on telling her if she wants to try and find the donor one day?'

She shuddered at the mere thought. 'If she ever decided to look, I was going to tell her that I used the donor excuse because I didn't want to admit that I conceived in a one-night stand. That I didn't want to tell her until she was older, because I didn't want her to think badly of me or worse, use it against me.' When Tristan nodded knowingly, Deb added, 'I never want Oscar getting his claws into her, playing mind games with her, or worse. Not even once she's an adult.'

'I understand. But don't you think she deserves to know the truth about where she comes from? Even if it's uncomfortable.'

'It's not just uncomfortable,' she argued. 'It's *awful*. Her father locked me in a room for two days. He treated me worse than an animal.'

Tristan passed her glass of wine back and took a sip of his own. 'So, what are you doing about work? Have you already resigned?'

'Not yet. I was hoping to get a job first. I had an interview at a medical centre in Parramatta this afternoon, but I'm not holding my breath. I don't think I was the only applicant, and I was still a bit of a mess after my run-in with Oscar.'

'If he's as dangerous as you think he is, then you should leave immediately.'

'I can't afford to.'

'I could help you,' he offered. 'Until you find something else.'

Part of her leapt at the idea, but she couldn't accept it so early in their relationship. 'Thank you, but if I get desperate, my dad will give me a loan.' Although he hadn't been a fan of the *idea* of Ramona, he loved her in his own way now and wouldn't let any harm come to them if he could help it.

'Okay,' Tristan agreed, 'but if you do need anything, promise me you'll ask. And promise if Oscar confronts you or you feel in any danger at work, you'll immediately resign. Replacement job or not.'

'I promise.'

He smiled and linked his hand through hers. 'Does anyone else know about this?'

She shook her head.

'Then I wish even more you'd told me earlier. I hate to think of you dealing with this all alone. We're friends and I want to be there for you. For the bad times as well as the good. I wish you'd confided in me. A problem shared is a problem halved and all.'

Somehow, Deb didn't think that was the case in this situation, but she appreciated his support, and his words brought a lump of emotion to her throat. 'I'm sorry. I want that too, I do, but I'm not used to leaning on anyone. Trust is … it's an issue for me.'

'And that's understandable, but I promise I'm going to prove to you that putting your trust in me is a good thing.'

She took a sip of her wine, desperately wanting to believe him. 'There is one other problem.'

His brow furrowed. 'Oh?'

'Quinn.'

'Your work friend? What's she got to do with any of this?'

'She thinks she's in love with Oscar.'

'What?!'

'You know how she'd been looking for that guy who helped her with her handbag?'

Tristan's mouth dropped open. '*No.* It's not him?'

'Yep.' Deb downed the rest of her wine and leaned forward to refill her glass. She'd worry about her downward drinking spiral later. 'You couldn't make this stuff up, hey?'

'Does she know?'

She shook her head. 'I was too shocked to say anything at first, and she's been on holidays this week, so I figured I had a bit of time to work out what to do. But now I think I've left it too long. I'm scared if I tell her, she'll tell Oscar about Ramona.'

'I thought you two were pretty close.'

'We are. She's my best friend.'

'Well, then, I don't think she'd break your confidence. It's not like they're even together, she's just got a crush. Whereas you and Quinn have history. You don't want something to happen between them, do you?'

'Of course not,' Deb said adamantly. Thinking about Oscar hurting Quinn like he'd hurt her made her want to march into The Energy Co and make it so he would never hurt anyone again. 'But it might never get serious,' she argued. 'Just because she likes him, doesn't mean anything will ever come of it. She hasn't had a serious relationship in the time I've known her. The moment a man starts to show real interest in her she freaks out. That's bound to happen with Oscar as well.'

Tristan ran a hand over his face and through his hair. 'Maybe, but I know if someone had information like that that could protect my daughter, I'd want them to tell her. Wouldn't you want the same if it were Ramona?'

Deb stiffened. 'Of course.' And Quinn was almost as important to her *as* her daughter.

That was the problem—by protecting one, she might be initiating danger for the other. She'd never felt more torn, more confused in her life.

'I always think honesty is the best policy,' Tristan said. 'And I understand why you don't want to reveal all to Ramona, but Quinn's a grown woman. I think you should trust your friendship and tell her before it's too late.'

As much as Deb hated to admit it, she knew he was right.

Quinn

'Good morning, girlfriend,' Quinn sang as she skipped into the payroll department on Monday morning carrying two takeaway coffees.

Deb looked up from her computer as Quinn deposited her latte on her desk with all the flair of a model on one of those TV game shows she'd loved watching when she was growing up. She couldn't help it—she was simply in a very good mood.

Although feeling guilty about the fact she wouldn't be able to visit Mrs D as much, it was good to be back at work. Now she just had to engineer an encounter with Oscar that didn't *look* engineered. Sadly, she'd not seen him again since last Wednesday night, no matter that she and Snoodles had walked past his house so much that eventually Snoodles had planted himself on the rug in Mrs D's front room and refused to move at all.

Deb picked up her latte and peeled back the lid. 'Thanks, and welcome back.' She downed some like it was her first drink after months in the desert. 'What did you do to yourself?' She gestured to the bandaid wrapped around Quinn's finger.

'Nothing.' She winked. 'But I need to come up with a good reason. I was going to say I cut it while chopping veggies, but I'm not sure it's possible to cut your little finger that way. I should have put it on my index finger instead. Any ideas?'

'Why on earth would you fake an injury?'

Quinn rolled her eyes. 'Remember the list? One of the suggestions was wear a bandaid because it'll make men stop to talk to you. I thought *he* might see it today.'

'You're not serious.' Deb's tone was scathing. She was never normally so biting.

'Are you okay?' Quinn asked.

'I'm fine. Just got a lot on my mind. Do you have time for a drink after work?'

'On a school night?' Quinn pressed a hand against her chest, feigning shock. 'Must be serious.' She lowered her voice. 'Is this about lover boy?'

'No.'

'Well, I did want to go visit Mrs D, but I can probably squeeze in a quick drink before then. Visiting hours don't finish until eight. Oh,' she clicked her fingers as she remembered, 'but I have to pick Snoodles up from doggy day care.'

Deb frowned. 'Doggy day care?'

'Yes. I got him in just around the corner, thank God. He's used to having company all day and if I left him alone at Mrs D's, there wouldn't be much of a house to return to.'

'How is Mrs Dagliesh?'

'Not much change. She's struggling to speak properly and they're not sure she's going to get back full use of her left side.' Her heart broke just saying this. Mrs D was so independent, and she'd hate having to rely on others moving forward.

'That's terrible. Are her daughters going to come home?'

'Yes, which should give her a boost. I've been in close contact with them since it happened. Neither of them could get away immediately but Crystal will be here Thursday afternoon and Michelle's going to make arrangements soon. It's likely Mrs D won't come home from hospital straight away. Best case she'll go into a rehabilitation centre for a while, worst case she's going to need permanent care. I think they're planning on Michelle being here by the time they need to work it all out.'

'Poor woman. I can't imagine much worse than a stroke.'

'Anyway,' Quinn said, needing to leave before she started crying. 'I'd better start work before Mr Carrot-Up-His-Arse catches me yakking. Let's do the park for lunch.'

'Sure. I'll meet you there—at our bench.'

'Okay.' Quinn found it slightly odd that Deb hadn't suggested they walk there together like always, but such thoughts were forgotten the moment she walked into digital marketing and found a small cardboard box wrapped with a silver ribbon on her desk.

She looked from Toby to Linc. 'D'you miss me so much you got me a present?'

'It was here when we arrived,' Toby told her. 'I wanted to open it but Linc wouldn't let me.'

'Thanks,' she said, as she dumped her things on the desk and plucked up the box. Good to know at least one of them had some social propriety.

'Looks like someone has a secret admirer,' Linc said, sharing an amused glance with Toby. 'Did you have a holiday fling or something?'

'No. It's probably from Deb.' They occasionally left each other little pick-me-ups.

Sinking down into her seat, she unwrapped the silver bow and was immediately hit with the smell of sugar. Donutty sugar? Her heart pulsed with anticipation as she lifted the cardboard lid and revealed the most beautiful donut she'd ever seen—satiny soft pink icing decorated with curls of white chocolate and fairy floss—and a tiny note that said nothing but 'Welcome back'.

It *had* to be him.

It was a work of art—almost too pretty to eat, but her sweet tooth got the better of her.

'Oh my God,' she moaned loudly through a mouthful. Both Linc and Toby raised their eyebrows.

She needed to thank Oscar asap. Was it too bold to go downstairs and turn up in his office? She didn't want to interrupt him during something important, but she had to acknowledge this sweet and generous gift.

She took another bite and almost orgasmed. Okay, so maybe that was a slight exaggeration, but this donut was heavenly.

'Do you mind eating more quietly?' Toby snapped.

Quinn ignored him as she wiped her mouth and placed the remains of the donut back in the box for later. Then she opened her email.

Good morning, Mr Darke
Do I have you to thank for the 'welcome back' gift on my
desk this morning?
Kind regards, Miss Paladino.

Knowing it could be ages before he replied, Quinn started sorting through the thousands of emails that had arrived while she was away. She'd set up an autoreply saying she was out of the office and encouraging people to direct their inquiries to Linc or Toby but, judging by the state of her inbox, barely anyone had listened. It was going to take all day to sort through it.

Less than two minutes later a new email landed, and she shrieked when she saw a reply from Oscar. Thankfully, Linc and Toby—earbuds back in their ears and eyes glued to their screens—didn't notice.

> *It is indeed a good morning, Miss Paladino. And I hope you*
> *like the donut. We couldn't have you being the only one*
> *who missed out, now, could we?*
> *I hope you enjoyed the rest of your holidays. How are*
> *Snoodles and your neighbour?*
> *Oscar.*

Quinn knew she should probably play it cool by not replying straight away, but she'd never been good at playing things cool and he *had* asked her a question. It would be rude to ignore it. She crafted a careful reply, telling him much the same as she'd told Deb. Again, his response came almost instantly.

> *I'm sorry to hear that. Let me know if there's anything I can*
> *do to help. I have to admit, I did enjoy meeting that dog.*

Quinn's heart swelled, not only at his very sweet offer to help, but at the fact he'd not even bothered to sign his name. In a matter of four emails, they'd lost all nods to formality—a sure sign that he already considered her a friend. She could be Bridget Jones to his

Daniel Cleaver, although he was far better looking than Hugh Grant and, even if he did like her, she doubted they'd exchange the kind of emails those two did. You could get in serious trouble for those kinds of shenanigans these days.

And besides, she'd rather be the Bridget to his Mark.

Debra

Deb's heart pounded as she saw Quinn walking towards her in the park. She'd struggled to concentrate on work and had almost called a rendezvous in the copy room but did not want to risk anyone overhearing this conversation.

'Hey.' Quinn flopped down on the bench beside her and started to unpack her lunch from her fancy cooler bag. 'I have had the best morning. Oscar left a welcome back donut on my desk and then I sent him an email to thank him, and he replied. He asked about Mrs D and even offered to help. He hasn't even met the woman and—'

'Quinn!' Deb shouted, causing her to startle.

She could not listen to another second of her friend gushing about Oscar. It sounded all too familiar. Donuts. Chummy emails. Offers to help little old ladies. He clearly had his eye on her. And if he was playing games with Deb, there was even the possibility he knew they were friends and was using Quinn to get to her. Either way, she couldn't let this childish crush continue a moment longer.

'There's something I need to tell you.'

'Oh God …' Quinn's smile fell from her face. 'What is it? Are you sick? Is Ramona? I can't handle any more bad news after Mrs D's stroke.'

'No, nothing like that,' Deb rushed to assure her. This was why she'd wanted to have this conversation in a bar, so she'd have some Dutch courage. 'Oscar is Ramona's father.'

'What?' Quinn recoiled as if Deb had hit her. 'He's your sperm donor?'

For a split second she thought about saying yes, but how would Deb explain that she didn't want him to know about the connection? How would she explain how *she* knew? She'd always said that Ramona was conceived through an anonymous donor.

'There never was a donor.'

'I …' Quinn fiddled with the large rainbow earring on her lobe. 'I don't understand.'

Deb squeezed her hand around the apple she'd brought for lunch like it was a stress ball, yet it did nothing to relieve anything. 'You know how I said I decided to have a baby because I was disillusioned with men and didn't want to wait forever for Mr Right?'

Quinn nodded.

'Well, that's not exactly the truth.' Deb swallowed and squeezed the apple even harder.

'Not exactly? Either it's true or it's not.'

'You're right,' Deb conceded. 'The truth is, I had a seriously deranged and abusive boyfriend who I met when I lived in New York.'

Quinn's eyes grew wide. 'You lived in New York? I thought you'd just been there on a holiday?'

She shook her head. 'I moved there in my mid-twenties to pursue a masters in psychology, and I met a guy—another Australian—at an Aussies in New York speed-dating event. I fell hard and fast for him and …'

As Deb spilled the story of Oscar's love-bombing, followed by his withdrawal, then more love-bombing, then jealousy, and finally the incident that had made her dump him once and for all, Quinn's face went pale. Deb could tell she didn't want to believe a word of it and, if she hadn't lived every moment herself, she might also think it sounded far-fetched.

When she got to the part about the camera, Quinn violently shook her head. 'Why didn't you go to the police? If he tied you up, there'd have been marks on your limbs. What about urine on the bed? I know women aren't always believed but those cameras would have been irrefutable evidence.' She paused, her eyes narrowing. 'Unless they weren't there?'

'What do you mean?' Deb snapped. It sounded like Quinn would rather believe a man she'd only just met over her best friend. 'Do you think I'd make this stuff up?'

Quinn shrugged. 'I don't know what to believe, Deb. Why are you just telling me this now? Why did you wait a whole week? You lied about Ramona. How do I know you're not just jealous of my friendship with Oscar and you're trying to—'

'Jealous! Why on earth would I be jealous?'

'Okay. Whatever. If it *is* true, don't you think Oscar deserved to know about his daughter?'

'No,' Deb said vehemently. 'He put me through hell when we were together, emotionally and physically. I wasn't prepared to risk my daughter to a monster like him. I left New York and never looked back. I raised Ramona completely on my own. I didn't want his money for child support, and I didn't want him anywhere near either of us. I still don't, and I don't regret what I did.'

'Oh my God! Last week when you were lurking around my street you weren't waiting for Ramona at all. You were scoping him out.'

'Guilty as charged.'

'You made me feel bad for asking you to tell me where he lives but you used that information for yourself! What were you planning on doing if I didn't turn up? Confronting him?'

'No.' Deb shuddered. 'I don't know.' She couldn't even really explain what she'd hoped to achieve, just that she'd felt compelled to go there. To check him out in his natural habitat.

'Is he why you've been wearing a scarf on your head and sunglasses whenever you're walking around the office? You're trying to hide?' Quinn's lip curled in clear disgust. 'Can't you see that's only drawing attention to yourself? You'd have been better wearing your old all-black clothes, letting your hair hang out and not wearing any make-up. Supposedly women *your* age are invisible anyway!'

'*My* age? I'm not *that* old.'

But Quinn didn't appear to be in the mood to argue this point. 'I can't believe you lied to me.'

The confusion and betrayal that flashed across her face hurt Deb to the core.

'I'm sorry, but I didn't know you well enough when we first met, so I told you what I tell everyone. After that, well, there didn't seem to be much point in coming clean. In my head, Oscar *is* nothing but a sperm donor.'

'You mean you didn't trust me,' Quinn retorted. 'I've told you every little thing about my life and you've held back this!'

'It's not like you've ever had anything traumatic to tell. You had a wholesome childhood, and your parents are not only still married but really love each other *and* you. You complain about your mum interfering in your business, but at least she gives a damn. Face it, Quinn, you've led a blissful life. You hardly even have to pay rent! The biggest thing you ever have to worry about is what colour to dye your hair!'

Quinn blinked. 'Is that really what you think? How you see me?'

Deb immediately regretted her tirade. The last thing she wanted was to hurt Quinn any more.

'No, of course not,' she gushed. 'I'm sorry, I'm not thinking straight. I think you're amazing and talented and kind and caring. Your life is the kind of life I want for Ramona, it's just—'

Quinn held up a hand and shook her head. 'I thought we were more than work colleagues, Deb. I thought we were friends. *Best* friends. And friends tell each other their deepest darkest secrets.'

'I did tell you my deepest darkest secrets. Everything except this. You know about my tumultuous relationship with my mum and dad, just not—'

'Just not the truth about the most important person in your life.' Quinn stood as if to leave. 'I guess I thought we were better friends than that.'

Deb grabbed her hand and pulled her back down onto the bench. 'We *are* those friends. Please don't go.'

She couldn't allow Quinn to leave, not yet, not when she was angry. She couldn't risk her walking back into the office and confronting Oscar with these accusations.

'Friends don't just tell each other things,' Quinn said, shaking her hand free. 'They also look out for each other. *If* what you're saying about Oscar is true, why didn't you warn me the moment he started work?'

'You can be angry at me all you like, but please be careful. I *am* telling the truth.'

Quinn scoffed. 'Why should I believe you? It's not like you've never lied to me before.'

'Okay.' Deb sighed. 'I deserve that, but I promise I'm telling the truth about this. Oscar is dark just like his name.' At the look of incredulity on Quinn's face, she continued to plead her case. 'He was a dangerous, manipulative man when we were together, and I have no doubt he's even more dangerous now. His charm is a front, you've got to believe me. In fact, I think he might be playing games with both of us already.'

'What do you mean?' Quinn asked uncertainly.

'The other day I got stuck in the elevator with him and Steve, but … he didn't recognise me.'

'How long were you together?'

'Just over six months.'

Quinn frowned. 'That doesn't make sense. If you were together that long, he'd remember.'

'I know. At first, I clutched onto the hope that maybe he really had forgotten me, but Tristan thinks—'

'You told *Tristan* about this before you told me? I thought you said things weren't even that serious between you. Guess that was just another one of your lies.'

'Quinn, please, you're being unreasonable.'

'*I'm* being unreasonable?' Quinn spoke so loudly a pigeon that had been pecking in the dirt a few feet away sprang into the air.

'That wasn't a lie,' Deb said. 'I only just told Tristan last night. I'd been too stressed to see him or talk to him, and when he came and confronted me, I unloaded. He made me realise I had to tell you, but I'm risking *Ramona's* wellbeing, possibly even her safety, by doing so. You have to promise me you won't say a word about her to Oscar.'

'So, let me get this straight. If it wasn't for Tristan, you'd never have told me.'

'I would have. Eventually. I almost said something in the copy room last Monday when you asked me to look up his details, but Lexi interrupted us.'

'Don't give me that bullshit,' Quinn fired, tugging her earring so ferociously Deb feared she might rip it right through her lobe.

'You've had a hundred chances since then. Even if you didn't run into me on my street last week, you could have messaged. You could have bloody called.'

'I know, I'm sorry.' Deb sniffed. 'I thought maybe I could just wait and see if anything developed between you and Oscar. If it looked like you were getting closer, that maybe he felt the same way about you, I *would* have said something, I promise, but I figured you might lose interest in him first. Like you usually do.'

The moment Deb admitted this she knew she shouldn't have.

'Oh my God.' Quinn looked at her like she was a stranger and her eyes glistened. 'You've just been humouring me. All the time we've known each other, I've been waiting for the connection I felt when I first met Oscar. I told you it was different with him, and I thought you of all people believed me.'

'It wasn't a case of believing you or not, but you've got to admit, the whole meeting someone random on the street and deciding they're your soulmate is a bit far-fetched. Life doesn't work that way.'

'Maybe not for you.' Quinn gave her a scornful look. 'But maybe that's because you've shut yourself up in your own little world for so long. Well, sue me for being optimistic and seeing the good in people. For believing in love at first sight.'

They sat there in silence for a few moments. Deb wasn't sure what else to say. Perhaps Quinn was right. Perhaps she did struggle to see the good in people. But so much of that was to do with Oscar. And her mother. It was hard when she'd had the experiences she had.

Quinn pressed her fingers against her forehead. 'None of this makes any sense. You think he's *pretending* not to know who you are? Why would he do that?'

'Who knows why Oscar does anything? He's a psycho! The only thing I know is that he's playing games. Even if it's a coincidence he turned up at The Energy Co—although I can't help wondering about the timing coinciding with me putting myself online—there's no way he doesn't recognise me. Best-case scenario, he decided not to say anything because he doesn't want me to tell anyone what he's like, but …' She paused for breath. 'Worst-case scenario, he knew I worked here when he applied for the job, or he recognised me that first afternoon in the office. When I was sitting next to *you*.'

'You think he's only being friendly to me because he's trying to get to you?' Quinn said in an unsteady voice. 'Is it that hard to believe that any guy would be into me without an ulterior motive?'

'Don't be silly, of course it's not. You're charismatic, smart, creative and beautiful. Your issue has never been not having men interested in you, rather that you're always wondering if the next guy you swipe left on will be better.'

'You mean swipe right.' Quinn pushed to her feet again before Deb could answer, then glared down at her. 'I can't believe this. You not only lied to me and to Ramona, but you've kept a man's child from him.'

'For very good reasons,' Deb snapped, standing as well, losing patience now. She felt like shaking Quinn. 'He's dangerous. I could not submit Ramona to an abusive parent.'

'You don't know Oscar would have been abusive.'

'After what he did to me, it wasn't something I was prepared to risk, but I don't need to justify myself to you. You don't have children, so you can't understand.'

'Okay then.' Quinn turned and stalked off.

Oh, no, no, no, no. Tossing the apple to the ground, Deb raced after her.

'Quinn!' she screamed, not caring about the looks they were getting from other park-goers. 'Quinn. Come back!'

Her friend didn't turn her head and, even walking, she was bloody fast.

Deb caught up to her at the traffic lights and thankfully the pedestrian crossing was red.

'You're not still going to pursue him, are you?'

'I don't know what I'm going to do,' Quinn replied coldly.

Deb's whole body trembled. 'You can't tell him,' she begged. 'Please. I'll do anything.'

Quinn folded her arms and narrowed her eyes. 'I'm not making any promises. I need time to think.'

And then the light went green and she charged across the street, leaving Deb standing on the pavement, once again struggling to breathe. As other pedestrians strode by, she reached out to steady herself on the sign post. Traffic whizzed past but all she could hear was her own heartbeat thrashing in her ears.

She yanked her phone out of her bag and called the office.

'Lexi,' she said when the receptionist answered. 'It's Debra Fast. I was out for lunch, and something's come up with my daughter. I won't be back in today.'

She hung up before Lexi could ask any questions.

Quinn

'Did you go for a run on your lunchbreak?' asked Linc as Quinn barrelled back into their cubicle. She was panting and sweating, not so much from exertion as shock.

'No,' she replied in a voice that warned him not to ask any further questions, before sinking into her seat and trying to lose herself in her work.

She'd lied when she said she needed time to think. Truthfully, she'd rather forget what Deb had told her, but like a nightmare you wake up from and immediately return to when you fall back asleep, their conversation refused to leave her alone.

Dark like his name, she silently scoffed. How long did it take Deb to come up with that one? Perhaps that's what she'd been doing this whole time when she could have been talking to Quinn.

After working on one Instagram post for an hour, she shot an email to her boss, saying she was going home with 'women's issues' and left her cubicle without even a goodbye to her colleagues. She walked the long way to the elevators, so as not to pass payroll, and swore as they took their usual sweet time to come. Down on the street below, she skated through the park and then up Oxford Street, trying to work off some of the tension that had formed inside her since Deb's confession.

She was still reeling from all her friend had said—that Oscar had locked her up like a prisoner for two days, stalked her, threatened to ruin her if she went to the police, filmed her without her consent—it sounded like something from a thriller novel, yet she knew these things happened. The difference was, usually people only heard about it when they'd escalated to murder.

Quinn shuddered—still unable to believe that Oscar could do any of these things—and stopped as she realised she'd ended up outside the hospital.

Mrs D was sleeping when Quinn got to her room, but a nurse she recognised from the weekend encouraged her to go in anyway.

'She'll probably wake up soon, and she was a little glum this morning so a friendly familiar face will do her good.'

'Glum?' Quinn asked. Maybe she should have taken another week off work to sit with her until her daughter could take over.

'It's not unusual.' He tapped the side of his head. 'The brain is impacted by the stroke and that affects behaviour and emotions. In Muriel's case, as far as we can tell, her mental capacity hasn't been affected too badly, but the connections from brain to mouth aren't operating properly, so she'll be feeling very frustrated.'

'Is there anything I can do to help?'

'Just be here for her. Tell her things about your day but try not to ask questions, because not being able to answer them could cause her to get agitated and upset.'

'Right.' Quinn nodded. It was the same advice she'd been getting since the beginning. 'I can do that. Thanks.'

'I'll leave you to it,' the nurse said with an encouraging smile.

Quinn dragged the lone visitor chair close to the bed and put her hand gently on Mrs D's. The older woman didn't even stir at the connection. Her skin felt cold, and she was almost as pale as the grey walls as she lay in the adjustable bed with its plastic cover, side rails and boring white hospital sheets.

The only sounds were the gentle whirr of medical machinery and muffled noises from out in the corridor. The silence gave Quinn too much time to think. She wished she could put the TV on, but the doctors and nurses had told her too much stimulation could be confusing for the patient. She glanced around for something to distract her and noticed that the two massive flower arrangements from Mrs D's daughters were starting to wilt. At least she could give the drooping blooms some water. She headed into the tiny sterile bathroom to fill a paper cup and was overjoyed to see Mrs D awake on her return.

She abandoned the water on the moveable table and scooped up her friend's hand again.

'Well, good afternoon, Muriel,' she said with a grin. 'Nice of you to finally wake up. I skived off work to come hang with you, you know?'

The moment she said this, she realised Mrs D might not have the mental capacity to find it funny but relaxed when the older woman's lips lifted slightly at one side. She gave her hand a squeeze and racked her mind for something to say. Not being able to ask questions or say anything that might distress her limited her options.

'Snoodles misses you,' she said eventually. 'At least I'm giving him the benefit of the doubt and telling myself that's why he decimated my slippers.'

'Oh … no.'

These words didn't come out of Mrs D's mouth, but Quinn's lip-reading skills told her this was what she meant.

'It's okay,' she rushed, kicking herself. 'They were cheap ones from Kmart anyway and now I've got an excuse to buy the fancy pair I've been eyeing off at Peter Alexander. Maybe I'll buy us a matching pair to wear on our movie nights.'

Mrs D didn't say anything, but her shoulders seemed to relax at these words.

'Speaking of movies, there's a new rom-com starring Selena Gomez coming out in a few weeks. We should go watch it together.' Positive thinking and all. 'Would you like me to massage your hands? They feel a little cold.'

Mrs D blinked once, and Quinn took this as a yes. Thankful for something to do, she dug some hand cream out of her bag and began. While she rubbed in gentle circles, she told Mrs D how she'd stripped the sheets in her spare room and made up the bed for Crystal who would be arriving on Thursday. But it was draining upholding a one-sided conversation, especially when her mind kept wandering.

Would Deb really concoct such a ridiculous lie? Could Quinn herself be so wrong about someone?

Lost in her own thoughts, she barely noticed when Mrs D's mouth moved, and a strangled noise came out.

'I'm sorry, I didn't quite catch that,' she said, leaning forward, desperate to comprehend.

'Yur fingy ... Burt.'

Her Burt? She followed Mrs D's gaze as she tried to work out who the hell Burt was, and registered her bandaid.

'Oh, my finger.' *Hurt, not Burt.* 'Don't worry. It's fine. Remember that list I told you about—the husband one? One of the suggestions was wearing a bandaid so eligible men stop and ask what happened.' She shrugged. 'Conversation starter, I guess. I was hoping Oscar would see it at work today but ...'

Her voice trailed off as the emotion she'd been trying to keep under control bubbled to the surface again. What exactly that emotion was, she didn't know. Was she sad, angry, disappointed or a confusing cocktail of all three?

She was hurt Deb had never trusted her enough to tell her the truth about Ramona and angry she'd insinuated Quinn was a silly spoiled brat who lived her charmed life up in the clouds. It wasn't her fault she'd had a good childhood, and it didn't make her shallow either. It didn't mean she couldn't empathise with those who'd been less fortunate.

Is that really why you're mad? Or is it because your hopes and dreams about Oscar have all been dashed?

Can't I be both? she silently retorted to her subconscious. *And sceptical?*

Thanks to the MeToo movement, Quinn knew that as a woman she was immediately supposed to believe accusations of abuse, but part of her wanted to believe that Deb *was* lying. It was better than believing all she'd said about Oscar.

She might have only known him a short while, but there'd been nothing in any of their interactions that would suggest he was anything but a sweet thoughtful man. He'd been lovely to Snoodles—didn't psychopaths usually hate animals? In his email, he'd even offered to help, and he'd given her the world's best donut because she'd been away when he delivered treats last week.

Then again, if she analysed that gesture without her rose-coloured glasses on, would she think it a little OTT? Maybe morning tea for his immediate team, but *everyone* in the office?

Was he too good to be true? And could Deb be right about him being nice simply because he wanted to use Quinn to get info on her?

I'm very good with names and faces.

That's what he'd told her last week when she mentioned Deb, yet Deb said he acted like he didn't recognise her. Quinn shivered. Now she thought about it, had that sounded a little sinister? Almost like a threat. Could it have been a warning? One she was supposed to pass on to Deb? *Argh.*

Mrs D flinched, and Quinn immediately let go. 'I'm sorry.' Distracted by her thoughts, she'd started to rub too hard. 'So sorry. I didn't mean to hurt you, it's just …'

No, she would not unload on her sick friend.

But she felt tears burning behind her eyeballs and turned her head, pressing the backs of her hands against her eyes to stop from crying.

'Geez, there must be something in the air in here,' she said with a forced chuckle.

When she thought she'd managed to avoid full-blown waterworks, she summoned a smile and looked back to Mrs D, only to find the older woman staring at her.

'It wh-at is?' Mrs D managed, her brow furrowing slightly.

Quinn shook her head. 'Don't worry. I'm fine. It's nothing. Really.'

Mrs D might not be able to communicate as well with her words as she once could, but she managed to give a stern look that reminded Quinn of the one her mother gave her when she knew she wasn't telling her the whole story.

She sighed. 'Looks like Oscar Darke might not be my Ride or Die after all. Turns out that Deb—if she can be believed and I'm still trying to work that out—had a relationship with him years ago.'

Mrs D blinked rapidly as if she was struggling to keep up, so Quinn slowed right down. 'I'm sorry. You know my friend from work I told you about? Debra? The one who was going to come watch movies at your place with her daughter? Anyway, she always told me Ramona was conceived via donor sperm but turns out that was a lie. Oscar is apparently her father. She never told him she was pregnant. She says he'd been abusive to her, and she didn't want to risk him finding out about their unborn child and possibly hurting her too. Deb says I should stay clear of him. She reckons he's dark, just like his surname.'

Her free hand drifted to her earring, and she fiddled with it as she always did when she was stressed.

'Darle?'

'Darke,' Quinn corrected. 'His name is Oscar Darke. I thought it was such a sexy name, but Deb reckons he's Darke by name, dark by nature.'

She tried to laugh it off, but as much as she desperately didn't want to believe it, what reason would Deb possibly have to make it up?

Mrs D tried to speak but her words came out in a slurred jumble. Quinn couldn't make head nor tail of them, but the expression on her face showed distress.

'Hey, it's okay. Don't worry about me. Whatever the truth, I'm a big girl and I can look after myself. All you need to worry about is getting rest and getting better.'

'Him. No.' Mrs D shook her head, at least that's what it looked like she was trying to do. 'Eh-Eh-Eh Ick.'

Eh? Ick?

Quinn paused, her heart aching for the poor woman who must feel so frustrated right now, and then it clicked. Maybe she was talking about her husband—Eddie. Her heart cracked even further. Mrs D's daughters were still on the other side of the world, and she missed her husband as well. Quinn could only imagine how alone she must be feeling. Perhaps talking about Oscar had reminded her of her own love.

'Would you like me to bring in a photo of Eddie? Maybe the one of you and him that's on the fridge?'

Mrs D sighed and closed her eyes as if exhausted. A tear slicked down her cheek.

Quinn had never felt so helpless in her whole life. It certainly put her own worries into perspective. She reached up and stroked the papery-thin skin of her forehead, trying to soothe her friend in the same way her mam had comforted her when she was young.

After a while Mrs D's breathing grew heavier, and she fell into slumber again.

Debra

Deb ran harder, faster, and further than she'd ever run before—it was either that or succumb to the desire to crawl into bed and drink until she passed out. It was only the thought of Ramona finding her in such a state again that had her putting on her sneakers instead. Over the last couple of months, she'd discovered running could clear her head unlike anything else, but it did nothing to ease her anxiety today.

She should never have told Quinn. What had she been thinking playing Russian Roulette with Ramona's life like that?

As she ran, she tried to call her friend, but all her efforts went immediately to voicemail.

'Dammit, Quinn! Be a grown-up and answer your bloody phone.'

Usually when she saw other joggers texting or scrolling on their phones while exercising, she'd inwardly shake her head, but today her fingers were working almost as hard as her feet.

Please, Quinn. Pick up.

I'm sorry.

Can we talk?

You have every right to be angry but please think of Ramona.

Please don't say anything to Oscar.

What would he do if Quinn decided to reveal all? Would he confront Deb at work? What if he found out where she lived and came to the apartment?

Worse, what if he bypassed her and hunted down Ramona? That thought made her feel as if she *had* been hit by a bus.

How far would he go? Having locked her in a room for forty-eight hours, as good as leaving her to die, Deb could only imagine what he might do to get revenge for keeping his daughter from him all these years.

News stories flashed into her head—dads shooting their kids, fathers driving children off bridges, men making their exes watch as they killed their children before setting fire to them. These disasters were reported almost as regularly as politicians behaving badly.

Desperate, she tried Quinn's number again, but of course, she didn't pick up. Deb tried the office instead.

'Good afternoon, The Energy Co, this is Lexi. How may I direct your call?'

'Hi, Lexi, it's Debra Fast,' she panted. 'Can you—'

'Are you okay? You sound like you've run a marathon. How's your daughter?'

'I'm fine. She's … fine. Can you put me through to Quinn, please?'

'Sure, one moment.' A jingle about the new wellbeing drink irritated her eardrums before Lexi returned to the line. 'Sorry, Deb, Quinn appears to have left for the day as well. You've got her mobile right?'

'Yes,' Deb said and then hung up.

Quinn, please. I'm desperate. If you don't want to talk to me, fine, but if you do tell him, at least give me a heads up.

Deb wasn't sure what she'd do if Quinn did but forewarned was forearmed and all that.

It was then she looked up and realised she had no idea where she was. Her feet were aching and her tongue so desperate for the water she hadn't had the forethought to bring that it darted out of her mouth to lick the sweat pouring down her face.

She collapsed onto the pavement and wept. This was all Tristan's fault. She'd never have told Quinn if he hadn't convinced her it was the right thing to do. How had she let some virtual stranger dictate her life like this?

I told her, she texted him. *And now she's not speaking to me. She'll probably tell Oscar.*

Her phone rang immediately.

'Deb, are you okay? What happened?' Tristan asked when she answered.

'I told her like you said I should, and she got mad and stormed off. I'm scared. I'm terrified she's going to tell Oscar.'

'Are you outside? It's hard to hear you.'

Until he mentioned it she'd barely registered the wind and the traffic shooting past. 'I'm running. At least I was …'

'Deb, tell me where you are.'

'I'm …' She glanced around, her surrounds unfamiliar. 'I'm not exactly sure. Let me check the map on my phone.'

'Geez,' he said, when she told him her location. 'Stay right there. I'm on my way.'

It took him twenty minutes to arrive and when he did, he pulled over on the side of the road, leapt out and jogged towards her.

'I can't believe you ran all this way?' he said.

'I needed to clear my head.'

'And has it worked?'

'No.' In fact, she felt more than a little woozy.

'Come on.' He offered his hand to help her up. 'Let's get you into the car.'

'Thanks.'

Wrapping an arm around her, Tristan ushered her into the passenger seat. 'Sorry about the dog hair. Hammer's usually my only passenger these days.'

'It's fine.' She kinda wished the dog was here—he'd been such a comfort during their conversation along the river.

As they drove, she put her head back and closed her eyes, too exhausted—mentally and physically—to speak.

When the car stopped, she opened her eyes to find they were in the driveway of a beautiful Federation-style house with an immaculately kept garden out the front. 'Where are we?'

'My place. It was closer,' he said, coming around to open her door. 'You look like you need a stiff drink and a bath.'

'A bath?' She couldn't undress and bathe in front of him, although her aching muscles kind of liked the idea.

'Relax,' he said, once again offering his hand. 'I'm not trying to have my wicked way. You've had a shock, and this will help, I promise.'

'Okay.' She was too weary to argue.

Hammer greeted them enthusiastically the moment they entered the house.

'Make yourself at home,' Tristan told her. 'I'll start running the bath and be back in a moment.'

Despite still being shaken, she had the wherewithal to look around. The house was decorated in warm tones with lots of photos and bright bold rugs on the floor. It wasn't pristine—there were shoes in the hallway and a jumble of dog leashes in a basket—but it was clean. She stepped into the living room, where two black cats sat side by side on a leather sofa and a large wedding photo hung in pride of place above the mantelpiece. Tristan and Marie, gazing into each other's eyes and looking blissfully in love.

'I should probably take that down,' he said, startling her as he came up behind her with a tumbler half-filled with amber liquid. 'You've had a shock. Get this into you.'

'Thanks.' She couldn't remember the last time she'd drunk whiskey, but it hit the spot, its warmth spreading through her like wildfire. 'You have a beautiful house.'

'I'm thinking of redecorating. The walls haven't been painted since the kids were little, but it's a matter of finding the time to work out what I want to do.'

Deb smiled as she sipped the drink.

Tristan took her hand. 'Come on.'

He led her down the hallway and then upstairs into his bedroom, Hammer trundling along behind them. Her gaze fell on the king-size bed with its blue-checked doona and her stomach tightened. When they entered the ensuite, she gasped at the sight of a gorgeous clawfoot bath, the water running as bubbles inched closer to the top.

'I can't remember the last time I had a bath.' Their rental apartments didn't usually have such luxuries.

'Well, I hope you enjoy it.' He smiled and gestured to the wall. 'There're clean towels on the rack, and I took the liberty of grabbing you a change of clothes from Tara's bedroom. I think they'll fit. I'll be downstairs when you're done, but take your time. Try and relax.'

'Thank you. I will.'

'Hammer, come?' Tristan barked as he turned to leave but the dog had settled itself on the bathmat and refused to follow.

'It's fine. He can stay,' Deb said, smiling down at him. Although a different breed, there was something in his eyes that reminded her of Doogie and provided a comfort she desperately needed right now.

Tristan shut the door behind him, and Deb removed her sweaty clothes, switched off the water and sank down into the bubbles. *Bliss.* Her overworked muscles relaxed in the warm water, and it was impossible not to feel slightly calmer while enveloped in the silky, vanilla-scented bubbles.

She sighed. If only she could stay in this bath forever.

She thought of Quinn again, and felt a bone-numbing sadness at the knowledge she'd hurt her closest friend. Would she ever be able to mend that rift?

And what if Quinn *did* tell Oscar?

Deb had never seen Quinn so angry and upset as she'd been in the park, but deep down she wanted to believe that once she'd calmed, she'd come around and realise Deb had never meant to hurt her. Her only hope was that Quinn wouldn't go to Oscar and confront him with Deb's accusations first.

When the water grew cool, her fingers began pruning and Hammer started whining at the door, she pulled the plug, climbed out of the bath, and wrapped herself in one of the soft, fluffy bath sheets. She shivered as she imagined this same towel wrapped around Tristan's naked body, then dried herself quickly and dressed in the clothes he'd left out.

A delicious aroma hit her the moment she started down the stairs, and she found Tristan in the kitchen, wearing an apron with 'Dog Dad' on it and standing over the sink washing up pots and pans.

'Been cooking?'

He turned and smiled at her. 'I made you my mum's macaroni cheese—it's what she used to make for me when I was studying for exams or when I was upset about something. Comfort food.' He nodded towards the breakfast bar. 'Take a seat.'

Deb did as she was told but couldn't find the wherewithal to speak. He'd cooked for her. Tears welled in her eyes.

'Hey, don't cry,' Tristan said, drying his hands quickly on a tea towel and then coming around to give her a hug. 'It'll be okay.'

That only made her sob harder. 'I can't remember the last time someone cooked for me.' For so long she'd been on her own with Ramona and she'd been the one doing the looking after. Even as a child she'd never had this kind of devotion. It felt unbelievably good to have someone taking care of her for a change.

He gave her another quick squeeze before scooping some macaroni cheese into a bowl. He also poured them each a glass of pinot grigio.

Deb gobbled up the food like a kid who hadn't eaten for days. 'This is so good.'

Tristan gave her a smug smile.

'Did you have to cancel any appointments to come get me?' Now that she had food in her stomach, she was starting to think straight again.

'I called in a favour from a colleague and she's covering my appointments this afternoon, but I would have cancelled if need be.'

The fact he'd have put her before sick animals made her feel both guilty and gratified.

'Do you want to tell me what exactly happened with Quinn?' he asked.

Deb took another sip of wine and then relayed their conversation in the park.

'So, you're not certain she's going to tell Oscar,' he said when she'd finished.

'For all I know, she's already told him. I'm thinking maybe it's time to go home, pack a suitcase, throw all our important documents into a car and move on again.'

Ramona would be furious—she'd miss her new friends and be devastated about the fashion program, but as long as she was safe, nothing else mattered.

'That's not the answer, Deb.' Tristan spoke so adamantly, she blinked. 'It's not fair on Ramona and it's not fair on you, either. You can't keep running away because of this man. You've let your fear of what he might do dominate your life for sixteen years. Maybe it's time to face him.'

It was easy for Tristan to say—he wasn't the one risking his kids or himself. She opened her mouth to respond, but he got in first.

'You're not the same person you were when you met him. You're more worldly, you've survived on your own, taking care of yourself and Ramona, and you shouldn't let scum like him rule your life.'

It sounded like Tristan had more faith in her than she did.

'Maybe you should even tell Ramona. That way, whatever happens, she'll be prepared as well.'

'No.' Telling Ramona was a last resort, something she'd only consider if she had proof that Oscar knew about her. 'She's not mature enough to handle the truth. And if I tell her, I know she'll want to meet him, no matter what I say about him.'

'Okay,' Tristan relented. 'You know her best, but whatever you decide, whatever happens, know that I'm here for you. You're not in this alone anymore.'

Deb put down her glass and reached across the counter to take his hand, overwhelmed with emotion for this kind, caring, beautiful man. 'Why do you want to be with me?' she asked. 'I'm a mess. My life is one big fat shitshow.' She laughed nervously as he met her gaze. 'And you could have anyone.'

'I don't want just anyone,' he said. 'At our age, everyone has baggage—this is yours. But I've smiled more in the short time we've spent together than I have in all the years that Marie's been gone. I know my heart. And it wants you.'

She thought about Tristan's baggage—his grief over the loss of his wife and the challenge of trying to work out how much of her to hold onto and how much to let go—and she realised she didn't want to run anymore.

Ramona

On Wednesday afternoon, Ramona was counting down the minutes until the end-of-day siren when an email landed in her inbox.

'Oh my God,' she muttered under her breath as she registered who it was from. She'd known it could be arriving any time soon, but now that it was here, she couldn't quite believe it.

'What is it?' Lucy whispered.

She now sat begrudgingly beside Ramona in most of the classes they shared, but this was the first time she'd so much as opened her mouth this period.

'I've just got the results from the DNA testing company.'

'Oh my goodness. Are you serious? Does it … tell you anything?'

'I don't know.' Ramona felt sick, suddenly unsure she should have done this. Her mum would kill her for going behind her back and she couldn't help remembering what Elijah said about the possibility of his dad being a deadbeat. Maybe hers was too? Then again, surely sperm donors had to meet certain standards? 'I haven't opened it yet.'

'Girls!' said Ms Lovegrove sharply. 'These equations do not require discussion. If you need any help, come and see me.'

'Sorry, Ms Lovegrove,' they chanted.

But while Lucy returned to work, Ramona could no longer focus on algebra. How could she think about maths when the answers to one half of who she was could possibly be sitting in that email?

Holding her breath, she opened it.

After a brief intro thanking her for using their company and wishing her the best with her 'connections', there were two sections. The first had a pie graph that showed her 'genetic ethnicity' and a map of the world highlighted in certain places. She was overwhelmingly Scandinavian and British with a touch of Eastern European, but it wasn't her ethnicity that truly interested her. Her gaze leapt down the page, her heart thudding, as she went to the 'matches' part of the report.

And there it was, right at the top: 'Parent/Child' and under that—Oscar Darke. Confidence: Extremely High. Relationship: Oscar Darke is your father.

Oscar Darke.

She read his name again and then tried it with her own: *Ramona Darke.*

It sounded far cooler than Ramona Fast, but then it hit her that this stranger's name belonged to an actual person. A person who—according to the DNA results—was her dad.

From all she'd read in the lead-up to the test, finding such a match first go was rare. There were multiple companies that provided this kind of testing and if her father had done one, it could have been with any of them, so she hadn't expected to hit the jackpot so soon and so easily.

'I'm going to be sick.' She pushed back her chair and ran from the classroom, not even bothering to make excuses to Ms Lovegrove.

Thankfully, the nearest bathroom wasn't far, and she made it to the sink before her lunch made a reappearance. It wasn't pretty, but the icky taste in her mouth was nothing on the icky feeling in her heart at having gone behind her mum's back.

The door opened and Ramona glanced sideways to see Lucy enter.

'Miss Lovegrove sent me to check on you,' she said, and then locked the door behind her.

'You might get in trouble for doing that,' Ramona managed.

'I don't care.' Lucy crossed the tiles to her side, then grimaced down at the mess in the sink. 'I'd ask if you're okay but that would clearly be a stupid question. Did you read the email?'

Ramona wiped her mouth and then nodded as she began to rinse out the sink. 'There's a parental match. It actually names my father.'

'Serious?' Lucy asked, her eyebrows creeping upwards.

Ramona opened her mouth to confirm but a wave of nausea came over her again and she turned, this time to dry retch into the sink.

'Were there any other matches?' Lucy asked, rubbing her hand gently on Ramona's back. 'Like cousins or ... siblings?'

Heartened by Lucy's touch, Ramona pulled herself together.

She took a deep breath and splashed her face with water. 'I didn't even get that far. I thought I wanted to know who my dad is, but I also thought it was a long shot. I thought maybe I'd find a second cousin or something and have time to work out whether to contact them or not and take this further, but ... his name was right there.'

'You don't have to do anything about it,' Lucy said. 'Not now, not ever if you don't want to.'

This relaxed Ramona momentarily until she remembered skimming the T&Cs when she took the test. 'I think he'll be alerted to the match as well. Anyone who's registered with the site gets an email when a new connection turns up. What if *he* contacts *me*?'

OMG. She was suddenly hyperventilating. Wanting to know about someone in theory turned out to be a lot different to finding information in real life.

'Take a deep breath,' Lucy said. 'And try and drink some water. You've only just got the match, you need time to digest it and work out what you want to do next. Even if he does message you, you don't have to reply—immediately or ever.'

Ramona nodded, turned on the tap again and formed her hands into a cup to try and get a drink. The cool water at least helped ease the horrid taste in her mouth.

'Thanks for coming in here,' she said to Lucy, 'but please don't tell anyone why I was sick.' She didn't want Sydney and the others to find out, even if they'd likely no longer care.

Lucy tilted her head to one side. 'Who exactly am I going to tell?'

Ramona gave a wry smile before sniffing and wiping her eyes. 'I know things haven't been great between us lately, and I'm sorry I didn't stick up for you right in the very beginning.'

'No, *I'm* sorry,' Lucy said. 'I'm sorry I didn't accept your apology. I wasn't sure I could trust you. I thought maybe you were only pretending to befriend me so you could feed stuff about me back to Malfoy, Crabbe and Goyle.'

Ramona snorted at the nicknames. 'I promise I'd never do that.'

'And I was also kind of punishing you. I guess that doesn't make me much better than them.'

'I get it,' Ramona said. 'I hadn't given you much reason to trust me. But I promise you, even if they hadn't banished me to schoolyard hell, once I saw the light, once I heard about just how much they'd done to you, I could never be friends with them again.'

Lucy grinned and threw her arms around Ramona, which must mean she was forgiven—only a true friend would hug someone moments after they'd spewed.

'So … if they're Malfoy, Crabbe and Goyle …' she said when they came apart, 'will you be the Harry Potter to my Ron?'

'Are you *crazy*?' Lucy grabbed hold of her thick frizzy ponytail. 'With hair like this, I'm definitely a Weasley. You'll have to be Harry Potter. You can borrow my glasses if you want.'

Ramona laughed.

'You gunna be okay?' Lucy asked, her expression turning serious again.

'I dunno.'

'Do you want to go back to class, or do you want me to take you to the sick bay and then grab your things?'

Ramona shook her head. 'They'll call Mum and then …'

'She'll want to know what's wrong?'

'Yeah. She's always been able to tell when I'm faking it or if I'm worried rather than sick.'

Lucy shrugged. 'It's almost the end of the day anyway. Come back to class and you can copy my answers.'

'Thanks.' Ramona sniffed and checked her reflection in the mirror. She looked awful, but she didn't care if that gave Sydney even more ammunition. She had Lucy onside again, and together they'd survive whatever the others threw at them.

Besides, she had bigger fish to fry.

'Do you think I should tell my mum?' Ramona asked as they headed back to class.

Lucy paused and turned to her. 'If that's what you want, maybe it's not a bad idea. If she sees you've gone to this much trouble to find out who your father is, then maybe she'll understand how important it is to you.'

'I think she'll probably just yell and shout and punish me for going behind her back.'

'Maybe at first, but parents sometimes fly off the handle before they come to their senses. After she's calmed down, maybe you can work out what to do next together? Maybe she'll go with you to meet this guy?'

'Does Jake ever fly off the handle?' Ramona asked, unable to imagine it.

Lucy smirked. 'He's a priest, not a saint.'

This made Ramona chuckle. 'I guess I'll think about it,' she said, feeling her tension easing. 'Thanks again for being here for me.'

'Don't mention it.' Lucy squeezed her hand. 'Now come on, we better get back before Lovegrove sends out a search party.'

The rest of the period went by in a blur, but Ramona did manage to come to one conclusion. Having information about her dad at her fingertips was scarier than she'd imagined, and she also felt the weight of guilt for going behind her mum's back to get it. When the siren finally rang, she headed for the train station as usual, but this time, instead of going home, she got out at Museum, just beneath The Energy Co building.

Debra

Deb's heart leapt as Quinn's head popped over the top of her cubicle late afternoon. The last couple of days had been hell. If it wasn't for Tristan, she'd have fallen completely apart.

Quinn giving her the cold shoulder was killing her. She dared not send an email because she didn't want to risk anyone else seeing it but neither did she want to confront her in front of Linc and Toby. The one thing keeping her sane was that she hadn't heard so much as a squeak from Oscar since the elevator incident.

Surely, if Quinn had told him, he'd have confronted her!

'Hello,' Deb said tentatively. 'How are you?'

'Ramona's here,' Quinn hissed, her eyes darting around.

Deb sat up straight as fear stabbed at her heart. 'What?' She leapt from her seat, scattering the papers on her desk onto the floor. 'Where?'

'I ran into her in reception. Lexi was just about to buzz you, but I said I'd handle it. I put her in the ladies' restroom and told her to stay put.'

'Did anyone else ... *see* her?' Deb's heart was racing so fast she could barely get the words out. They both knew what she really meant was, did *Oscar* see her?

'I don't think so. I'll keep him distracted downstairs while you get rid of her,' Quinn whispered.

Then, without another word, she turned and headed back the way she'd come. Deb stood frozen for what felt like eternity before finally snapping into action.

Ignoring the papers scattered at her feet and the bewildered looks from her colleagues, she raced down the corridor towards the bathroom.

'Where's the fire?' asked No Mates Nate as she almost barrelled into him.

She didn't reply and arrived in the restroom moments later to find Ramona exactly where Quinn said she'd be. As the door thunked shut behind her, she took a brief moment to scan the cubicles to check they were alone before asking, 'What on earth are you doing here?'

Ramona blinked. 'I'm just ... visiting. I thought I'd surprise you and maybe we could catch the train home together. I *thought* you'd be happy to see me.'

Her breathing still ragged from the shock and her mad dash down the corridor, Deb felt awful. 'I'm always happy to see you, sweetheart, it's just ... remember I told you I'm working late tonight?'

'No,' Ramona said flatly.

Deb frowned. 'I'm sure I did.'

'How late are you gunna be? And why?'

'Today's my last day, remember? I told you about the job offer I got yesterday.' The moment she'd accepted, she'd handed her resignation to Shaun.

'Yeah, but I didn't know you were finishing today.'

Deb struggled not to show her frustration. Did Ramona ever listen to anything she said? Or had her head been so full of Oscar that she'd forgotten to mention it? 'Yes, I decided to take my notice as holiday leave, so I need to wrap up everything before I leave tonight.'

If she had to stay until midnight to get it all done, well, that was a price she was willing to pay.

'Oh, right.' Ramona nodded. 'Sorry, I forgot.'

'It doesn't matter.' Deb grabbed Ramona's arm and started tugging her towards the door. 'I'm not exactly sure what time I'll be home, but I left dinner for you in the fridge. You just need to heat it up in the microwave.'

At least she'd had the forethought to do that.

Ramona dragged her feet. 'Can I stay here and help you?'

'Help me?' Deb scoffed, fear strangling her at the thought. 'What do you know about numbers?'

'I didn't mean I could do your actual work, but maybe I could do some photocopying, help you file stuff, or just offer moral support.'

'No.' Deb took a quick breath. 'That's a lovely offer, but you need to get out of here. Come on.'

Ramona yanked out of her grip. 'What's going on? Usually you hate leaving me home alone at night.'

'Nothing, I've just got a lot of work to do, and I'll do it faster without an audience. Besides, haven't you been asking me for more responsibility? For me to trust you. This is me giving you the chance to prove you don't need a babysitter.'

'Bullcrap.' Ramona folded her arms, standing her ground. 'Both you and Quinn are acting weird. Why didn't she just take me to your office?'

For once, Deb wished her daughter was a little less whip-smart. 'We're not supposed to bring our kids into the office except on special days,' she lied. 'I need a good reference, so I can't be seen to be breaking the rules just because it's my last day.'

'Why do you need a reference if you've already got another job? And why should you care what your boss here thinks—he's the one getting rid of you, right? Isn't that what you told me? Something about a restructure?'

Deb swallowed. This was the problem with lying—the more you told, the easier it was to get caught out. But sometimes white lies were necessary for the greater good. 'It's never good to burn bridges. But I promise I'll make it up to you later.'

'Fine,' Ramona relented. 'I'll go. I wouldn't want to stuff things up for you.'

Deb ignored her sarcastic tone and pulled her into a hug. She pressed a kiss against her forehead, silently praying Quinn still had Oscar under guard. 'Come on, I'll see you out.'

Ramona didn't say a word as they walked to the elevators and Deb was too busy keeping an eye out to speak. She glanced at reception as they waited for the elevator, shuddering as she imagined what might have happened if Oscar had been there when Ramona arrived.

'I can make my own way down,' Ramona said.

'I'll walk you to the station,' Deb insisted. She wouldn't breathe easy until she saw her daughter safely out of the building and onto the train.

Today they'd come too close to calamity. She berated herself for still being here—she should have vanished the moment Shaun introduced Oscar.

'Have a good afternoon, honey,' Deb called, trying to keep her voice light as she waved Ramona through the ticket gate.

'Good luck with getting all your work done,' she replied despondently, before disappearing into the crowd.

It wasn't until she was on her way back that Deb wondered about Ramona's reason for visiting.

Quinn

She's gone. You can abandon your post and come back up now. Thanks.

Quinn read the message and then glanced over to Oscar's office where the door remained shut. *Thank God.* She'd offered to distract him on instinct but had no idea how she was going to do that if need be. Ever since she'd heard Deb's accusations, she'd been avoiding them both. Sliding her phone into her pocket, she headed back to her desk and had barely sat down when Deb arrived.

'Thank you,' she gushed, throwing her arms around Quinn. 'I'm guessing this means you haven't told him?'

'Told who what?' asked Linc, who, despite permanently wearing earbuds, had supersonic hearing at the most inconvenient times.

'No one,' Deb said.

'Nothing,' Quinn barked at the same time. 'Mind your own business,' she added, then turned back to Deb. 'Can you meet for a drink after work?'

'I'm sorry, I'd love to, but I've got a new job. Today's my last day here and I've got lots to wrap up before I can leave. Maybe we can catch up on the weekend?'

'What?' Quinn barely registered the hope in Deb's voice—her news felt like a punch to the gut. Her best friend was leaving, and she hadn't even told her? Then again, perhaps Deb would have mentioned something if Quinn had bothered to answer her calls these last couple of days. 'You're leaving because of …'

When her voice trailed off, Deb nodded.

'I'm gutted, but congrats on the new job,' Quinn said, refusing to leave things tense between them. 'How about one last rendezvous for old times' sake?'

Deb grinned and followed her down the hallway to their sacred meeting place. The moment they were inside, they both spoke at once.

'I haven't told him and I'm not going to,' Quinn said, having come to this decision only fifteen minutes ago.

'I'm so sorry for hurting you but *thank you*.' Tears accompanied Deb's words. 'I owe you one—hell, I owe you a million. Anything you need, just say it.'

Quinn looked around for a tissue but there were only reams of paper. 'First thing you can do is stop crying. Ramona's safe. You're safe.'

'What about you?'

'What about me?'

'I'm guessing you must believe me about Oscar, because if you didn't …' Deb sniffed. 'Well, you wouldn't have felt the need to hide Ramona, so I hope that means you're going to stay clear of him.'

Quinn sighed and leaned back against the copier. 'I didn't want to believe you. I've thought about nothing else the past couple of days and honestly, it's almost impossible to wrap my head around who you say he is. I've always trusted my gut about people, and something still doesn't sit right for me, but … this afternoon, when I saw Ramona, the evidence spoke for itself.'

She'd been undecided on what exactly she was going to do until she'd seen Deb's daughter coming out of the elevator and her golden caramel hair had glinted under the artificial lights. Then she'd caught her eyes, and it was like seeing a younger, female version of Oscar. She'd gasped, unable to ignore the facts any longer.

Instinct had kicked in. She had to get Ramona out of there, just in case.

'I know one thing for certain—you're not lying about Oscar being her dad.'

'I'm not lying about *any* of it, I promise,' Deb said vehemently. 'The only reason I ever lied about the donor is because—'

'I know, I know,' Quinn cut her off. 'You were trying to protect her, and I might not be a mother myself, but I would do anything to protect the ones I love. And, although I'm disappointed you never thought you could trust me, deep down I know you care about me too.'

Deb blinked as she choked out the words, 'I do. So, so much.'

'Which means … I guess I have to believe what you're saying about Oscar.'

'So you're not going to pursue him anymore?'

When Quinn shook her head, Deb let out a great big sigh and Quinn could tell her relief wasn't simply that the secret was safe, but also for her.

'I'm sorry.' Deb looked genuinely stricken. 'I wish Handbag Dude had been anyone but him.'

'Me too,' Quinn said sadly.

'But trust me, you do not want to waste tears on that man. You're far too good for him.'

At that, Quinn felt her eyelids growing hot and gummy. She'd been too angry to cry until now, but she was just so tired of hoping and dreaming of love. 'I'm allowed to be disappointed,' she said fiercely. 'I know you think it's silly, but I really thought I'd found my person.'

'I'm sorry.' Deb reached out to touch Quinn's arm. 'But I know there's someone wonderful out there for you. Maybe you should go back on the apps?'

That thought only made Quinn feel more tired. And pathetic. She shook her head. 'No. I'm done. Life's not a romance novel and not everyone gets a happy ever after. I've got a great family, good friends ...' She smiled at Deb, indicating that all was forgiven, and she was including her in this category. 'That's enough.'

The door swung open, and Lexi entered. 'Do you two ever do *any* work?'

'I do, but Deb's a total slacker,' Quinn joked, hoping her voice didn't crack, as Lexi shuffled into the cubicle. 'She leads me astray.'

Deb snorted as they walked out into the corridor.

'God I've missed that sound,' Quinn said.

'Does that mean we're okay then?' Deb asked as they lingered outside the copier room. 'It was going to be torture leaving with you still angry at me.'

Quinn's heart grew heavy again. 'Please tell me you're not really leaving?'

'I don't have any other choice. I can't work in the same office as ...' Her voice trailed off.

'I'm going to miss you like crazy. Who am I going to send inappropriate emails to during office hours now?'

Deb laughed through a sad smile. 'You can still email me. In fact, I demand it, and we'll catch up on the weekends. You can fill me in on all the gossip.'

She nodded, but it wasn't going to be the same. 'Who am I going to have Friday dumplings with? Who's going to fix the copier when I break it?'

'You haven't needed my help with that since that first day we met.'

'That's beside the point.' Quinn pouted as she pulled Deb into a hug. 'I guess you don't want me to throw you a farewell party?'

'Hell no! Shaun suggested goodbye drinks, but I convinced him not to bother. I want to slip away as quietly and discreetly as possible.'

'How did Shaun take your sudden resignation?'

'He tried to convince me to change my mind, but I was firm. Once he realised I wasn't sticking around, he wished me well. If anyone asks after me once I'm gone, please tell them we've lost touch.'

'I will,' Quinn promised. 'As long as you promise that we don't.'

'Never.' Deb bit her lip a moment, then, 'But right now I have to go back to my desk. If I stay here chatting any longer, I'll start bawling and I won't get out of this place till after midnight.'

She turned and hurried back towards the finance cubicle before Quinn could say another word.

Although Quinn also returned to her desk, she couldn't settle. She didn't mind her job but the absolute best part of being at The Energy Co was Deb. The days would drag, and the office antics wouldn't be as fun without a work wife to debrief with. She'd have to start going out for lunch with Linc and Toby, if they let her, or find herself another work wife.

Lexi? *She'd be on maternity leave soon.* Samira? *As if.*

No one would ever meet the grade because Deb was simply irreplaceable. And it wasn't right that she'd been forced out and Oscar—who had abused her, cheated on her, stalked her—was sitting at his desk below, fooling everyone with his charm and donuts.

Quinn's jaw clenched and she yanked at the tiny pink rollerskate dangling from her ear.

But maybe ...

She sat up straight, her mind ticking fast the way it did whenever she had a shiny new idea for a campaign.

Maybe it wasn't too late for Deb to get revenge.

Ramona

Ramona wiped her eyes as she got off the train and headed straight for Elijah's house. She was hurt and angry by the way her mum had ushered her out of the building. Who cared if she was busy? That didn't mean she had to treat her own daughter like a corrupt employee being banished by security. She'd been so preoccupied these last few weeks, but she wasn't the only one with problems.

How would she react when Ramona told her she'd tracked down her donor? Maybe it would be good to give her the news when she was distracted by other things. Maybe she'd forget to be mad, but it could just as likely go the other way.

Anyway, it was far too important a conversation to have when she wasn't in the right frame of mind, so Ramona decided to wait until tomorrow, or even the weekend, when Deb was relaxed and on holidays between jobs.

But she had to talk to *someone*.

She lifted her hand to use the old iron knocker on Elijah's front door.

'Hey, what's wrong?' he asked the moment he opened it.

Ramona loved that he only needed to look at her to know how she was feeling. 'I found my dad,' she whispered, not wanting Barbara to hear.

His eyes bulged as he pulled her inside. 'It's okay, Gran's at lawn bowls. You really found him?'

'Uh huh. Can I have a glass of water, please?' She'd been so consumed with the results of her DNA test that she hadn't had anything to drink or eat since throwing up a few hours ago and now she was parched.

'Sure.' Elijah poured her a glass of water from the fridge and then grabbed a tin of biscuits. 'Let's take these to the sunroom and you can tell me all about it.'

After downing all the water, she went over to Frodo's cage and let him out. He jumped onto her finger, and she sank down onto the couch where Elijah joined her after releasing the other birds.

'I got the results of the DNA test,' she said. 'And there's a paternal match. Apparently, my father is called Oscar Darke.'

'That was quick.'

'I know,' she sighed as she tickled Frodo's chest. 'I don't think I ever really thought I'd find him. Seemed like a long shot.'

'Are you going to contact him? I mean, you can, right? Through the website?'

'Yep. And he'll be notified of the match too.' Her stomach turned over but she reached for a bikkie, hoping to distract it. 'So ... he might contact me.'

'Do you want him to?'

'I don't know.' She rubbed her lips together, thinking. 'I guess so.'

'Have you googled him?'

'Huh?' It took a second for her to register Elijah's words. 'Oh my God. Why didn't I think of that?'

He smirked. 'Because I'm a genius and you're … in shock. Do you want me to do it?'

Ramona thought a moment and then nodded. 'But don't tell me if you find anything terrible.'

'Deal.'

She tried to distract herself playing with Frodo while Elijah typed her father's name into his phone, but she couldn't take her eyes off him, and her heart clenched when his beautiful face twisted into a frown.

'What is it?' she hissed, scaring Frodo who flew off to join his friends. 'Is he an axe murderer? Has he committed fraud? Is he on the run from the law?'

Was it too much to hope that her father was a billionaire who owned a private island in the Bahamas and donated money to refugees or something?

Elijah looked up, his expression confused. 'Well … I've found a LinkedIn account. If this is him—and I'm pretty sure it is—he … he works at The Energy Co.'

'What?' There had to be some mistake, or this was a crazy coincidence. 'You mean …'

He nodded. 'With your mum.'

'How long does it say he's worked there?'

'Only a couple of weeks. According to this, his last job was in New York. Has your mum ever been to America?'

'Not that I know of. Maybe you've got the wrong guy? Surely there's more than one Oscar Darke on the internet.'

'Maybe,' he said, angling his screen towards her, 'but I bet they don't all look exactly like you.'

Ramona peered closer at the screen and then sucked in a breath. She had to admit Elijah was right. It was like looking at an older male version of herself. A lump lodged itself in her throat. 'That's my dad.'

'I think so,' Elijah said, squeezing her hand.

She barely registered his touch. 'Do you think he looks nice?'

'Well, it's hard to tell someone's personality from a tiny profile picture, but he has honest eyes and a warm smile. Just like you.'

Ramona's heart swelled until she remembered The Energy Co thing. 'Oh my God, that's why Mum's been acting weird the last couple of weeks. Ever since we found her drunk that night, she's been on edge, distracted. And I *knew* there was something fishy going on this arvo.'

She told him how she'd gone to tell Deb about the test results and that Quinn had found her in reception and whisked her off to the bathroom to make her wait there.

'That's why she's changing jobs. I bet there's no restructuring going on at all. And, if she's leaving because of him, then that means she knows who he is! And if she knows who he is, then that means I *wasn't* conceived via an anonymous donor.'

Angry heat flushed through her body at the realisation that her mother—the woman who supposedly valued honesty above all else—had lied to her. Not just today, not just this last couple of weeks, but her whole damn life.

'Maybe he donated sperm before he went to the US,' Elijah said. 'It could just be a fluke they're working at the same place.'

'Do you really believe that? It's too much of a coincidence that she starts acting weird and leaves her job just after he arrives.'

He hesitated a moment. 'Do you think maybe she and this Oscar dude knew each other when they were younger and he agreed to give her sperm?'

Either that or ... they were in a relationship, but that would have meant Deb spent time in America too. Maybe he didn't want to have a baby and so she decided to go it alone. Maybe that's why she'd never mentioned her overseas trip. Because his rejection hurt so much and she didn't want Ramona to feel rejected as well.

Or maybe ... maybe her mum had lied to Oscar Darke too. Maybe he didn't even know Ramona existed and him turning up at The Energy Co threw a spanner in Deb's deception. That's why she was doing everything she could to keep them apart.

Ramona had never felt such hurt and betrayal in her life.

'I don't know what to think.'

'Maybe you should just ask her?' Elijah said, offering her another cookie.

She shook her head, she couldn't eat at a time like this. 'So she can lie to me again?'

He raised an eyebrow and nodded towards his phone, where the image of her supposed father still filled the screen. 'This photo would be fairly hard to deny, even without the DNA results.'

'You clearly don't know my mother. She's obviously been lying to me most of my life, why would she stop now?'

'You don't know that for sure.'

'Yes, I do. She knows it's him. And she doesn't want me to know.'

'So, if you're not going to talk to her about it, what are you going to do?'

'I'm going to message Oscar.'

Quinn

Deb looked up from her desk as Quinn walked into her cubicle later that night. 'What are you still doing here?' she asked.

'I'm not *still* here, I'm back.' Quinn held up a bottle of wine and a takeaway bag. She dropped them on one of the desks and then flopped into a seat. 'And I bought dinner and booze.'

'That's so sweet, but I'm almost done, and I probably should get home to Ramona.'

Quinn shook her head as she unscrewed the top on the bottle of sav blanc. 'You can hang out with that gorgeous girl anytime. This will be our last official work chat and if you won't let me throw you a proper party, the least you can give me is one final drink and dinner.'

'Okay, you've twisted my arm.' Deb grinned as she switched off her computer.

Quinn noticed the photo of Deb and Ramona had already gone. She handed her friend a glass and begun to unpack the dumplings. 'When I told Sami what these were for, he almost cried. He said to say goodbye and told me to tell you to make sure you visit whenever you're in the city. Where is your new job anyway? Please tell me it's close by. Maybe we can still meet for lunch?'

'I'm sorry, it's at a medical centre in Parramatta.'

'*Parramatta?* You may as well have taken a job on the moon.'

'Sorry,' Deb said, taking a sip of wine.

'Hmm … I've been thinking. Maybe,' Quinn began, excited to tell Deb her plan, 'you don't have to leave after all.'

'What do you mean?'

'You only just resigned. I'm sure Shaun won't mind if you tell him you've had second thoughts.'

'But I haven't. I *can't.*'

Even though there wasn't another soul as far as the eye could see, Quinn leaned close and lowered her voice. 'What if we make Oscar leave instead?'

Deb's glass stilled on the second trip to her mouth. Her eyes narrowed. 'I told you, I'm not reporting him to Shaun or to the police.'

'That's not what I'm suggesting. Get some of this grub into you and I'll explain,' Quinn said, passing over one of the containers and a large plastic spoon. She grinned wickedly. 'I'm going to seduce him.'

'What? No! You promised you'd given up on that idea!'

'Calm your farm,' Quinn said, holding up her hand. 'It's going to be a ruse.'

Deb blinked. 'What do you mean?'

'So first, I'm going to wheedle my way into his life. He's already offered to help with Snoodles. I'll take him up on that offer, and I'll start spending more time with him, and hopefully, he'll make a pass. I'm pretty sure he's been flirting already.'

'Of that I have no doubt.' Deb downed almost her whole glass of wine in one go. 'But how exactly is that going to make him leave? You think he'll quit his job in order to have a relationship with you? Highly unlikely. But even if he did, then what would you do? Dump him?'

'Look, I know you don't want to confront him or report him for what he did to you, but if I can provoke him ... If we start dating, but then I make him think I'm losing interest, or maybe seeing someone behind his back, then there's every chance he'll try something with me like he did to you. Then *I'll* report him to the police, and to Shaun. And when I do, I bet other women will come forward. You can't be the only one.'

'No fucking way,' Deb said, and Quinn jerked backwards because her friend very rarely swore. 'Do you realise how crazy that sounds? Okay, so there probably *are* others, but even if he did take your bait, this plan of yours could take a couple of months. I can't just hang around hoping he doesn't recognise me. Besides, I won't let you put yourself in danger for me.'

'I won't be,' she argued. 'Because I'll know from the start what I'm getting myself into. I'll keep you posted whenever I'm at his place or going to be alone with him, so if you don't hear from me within a certain time, you can call the cops and—'

'No,' Deb said again before Quinn could finish. Her knuckles were turning white around the glass. 'I've already quit. I'm not going back on this decision. *Please*, Quinn, we just need to leave things alone.' Her voice was shaky as she added, 'Promise me you'll forget this ridiculous plan and just steer clear of Oscar Bloody Darke.'

Quinn sipped her drink as she contemplated her answer. 'Okay,' she said eventually. 'I promise.'

Sometimes a small lie was necessary for the greater good. This wasn't just about Deb being able to stay, it was bigger than that. It was about refusing to let men continue to walk all over women. Even if she couldn't keep Deb at The Energy Co, the least she could do was make it so Oscar couldn't stay either. She couldn't stand the thought that he might hurt someone else the way he'd hurt her friend. Vulnerable women, who, like Deb, were too scared to report him.

Well, Quinn wasn't scared, and it was time to enact revenge.

'Thank you.' Deb finally started digging into her dumplings. 'Man, I'm going to miss these.'

Quinn nodded and blinked away tears as she started on her own.

'How's Mrs D?' Deb asked after a few moments of silence.

'She's recovering, but much slower than they'd hoped. Today's the first day I haven't seen her.'

'You brought dinner for me instead?'

'I was going to have the night off anyway. She's had a rough few days, getting really distressed whenever she tries to speak. After I saw her on Monday, I decided to bring her some photos from home to try and make her feel better. Last night a nurse told me she'd made a breakthrough in physical therapy, and she seemed happy with the photos, but I wasn't there five minutes before she started trying to talk and got frustrated—she knows what she wants to say, she just can't make her mouth say it.' Quinn sighed. 'It was heart-wrenching to watch and I'm not sure I'm doing any good being there. I thought maybe we both could use a break. Her daughter's arriving soon so that should help.'

'Poor woman,' Deb said. 'A stroke has to be one of the most awful things that can happen to you. It must feel like being trapped inside your own body.'

Quinn nodded, but she didn't want to dwell on that on Deb's last night. She'd much rather hear what was going on between her friend and the handsome vet. 'Tell me about Tristan. It sounds like you guys are getting closer?'

Deb's face flushed and her smile rivalled that of the Cheshire cat. 'Yes. He's amazing. I honestly don't know what I've done to deserve him. I haven't exactly made things easy for him. Most men would have given up after the stuff I've told him and the way I ignored him for the better part of a week, but for some crazy reason, he seems to like me.'

'That's not crazy at all,' Quinn said, refilling their glasses. 'You're a very likeable person, Debra Fast. I practically fell in love at first sight too.'

'Thanks.' Her eyes glistened again. 'If it wasn't for you, I'd never have stepped out of my comfort zone and I'd never have met him.'

'That's what friends are for.'

Deb lifted her glass. 'Amen. To friendship.'

They clinked and Quinn added, 'And many, many, *many* years of it to come.'

'Speaking of …' Deb put her wine on her desk and opened a drawer. It was empty except for a tiny box, wrapped in shiny pink paper. 'This is for you. I was going to leave it on your desk when I left but …'

Quinn took it and eagerly unwrapped it. 'I'm sorry I didn't get you anything.'

'What do you call dinner?' Deb asked, as Quinn peeled back the tissue paper inside and gasped at the pair of clay earrings—one a bowl of dumplings and the other a wineglass.

'Oh my God. Did you make these?' she said as she lifted the dumplings and admired the detail.

Deb nodded. 'Yes. I've been crafting quite a bit to try and distract myself from all the stress. It's been therapeutic. And I wanted to give you something to commemorate our best times together. It was either those or a tiny pair of photocopiers.'

'I'd proudly wear photocopiers on my ears if you made them,' Quinn laughed, removing the rollerskate earrings and replacing them with the ones from Deb. 'Seriously, these are amazing. *You* are amazing.'

'Thanks. I've been thinking about what you said about trying to sell some of my stuff. The idea is terrifying, but I thought maybe I'd give it a try. Try and build a little sideline business. That's if you really think anyone would be interested.'

'Hell yeah, they would.' She grinned and took a selfie for Instagram. 'I'm never taking these off.'

'Thanks.' Deb's face grew sombre. 'I truly am sorry for not being a hundred per cent honest with you. You mean the world to me, and I hate that I hurt you.'

'Stop. I love you, girlfriend. It's all good. We'll never speak of it again.'

'I love you back, and let's never speak of *Oscar Darke* again either.'

In reply, Quinn lifted her glass and took another sip.

All was *almost* right with the world.

Ramona

Ramona let herself into their apartment on Thursday afternoon, forgetting, until the mouth-watering aroma of freshly baked goods hit her, that her mother was now on a week's annual leave before starting her new job. *Dammit.* After yesterday's discovery, she was still angry at Deb's deception but wanted to hear from Oscar before she confronted her.

'Welcome home, sweetheart. How was your day?' Deb asked as Ramona stormed into the kitchen on the hunt for an after-school snack.

'Fine.' She spied raspberry and white chocolate muffins sitting on the cooler. They were her favourites, but her mum rarely had time to make them.

Deb gestured to the muffins. 'Help yourself.'

Ramona's stomach battled with her brain. Were these simply because her mother had time between jobs or were they an attempt to apologise for her recent weird behaviour? Part of her wanted to reject them, but in the end, hunger won out.

'Don't have too many as I've also got a pie ready to go in the oven,' Deb said as Ramona grabbed two warm muffins.

'The pie with the Vegemite in it?'

'That's the one,' Deb said with a smug nod. 'Your favourite. And I bought a tub of that expensive cookies and cream ice-cream for dessert.'

Definitely guilty behaviour. 'What's the special occasion? Your new job?'

'Does there have to be a special occasion for me to spoil my favourite daughter?'

Ramona inwardly rolled her eyes. That would have been corny even if she wasn't furious. 'Can Elijah come for dinner?' she asked through a mouthful of muffin.

'Oh, sweetheart ...' Deb wiped her hands on the stupid apron she was wearing. 'I thought it might be nice for us to have some one-on-one time tonight. It's been so long since we properly hung out.'

And whose fault was that? Ramona wanted to shout but managed to curb her tongue. She didn't want her mother to suspect anything was going on.

'Tristan's taking me out for dinner tomorrow night to celebrate my new job, so you can see Elijah then, but only if you're in public. If you're alone it needs to be at his place, so his grandma can chaperone,' Deb said with a wink.

'Ew. I told you we're just friends,' she lied—if it was good for the goose, it was good for the gosling. And it pissed her off that her mum just expected Ramona to fit in with her plans. Speaking of lies ... 'So how's the restructure at The Energy Co going? Has anyone actually lost their job yet?'

'Umm ...' Deb looked into the oven pretending to check on the pie, even though it wasn't even on yet. 'I think the powers that be are still making their decisions, but that's not something we have to worry about now, is it? Anyway, have you got much homework?'

'A little, but I'll do it soon,' Ramona snapped, grabbing another muffin.

'I wasn't insinuating that you wouldn't, I was just wondering if you have time to help me with something?'

'What?' If her mum wanted her to do the dishes when she was the one who'd decided to play restaurants, she had another think coming.

Deb smiled as she pointed through to the dining room table, which was once again covered in craft stuff—mostly the clay she'd been playing with lately. 'I gave Quinn some earrings I made for her, and she thinks I should make more to sell. She said there's lots of makers running small businesses on Instagram and I thought I might give it a go, try to bring in a bit of extra cash. Could you help set me up with an account. Please?'

'*You're* going on social media?'

'Not me, exactly. I'll need to come up with a business name. But I was going to make a private account first just so I could check out some other makers. So, will you help?'

Not feeling very charitable, Ramona said, 'I'll see if I have time. Depends on my homework.'

'I thought you didn't have much?' called Deb as Ramona headed into her bedroom.

Ignoring her mother, she shut the door and flopped onto her bed, then after ten seconds of glaring at the ceiling, grabbed her laptop out of her school bag and propped it on her knees. The DNA testing site was already open—since sending a message to Oscar Darke yesterday afternoon, she'd been checking it constantly all through the day—but when she refreshed it, she was once again disappointed.

She texted Lucy: *Still no reply.*

The three little dots appeared immediately and seconds after: *It's not even been 24 hrs. He probably doesn't check the site regularly.*

While Ramona wanted to believe this, she knew he'd have been sent a notification to his email when they matched. And didn't everyone—especially businessmen—check their emails regularly?

I just feel so helpless.

Be patient. I'm sure he'll reply soon.

But patience wasn't her virtue, and what if he didn't? Then what? She supposed she could go into The Energy Co and ask to see him, but even though Deb wasn't there anymore, Quinn could easily intercept her again.

If only I knew where he lived—then I could go confront him at his house.

It might even be better to catch him unawares—in case he too was a liar like her mother.

Have you tried the phone book?

The phone book? Is that even still a thing?

Ramona remembered finding a massive book with flimsy, dirty pages at one of their old rentals and marvelling over it when her mum explained what it was.

Lucy sent a LOL emoji. *Of course, it's just online now.*

He's not listed, Ramona replied after searching the White Pages online directory. *There's a number of Darkes in Sydney but none starting with O.*

Bummer.

Lucy changed the subject to their fashion project—they'd started working on their pattern today and tomorrow afternoon were going shopping to buy the material for their gown.

While they were chatting, a message appeared from Elijah: *Hey Pretty Boy—you coming over this arvo? X*

Even when she was feeling sad and cranky, he never failed to make her heart sing, especially when he used his special nickname for her.

*I can't. *sad face emoji* Mum's home and she wants to bond. *vomit emoji***

LOL emoji What about tomorrow? I know its cheesy, but do you want to go bowling?

Bowling. *LOL emoji* *LOL emoji* * LOL emoji* Hell yeah. I love those goofy shoes.

And at least it might take her mind off Oscar Darke for a while.

Awesome.

Oh, but I'm going shopping with Lucy after school, so I'll be a bit later home than usual.

No worries. Say hi to Luce for me. So good you guys are talking again.

Ramona's phone rang in her hand, and she startled at the sound—nobody ever called her except her mum, and she was out in the kitchen playing domestic goddess.

It was Lucy—maybe she wanted to talk about their project? Still, Ramona answered tentatively, 'Hey. What's up?'

'I was thinking about the White Pages and the other Darkes that are listed. I don't think it's that *common* a name, so there's every chance that one of them is related to your dad.'

Ramona sat up straighter. 'Lucy, you're a genius. I can call them and ask if they know an Oscar Darke.'

'Well, yes, that's what I thought initially, but then,' Lucy's voice grew more animated, 'I truly did have a genius idea.'

'What is it?'

'I know you don't want to go into The Energy Co because of your mum's friend, and ambushing him in his workplace might not be the best idea anyway, but what if you call reception, pretend to be your mum and say that Oscar did something kind on your last day and you want to have a gift delivered to his house. Then you'll have his address and can do what you want with it.'

Ramona thought about what that would be—even if she didn't have the guts to confront him immediately, she could stake out his place, wait for a glimpse of him. Just seeing him in the flesh would be good. She might also be able to work out if he lived with anyone else. Maybe he was married. Maybe he had other kids. Her *siblings*. She shivered, half-excited, half-nervous at the prospect.

'Why wouldn't I just send it to the office?'

'I dunno. Maybe you don't want everyone else to see. Hopefully the receptionist won't think of that, and if she does, well, we'll try option two—calling all those Darkes in the White Pages. But I think this is worth a shot, don't you?'

'Yes.' It was the best plan either of them had come up with so far. 'Do you really think I can get away with pretending to be Mum?'

'You sound exactly like her. You know you do.'

'Thank you, Lucy,' Ramona gushed. 'It truly was my lucky day when I got paired with you.'

'You better believe it.'

Quinn

To: Oscar.Darke@theenergyco.com.au
From: Quinn.Paladino@theenergyco.com.au
Subject: Snoodles
Hi neighbour—Happy Friday. Hope your second week
was a dream. I'm still dreaming of that donut. Anyway, just
wondering if you meant it when you said you'd be happy to
help with Snoodles if need be?
☺
Quinn

She couldn't believe Deb had only been gone two days. The office was deadly dull without her. Quinn already missed their copy-room rendezvous, and this morning when she'd only had to order one cup of coffee, she'd almost burst into tears right there in the queue. Every time she caught a glimpse of Oscar across the office or heard someone singing his praises, her resentment simmered and her determination to get revenge for Deb grew stronger.

She'd tried to talk to him in the staff kitchen, but the one instance they were both there at the same time, Samira had also been buzzing about, flirting outrageously. Honestly, that woman had no scruples. Not only was she married and having Mikael as a side dish, now she had her eye on Oscar too.

In the end, Quinn decided the best thing to do was get to him outside of the office.

Howdy indeed, neighbour—great week. Feel like I'm really getting in the swing of things now. And there are plenty more donuts where they came from. Regarding Snoodles— what can I do? Pick him up from doggy day care? Feed him? Help him pick up bitches in the park?

She laughed despite herself and then remembered she wasn't supposed to like him anymore.

Trust me, he doesn't need your help picking up! Women flock to him—both two and four-legged. But I was wondering if you had time to walk him tonight? I want to visit Mrs D, but Snoodles goes bonkers if he doesn't get a proper walk the moment I pick him up from doggy day care.

All lies. Usually, he came home exhausted after playing with all the other dogs and Crystal had arrived this morning from England, so Quinn had decided to step back to allow her and Mrs D to spend time together. She'd visit again tomorrow, but tonight—assuming Oscar came to the party—she had other plans.

She waited with bated breath for his reply and then smiled smugly at her computer as she read it.

A walk with the big guy would be my utmost pleasure. I'm knocking off in an hour. Just bring him round to my place when you're ready.

Quinn replied and then sat back in her seat and rubbed her hands together.

Operation Oscar had officially begun.

*

An hour after she'd dropped Snoodles off at Oscar's place, Quinn picked up a bag of takeaway from the local Chinese restaurant and headed back.

She found the two of them sitting on his front porch, Snoodles gnawing contentedly on a bone and Oscar nursing a bottle of beer. He was wearing a plain black T-shirt, running shorts and his feet were bare. Good golly, even his toes and the hairs on his legs were sexy.

'Hey. How's the patient?'

Quinn shot him a faux smile. 'She's slowly getting there. Speech is coming back a bit more each day.' At least this was true—she'd got a text from Crystal that afternoon telling her so. 'Did Snoodles behave for you?'

'Yeah.' He grinned at the dog. 'Wasn't at all crazy like you insinuated. In fact, our walk was quite sedate.'

Quinn shrugged. 'Guess he had an exhausting day at day care. Anyway, thanks so much for taking him out. I bought you some dinner to say thanks.'

'You didn't have to, but thank you. I hadn't even thought about what to eat yet.'

She'd been banking on that. 'You're welcome.'

He pushed to his feet, accepted the proffered paper bag and peered inside. 'Geez, there's enough here to feed an army. Want to join me?'

'Oh … I …' Quinn faltered. 'I wouldn't want to intrude. You probably just want to relax not dine with a colleague.'

He raised an eyebrow. 'Have you eaten yet?'

She shook her head.

'Well, then, please join me. As a neighbour, not a colleague.' He smiled as he gestured at the front door.

'Shall I take Snoodles home first? We can't leave him out here or he'll bark at every passer-by.'

'Nah, don't bother. He can come too.'

She was about to protest that the dog might destroy his furniture, but then remembered that was the least of her worries. And having Snoodles with her would be good security. However much the dog liked Oscar, she couldn't imagine him allowing him to hurt her.

Despite Snoodles' presence, a shiver scuttled down Quinn's spine as she stepped inside and Oscar closed the door behind them. When he touched a hand to her back to usher her down the hallway, it was everything she could do not to cower. After promising Deb she wouldn't do this, she couldn't tell her where she was, but she hadn't told anyone else either. Suddenly she wished she'd mentioned it to Dec.

'Why don't you take the food into the living room,' Oscar said, indicating a door to the side as he handed her back the paper bag. 'I'll grab us some bowls and cutlery. And can I get you a beer or a glass of wine?'

Quinn thought she should turn down both as she needed to keep her wits about her, but she didn't want him getting suspicious, and she could hardly say she didn't drink because they'd already shared a beer. 'A glass of wine would be lovely,' she said, then scurried into the living room.

Snoodles followed her, his bone between his teeth. Quinn was worrying about bits of it staining the plush cream carpet when her gaze fell upon a beautiful and shiny piano sitting in the corner, a wedding photo perched upon it. Thinking it must be a photo of his parents, she went to take a closer look and gasped as she realised the man in the picture—the *groom*—was Oscar himself.

Holy shit.

Standing beside him, holding a piece of what looked like red velvet cake to his mouth, was a curvy blonde with a short, choppy bob, dressed in the most divine pale pink gown. The hairs on the back of Quinn's neck prickled as she glanced around the room. There were several other photos on display, many of Oscar and this woman. His bride.

But where was she now? Why wasn't he wearing a ring? Were they divorced? Had he left her in New York? Had she died? Had he *killed* her?

'Hope sav blanc's okay. I'm not much of a wine drinker but I bought this for when my mum drops in.'

Quinn jumped at the sound of his voice and spun around, her cheeks heating as if she'd been caught doing something she shouldn't.

'That's fine,' she said, taking the glass. She wasn't quite sure how to play this—should she ignore the photo or ... 'You're married?'

A sadness filled his face and he slowly nodded.

'Is she ... is she alive?'

'Yes.'

Quinn felt like she'd been sucker-punched. 'So you're divorced? Separated?'

'No.' Oscar took a long gulp of beer.

'Then, I don't understand. Where *is* your wife?' She waved her hand around as if expecting a woman to jump out from behind the piano.

'Do you want to take a seat and I'll explain?'

Something told Quinn she should probably take the dog and leave, make an excuse about an engagement she'd forgotten. But hadn't she come to investigate? Without another word, she placed the takeaway bag on the coffee table and sat on an armchair, avoiding the couch in case he sat beside her.

He lowered himself onto it and leaned forward to start unpacking the food. Was he stalling? Coming up with a story?

'Dig in,' he said eventually, handing her a bowl and gesturing for her to help herself.

Quinn took the bowl but didn't make a move towards the food. 'You were about to tell me about your *wife*?' she prompted.

'Olivia. Her name's Olivia.' He ran a hand through his hair. 'And she's sick.'

For some reason, this was the last thing she'd expected him to say. 'What's wrong with her?'

'She's got early-onset Alzheimer's disease.'

'Oh.' Quinn's mind had immediately jumped to cancer, but somehow this seemed even worse. 'How old is she?'

'Thirty-eight.'

'Shit.' She couldn't help herself, her heart cracked despite the fact she wasn't sure how much to believe. Deb had said that in hindsight she questioned almost everything he'd ever told her. 'So young.'

He smiled sadly. 'Yeah. That's why we moved back to Australia, so we could be closer to her family, and mine, so we could all care for her as long as possible. But ... she deteriorated rapidly and a few months ago ...' He paused and blinked as if fighting tears—he was either a very good actor or at least some of this tale was true. 'We had to put her into full-time care. I feel so guilty that I couldn't take care of her myself, but she needed more than I could give.'

'My goodness, Oscar, that's just ...' Again, Quinn was lost for words, not simply because no words seemed adequate for such tragedy but because this information had thrown her for six.

'Fucking awful,' he finished and then chuckled, not in a funny-ha-ha kind of way but in an 'if I don't laugh I'll cry' way. 'It's a brutal disease in the elderly but even more tragic in the young. It just happened so fast. She hardly recognises me when I go visit now. Sometimes she's still happy to hang out, but other times she cowers away from me, screaming and crying that I'm about to hurt her.'

He paused and took a swig of his drink. 'The staff have to calm her down. It's heartbreaking that she feels safer sitting in a communal living room than with me.'

Quinn couldn't help but wonder if that's because he'd hurt her during their marriage.

'I was going to go see her tonight, but then you asked me to walk Snoodles. I've got a few other things on my mind at the moment ... and to be honest it was a relief to have an excuse to give visiting a miss.' He looked up from the table and into her eyes. 'How much of a bastard does that make me?'

Quinn didn't answer. She hadn't come here to start feeling sorry for him. Nor did she care what else he had bothering him. 'Does she have a history of this in her family?' she asked instead.

'No,' he said glumly. 'It came as a total shock.'

It was time to start eating, if only for something to do while she worked out her next move. If this was true, Quinn could only imagine how hard Oscar's life must now be. He was married to a

415

woman who couldn't truly be a partner, yet neither could he freely move on with someone else. How long did people with early-onset Alzheimer's live?

Was this fate's way of getting revenge for the way he'd treated Deb?

If it wasn't true, he deserved a bloody Academy Award!

'Tell me about her? Where'd you meet?'

He leaned forward to start dishing food into his bowl. 'When we were both living and working in New York. Olivia was an editor at a big publishing house. We met at a local Aussie pub. It was a real cheesy place, you know the type—they pretty much only sold Fosters, the bartenders wore Akubra hats with corks hanging from them, and most of the patrons weren't even Australian. Except this one night a month when they ran speed dating for Aussies wanting to date other Aussies.'

The hairs on Quinn's arms flickered. 'Speed dating?'

'Yeah.' Oscar went on, seemingly—*hopefully*—oblivious to her shock. 'Five minutes to get to know someone. I went along for a laugh with a mate, never thought for one moment I'd actually meet the love of my life.'

Quinn lifted her wine to her mouth and took her first long gulp. Not that she thought Deb was a liar—Ramona was evidence of that—but this couldn't be a coincidence.

'How long have you been together?'

'Almost eighteen years.' He smiled wistfully. 'Married for seventeen.'

Quinn's blood went cold. Ramona was fifteen. He must have had an affair with Deb when he was already married.

Suddenly wondering if she'd bitten off more than she could chew, Quinn fought the urge to flee. *Stay. Now you're here, you need to gather as much information as you can.*

'So.' She swallowed. 'Olivia—what's she like?'

Oscar finished his mouthful then rested his bowl in his lap. 'She was fantastic. I guess we were a case of opposites attract. I'm more comfortable in a small group of close friends but Liv was always the life of the party, always collecting new friends and dragging me out to dinners that I didn't want to go to but ended up enjoying well enough. She met some very interesting people in the publishing world. Sometimes I wondered what she saw in me, why she'd chosen me when she could have had the pick of all these swanky author types.'

Oh, I can imagine exactly what she saw in you, Quinn thought, and it wasn't just his good looks. Looks only got you so far; surely he knew he had a certain charisma?

As he told her more about his and Olivia's life together, she couldn't help noticing he spoke about her in the past tense, as if he were already a widower. Already grieving. Yet he spoke so tenderly and even a little tearfully that she kept forgetting why she was here. Kept forgetting the fact he was actually a monster.

'You never had kids?' she asked.

'No.' He looked wistfully into his bowl. 'We both wanted them, but we thought we'd establish ourselves first. Liv wanted to be far enough along in her career that taking maternity leave wouldn't set her back. I wanted to move out of our apartment, buy a house. We started trying when she was thirty-two, but it didn't happen. After a year we had all the tests—turned out a lot of her eggs had a chromosomal problem. We did a few rounds of IVF but they didn't work, and then ...'

'And then she was diagnosed?' Poor Olivia sounded like she'd had quite the bad luck.

'Yeah,' he sighed. 'So that was the end of that. Life suddenly became all about making sure Liv had the best treatment and care.'

'I notice you don't wear a wedding ring. Is that because you don't want to have to explain to people about Olivia?'

He shook his head. 'I haven't worn one in years. I get dermatitis, wearing my ring aggravates it. I wanted to keep it on anyway, but Olivia told me I was being ridiculous—she trusted that I'd never cheat on her, with or without a ring.'

Except he *had*, because while he'd been married to Olivia, he'd slept with Deb. Conceived Ramona. That fact brought Quinn back to her senses. Olivia was the one she should be feeling sorry for. Who knew how many times he'd cheated on her, what else he may have done to her?

'I didn't decide *not* to tell anyone at work about my wife,' he continued. 'It's not like it's a state secret or anything, but it's a tough subject and not something I want to open with. Shaun knows, but aside from him, you're actually the first person from The Energy Co that I've told.'

'I'm honoured,' she said, summoning a fake smile. 'And if you don't want me to, I promise I won't tell another soul.'

Except maybe Deb—what would she make of this?

She'll be angry at you for coming here and doing what you promised you wouldn't. She'll assume he's lying about this also. Say he's telling you a sob story to get you to feel sorry for him. Make you let down your guard. Could that be true? *Maybe Olivia—if that even was her name—was away for work.*

Lost in thought, Quinn almost missed what Oscar said next. 'I'm sorry, what was that?'

He smiled and stretched out his leg, nudging her shoe with his foot. 'I said, thank you. Thanks for dinner, but mostly thanks for listening. I do like you, Quinn, and I'm sorry if I gave you the wrong idea. Under other circumstances, and also if we didn't work together, I'd be asking you on a date. I hope we can become good friends instead.'

Oh God. Quinn's stomach tightened at the way he was looking at her. Two weeks ago, this was almost exactly what she'd wanted to hear, but she couldn't allow his sad story to sway her. Even if his wife did have a terrible illness it didn't mean he hadn't also done what Deb had said.

'I'm really sorry if this confession has made you uncomfortable,' he added.

She swallowed. 'No, it hasn't. I'm glad you felt you could confide in me. And I would very much like to be friends.'

'Thank you.'

He lifted his bottle of beer and leaned towards her. 'To friends.'

'Yes, to friends,' Quinn said as she reached across the coffee table and clinked her glass against his.

Debra

'I hope you don't mind,' Tristan said when he picked Deb up for their celebratory date, 'but I decided to make dinner for you at my place instead.'

'Oh, no, of course I don't mind—especially if your macaroni and cheese is any indication of your cooking skills. Will Tara and Tom be there?'

She was excited to meet Tristan's kids, but she'd also been looking forward to an evening with just the two of them. Talking, enjoying good food and wine, and getting to know each other even better.

'No. They both had other plans this evening, so we'll have the house all to ourselves.'

She felt a jittery zing at his words. They hadn't slept together yet, but things had become serious much more quickly than she'd imagined. Him running a bath for her the other day and then cooking comfort food had felt weirdly intimate, and she'd be lying if she said she hadn't thought about taking things further.

'What are we having?' she asked, trying to banish such thoughts. She didn't want to put so much pressure on herself that she couldn't even make conversation.

'That's a surprise,' he said, 'but I guarantee you'll like it.'

'Anything that I don't have to cook myself is always a win.'

The moment Tristan opened his front door, Hammer barged out, his tail wagging as he jumped up at Deb.

'Hey, gorgeous,' she said, taking a moment to rub his chin and belly. 'I'm happy to see you again too.'

When the dog had calmed, Tristan took Deb's hand and led her into the dining room.

'Wow, you've gone all out,' she said.

The table was set like something from an interior design magazine, with a black tablecloth, fabric napkins, crystal glassware, crisp white plates, candles and a beautiful vase of gerberas in the middle.

'You can take the flowers home later,' he said, pulling out a chair, 'but for now, take a seat and let me wait on you.'

'No arguments here,' she replied, unable to remember a time where she'd been waited on by anyone not on a restaurant's payroll.

Tristan lit the candles, dimmed the lights and popped a bottle of champagne he'd had resting in a fancy ice bucket. He poured her a glass and then disappeared into the kitchen, returning with platters of sourdough bread, cured meats, slices of pear and apple, some tiny meatballs, roasted Brussel sprouts, potatoes and steamed vegetables.

'Now for the final touch,' he said, before retreating again, leaving her bemused at the odd assortment.

'Voila.' He carried out a gorgeous white ceramic pot with a handle on one side and a rack underneath with a tiny burner. It was then Deb noticed that instead of cutlery, there were fondue forks.

'Oh my goodness. Is that what I think it is? My mum used to make fondue.' She let out a half-laugh. 'I didn't think anyone still did.'

He smiled as he put the cheese fondue in the middle of the other food. 'So you do have some fond memories of your mother?'

'Yeah.' She swallowed. 'I guess that's what makes what she did such a betrayal. Sometimes she was a really fun mum—we used to cook together, go to the park and play that game where you look up at the clouds and say what you think they look like. I thought she loved us, I thought she loved me. And yet how can you just walk away from someone you love?'

'Is that why you studied psychology?' Tristan asked.

'What do you mean?'

'To try and get an answer to that question. About what makes someone abandon their child like your mother did.'

'Yeah … Maybe. I never really thought about it like that, but I did want to work with kids who didn't have the best childhoods and that probably stems from my own. I wanted to help children who are working through trauma and issues they simply can't comprehend.'

Tristan smiled warmly. 'And have you ever thought of finishing your masters? Of picking up your career where you left off.'

She snorted. 'It was hardly a career.'

'But it could have been,' he said. 'And I think it still could be. You told me you don't understand people and so how could you help? But I think what you really mean, is that you don't understand *bad* people.'

'I'm not sure I'm following.'

'You don't need to know the workings of a psychopath's mind or even understand neglectful parents to help kids or adults. You understand how it feels to be someone who has experienced trauma and I think you'd have a lot to offer others who've also been through something awful.'

Tristan let his words hang in the air a few moments and Deb took a sip of her wine.

'I know you say you like payroll,' he added, 'but would you be doing it if you hadn't met Oscar and got pregnant?'

'Probably not,' she had to admit. But she *had* met him, and since then her life had been focused on Ramona—on providing for her, on keeping her safe. But Ramona was getting older now, becoming more independent, and maybe Tristan had a point. Did she have something to offer?

He merely smiled knowingly.

'Can we talk about something else now?' she asked. Unsure whether the kick in her heart was nerves or curiosity, she vowed to give his idea some thought.

He nodded and raised his glass to clink hers. 'Anything you want.'

She told him about her new earring venture and how Ramona had reluctantly set her up on Instagram the night before. 'I think she's scared I'll start following all her friends.'

Tristan made her laugh with stories of his clients—the crazy cat ladies, dog breeders who had whole storeys of their houses reserved for their prized animals, and a couple who were divorced and currently in an expensive legal battle over custody of their pet snake.

When she thought she couldn't possibly eat another bite, Tristan said, 'Shall we play a game of Scrabble before dessert?'

'Dessert?'

He nodded. 'Chocolate fondue.'

'Then definitely, let's play Scrabble first. I don't think I could eat another bite right now.'

'Why don't you take another glass of bubbles into the living room and get the board ready—it's on the coffee table—while I clean up.'

Deb gestured to the table. 'I can't leave all this mess to you.'

'Yes, you can,' he said, squeezing her hand. 'I told you, tonight is about me waiting on you.'

'Fine,' she relented, glowing inside and probably out, 'but I'm going to repay the favour soon.'

'I'll hold you to that.'

While Tristan cleared everything away, Deb took their glasses into the living room, but something distracted her before she got to the Scrabble board.

Oh my. The large wedding photo above the mantelpiece was gone. He'd replaced it with a canvas of a highland cow, painted in a plethora of colours. She pressed her hand against her chest, knowing how much of a big move this was. How did his kids feel about the removal of their mother?

She knew Tristan would never forget Marie—she wouldn't expect him to—but this was a clear sign that he was ready to make room for someone else and she couldn't be happier that he'd chosen her.

Not wanting him to catch her beaming at the cow, she sat on the couch and began unpacking the board. 'I warn you, I'm impossible to beat,' she teased when he joined her a few minutes later.

'Is that a challenge?' he asked as he started distributing the tiles.

Despite playing against each other, they sat next to each other, the game board in front of them on the coffee table. Deb didn't really care if she lost, it was simply nice to be spending a Friday night sitting here with him. For the last couple of months she'd mostly spent them alone with Ramona closeted away in her bedroom.

'Hunk,' she said. It wasn't a long word, but it was the best she could do with what she had.

Tristan winked at her. 'Are you trying to tell me something?'

She laughed and gestured to the board. 'Well, go on, can you beat that?'

He scoffed—'Easily'—and laid out the letters N-O-O-K-Y.

'That's not a word!'

'Sure it is.' He stood, went across to the bookshelves and plucked out a dictionary. 'Here. Look it up.'

Deb flicked through the pages till she got to the right one and then blushed as she read the definition. Closing the book, she scrutinised her tiles and almost shrieked with glee when she realised she could spell 'snog'.

'Are you *sure* you're not trying to tell me something?' Tristan asked, leaning a little closer.

She licked her lips and leaned closer still. 'I don't know. Are *you*?'

'What would you say if I was?' His voice was low, and his breath tickled her lips.

'This,' she said, closing the tiny gap between them as she pressed her mouth against his.

*

'Is that the first time you've slept with anyone since Marie?' Deb asked much later when they were snuggling on the couch. If it weren't for the way her body still thrummed from his touch, she wouldn't be able to believe they'd had sex.

He nodded. 'And you, since ...?' She was grateful he didn't say his name.

'Yes. Were you thinking about her while we ...?' She blushed—what a stupid question. She wasn't thinking straight. 'I'm sorry. You don't have to answer that.'

'No.' He cupped her face in his hands and stared right into her soul. 'I was not thinking about my wife while we made love, Debra.

I've barely been able to think about anything but you since we met. At first I felt guilty about that, but now all I can feel is happy, and I want to make you happy too.'

She pressed her forehead against his. 'You do.'

'I wish you could stay the night,' he said when Deb finally thought she'd better make a move. 'I want to fall asleep, wake up at 2 am, make love to you again and then bring you breakfast in bed in the morning.'

Just those words sent ripples of pleasure through her. She loved that he didn't only want to ravish her, but also cherish her, and she wanted to cherish him right back. 'That would be wonderful, but I need to get home to Ramona.'

'I know. One step at a time, hey?'

Ramona

'This must be it,' Elijah said, looking up from his phone as they slowed across the road from a terrace house in Darlinghurst on Saturday morning.

It was such a trendy neighbourhood and, just like she had at Sydney's, Ramona felt completely out of place. On the train, Elijah had been trying to distract her nerves with facts about the suburb. 'It used to be that one in five couples who lived there were men in same-sex relationships.'

'Do you think my dad's gay?' Ramona had asked.

He shrugged. 'Could be. Would you care?'

'No. It's just I never thought about that possibility. Maybe that's why Mum lied about him?' Every time she thought she'd exhausted the options, another popped up.

'Maybe. Hopefully you'll have some answers soon.'

They'd met Lucy at Kings Cross station and walked the short distance to the address the receptionist had given them when Ramona had called The Energy Co yesterday pretending to be her mum.

'Your dad must be quite wealthy,' Lucy said now as they eyed the house with its ornate, white cast-iron balcony railings on the second storey and the low, spear-headed iron fence at the bottom.

'Yeah,' Elijah agreed. 'Even if he rents, this place has gotta cost a bomb.'

'I guess he's really good at selling things,' Ramona said, barely noticing the house at all. Today she only had room for thoughts of her father.

Would they get a glimpse of him? Would she *meet* him?

'What do you want to do now?' Elijah asked. 'Shall we wait and watch for a while, or do you want to knock?'

Her heart shot to her throat at the thought, but now they were here, she didn't want to walk away either. What would be the point of doing the DNA test, of going to the trouble of hunting down Oscar Darke's address, if she fled like a scaredy cat?

'Yes,' she said, trying to summon courage. 'Let's do it.'

'What are you going to say if he answers the door?' Lucy asked.

'I guess I'll tell him who I am and ask if he'll answer some questions.' Ramona sucked in a breath and inclined her head towards the front door. 'Let's do this before I chicken out.'

She marched through the gate and jabbed her trembling finger against the doorbell. The pounding of her heart halted, and she froze as she heard the sound echo throughout the house.

The three of them stood on the porch in silence as they waited. And waited.

'Maybe he's not home?' Lucy said eventually.

'Yeah.' Elijah moved to the window and peered through it. 'Looks nice inside. Neat, but like a home. There's a big piano. Maybe he plays? And hey, is that a wedding photo?'

Ramona nudged him aside so she could look. Sure enough, on top of the shiny piano there was a framed photo and although it was hard to tell in the dim light, it definitely appeared to be of a bride and groom. *Not gay then*. But married. That wasn't a great surprise—Oscar had to be at least her mum's age—but for some reason this confirmation freaked her out.

What the hell was she doing here? He hadn't responded to her message, which likely meant he didn't want to have anything to do with her. Why hadn't she taken the hint? His wife probably didn't even know Ramona existed. What if she was the result of an affair?

'Any sign of kids?' asked Lucy, still standing a little back.

'Not that I saw,' Elijah replied.

But Ramona barely heard them. She needed to get out of here before Oscar came home. Or worse, his wife. What would she say to *her*?

At that moment, the gate creaked behind them and every bone in Ramona's body froze. Somehow, she found the courage to turn around, and standing there was a tall man with mussed caramel-coloured hair, eyes the same unique aqua as hers, black glasses and a neatly trimmed beard.

Her stomach somersaulted and she heard her friends inhale quickly beside her. Oscar looked even more like her in person than he had in his LinkedIn photo.

'Are you Oscar Darke?' she blurted.

'Yes.' A brief pause. 'You must be Ramona?'

He knew her name. Which meant he knew who she was. He'd obviously got her message. She felt a pinprick of hurt that he hadn't responded, but right then, other emotions were stronger.

This was her father. All her life she'd wondered what he looked like. If she'd ever meet him, and here he was, standing right in front of her.

'How old are you?' he asked, frowning slightly.

'Fifteen. Almost sixteen.'

His frown deepened. 'I thought you had to be at least eighteen to do a DNA test?'

'I lied about my age because I was desperate to meet you,' she retorted, not about to let a parent who'd been absent her whole life reprimand her.

A long, totally awkward silence followed, as if Oscar were trying to gather his thoughts. Ramona could hear her heart pounding again and her hands were clammy. She could not stop staring at him. This was so surreal.

'Well, hello then, Ramona,' he said finally, his frown morphing into a warm smile. 'It's a pleasure to meet you.'

He stepped forward and offered his hand, which felt weird because they were so closely related, but also somehow right because they knew nothing about each other.

She slipped her hand into his and swallowed tears as he looked down at her.

'And who are your friends?' Oscar asked, turning his smile on Lucy and then Elijah.

Ramona didn't speak. Elijah squeezed her other hand as he said, 'I'm Elijah, Ramona's boyfriend.'

She felt her cheeks flush. It felt weird to hear it, but even weirder that her dad knew about their relationship before her mum.

'Nice to meet you too,' Oscar said as they shook hands.

'And I'm L-Lucy, her best friend.'

Oscar shook her hand as well. 'Well, would you like to come in for a drink? I have—'

'Yes, please,' Ramona said before he could finish.

He ushered them inside, through the living room, then the dining room and into the kitchen at the very back.

'Now, tea, coffee, water, OJ, or an energy drink?'

Ramona didn't remember answering as she was too busy scrutinising her surrounds, looking for signs of his wife or kids, but a glass of orange juice appeared in her hand as Oscar said, 'Shall we go out to the courtyard?'

They sat in cane chairs at the heavy stone outdoor table and Ramona decided to speak before anyone could launch into small talk. 'I take it you got the message I sent Thursday night?'

Oscar nodded, his long fingers wrapped around his glass. They even had the same shaped fingernails. 'Sorry I haven't replied. I could tell you I was busy at work, and while I have been, that's not the reason. To be honest, your message came as quite a shock and I ... I was nervous.'

That endeared him to her. 'So, you didn't know I existed?'

He deliberated a few seconds. 'No. That's why I needed a few days to wrap my head around the idea, but I would have contacted you. In fact, I was probably going to do it this afternoon.'

Ramona nodded, deciding to give him the benefit of the doubt. It *had* only been a few days since she'd reached out. But surely someone who'd donated sperm wouldn't be so shocked by such news?

'How'd you know where I lived, by the way?' he asked.

'We looked up your LinkedIn profile and found out where you worked. I called up and pretended to be another employee and asked for your address.'

'I see.' He actually smiled. 'I'll have to speak to them about handing out employees' contacts so freely, but I admire your ingenuity.'

'It was Lucy's idea. And Elijah was the one who thought to look you up on LinkedIn. Without them, I'd probably still be waiting for your reply.'

'Nothing like good friends.'

'Anyway,' Ramona said, not wanting to get off track. 'You're married?'

Oscar frowned again. 'Have you guys considered opening a private investigating business?'

Elijah chuckled. 'We saw the photo on your piano.'

'Ah, right. Yes, I am. If it wasn't for Olivia, you might not have found me. She gave me a DNA test for Christmas a few years ago. It was a bit of fun. At the time, everyone was doing them, hoping to discover family secrets. We were disappointed when neither of us found anything exciting. Although it looks like that wasn't the case after all,' he said with a grin.

How could he sound so flippant about this?

'W-where's your wife?' Lucy asked, pausing between sips of a drink from The Energy Co that was turning her teeth blue.

He sighed. 'Olivia has Alzheimer's disease.'

They all gasped.

'She needs full-time care, so she doesn't live with me anymore. I was visiting her this morning, which is why I wasn't home.'

'Isn't that only for old people?' asked Lucy.

Oscar shook his head sadly. 'Hers is early-onset. It can affect people as young as thirty.'

'I'm so sorry. That's awful.' Elijah said what they were all thinking.

Ramona felt bad bombarding Oscar with questions after that, but she couldn't let sympathy get in the way of finding answers. 'Do you and Olivia have any kids?'

'No.' He shook his head. 'But I always wanted them.'

'How long have you been married?'

Oscar took his time answering what should have been an easy question. 'Seventeen years,' he said with a grimace.

'So you were married when I was conceived. Did you ... have an affair?' This was one of the options Ramona had pondered. *If* her mum had lied about the donor sperm thing, that reason seemed the most likely. Perhaps she didn't want to be a home wrecker.

432

'Does your mum know you're here?' Oscar asked.

Ramona glanced at her friends. 'No,' she admitted. 'As I said, I forged my age on the DNA test. She'd never have allowed it, but I deserve to know where I come from. And since Mum won't tell me the truth, I thought maybe you could.'

'I'm sorry,' he said, 'could you tell me your mother's name?'

'Debra Fast. Ring any bells?'

'I wish it did.'

Ramona felt anger welling inside her. 'Exactly how many people did you cheat with that you can't remember her?'

'I …' Oscar gulped down some water. 'What exactly did she tell you about us?'

Ramona sighed. Oscar seemed to be trying to glean information that would help him concoct a story. Although she'd liked him on sight, she was beginning to have her doubts.

'Mum told me I was conceived through donor sperm.'

He blinked rapidly and then burst into a smile, shaking his head and half-scoffing. 'Yes, that makes sense. I completely forgot. I decided to donate before I went to New York.'

Ramona, Lucy and Elijah exchanged a look—she could tell neither of them believed him either. Giving away your sperm wasn't the kind of thing you did on a whim and then forgot about. *Was it?*

'Why?' she asked simply.

'I … ah … I just thought it would be a good thing to do.' He paused again, then added, 'I think I read an article about couples struggling with infertility and figured it was something I could do to help.'

That would make him a saint! *If* she believed him.

'Right,' Ramona said, pushing back her seat. 'Thanks for the orange juice.'

'You're leaving already?' He sounded slightly disappointed.

She faked a smile. 'I don't want to take up any more of your time. Thanks for the drinks.' Then she turned on her heel and fled.

Her friends and Oscar hurried after her through the house and outside.

'Thanks for coming,' he said as she reached the gate. 'Hang on.' He pulled out a business card and thrust it at her. 'Call or message me any time. And maybe you can get your mum to call me?'

Yeah—then the two of them could get their heads together and make sure their stories matched.

What the hell was going on here?

'Well, that was a waste of time,' Ramona exclaimed, her eyes stinging with tears as they walked back towards the station.

'Not completely,' Lucy said, 'at least you now know who your dad is and you've met him. He seems nice and it sounds like he'd be happy to meet you again.'

Hmm. Ramona wasn't sure whether she wanted to see *him* again. 'Did you buy his story? I don't know if he did donate or if he and Mum were actually together, and if so, under what circumstances.' She threw her hands up in the air, exasperated. 'I don't know anything!'

'Does it matter that you don't know exactly *how* you were conceived?' Elijah asked. 'When you did the DNA test, you wanted to find your father so you could know the other side of your family. And you have. That's obvious just looking at the two of you.'

'It *matters* that I'm being lied to by the two people in my life who are supposed to care about me more than anyone else.'

'Maybe they're lying to you for a good reason,' Lucy suggested.

Ramona glared at her. 'And what exactly would that be?'

Her shoulders slumped and she sighed. 'I d-don't know. I'm sorry.'

'No, I'm sorry. I shouldn't have snapped at you. I just … I just feel so … so lost. I have no idea who I am.'

The tears she'd been fighting finally broke free.

Elijah put an arm around her. 'Hey, you're Ramona Lee Fast and you're smart and kind and funny and have the best taste in fashion of anyone I know. Frodo adores you too and he has impeccable taste.'

'He's right.' Lucy smiled. 'You're awesome. My life's so much better now you're in it.'

She appreciated her friends were trying hard to make her feel better but no matter what they said, nothing could lift her mood until she knew the truth.

'It's time,' she told them through her sobs.

'Time for what?' they asked in unison.

'Time to confront my mother. Before this Oscar guy finds her and they have the chance to coordinate their stories.'

Quinn

'Morning.' Quinn kissed Mrs D on the cheek and lifted a hand to Crystal, who she'd officially met on Thursday night. 'How's the jet lag?'

She groaned and rolled her eyes. 'I thought I was coping well until I woke up at 3 am and couldn't get back to sleep.'

Quinn gave her a sympathetic smile, then turned back to Mrs D. 'You're looking much brighter today.'

'That's cos you got good news this morning, didn't you, Mum?'

Mrs D nodded slowly and managed to say 'yes' quite clearly.

'Oh?' Quinn asked, lowering herself into a plastic chair.

'Mum's being transferred to a rehabilitation hospital on Monday,' Crystal explained. 'They'll be able to give her more specific therapy there and help her get ready for ... for the next step.'

Sadly, Quinn knew it was unlikely her friend would be able to return to living by herself, but they didn't want to discuss that in front of her just yet. Mrs D's primary focus needed to be on getting back her speech and movement.

'They even said we might be able to bring Snoodles to visit there,' Crystal added.

'Wow, that's awesome,' Quinn said, already wondering how on earth they'd be able to keep the demon under control in such a place.

'Os-car?'

Crystal leaned closer to Mrs D. 'What's that, Mum?'

Mrs D lifted her left hand—on the good side—and pointed to Quinn. 'Tell ab-out Os-car.'

Crystal frowned but Quinn immediately understood. 'Oh,' she half-laughed when it wasn't really a laughing matter at all. 'She must want me to tell you about Oscar.'

'Who's Oscar?' Crystal asked.

'Just this guy I had a bit of a thing for.' Now that her hopes had been so tremendously dashed, it was embarrassing to admit how crazy she'd been about someone she barely knew. Someone who'd turned out to be a total arsehole. 'Your mum knew how much I was into him, but a few days ago, I discovered something terrible. He used to be in a relationship with my friend and he was controlling and emotionally abusive. Once he locked her in a room for forty-eight—'

'No!'

They both startled at the exclamation from Mrs D. She was shaking her head.

Quinn again felt chastised—she didn't know what she was doing wrong but once again her friend appeared agitated by her visit. 'I'm sorry,' she said. 'I thought you—'

Mrs D interrupted, now tugging at Crystal's arm. 'Darle. Os-car Darle.'

'You don't mean Oscar Darke?' Crystal looked to Quinn, her eyes widening. 'Is that this guy's name?'

'Yes,' she replied warily. 'Do you know him?'

'Well, I used to—we lived on the same street growing up and went to school together. Now we just have mutual friends.'

'He just started work in my office.' Quinn quickly brought up Oscar's LinkedIn profile on her phone and showed Crystal. 'That must be a few years old, but he hasn't changed much. Is this who you're talking about?'

Crystal stared at the photo. 'Yeah, that's him. All the girls had mega crushes on him.'

'Eh-ric. Tell her Eh-ric,' Mrs D said, her tone urgent. 'Can't be … Os-car.'

Crystal turned back to Quinn. 'Mum's right. The man your friend described doesn't sound anything like Oscar, but it sounds exactly like his twin brother, Eric.'

Quinn's stomach dropped. 'Eric?' She looked to Mrs D. 'Oh my God. On Monday, I thought you were saying Eddie, but you were trying to tell me.'

The old woman nodded sadly.

'So, let me get this straight, Oscar has a *twin brother*?'

'Yes,' Crystal said. 'Total psycho. He even had issues at school. They're identical so Eric was just as good-looking as Oscar, but he didn't have the same intelligence or way with people. He was always competitive with Oscar, but not in the healthy way that's natural between siblings. Anything Oscar had, Eric wanted, and if he couldn't have it, he'd try to sabotage it. One year, Oscar made the state running team and Eric *accidentally*'—she made air-quotes—'tripped him up. He broke his ankle. Couldn't run at all for months.'

Oh my God.

'But …' Quinn shook her head slightly, struggling to digest this news. 'Oscar told me he was an only child.'

Didn't anyone tell the truth anymore?

'From what my friend Sharon heard, he considers himself one now. He's cut Eric completely out of his life and so have their parents. You can't blame him after what the man did to Oscar's wife.'

Deb's stomach clenched. 'What did he do?'

'It's absolutely awful. Unthinkable. The poor woman is suffering from early-onset Alzheimer's. From what I've heard, one day Oscar popped out to the shops to pick up some groceries and left Olivia with Eric.' Crystal rubbed her forehead, clearly distressed by what she was about to say. 'He raped her.'

'What?!' Quinn gasped.

'It's unclear whether he forced himself on her or somehow tricked her into thinking he was his brother, but Oscar forgot his wallet and came home to find them in the act.'

'Oh my God. What kind of psychopath is this Eric? If I were Oscar, I'd have killed him.'

'Sounds like he came pretty damn close. Neighbours heard the commotion and called the police, but once they'd worked out what happened, the charges against Oscar were dropped.'

'Please tell me Eric is in jail?'

'Yes. Seven years. Only recently convicted. I think they should have locked him up and thrown away the key this time. Some people can't be reformed.'

'He's been in jail before?'

'Oh yeah … over the years he's been involved in heaps of petty crimes, drink-driving, even some white-collar crime, although I hear he wasn't particularly good at that. He's been in and out of prison ever since he came back to Australia after his brief stint trying to make it in New York like Oscar.'

'Holy shit,' Quinn said as realisation dawned. 'This is absolutely nuts!' She tried to put the pieces together. 'So Eric was in New York too? Could that mean *he's* Deb's ex-boyfriend, not Oscar? Maybe he conned her too!' However confusing and crazy this sounded, they couldn't both be such bad eggs. 'Has Eric ever pretended to be Oscar?'

'You mean aside from that time with Olivia?' Crystal nodded. 'When we were kids he used to do it all the time. He tried it on with teachers at school, and even once with a girl Oscar was dating. She only realised it wasn't Oscar when Eric tried to kiss her.'

Quinn screwed up her nose at the thought.

'I don't know about in adulthood, but I wouldn't put it past him. Oscar always had a good career and did well at work, while Eric didn't finish uni and could never hold down a job. It probably sounded better when he was trying to pick up to say he was a successful sales manager at a major corporation than what he usually was—between jobs or doing something illegal. As to why he used Oscar's name? Probably in case anyone googled him.'

'Wow.' It was suddenly all making sense. No wonder Oscar hadn't recognised Deb, he'd actually never *met* her before starting at The Energy Co. 'I don't believe this. It's like something out of a psychological thriller. Or a soap opera. Or one of those insane telenovelas.'

Quinn was trying to process this revelation. She'd known from the moment she'd first laid eyes on Oscar that he was a good soul— how many people had walked past her on the footpath that evening before he stopped to help? And, after she'd heard everything he'd been through—all he was still going through with Olivia—she only believed it more.

'How was none of this in the news?' she asked. Even if she didn't know the people involved it was the kind of thing she'd remember if it made the headlines. Surely Deb would have seen it too.

'I asked the same thing. Michelle and I called Mum as soon as we heard about it on the old school grapevine to see if she knew, but she hadn't heard a thing. Turns out the court issued a suppression order due to the nature of the crime and Olivia's illness. They protected her in the same way minors are protected.'

Quinn jumped up from her seat. 'I need to call Deb.'

Debra

Deb's phone woke her from a rather nice dream. She smiled when she saw the caller was Quinn. Wait till she told her why she was still in bed at eleven o'clock in the morning. Who knew making love could be so exhausting?

'Missing me already?' she said by way of a greeting.

'I don't think Oscar's your ex. Which means he's not Ramona's father!'

'What?' Deb sat up in bed and glanced at the open door, hoping Ramona was still asleep. 'I ... I ... *What?*'

'He's a twin,' Quinn blurted. It sounded like she'd been exercising. 'Mrs D's daughter went to school with Oscar and Eric.'

'What?' Deb shook her head. 'But Oscar doesn't have any siblings.' Even as she said this, she realised that could easily have been just another one of his lies.

'That's what the real Oscar told me too, but turns out he disowned his brother. The man you met in New York must have been Eric. It all makes sense now that I've got all the pieces. Eric has always been jealous of Oscar who has always been more well-liked and far more successful. My guess is he didn't have a job when he met you, so he pretended to be his brother, who had a good one. Sounds like you weren't the first girl he fooled this way.'

'Hold on, slow down. Why would he do that?'

'Well, they're identical so if you checked out who he was—looked him up on the web or something—you'd have seen his *brother*. And being in a good job would probably have been better than admitting to being the no-hoper he clearly is.'

'This is insane,' Deb said, all the while thinking it made sense. Crazy sense, but sense, nonetheless. 'I wonder if the apartment we went to belonged to the real Oscar?'

'Highly likely.'

'He must have only taken me there when his brother was away. And, oh my goodness, that's why Oscar didn't recognise me in the elevator.'

'Exactly. Looks like you never had any need for a disguise, and you didn't need to resign.'

Deb couldn't think about that right now. 'What did you say Oscar's twin's name is?'

'Eric.'

'So where's Eric now? Please tell me he's still in America.'

'Afraid not, but you don't need to worry about running into him on the streets for quite some time.'

'What do you mean?'

'He's in prison.'

'What?' *Prison!* Deb's relief was quickly followed by curiosity. 'What for?'

'Raping Oscar's wife.'

Oscar was married? *But ...* Deb sucked in a breath and shook her head. 'That's terrible.'

'It's worse than terrible—Oscar's wife, Olivia, has early-onset Alzheimer's. They're not sure if Eric just downright took advantage or if he tricked her into thinking he was her husband.'

'Oh my God.' Now *that* sounded exactly like the man she knew. 'Hang on, how do you know all this?'

'I told you. I learned some from Mrs D's daughter, but the rest from Oscar. I went to his house last night and—'

'What were you doing at his house? You told me you were going to leave it all alone!'

'None of that matters now.' Quinn sounded exasperated. 'The important thing is, Oscar is not Ramona's father. I've got to go back to Mrs D, but I thought you should know. I'll see if I can find anything else out and chat later, okay?'

'Okay. Thank you.'

After she hung up, Deb stared at her phone before finally climbing out of bed. The apartment was eerily quiet, and when she checked Ramona's bedroom it was empty. Deb guessed she must be down the road hanging with Elijah and the budgies and was grateful for a few moments' reprieve to try and digest what Quinn had told her. If Oscar wasn't Ramona's father, then her worries about him appearing at The Energy Co had been unfounded, her resignation in vain. As far as she knew, this Eric still had no idea about their daughter. Even better, he was currently in jail, unable to hurt either of them.

Although the news should have taken a load off her anxiety, something still niggled inside her. An ominous feeling that made her stomach queasy. Hoping caffeine would help, she headed into the kitchen to make coffee and found a note next to the machine.

Gone to the city with Elijah to hang out with Lucy. Will be back before dinner.

Normally she'd be irritated that Ramona hadn't woken her to ask permission, but today she was too distracted to summon such emotion. As the coffee machine worked its magic, she typed a quick message back: *Hope you're having fun. Love you.*

And then she took her mug to the lounge room and fired up her laptop.

Eric Darke.

She couldn't find anything on Google about the rape, but there were numerous small articles about other crimes Eric had been involved in over the years, including a few photos of him at various ages. Identical was an understatement! Knowing now exactly what vile things Eric was capable of felt like vindication for never telling him about Ramona.

How many other women had he taken advantage of, *abused*, between her and Olivia? Had her silence made it easier for him to get away with depraved behaviour?

It suddenly hit her that if Oscar wasn't Ramona's father, then it changed things for Quinn too. The man who'd helped her, the man she'd fallen so hard and fast for, wasn't the man who'd abused Deb, but he *was* still married, which meant there was no future for the two of them.

She was thinking it all over when the door opened and Ramona stormed in, her face red from crying.

'What's wrong?' Deb asked, snapping her laptop shut. 'Did something happen with Lucy and Elijah?'

'We went to meet my father.'

'What?!' Cold terror flooded her body. Ramona had met *Eric Darke*? It was a good thing Deb was sitting down because her limbs suddenly turned to jelly and black dots floated in front of her eyes. 'You went to the *prison*?'

'Huh?' Ramona looked at Deb as if she'd spoken in tongues. 'What the hell is going on, Mum? Why would you think my dad is in prison? I thought I was a donor baby, but I'm fairly certain the man the DNA test told me was my father has never donated sperm in his life. And if I was the result of anonymous donation, then you wouldn't know where he is either! So what are you talking about?'

'You did a DNA test?'

Ramona nodded.

'Why didn't you tell me? How did you even order it? Didn't you need a credit card?'

'It doesn't matter,' Ramona spat. 'We're talking about *your* lies, not mine. Look me in the eye and tell me the truth! You didn't use an anonymous sperm donor, did you? You recognised Oscar Darke when he turned up at your work and you freaked so bad you quit. So *how* do you know him and *why* did you think I'd gone to a prison?'

'That's who you met today? *Oscar?* He's the one the DNA test said was your father?'

'Yes.'

'Thank God,' Deb exhaled.

'What do you mean?' Ramona sounded like she was losing patience. 'None of this makes sense. Oscar was married when I was conceived, so did you have an affair and keep your pregnancy secret?'

Deb opened her mouth, not quite sure what she was going to say, but again Ramona got in first.

'Something weird is going on here and if you don't tell me what it is, if you don't tell me the truth, I swear I'll never forgive you.'

Her little girl looked wilder and strangely more mature than she had before. Although Deb still desperately wanted to protect her, if she'd gone to such extremes to find her father, maybe it was finally time to come clean.

She swallowed and patted the vacant spot on the couch beside her. 'Sit down. I promise, I'll tell you everything.'

Ramona looked like she wanted to argue. In the end her need to know won out, but she sat as far as possible from Deb as she could.

'I met your father when I was studying in New York,' Deb began, telling Ramona as much as she could stomach. 'He swept me off my feet, made me feel truly loved for the first time in my life. But it was all a lie. He didn't really love me. I don't think he was capable of such a thing. He charmed me into falling in love with him and then he started to control me. He made me believe things about himself, about other people, even about me, that weren't true.'

She couldn't bring herself to tell Ramona about the traumatic forty-eight hours that had scarred her for life but did say that after she'd tried to end things, he'd planted cameras in her bathroom.

'When I found out I was pregnant, I quit my job, bought a plane ticket home and swore I'd do whatever it took to protect you from having such a monster in your life.'

Ramona didn't say a word until Deb neared the end of her story. 'And that monster was Oscar?'

Deb fiddled with the band of her watch. 'I thought so until about an hour ago.'

'What happened an hour ago?'

'Quinn rang. She discovered something I didn't know. You're right—I left The Energy Co because Oscar started there. I was terrified that if I stayed, he'd find out about you.'

'So, I'm really not a donor baby?' Ramona said, her voice small, her expression more fragile than a porcelain doll's.

'No,' Deb whispered with a small shake of her head. 'I'm so sorry. I told you that because I didn't want to burden you with the truth. I never realised how much you wanted to find out.'

'That's because every time I raised the issue, you brushed me off. What were you going to tell me when I was eighteen and legally able to try and find my donor?'

Again, Deb opened her mouth, but Ramona held up her hand. 'It doesn't matter. Probably more lies. Tell me the rest.'

'The *rest*?'

Ramona rolled her eyes. 'What did Quinn discover?'

'Well, it turns out Oscar is an identical twin.'

'What the?! Seriously?'

Deb nodded. 'I know. Surprised me too. He has a brother called Eric, who apparently has a history of fooling people and pretending to be Oscar. They were both in New York at the same time as me, and Eric sounds much more like the person I was in a relationship with. It would also account for why Oscar didn't recognise me at all when we met at work, but—'

'But what?' Ramona demanded.

'You said your DNA test led you to Oscar, so I don't know—'

'I'm pretty sure identical twins have the same DNA,' Ramona interrupted. 'We've been studying genetics in science.'

She whipped out her phone and madly started tapping. A few moments later, she nodded. 'Yep. The place I ordered my test from says that their testing is almost failsafe, except in rare cases of a sample switch when two people take their tests together, or in the case of identical twins. Their children are a unique case—cousins appear as half siblings and the twins appear as parents of both sets of kids. So I guess that means it's possible this Eric guy is my dad and the test got it wrong. It would certainly explain why Oscar seemed so confused today.' She paused a moment. 'What's he in prison for?'

'He …' Deb took a deep breath. No conversation had ever been as hard as this one. She'd barely had time to wrap her head around it herself. 'He hurt Oscar's wife.'

Ramona blinked. 'What do you mean hurt?'

'Oscar's wife ... she has early-onset Alzheimer's disease.'

'I know. He told us. It's awful, but what did Eric do to her?'

'Eric, he ... he took advantage of her.'

'Mum!' Ramona screamed. 'Don't try and protect me anymore. I'm not a baby. I'm almost sixteen. I deserve to know the truth and I can handle it. *How* did he take advantage of her?'

Deb struggled to say the words. 'He raped her.'

'What? No.' Ramona wrapped her arms around herself and rocked a little. 'It can't be true.'

'I'm sorry, honey.' It broke Deb's heart saying all this to Ramona. That's why she'd done all she could to protect her from the truth, but now there was no chance of closing Pandora's box.

She slid along the couch and tried to hug her, but again Ramona pushed her away. 'Don't touch me.'

'Honey, please ...'

She sprang from the couch. 'You lied to me. All these years when I tried to ask you questions about my father, you looked me in the eye and lied. *You!*' Tears streamed down her face as she hurled her accusation. 'You who's always gone on about the truth being so *fucking* important. When I went behind your back to get social media, you made me feel like the lowest of low, and yet you lied to me my whole life. You're such a hypocrite.'

'I'm so sorry, but you've got to understand, I did it for your own—'

'Don't give me that bullshit.'

Deb flinched. 'It's not bullshit. Please,' she pleaded, 'will you just listen to me?'

She had to convince Ramona that everything she'd done, everything she'd withheld, had been for the right reasons.

'Listen to you? Right now, I can't even stand to look at you.' Ramona fled to her bedroom and slammed the door.

Although it went against the grain not to chase after her, Deb held back. Ramona needed time to calm down before they tried to talk about this again.

Five minutes later, she appeared with her school bag slung over her shoulder, the pink teddy she still slept with every night tucked under her arm, and a recycling bag in each hand.

'Where are you going?' Deb asked, her heart clenching.

'After all I've discovered today, you're the last person who deserves an explanation. But if you must know, I'm going to stay with Elijah!'

Ramona slammed the front door so hard the noise reverberated around the whole apartment and Deb burst into tears.

She'd told her the truth, just as she'd wanted, but what if her daughter still never forgave her?

Ramona

'My dad's a rapist,' Ramona blurted to Elijah the moment he opened his front door.

'What?'

'He's in jail.' She was so upset she didn't even care if Barbara heard. She didn't care if *all* the neighbours heard.

'But … I … *how*? We met your dad today.'

She shook her head. 'That's not him. That's his twin brother. My father's name is Eric.'

'Twin brother? Wow,' Elijah said as he drew her into his arms. 'How'd you find that out?'

She sobbed against his shoulder, her words mingling with her tears as she tried to explain what had gone down with her mother. 'I hate her so much!'

Elijah pulled back and frowned. 'What? Why? It's not Deb's fault your father is an a-hole. Sounds like she was lucky to escape him.'

Ramona glared at him. 'She lied to me. She's made a fool out of me. All these years she told me I was a donor baby and that's what I've told everyone else. I kinda felt like it made me a bit special, when really, I'm not special at all. I'm nothing but the child of a criminal. A rapist.'

She had Eric's genes. This awful, awful man who treated women in the worst possible way was who she'd imagined one day meeting and bonding with, fantasised about bringing to school events. Imagine bringing Eric to SLC and introducing him as her father? Not that she could because he was behind bars! What would Sydney and her groupies do if they discovered that news? They treated Lucy like a leper because her dad was a priest; how much worse was a rapist?

'I'm sure your mum was just trying to protect you,' Elijah said. 'She loves you.'

'Don't make excuses for her. You don't lie to people you love. All my life she's gone on about us being on the same team, about being honest and open with each other, and all my life she's kept this from me. There's no excuse.'

He nodded glumly. 'Do you want to come inside, have something to eat? Gran cooked up a big batch of melting moments this morning.'

She realised she hadn't eaten since that morning—maybe some sugar would help her think straight. 'Yes please. Is Barbara here?'

'No, she's at book club this afternoon. Come on.' Elijah took her hand and led her into the kitchen, where they grabbed the biscuit tin and a couple of cans of lemonade from the fridge and took them out into the sunroom. As had become their ritual, he freed the birds and then sat down on the couch next to Ramona who was already chomping into her first biscuit.

Frodo flew across and sat on her shoulder, nuzzling her neck in his usual way. She wasn't sure if he was offering affection or simply trying to steal a bit of her cookie.

'You have the right idea,' Ramona said as Elijah cracked one of the cans and handed it to her.

'What do you mean?'

'Not wanting to find your father. I wish I'd never done the stupid DNA test. I guess I thought because I was conceived by donor sperm, my dad had to be someone with a good heart, but it turns out half my DNA is pure evil. What does that say about me? Maybe I'm capable of horrific things.'

'That's ridiculous,' Elijah said, his tone almost fierce. 'I might not have known you long, but I know you, and you have a good heart.'

'No, I don't.' Tears blurred her vision as she thought about how long she'd taken to stick up for Lucy. 'I let Sydney, Nyra and Kenzie say all sorts of horrible things about Lucy. I resented being matched with her at first.'

'But then you realised what was happening and stood up for her, even though it made your life hell. Someone evil wouldn't have done that.'

Ramona didn't even hear him. 'And I've done some awful things in my life. When I was little, I stole lollies when we went to the supermarket cos Mum would never buy them.'

'Everyone shoplifts at some stage. It's almost a rite of passage.'

'Did *you*?'

His expression gave her the answer. Elijah was far too good for the likes of her. She needed to make him understand what kind of person she was, deep down.

'When I was about seven, we had a neighbour with a baby. I used to play with her out in the garden while her mum was hanging the washing. Sometimes when her mum wasn't looking, I'd pinch her, hard, just to make her cry. And I liked it.' She put down her can, unable to stomach anything else.

'All kids are naughty. But you don't do things like that now. And you can see it was wrong. Maybe you were just wanting attention or something?'

She shook her head. 'No. I always had Mum's undivided attention. Oh my God, that's probably why no one ever liked me at my other schools—they could feel the evil radiating off me. Maybe Sydney saw a kindred spirit?'

'Now that's just ridiculous,' Elijah said, pulling her in for a hug. 'I know you're upset—you've every right to be—but I won't let you think such horrible, untrue things about yourself.'

But there was nothing he could say to convince her. Of course he'd see the best in her, that was what he was like. 'Do you think I could stay here for a bit?' she asked, snuggling into him.

'Sure. We can watch a movie to take your mind off all this before you go home.'

'Home?' Ramona pulled back and blinked. He'd misunderstood. 'I can't go home. I need some space. If I go back, Mum will just want to talk about this. She'll try to get me to forgive her and I'm not ready to do that. I'm not sure I'll ever be ready.'

'You want to stay here overnight? Indefinitely?'

She nodded.

Elijah sighed. 'I wish you could, but Gran would never allow it—she'd be worried we'd sneak into each other's beds during the night.'

That made Ramona smile for the first time since her life had imploded. Adults always thought teenagers had no self-control.

'Could you stay with Lucy?' Elijah suggested.

'Yeah, maybe. I'll message her.' Yet even as she pulled her phone out of her pocket, she realised she didn't want to go to Lucy's. Or rather, she didn't deserve to. Lucy was as pure as Elijah. They'd both be better off without her.

Ramona had never felt so alone in her life. Although she and Deb didn't have a massive family, at least they'd always had each other, but now that family seemed far too small. She didn't even have an aunt, cousin or grandparent she could turn to.

Perhaps she should go to Oscar. He was her uncle after all. Then again, he'd lied to her as well.

She pretended to text Lucy and then told Elijah she'd said yes.

'I'll come with you to her place,' he offered.

'You don't have to—you've already been to the city and back today.'

'Ramona,' he said, taking both her hands and looking down into her eyes, 'I'm coming. I'm not letting you travel alone when you're so upset. Just let me put the budgies away.'

'Please, Elijah,' she said firmly as he stood, 'I need to be alone for a bit.'

Hurt flashed in his eyes but then he nodded. 'Okay. If you're sure. But I'm walking you to the train, and you have to promise you'll call if you need me.'

'I will.' She forced a smile. 'Thanks.'

Elijah helped Ramona carry her things to the station and then she reached up and kissed him on the cheek, tears prickling her eyes as she wondered if this was goodbye.

Debra

Deb called Quinn to update her on everything that had happened and then tried to keep busy doing her usual Saturday routines, telling herself that Ramona was only down the road and in good hands with Elijah. If there was ever a time Ramona needed a friend, it was now.

She'd sent her a message not long after she'd stormed out:

I love you, sweetheart. Please never forget that and know that everything I've done was because I wanted to protect you.

But when it started to get dark and Ramona still hadn't replied, Deb couldn't bear it a second longer. How much time was she supposed to give her before she tried to make her listen again?

She wanted to tell Ramona she understood why she'd gone behind her back to do the DNA test and she was so, so sorry for what she'd discovered. She wished she'd had better judgement when it came to men, but even though her relationship with Eric had been a nightmare, she'd never regretted keeping Ramona. Not for one second.

Deciding to use the excuse of making sure Barbara was okay with Ramona staying the night, she walked the short distance to Elijah's place.

'Hi, Barbara,' she said when the older woman opened the door. 'Can I speak to Ramona please?'

Barbara's brow creased, highlighting her wrinkles. 'She's not here.'

'But she came over hours ago and ...' Deb's voice trailed off as fear gripped her heart.

'Come in,' Barbara said, opening the door wider. 'I'm sure Elijah knows where she is.'

They found him in the lounge room watching some animal documentary and eating from a packet of salt and vinegar chips. She caught his wary gaze before he covered it. 'Hi, Deb.'

'Did Ramona come see you this afternoon?'

He hesitated. 'Um ... yeah.'

'And do you know where she is now?' She could tell from the look on his face that Ramona had told him everything and he didn't want to break her confidence. 'Elijah, I need you to be honest with me. I know she's upset, and I'm worried about her.'

'She's fine,' he said eventually. 'She just needed some space, so she's staying with Lucy.'

'Lucy?' She tried to swallow her anger that Ramona had gone all the way to Glebe without telling her. This was getting out of hand. 'Okay, well thank you.'

'What are you going to do?' Elijah asked as she turned to go.

'What am I going to do?' she shouted in frustration. 'I'm going to go talk to my daughter and see for myself that she's safe.'

'I really think you should just give her tonight at least. She's hurt and she's angry, and she needs to calm down before seeing you again.'

Deb glared at him. 'Is that what you think? Well, forgive me for not taking parenting advice from a sixteen-year-old boy.'

'Good luck,' Barbara said, hurrying after Deb to see her out of the house. 'Parenting isn't for the faint-hearted, that's for sure.'

Deb knew that Barbara was speaking from experience, but she didn't have time for group therapy. What must Lucy's father think about Ramona suddenly turning up on his doorstep with all her things? Had Lucy and Ramona told him why she was there?

As she hurried home to get the car, she tried calling Ramona, but the call went straight to voicemail.

She texted instead: *If you don't call me immediately, I'm driving into town to come and collect you. I know you're angry but you're my daughter and you're only fifteen years old, which means I need to know you're safe.*

Like the call, the message went unanswered, but Deb was already on her way. She cursed herself for not having the forethought to have asked Ramona for her friends' parents' numbers. That was the problem with teenagers having mobile phones—they could organise everything themselves so there wasn't any need for parents to know each other until something drastic happened. Jake was the only parent from SLC she'd met, and only once when she dropped Lucy home weeks and weeks ago.

Halfway there her phone rang and she almost swerved off the road. *Ramona?* Her hopes were dashed when she saw the caller was Tristan.

'Hey, good-looking,' he said when she answered. 'I know you're with Ramona tonight, but I couldn't resist hearing your voice. Last night was—'

'Ramona's run away to her friend's place,' she interrupted.

'What? What do you mean run away?'

The revelations of the last few hours spilled out.

'Why didn't you call me when she left?'

'I thought she'd just gone to Elijah's. Besides, I had other things on my mind and it's not like we're married. You're not Ramona's father.'

'I know. I'm sorry. I just want to be there for you if you're upset.'

Deb heard the hurt in his voice, but the truth was she still wasn't used to relying on anyone and right now she didn't have the mental energy to feel bad about this. 'I'm heading into the city to her friend's place. I'll call you later, okay?'

'Okay, good luck,' Tristan said before hanging up.

She turned on the radio but couldn't have recalled any of the songs she heard. The events of the day kept playing over and over in her head. Initially, she'd been so relieved to hear that Ramona hadn't met Eric but now, alone in her car with no other distractions, she started to wonder what Oscar had been playing at.

If the whole twin story was real, even if there had been some sort of mix-up at the DNA testing company, why didn't he set Ramona straight? Why had he let Ramona believe he was her father when he must know he couldn't be?

It didn't make sense and it didn't sit right in her gut. What if they were both psychopaths?

This thought had her gripping the steering wheel as a cold terror flooded her body. The last sixteen years she'd spent running from Oscar—or rather the man she'd believed to be Oscar—and yet ... the truth had finally caught up with her.

Deb glanced at the time on her dashboard. Although it was getting late, Ramona was safely at Lucy's place and maybe it would be good if Deb got a few more answers before she spoke to her. In the moment, Elijah's words about Ramona being hurt and angry had aggravated her, but now they simply made her heart ache.

Poor Ramona must be so confused.

Decision made, she pulled over to put Oscar's address into her GPS. Ever since the day she'd looked up his contact details, it had been imprinted in her head. It didn't hurt that he lived on the same street as Quinn.

Fifteen minutes later, she slowed in front of his house and stared at it a few long moments before switching off the ignition and climbing out.

Was she really going to do this?

To face Oscar Darke. Whoever he was.

Her heart froze, but the voice in her head told her to keep going. No matter how terrifying, it was finally time to face her demons and work out who exactly she was dealing with. It was time to be brave. For her daughter.

The cast-iron gate creaked as she entered the pretty courtyard, the light from a nearby streetlamp shining a path to the door. Her breath quickened as she knocked.

It opened promptly and Oscar appeared. 'Hello?' he said, his expression confused.

She stared long and hard. Of course, she'd seen him in the office—they'd been up close and personal in the elevator—but now she'd been told he was a twin she couldn't help looking at him differently. Scrutinising any tiny difference she might not have noticed before. Was that a slight dimple on his chin? It was hard to tell.

'Hang on ... do I know you?' He frowned then clicked his fingers. 'You're the woman from the elevator! Denise, right? How can I help you?'

'Actually, it's Debra,' she corrected. 'Debra Fast.'

She saw realisation dawn in his aqua eyes. 'You're Ramona's mum.' He cleared his throat. 'Wow. She didn't mention you worked at The Energy Co as well. I'm glad you've come. She left in a hurry, and I was worried about her. I wanted to talk to you, to check she was okay, but couldn't find a listing in the White Pages or online.'

'I've always kept my number private,' she said, her fear slowly evaporating. This wasn't her ex. Oscar and Eric might look the same, but that's where their similarities ended. He genuinely seemed concerned about Ramona, whereas Eric—it was going to take some time to get used to that name—was only ever concerned about himself.

'Do you want to come in so we can talk?'

'Yeah, that'd be good.'

'Great.' Oscar gestured for her to head inside. 'Can I get you a drink? I've got beer, coffee, tea.' He hesitated. 'Or would you rather a whiskey?'

'I'll have a coffee, thanks.' She was slightly tempted by the whiskey but didn't want to turn up to the priest's house later smelling like a distillery.

Oscar closed the door behind them and she found herself in his living room. 'Take a seat,' he said, pointing to the couch, 'and I'll grab the drinks.'

She glanced around, her gaze catching a wedding photo atop the piano. Unable to resist, Deb took a closer look.

'Do you take milk?' he called from the back of the house. 'And sugar?'

'Yes, to milk, and—' She was about to say no to the sugar but decided to make an exception today. 'One sugar, please.'

Oscar's wife was so young. Obviously the photo must have been taken a few years ago, but it didn't seem possible that someone about Deb's own age could have been struck by such a cruel, debilitating disease.

'Here you are.' He handed her a mug as he came to stand beside her.

She took it from him. 'Your wife's beautiful.'

'Inside and out,' he said sadly.

'I heard she has Alzheimer's.'

'Ramona told you?' he asked, before taking a sip of his coffee.

She shook her head. 'Quinn. She called me this morning. You see ... I never knew Eric was a twin. He told me he was an only child, so when you turned up at The Energy Co I freaked out. I thought you were him.'

'I'm sorry.' He scratched his head. 'How does Quinn know I'm a twin? I feel like I've started watching a TV series in season two. Can you catch me up a little?' He gestured to the couch and they both sat.

Deb went right back to the beginning. 'I met Eric in New York, at a speed-dating for Aussies event.'

'No kidding. That's where I met Olivia. Eric never told me he went.'

'Probably because he was using your name. Or at least that's how he introduced himself to me. Your name, your job, I think he even took me to your apartment a couple of times.'

Oscar winced.

'You don't sound surprised?'

'I wish I could say I was, but you weren't the only one he tried it on. I found out when a woman came to my office one day to surprise me with a picnic lunch. It got pretty messy when the receptionist told her I was out with my wife. The woman waited until I returned and then she laid into me. I'd never seen her before in my life, but she thought we'd been in a relationship for two months.'

'He often accused me of cheating on him when I'm fairly certain he was cheating on me,' Deb said.

Oscar nodded. 'Once Olivia found a pair of lacy knickers under our couch cushions.'

Deb swallowed, not about to admit that she'd lost numerous knickers during the brief time she'd been with Eric. Every time they slept together, he'd insist on keeping them; she'd thought it sexy in the beginning but now she could see it for the sick trophy it was.

'That's when we realised,' he continued. 'He'd been using our apartment when we were away or out at work. He actually stayed with us in the beginning, but he made Olivia uncomfortable. After a couple of months, we asked him to leave, and that's when we discovered he'd lost the job he got his visa for. He was living in the States illegally and we told him we wanted nothing to do with it. We thought he'd gone back to Australia until the picnic basket woman came into my office. Then we realised he must have still been around, but we didn't see him until Liv found the knickers. Then I tracked him down and told him to grow up and go home.'

'Wow. I wonder if that was before or after I was with him?'

Oscar shrugged. 'I'm not sure exactly, sorry. So many years later, the timing has blurred.'

'It doesn't matter.' Deb finally drank some coffee.

'Did he know you were pregnant?'

'I ... I don't actually know.' She told him about Eric locking her up, her trying to leave him and then finding cameras the day she did the test.

'Jesus.'

'As well as a baby, he also left me with an STD, confirming my suspicions he'd been cheating. I didn't want anything to do with him. I didn't want someone like him in my child's life.'

'I'm so sorry he put you through that.'

It wasn't Oscar's fault, but she appreciated his words. 'You don't need to apologise, I'm the one who should be apologising to you.'

'What? How do you figure that?'

'Quinn found out what he did to Olivia as well.'

Oscar's face fell. She'd never seen anyone look so despondent. Or was it anger?

'I can't even ... If I'd reported him all those years ago rather than running, maybe ...'

'No,' Oscar interrupted. 'Don't think like that. This is not your fault. I could blame myself for not insisting he got help earlier. And for years I did, so did my parents—there were so many signs growing up that he wasn't quite right in the head and needed serious help.'

As he told her about how Eric had treated him and his parents over the years, Deb realised she had so much in common with this man who, until that day, she didn't even know existed. He'd once loved Eric too, only he'd been betrayed and let down by him over and over again.

'Maybe I should have tried harder, maybe my parents should have, but in the end, we realised it's all on him. He had a good childhood, he wanted for nothing, and I helped him as best I could over the years, and how did he repay me? He raped my wife.'

Oscar glanced over at the photos on the piano and Deb saw the veins in his neck pulse as his tone grew more and more irate. 'After the conviction, he was diagnosed with narcissistic personality disorder, but even knowing that I can never forgive him. He's dead to me. As far as I care, that motherfucker can rot in jail. I completely understand why you tried to protect Ramona from him.'

'Is that why you admitted to being her father today?'

'Yeah. When I first got the notification from the DNA company, I thought maybe I'd fathered a child I didn't know about before going to New York. I promise I'm not anything like my brother, but I did sleep with a few women in my late teens and early twenties. There was a woman I had a one-night stand with just before I left Sydney ... we didn't exchange last names or any other details. I guess I thought maybe she had a baby.'

'Must have been a shock,' Deb said.

'At first, but I gotta admit, I felt a little excited at the prospect, and that brought some guilt.'

'What do you mean?'

'Liv and I couldn't have kids, and it felt wrong that I might get what she never would. It also scared the hell out of me. I was terrified I'd meet Ramona and be a disappointment, or that she might hold some kind of grudge against me.'

Deb smiled. 'But then Ramona turned up and you realised the age didn't fit?'

'Yeah. I knew it was her instantly, but she looked so young. Too young. I asked her age and she confirmed it. That's when I guessed what must have happened. At fifteen, there was no way she could be mine, which left only one alternative.' He paused and Deb saw his grip tighten on his mug. 'I was so fucking angry that Eric—the last person on earth who deserves to be a father—had a daughter and I never would, but that quickly made way for something else. Fear. Fear that Eric would hurt Ramona if he found out about her. I didn't really think it through, I just said what I could to protect her because no way in hell did I want to be responsible for my brother ruining another life.'

'None of this is your fault,' she said, grateful for the way he'd tried to help.

He shook his head as if he didn't believe her. 'Anyway, I don't think she bought my story.'

'She might have, if I didn't accidentally let slip what I'd just found out about you being twins and Eric being in prison.'

'Poor girl.' Oscar put down the mug and rubbed his forehead. 'How's she doing with that information?'

'Not great. In fact, she went to stay with a friend. I was on my way to see her when I decided to drop by here first.'

'Guess you got my address because we work together?'

She nodded and gave him a sheepish smile as she stood. 'Perks of being payroll manager.'

'Well, I'm glad you came,' he said, standing too. 'I understand why you did what you did, and I commend you for keeping Ramona away from Eric. She's clearly an amazing girl. You've done a wonderful job of raising her alone.'

'Thank you,' she whispered, tearing up a little.

'But you don't have to be alone anymore. I'd love to be a part of Ramona's life, if she wants it and you'll allow it. And I know my parents would love to meet her too. I think they'd given up on grandchildren.'

'But what about Eric?' Deb interrupted, a chill skating down her spine as she said his name.

He shook his head. 'None of us have anything to do with him anymore, so you don't need to worry on that front.'

'We'll have to see,' Deb said, not wanting to make any promises. 'Ramona's very angry right now. I think she might need some time to come to terms with … with everything before she makes any decisions.'

Because as hard as it was, Deb now realised her little girl was growing up and this would be her decision to make.

Oscar smiled as he opened the front door for her, but she just stood there staring at him. 'Debra?' he asked. 'You okay?'

'I'm sorry.' She blinked and shook her head slightly. 'It's just … you look exactly like him.'

'I know,' he said. 'But I promise I'm not.'

Quinn

'We really need to stop running into each other like this,' Oscar said as Quinn closed Mrs D's gate behind her and almost bumped into him on the footpath.

Her mouth went dry at the sight of him in black sports shorts and a blue T-shirt. 'You going for a run?'

'Yeah.' He pushed his hair back out of his face.

God, he was hot. Quinn cursed her thought—it was a sin to lust after a married man, but her body was still catching up to her brain. *Dammit*.

'It's been a bit of a day,' he added, 'and I needed to get out and try to clear my head.'

'Did it work?'

He sighed in reply. Never had anyone looked more in need of a friend. 'Not sure. I've only just set off.'

Quinn should probably let him get on with his run, but she felt compelled to talk about all she'd discovered today and was trying to work out how to broach the subject when Oscar spoke.

'I can't believe your neighbour Mrs D is Mrs Dagliesh. It should have clicked. I went to school with her daughter, Michelle, but I guess you know that now.'

Quinn nodded sheepishly. For some reason she felt guilty.

'I didn't know she still lived here,' he said. 'My parents kept their house as a rental but moved out to the suburbs years ago.'

'I've just had dinner with Crystal, her other daughter. Michelle's coming home soon. Sadly, it doesn't look like Mrs D will be able to come back here and live alone, even after rehab.'

'I'm sorry to hear that. Will she have to go into care?'

'No. Crystal and Michelle can't bear the thought of putting her into a nursing home, so they're going to move her to England where they both live now.'

This news had hit Quinn harder than she thought it would, even though it would be wonderful for Mrs D. Maybe it was all the revelations of the day, or maybe it was simply that she was going to miss her friend like crazy. With Deb gone at the office, she couldn't bear the thought of any more changes.

'You okay?' Oscar asked, frowning down at her.

'Yeah.' She swallowed as emotion swelled in her throat. 'They've asked me to adopt the big guy.'

He glanced towards the house. 'Snoodles?'

'Ah huh. Apparently, Crystal and her wife have two cats and Michelle's husband is allergic. But I can't take him because Darpan, my brother's husband, is also allergic.'

Quinn chewed on her bottom lip. Losing Mrs D was going to be bad enough but as much as Snoodles had been a pain in her arse when they'd first started walking, even his naughtiness had grown on her and she really did adore him. The thought of him going to live with strangers left her cold.

'If I could afford my own place, I'd take him in a second,' she added. 'I've been thinking of moving out for a while, but I can't guarantee I'll be able to find anywhere that lets me have pets in time.'

'I'll take him.'

She blinked. 'What?'

Oscar grinned. 'I'd love a dog. Granted, he's slightly bigger than I'd probably have chosen myself, but it'll be good to have someone to go running with and company when I'm slothing about on the couch watching TV.'

Quinn couldn't help wishing she could be that somebody. She twisted the heart earring dangling on her lobe. 'Wow. That's such a generous offer. Crystal is jet-lagged and was going to head straight to bed, but I'll let her know tomorrow and maybe you can get together to work out the logistics.'

'Sounds good to me. Well, I guess I'd better let you go. It's getting chilly out here.'

'How are you, Oscar?' she asked, not wanting him to go without making sure he was okay. 'Ramona turning up at your place must have been quite the shock.'

He shrugged. 'Yes and no. I got a message from her earlier in the week through the DNA testing company, but I had no idea she knew where I live, so coming home to find three teenagers on my doorstep was quite the surprise. And her age shocked me. It was then that I realised she couldn't be mine.'

Quinn nodded.

'I actually almost told you about her last night—not that I knew your connection to her then, but I just really wanted someone to talk to about it.'

'Oh? Why didn't you?'

He shoved his hands in his pockets and looked down at his feet. 'It felt like a betrayal. Liv's always been the one I share my problems with, yet she can't really help anymore and ...'

'Hey ...' Oscar's despondence broke her heart and she stepped forward and put her hand on his arm. 'I'm happy to be an ear whenever you need one.'

'Thanks. Deb and I just had a good chat but—'

'Deb came here?' She'd called Quinn earlier that afternoon but mentioned nothing about visiting Oscar.

'Yeah, she was on her way to pick Lucy up from a friend's and wanted to grill me on my intentions I think.' He chuckled. 'Not sure how much you know but I kinda let Ramona believe she was mine when she visited. She's a great kid and I'd have been proud to call her my own.' He paused a moment, then, 'Did you know when you came over last night about my connection to Deb? Or rather, the connection you thought I had?'

'Yes.' Quinn's hand once again went to her earring and she shivered. 'She told me everything.'

'Geez.' He looked gutted. 'You must have thought I was a monster.'

'Honestly? I didn't know what to think. None of it made any sense to me.'

He glanced at his watch. 'Look, I know it's getting late, but do you want to go get a drink or something?'

Quinn felt torn. Part of her wanted this desperately, and she could tell he needed to debrief, but the more sensible side of her told her it wouldn't be a good idea, even if she had just offered her ear.

Her phone rang before she could reply, and she tugged it out of her pocket. 'Speaking of Deb. This is her. I'd better answer it.'

Oscar nodded. 'Of course.'

'Hey, Deb, what's up?'

Debra

Deb parked in front of the cemetery next to Lucy's house and made her way through the quaint solar-lit garden to the front door of the rectory. She felt much calmer after her conversation with Oscar but still knocked loudly and urgently, desperate to see Ramona.

'Good evening, Deb,' Jake said warmly as he registered her standing on his doorstep. He peered past her as if expecting someone else. 'Isn't this a lovely surprise. Did Lucy forget to tell me she and Ramona arranged a sleepover or something?'

Deb frowned, her renewed calm evaporating. 'Isn't Ramona here?'

Jake's smile dropped. 'No. It's just me and Luce.'

Oh my God. Her heart went numb. 'But … Ramona came here this afternoon?' It was half-statement, half-question.

'I … No. I'm sorry but she didn't. They went out together this morning, but Lucy came home alone just after lunch, and she's been here ever since.'

Deb burst into tears.

'Hey.' Jake wrapped an arm around her and ushered her into the house. Lucy looked up from where she was sitting on the couch and immediately muted the TV. 'Can you put the kettle on and make Debra a cup of tea please?'

'Wh-what's going on? What's wrong?' Lucy asked, slowly rising.

'Where's Ramona?' Deb demanded, pulling away from Jake.

Lucy blinked. 'I'm s-sorry, but I don't know. I … I … thought she was going h-h-home to talk to you about … about her father.'

Much to Deb's distress, she believed the girl—but if Ramona wasn't here, where was she? 'Can you try to call her for me?'

'I can but I already s-sent her some messages asking how things went and she hasn't … r-r-replied.'

'Please?' Deb begged.

Lucy nodded, then reached to the coffee table and picked up a phone. Deb leaned over her, making sure she really was trying Ramona. The room went quiet as Lucy lifted her phone to her ear.

'It went straight to voicemail,' she said, her tone both apologetic and anxious.

'Shit.' Deb covered her mouth with her hand as dread filled her.

'Was she upset?' Jake asked.

'Yes. She found out who her dad was this afternoon and she's angry at me because …' Guilt and shame swamped her but she couldn't focus on that right now. 'Because I hadn't told her everything about him. But none of the why matters, we need to find her!'

'Is there anyone else she might have gone to? A family member? Another friend from school?'

'I don't know, we don't have any family nearby.' Deb looked to Lucy. 'Could you call your other school friends, check with them?'

Lucy shook her head. 'I don't have the … n-n-numbers of anyone else from school, but I'm sure Ramona wouldn't have gone to them anyway. They all hate us.'

'They *hate* you?' That caused Deb to pause a moment. 'Since when?'

'Well, they've always hated me,' Lucy admitted as if this were no great loss, 'but when Ramona befriended me, they ... c-cut her off too. She won't go to any of them.'

How did Deb not know any of this? Had she been too hung up on Tristan and then the Oscar thing to notice her daughter was unhappy?

'Lucy,' Jake said, 'how about you go make us all a cup of tea?'

Jake's calm, however well meaning, infuriated Deb. How would he feel if it were Lucy missing? 'I don't have time for a cup of tea! I have to go find Ramona.'

'And where are you going to look first?' he asked.

She swallowed. 'I ... I ... don't know.'

He nodded. 'Then let's sit down and form a plan. When was the last time you saw her?'

Deb all but fell into the couch, her legs barely holding her up anymore. 'Um ... about seven hours ago.' Her stomach cramped as she thought of all that could have happened in that time. It was dark out now and Ramona could be anywhere. With *anyone*.

'I think we should call the police,' Jake suggested, already pulling his phone out of his pocket. 'They can put an alert out for her. She can't have gone too far and if she is staying with someone, hopefully their parents will see the news and call in.'

Deb nodded, unable to believe this was happening.

Lucy returned with a tray of tea and biscuits as Jake and Deb were explaining to the woman at the emergency call centre what the problem was.

'We'll send someone round immediately,' she promised. 'In the meantime, find some photos we can use and call everyone you can think of who she might have gone to.'

The call ended and Jake pulled out a pen and paper. 'Let's make a list of who to call.'

'I can really only think of Elijah, but I saw him before I left—he was the one who told me she was here.'

Jake frowned. 'Could he have been lying?'

'I … I don't know.'

'Why don't we try him again?'

'I don't have his number.'

'I do,' volunteered Lucy. 'Use my phone,' she said, pushing a button and then handing it to Deb.

'Hey, Luce, how's Ramona?' Elijah answered.

'It's not Lucy, it's Debra,' she said. 'And Ramona never got here.'

'What?' She heard the panic in his voice, but could she trust him?

'I need you to be honest with me, Elijah. Do you know where Ramona is? Don't lie to me.'

When Deb started shouting at him to tell the bloody truth, Jake took the phone and spoke calmly to him. Forcing deep breaths, she wrung her hands together until Jake hung up.

'The boy's telling the truth,' he said. 'He's as worried as we are now he knows she didn't come here. He says he tried to call her after you left, and it went to voicemail. He's going to go check your place and then start looking around the neighbourhood. I told him we'll keep him updated.'

Deb pulled at her hair. It was one thing for Ramona not to pick up for her, but to ignore Lucy and Elijah … Before she could voice her fear, the doorbell rang.

Lucy ran to answer it and seconds later two cops appeared, introducing themselves as Senior Constable Dyer and Constable Tsiolkas. Lucy poured them cups of tea while Dyer peppered her with questions and Tsiolkas scribbled notes in his little pad.

'You'd had an argument before Ramona left, is that right?' asked Dyer.

'Yes.' Deb clenched her jaw. How many times did she have to go over this? They weren't going to find Ramona sitting here.

'And what frame of mind would you say she was in when she left?'

That sounded a little accusatory and Deb's chest squeezed as she realised what they were considering. *No.* Ramona wouldn't ... would she? Oh God, if anything happened to her, she'd never forgive herself.

'*Please*,' she said, 'I've told you all I can. Can you just start looking for her?'

The senior constable nodded. 'I think we've got enough for now. Constable Tsiolkas has already circulated the photos you gave us. I suggest you keep contacting anyone you can think of that she might have gone to, and also put an alert out on your Facebook notifying your friends and asking them to share it. We'll get one up on the police social media asap, but the more people who know we're looking for her the better.'

'I don't have Facebook,' Deb said.

'No worries. Just do your best. We'll send round a local officer to check if she's gone home yet, but you might want to head there too because it's most likely that's what she'll do. Eventually.'

'Luce and I will call you immediately if she turns up here,' Jake promised.

'I can't just go home and sit and wait,' Deb cried as the police left. 'Lucy, can you call Elijah back and ask him to wait at the apartment and call me if she returns?'

'Yes, of course.'

'What are you going to do?' Jake asked.

'I'm going to drive around looking for her.' She snatched up her bag, already digging out her car keys.

'I don't think you should drive in the state you're in,' said Jake.

'I'll be fine,' she replied, then suddenly thought of something. 'Quinn has Facebook! And thousands of followers.' Barely before she'd finished the thought, her phone was at her ear and she was calling her friend.

'I'm on my way,' Quinn promised after she quickly explained what was going on.

'My friend's coming here,' Deb told Jake. 'She'll do the social media stuff and then she'll drive with me.'

'Good,' he said, clearly relieved that she wasn't about to head out on her own.

Feeling slightly better now that Quinn was coming, Deb called Tristan.

'Hi there,' he said.

'Ramona's not at Lucy's,' she explained. 'I'm so sorry about brushing you off before, but could you help me now?'

'You name it and I'll do it.'

'Well, Elijah is going to go sit at the apartment in case she turns up, but do you think you could start driving around the area and keep an eye out? The police are going to find out if she got on the train like she said she was going to, but until we know for sure, Quinn and I are going to drive around here where she said she was heading and then, I guess …'

Her voice trailed off—she didn't want to think about what she'd do if they didn't find Ramona.

'Of course,' he said. 'We'll find her. I promise.'

Even though that was a promise he didn't have any right to make, Deb felt heartened by Tristan's words. 'Thank you,' she said. 'I'll stay in touch.'

'I've called the after-hours number for SLC,' Jake said as she hung up. 'They're going to post to their Facebook and Instagram accounts and send an urgent email out to all parents. They said to let them know if there's anything else they can do to help.'

'Thank you.' Deb nodded, feeling so bloody helpless. Where on earth was her daughter? Terrible thoughts flashed through her head as she contemplated all the horrible possibilities. There must be something else she could do.

'Would you like me to pray while we wait for your friend?' asked Jake.

Deb's instinct was to say no, but she found herself nodding instead. If God was real, she hoped he'd forgive her for overlooking him all these years and answer the only prayer that had ever mattered.

Please Lord, bring Ramona home safely.

Ramona

Ramona's phone had died what felt like hours ago—in her haste to pack, she'd totally forgotten her charger. What an idiot. Not that she'd have anywhere to plug it in, but she might have found a lone power point somewhere in a shopping centre or train station. She bought herself the cheapest meal you could get at Macca's and ate it down by the harbour, dangling her legs over the water's edge as she wondered what the hell to do next.

Although she'd been wandering round the city all afternoon, come nightfall things started to get scary—a few scruffy-looking men had already approached asking for money or cigarettes and the way they'd leered at her made her scalp prickle.

Was Eric—*her dad*—like them? Before he was in prison, did he prowl the streets looking for prey? Was Olivia his first rape victim or just the first he'd been caught for?

She didn't want to think these thoughts, but they wouldn't leave her the hell alone.

As it was a Saturday night, there were people everywhere, but they were mostly dressed up to the nines, many half-drunk already—she doubted they'd notice if something happened and she needed help. She contemplated going home, but then she remembered her mother and her anger raged all over again.

How dare Deb lie to her all these years! She understood not telling a toddler or a child about why she'd run from Ramona's father, but she hadn't been a child for years. There'd been many times recently she'd tried to raise the subject of her dad—any of those times would have been the perfect opportunity to come clean; instead she'd perpetuated the lie.

The worst thing was she didn't think her mum would ever have told the truth if her hand hadn't been forced. Deb had bargained on the fact Ramona would never follow through on contacting the donor register.

What would she have done when she did? Come up with some crazy lie about why Ramona wasn't on it?

No, she wasn't going back.

If only she'd followed through on getting a part-time job, she'd have more than twenty dollars to her name. Maybe then she could get a room in a cheap hotel or something. As that wasn't an option, she considered a homeless shelter for women and kids. There had to be something like that around here. Only last term at school they'd had a fundraiser for a local refuge. But then again, if she went there, there'd be a social worker asking all sorts of questions. They'd probably even contact Deb. She shuddered. Perhaps she *should* have gone to Lucy's. At least there she'd be safe, but she still felt icky about telling Lucy and her dad the truth about her father. Sure, priests were supposed to be all forgiving, but what parent would want their daughter hanging out with the daughter of a rapist?

Once again, she thought of her other friends—well, the ex-ones from SLC. Although Kenzie had stopped talking to her along with Sydney and Nyra, she hadn't sent any horrible messages or actively made her school life hell. Maybe she'd let her stay at her place for a night or two … but this possibility was short-lived. Ramona didn't know where Kenzie lived, and with her phone dead she couldn't message her anyway. She guessed she lived reasonably close to school, although probably not anywhere quite as flash as Sydney's suburb; Kenzie *had* mentioned feeling like a pleb whenever she went there.

Suddenly she remembered something else Kenzie had said that night—about Sydney running away to the pool house. It would be the perfect place to hide out, but would it be locked? Would she even be able to get past the perimeter security?

Doubting the answer to either of these questions would be yes, a night in a park in Bellevue Hill would be better than a park in the inner city anyway. Decision made, she started towards the station and caught the next train to Edgecliff. Sydney's house was a fair walk from there and by the time Ramona slowed in front of the mammoth entry gates, her feet felt like they were about to fall off and her shoulders hurt from lugging around her bags.

She hid behind a tree out the front of Sydney's property and stared up at the gates and the house beyond, trying to work out how to bypass them. A lush green hedge stood tall on either side of the gates, but the fence behind it wasn't that high. There was only a smattering of lights on in the house and Ramona guessed from her visits there that the lights were Sydney's and London's bedrooms. Hopefully Mr and Mrs Jamison were out.

Her heart thudded as she threw her bags over the hedge and waited to see if an alarm would go off. When nothing happened, she squeezed through the hedge and heaved herself over the fence, breathing a sigh of relief when she landed on the other side. Sneaking to the backyard was easy and then she tiptoed towards the pool house, the water glittering beneath the moonlight. She held her breath as she tried the door handle and couldn't believe her luck when it opened. She dumped her stuff inside and shut the door quickly behind her. Although she didn't risk turning on the lights, her eyes adjusted quickly to the dark and—*wow*—she couldn't believe what she saw.

This place was like a five-star hotel. In addition to the pool table, there were plush leather armchairs and a bar area with a fridge containing actual food and drink. Ramona almost cried at the sight.

She helped herself to a can of Diet Coke and a packet of Twisties and then flopped onto one of the couches. An enormous TV screen beckoned but she dared not turn it on for fear of alerting someone. The stress and tension of the day finally caught up with her and she drifted into a restless slumber, only to be woken by the creak of the door.

A silhouette of a figure stood in the doorway. The door thunked shut and almost immediately the room lit up with the flashlight from a phone.

'No fucking way,' spat Sydney, her eyes narrowed.

'What are you doing in here?'

'Uh.' Sydney perched one hand on her hip. 'I *live* here. More to the point, what are *you* doing here? And why have you run away?'

Ramona's stomach clenched. 'How'd you know I've run away?'

'Are you kidding?' Sydney scoffed as she dropped her hand to her pocket and pulled out a vape pen. 'Your face is all over social media. It's all anyone's posting about tonight.'

'What? Really?'

'Uh huh. The police have put you on their Insta and everyone's sharing it.' Propping the pen between her teeth, Sydney opened her phone, tapped it a couple of times then showed Ramona.

Her eyes boggled as she stared at the image of herself on the screen. 'But ... I told Mum I was staying at Lucy's.'

Sydney shrugged and flopped onto the couch beside her. 'Guess she discovered you weren't. Why *didn't* you go there? Isn't she your bestie now?'

'Because she's too good for me. I don't deserve a friend like her.'

Sydney clicked her vape pen a few times in rapid succession until it lit up. 'The fuck you talking about?'

'I found out about my dad. He's a rapist,' Ramona blurted.

'Fuck.' Sydney lowered her pen a moment. 'Are you serious?'

'Do you think that's the kind of thing I'd joke about?'

They sat there in the relative dark—Sydney vaping and Ramona contemplating the fact that her mum had called the police. If only her phone wasn't flat, she could call Lucy and see if she knew anything. Shit, did Elijah know she was missing as well?

Ramona felt a pinprick of guilt and that only annoyed her—Deb was the one who should be feeling guilty!

'Well, you gunna fill me in or not? Is this something to do with the DNA test?'

Although Sydney was the last person Ramona wanted to share all this with, she felt she owed her after sneaking in here and stealing food and drink. 'I'll tell you, but first, do you have a phone charger I could borrow?'

Sydney stood up and disappeared behind the bar, reappearing with a charger. 'There's a power point on the wall behind the couch.'

'So, you know how I thought I was a donor baby? Turns out Mum lied to me about that my whole life,' she began, after plugging in her phone. It was so dead it would be a while before she could message Lucy and Elijah.

482

'Wow.' Sydney inhaled long and hard on the pen and exhaled vapour as Ramona came to the bit about discovering Eric was a rapist. 'That's some story.'

If only it *was* a story, Ramona thought as her phone began to go psycho with alerts. Hundreds of missed calls and messages.

'You were right about why I bullied Lucy.'

'Huh?' That was the last thing Ramona expected Sydney to say and it drew her attention away from her phone.

'I'm jealous of her,' she admitted. 'Her father actually cares about her.'

Ramona frowned. 'I'm sure yours does too.' And at least he knew she existed. At least *he* wasn't in jail.

'From the outside my family looks perfect—parents still married, big house, latest stuff ...' Sydney's voice trailed off. 'But it's all a big fat lie. My parents hate each other. I don't only come out here to vape but to get away from the fighting. You want some?' She offered the pen to Ramona.

'No thanks. Do you mean *arguments*?'

Sydney sighed. 'No, actual fights. There's been times I've thought Dad was going to kill Mum, but she often gives as good as she gets.'

'Does he ... does he hurt you? Does *she*?'

'No, Mum barely even acknowledges London and me except on her Instagram account, and Dad knows if he ever laid a finger on us, I'd run away and tell the world what he's really like. Instead, he buys my silence with designer shoes and handbags.'

Ramona couldn't believe her ears. 'Your mum's never tried to leave?'

Sydney laughed as if this were the funniest thing she'd ever heard. 'Mum thinks a few bruises and black eyes are a small price to pay for everything else he gives her. She only cares about money and appearances, way more than she cares about me and London.'

'But what's that got to do with Lucy?'

Sydney inhaled and exhaled again. 'The first day of high school, I saw Lucy with her father. It was clear he really loved her and that they have a strong relationship—something I'll never have with either of my parents—and something inside me snapped. I did the only thing I knew to make myself feel better—I gave Lucy something to feel bad about. You're right. I'm an absolute bitch,' she said matter-of-factly. 'You sure you don't want some?'

Ramona shook her head.

'So what are you going to do now?' Sydney asked.

'I dunno. Right now, I hate my mother so much, I feel like she deserves to stew a little longer.'

Not that she could stay away forever. Even if she had access to her savings, they wouldn't last long, and as soon as she was found she'd be taken home.

'Look,' Sydney began, 'I won't tell anyone where you are. I know all about shitty parents and mine never come down here so you can hide out as long as you like …'

'But?' Ramona asked.

'But your mum doesn't sound like she *is* a shitty parent.'

'You've only met her once.'

'Yes, and I saw how happy she was to see you when she picked you up from here, and I've seen those yummy salad sandwiches she makes you for lunch. It's clear she only made up the donor story because she didn't want you to freak out about your dad, which— no offence—you have.'

Ramona opened her mouth to object but Sydney held up a hand and barrelled on. 'Your mum obviously chose to have you when she could have had an abortion, and it also sounds like she did it with little support. I think that's pretty damn gutsy, and it shows how much she wanted you. Honestly?' Sydney shrugged. 'That's a lot more than a lot of kids can say.'

Ramona struggled to wrap her head around the fact that Sydney—the most popular girl in school, the one who never seemed to want for anything—was lacking the most important thing. Something that, until today, Ramona had never questioned.

'You think I should forgive her?'

Sydney shrugged again. 'Up to you, but if she called the police she must be out of her mind. I doubt my olds would even notice if I disappeared. I sleep in here some nights—I've even snuck Blake in—and the only time they realised was because London dobbed.'

'That's awful,' Ramona said.

'Yeah, she can be a total little shit when she wants to be.'

'I meant the fact your parents don't notice you're gone.'

'Oh right. Well, it is what it is. There are a few perks.' Sydney leaned back into the couch and inhaled again.

Ramona thought she should probably try to get her to talk about her parents again, encourage her to do something about it. But what? Feeling in over her head, she tried a different tack. 'You know, deep down, I reckon you're actually a pretty good person.'

'What do you mean?' Sydney laughed as she peered over the top of her vape pen.

'You can see you were wrong, which means you can make a different choice. You can apologise to Lucy. You don't *have* to be a bitch.'

'Hmm ... maybe.' Sydney's expression grew distant for a few moments, before she shook her head and looked back to Ramona. 'Anyway, shall I go get you a pillow and blanket or are you calling your mum?'

Debra

Deb, Jake and Lucy were waiting anxiously on the rectory porch when Quinn arrived in an Uber. No wait—it wasn't an Uber, it had parked, and Oscar was also getting out.

'Thank you for coming,' she gushed, as Quinn hugged her. 'If something happens to Ramona, I'll never forgive myself.'

'Nothing is going to happen to her. She's a smart girl. She won't have done anything stupid and we're going to do everything we can to find her. The police have already posted Ramona's photo to their social media, and I've shared it far and wide and asked everyone I know to do the same.'

'Thank you.'

'And now we'll search all bloody night if we have to.' She pulled back and gestured to Oscar. 'He's going to drive around too.'

He smiled sympathetically and lifted his hand in a wave. 'Hey, Debra.'

'Hi,' she managed as Jake stepped forward and introduced himself.

'And this is my daughter, Lucy,' he added, wrapping an arm around her.

'Ramona's b-best friend,' she clarified.

Quinn reached out and squeezed her hand. 'Right. Shall we go?'

'Yes.' Deb gave Quinn her keys and they all agreed to keep in touch and let each other know as soon as there was any news. Her phone rang as Quinn was pulling out of the cemetery car park. 'Tristan, hi.'

'Any news?'

'No,' she breathed, failing to swallow the lump in her throat. 'She's not shown up there?'

'Afraid not. Elijah is standing guard in front of your place and I'm driving up and down every street. Do you think I should start knocking on doors?'

Deb glanced at the time on the dashboard. It was now almost ten o'clock. People might be in bed. 'Yes, that would be wonderful. Shall I send you a photo of her?'

'I've got the one the police posted on Facebook. I've shared it and so have Tara and Tom. They're driving around the nearby suburbs as well.'

That brought more tears to Deb's eyes. She hadn't even met them yet. 'Thank you and thank them,' she managed. 'I better go. I want Ramona to be able to get through.'

'Of course. Call me as soon as you hear anything.'

'He sounds pretty lovely,' Quinn said. 'I hope I get to meet him soon.'

Deb didn't reply. Right now, she was unable to think about anything beyond finding her daughter.

They drove a little in silence, Quinn haphazardly turning down streets, Deb staring out the window, her heart leaping every time she saw a figure ahead, then sinking further into despair each time it was just some random teenager with a similar height and build.

Where the hell was Ramona?

After a while the quiet got to her. She couldn't stand her own thoughts. 'I can see why you're smitten with Oscar,' she said, glancing at Quinn. 'I met him this afternoon.'

A sad smile crossed her friend's face. 'Yeah, he told me. I ran into him tonight when I dropped Snoodles off. He was out running; apparently he needed to clear his head. We got talking … in fact, we were just about to go for a drink to debrief when you rang. He offered to drive me.'

Until that moment, Deb hadn't even thought about why or how he'd come. 'That was sweet of him.'

'It sounds like he wants to be in Ramona's life. And I reckon he'll make an awesome uncle. That's if you let them get to know each other.'

'I've got nothing against Oscar,' Deb said. 'He's been hurt by Eric even more than I have, but right now my only concern is finding my daughter.'

'Of course.' Quinn gestured ahead as they came to a T-junction. 'Left or right?'

Deb shrugged—they may as well be gambling on a photo on Tinder. They'd already been driving for what felt like forever. They'd crawled the streets around SLC and she wondered if they should be driving back towards home, but she was scared to make a decision for fear of making the wrong one.

They drove in silence a little while longer, both of them staring out the windows.

'I'm no better than my own mother,' Deb realised. 'No wonder Ramona hates me.'

'She doesn't *hate* you,' Quinn said firmly, 'she's just angry. You've never intentionally hurt her, physically or emotionally. She'll come round.'

Deb wasn't so sure. 'I've lied to her her whole life. How did I ever think that was okay? I grew up hating my mother and I can't bear that Ramona's and my relationship might end up the same way.'

'We all tell lies, big and small, but I don't need to have met your mother to know that you are nothing like her. Ramona is lucky to have you.'

'Sadly, I don't think Ramona sees it that way.' And Deb didn't blame her. Quinn didn't understand what it felt like to have a parent truly let you down, but she did. 'If only she'd never taken that stupid DNA test. Those kits wreak havoc with people's lives.'

'Maybe,' Quinn agreed, 'but they're not all bad. I've heard happy stories too.'

Deb froze suddenly as a thought landed. She looked to Quinn. 'Could she have gone to the prison?'

'No.' Quinn shook her head adamantly. 'And even if she did manage to find out which one he was in, surely they wouldn't have let her in without an adult?'

Deb certainly hoped not.

Her phone rang again. 'Oh my God. It's her!' Her heart halted as she fumbled to answer. 'Ramona! Thank *God*! Where are you?'

'I'm at Sydney's,' she admitted, her voice shaky.

'Are you okay?'

'Yes. I'm so sorry.'

'Oh, darling, if anyone should be apologising, it's me.' As tears of relief streamed down her cheeks, she added, 'I'm just glad you're okay. Quinn and I are about twenty minutes away, but I'll be there as soon as I can.'

'Quinn?' asked Ramona.

'Yes, she's been helping me look for you.'

Quinn leaned near to the phone. 'Hi, Ramona.'

'Oscar's out looking too,' Deb added, 'and Jake and Lucy, Elijah and even Tristan. We've all been so worried. We all love you so much.'

'Oscar's been helping?'

'Yes. I met him tonight. He's lovely. I better call everyone now and let them know you're okay. See you soon, my darling.' She looked at Quinn. 'Ramona is safe!'

Quinn nodded. There were tears snaking down her cheeks as well.

Deb kept herself busy calling Jake then Tristan, who she asked to give Elijah the good news. The relief in both men's voices made Deb feel less alone than she ever had before. It had always been just her and Ramona against the world, but in the last few years she'd found Quinn, and now their little circle was growing. Jake, Lucy, Tristan and Elijah might not be blood, but they already felt more like family than her own ever had.

'You better let the police know,' Quinn said.

'Oh golly, of course.'

'And I'll call Oscar when you're done,' she volunteered, failing to keep the longing from her voice.

Poor Quinn.

The police were pleased to get the good news about not having to add Ramona to their long missing persons list, but told Deb they'd come to Sydney's place as well just to check she was okay and officially close the case.

Quinn was on speaker phone to a very relieved Oscar when she slowed in front of Sydney's huge house. Deb couldn't care less whether it was a palace or a pigpen, she was simply delighted that Ramona was sitting on the kerb exactly where she said she'd be.

She flung open the door before Quinn had even stopped and ran towards her. Ramona ran the last few steps into Deb's arms. They were both crying—Deb didn't think her eyes had been dry longer than two minutes in the last six hours and she didn't ever want to let go.

They were still sobbing and clinging to each other when a police car pulled up behind Quinn's. Deb forced herself to loosen her hold on her daughter as they turned to face the approaching officers.

'Well, this is a sight for sore eyes,' said Senior Constable Dyer. 'Nice to meet you, young lady. You gave us all quite a scare this evening.'

'I'm sorry, officer,' sniffed Ramona.

Dyer waved a hand as if this was just a regular Saturday night. 'Let's not mention it again, but next time you think of running away ... don't.'

Ramona grinned through her tears. 'Deal.'

Quinn emerged from the car as the police officers were getting into theirs. 'Oscar's almost here. He's going to pick me up so you two can head straight home.'

Deb raised an eyebrow but simply said, 'Okay. Thanks.' Then she turned to Sydney who was sitting on the kerb, vaping while texting madly on her phone. 'Thanks for looking out for Ramona.'

Sydney looked up as if surprised anyone was talking to her, then hid the vape pen behind her back. 'No worries, Mrs Fast. She's a good friend.'

Oscar joined them as Sydney retreated to her mansion. He looked almost as relieved as Deb felt to see Ramona.

'Well,' he said as he walked up, 'we meet again. Twice in one day. People will start to talk.'

'Hi,' Ramona said as she gave him a sheepish wave. 'Sorry if I scared you too.'

He reached out to ruffle her hair. 'I'm just glad you're okay.'

Deb took Ramona's hand. 'Come on, sweetheart, let's get you home to bed.'

After quick hugs goodbye all round, Quinn and Oscar climbed into his car and Ramona and Deb into hers.

'Can we go through the drive-thru and get a McFlurry from Macca's on our way back?' asked Ramona as she clicked her seatbelt into place.

'Sweet girl, we can get anything you want.'

'What about a pony?'

Deb chuckled. 'Don't push your luck. 'Besides, aren't we getting a budgie?'

'Yes.' Ramona grinned. 'It's gunna be awesome.'

Deb wasn't sure Ramona wanted to talk about what had happened today and she didn't want to push her. There'd be plenty of time tomorrow or the next day—she was simply happy to have her back. They parked the car and sat in comfortable silence, watching the late-night traffic zoom past as they ate their McFlurries. Deb had just about finished hers when Ramona spoke.

'I'm scared I'm like him.'

'What? You mean your father?' When she nodded, Deb stuck her spoon in the near-empty cup and turned to properly face her. 'You are *nothing* like him. You are sweet, and kind, and caring, and—'

'But didn't you ever worry that I would turn out like him? I've got half his DNA.'

'And you've also got half of mine, yet we're different in so many ways. You're your own person and you can shape your life however you want to.'

'I just said something similar to Sydney actually.'

'Oh?'

'Yeah.' Ramona told Deb that Sydney and her friends had bullied Lucy and then done the same to Ramona when she'd chosen to stand up to her. 'I told her she could choose not to be a bitch if she wanted to.'

Deb smiled, so proud of her daughter. 'See, you're a good person. I believe it, and you need to as well.'

'Trust me, I've had plenty of dark thoughts.'

Deb took Ramona's hand in both of hers. 'Oh, angel, it's human to have dark thoughts, and I hope you know you can talk about any of them with me. I'll always be here whatever you need.'

'Thanks.' Deb was about to start the car to head home when Ramona spoke again. 'Mum, why didn't you have an abortion when you found out you were pregnant?'

Her heart twisted inside out, but she'd promised herself no more dancing around the truth.

'I won't lie,' she said. 'I thought about it for all of about five minutes, but I wanted you, Ramona. Even though I wanted to get away from Eric, I knew you were the best thing that would ever happen to me, and I wanted to create a family. I wanted to prove that I could be a good mum, despite the example I had growing up. I'm not sure I've succeeded, and I'm sorry I kept the truth from you all these years, but I promise—'

'Mum,' Ramona interrupted. 'You're nothing like your mother either. I can't believe she just abandoned you. She must have rocks in her head.'

'Something like that,' Deb agreed.

'And I know I was angry and hurt, but I understand why you did what you did. I'm actually grateful.' Ramona leaned in close and gave her a hug. 'If I ever have kids, I'll be happy if I'm half the mum you are.'

Deb thought her tears were spent but at Ramona's words another wave broke free. It was the best compliment anyone had ever given her. 'Thank you, my darling. When the time comes, I know you'll be a great mum, but I'm not quite ready to be a grandma yet, okay?'

Ramona laughed. 'Don't worry, I have lots I want to achieve before I even *think* about babies.'

'Good.' Although Deb hadn't planned to have this conversation tonight, now that they were talking openly about their fears, she had to say it. 'You know, if you want to meet Eric, I … I understand. And I want you to know I'll support you.'

'I don't want to meet him.' Ramona looked aghast. 'I'm just going to go back to pretending he never existed. As far as I'm concerned, Eric *is* nothing but a sperm donor. But I would like to get to know Oscar, and maybe my grandparents, if you don't mind?'

The sweet release of relief gushed through her body. 'I don't mind at all.'

'I love you, Mum.'

'Aw, darling, I love you too. Always and forever.'

'And you're right, all I need is you.' She paused a moment, then added, 'And Lucy. And maybe Elijah too.'

Deb grinned, happy her daughter finally had such good friends and weirdly excited by the prospect of her having a boyfriend. It showed Ramona was growing up and Deb's own fear of men hadn't rubbed off. 'So, things might be serious between you and Elijah after all?' she asked.

Ramona's cheeks coloured. 'Yep. I really like him, Mum. I've never felt this way about anyone before.'

'That's wonderful.' Deb turned the keys in the ignition. 'Now, let's go home, where we both belong.'

*

An hour or so later, long after Ramona had collapsed into bed from emotional exhaustion and Deb was nursing a glass of wine as she tried to process the events of the day, her phone buzzed with a message. She smiled as she read it:

Are you awake?

Yes.

Fancy a visitor?

Her heart leapt. *I'd love that.*

Then buzz me up.

She hauled herself off the couch, went to the window and looked down. There was Tristan, standing patiently at the entrance of the building. Her heart turned over in her chest at the sight of him and she rushed to press the button to let him in.

Flinging open her front door, she heard the sound of heavy footsteps on the stairs and then he appeared—his broad shoulders, his dark hair and the smile that made her body feel like honey.

He held up a carton of cookies and cream ice-cream. 'I thought you might need this after the night you've had.'

She laughed and pulled him inside. 'Thank you. I'm so glad to see you.'

The door thunked shut behind them as their lips met in a kiss that made Deb feel as if she'd finally come home.

'Care to join me in a glass of wine?' she asked when they broke apart.

He raised one eyebrow. 'Does wine go with ice-cream?'

She shrugged. 'Who cares? We're grown-ups—we can eat whatever we want, whenever we want, with whatever we want.'

'Good point.' He grabbed two spoons as Deb poured him a glass of sav blanc and they took the lot to the couch.

'I'm sorry I was so short with you today,' she said.

He squeezed her hand. 'It's fine. You were worried about Ramona. I get that. I'm a parent—my kids will always come first as well. But I'm here for you if you ever need help or support, or just a shoulder to lean on.'

Deb leaned towards him and took his face in her hands. 'What on earth did I do to deserve you?' she asked, kissing him long and slow before he had the chance to reply.

Whatever it was, she thanked the gods for sending him to her and couldn't wait to see what the rest of their lives had in store.

Epilogue

Two months later

Although cold, it was a beautiful evening as Deb, Tristan and Elijah walked from the car park through the immaculate gardens to the grand entrance of SLC for the fashion show.

'Geez,' Elijah said, gawping up at the Gothic Revival style building. 'This school is even fancier than I imagined. Maybe I should have bought a new pair of jeans.'

Deb smiled. 'You and your jeans are perfect as they are.'

Once inside, they were greeted by a smiling blonde in SLC uniform, who directed them through the courtyard to the great hall, which had been transformed into something that looked right out of Paris or London Fashion Week. The school orchestra was set up on both sides of the stage and a catwalk extended from the middle. Tristan and Elijah nabbed a table in prime position and then put their jackets on the other seats to save them for the rest of their group.

Jake turned up with two older couples who he introduced as his parents and his late wife's parents. His mother-in-law, Jennifer, had stunning auburn hair, which she'd assume was dyed to cover greys, if it weren't exactly the same shade as Lucy's. Not long after, Quinn pranced into the room with Oscar following closely behind. She was wearing a dazzling dress that included almost every colour under the sun and her hair was multicoloured to match. Deb waved them over and was delighted to see she was also wearing the earrings she'd made her.

'You'll never guess the latest gossip from work,' Quinn said as she greeted Deb with a hug and managed to grab a glass from a passing waiter at the same time.

'Tell me!'

Quinn took the seat next to Deb. Oscar sat between Elijah and Tristan. 'I told you to guess.'

Deb rolled her eyes. 'You also told me I wouldn't be able to.'

'Fine.' Quinn took a sip of her drink and then glared at the glass. 'What kind of poison is this?'

'It's sparkling apple juice—this is a school function,' said Deb with a laugh, then prompted, 'The gossip?'

'Toby and Linc are an item. They just announced their engagement.'

'What? No way. I thought they hated each other!'

'Hate is a strong word. It was more bickering between an old married couple. And,' she added, 'I think the bickering was a red herring to put us all off their scent.'

'Wow.'

'And that's not the only news. They've both resigned. They're tired of Mr Carrot-Up-His-Arse not appreciating them, so they're starting their own freelance digital marketing company. They actually offered me a job, but I turned them down.'

'You're staying at The Energy Co with Oscar?' Deb asked, glancing over at him. He and Quinn weren't a couple—both far too respectful of Olivia for that—but they'd become good friends, and Deb hoped one day they'd be able to act on the feelings that were obvious between them.

Quinn shook her head. 'Actually, I'm handing in my notice as well. That place is no fun without my work wife, and I've decided to follow my childhood dreams. I've got myself a hairdressing apprenticeship and I'm starting at TAFE next semester.'

'Oh my God, that's fantastic,' Deb said, giving Quinn another hug.

'Anyway ...' Quinn beamed. 'Enough about me, how are you and lover boy?'

Deb pressed her finger against her lips and blushed. 'Shh. Now is not the place.'

But the truth was things were better between her and Tristan than she could ever have imagined. Ramona, Tom and Tara had met, and Ramona loved talking fashion with Tara while she and Tom shared a passion for old movies and would try and stump each other with trivia when the five of them got together for a meal.

'But I have some news as well.'

'Oh?' Quinn quirked a perfectly preened eyebrow.

'I've been accepted into a master's degree in psychology starting next semester.'

'Girlfriend!' Quinn squealed, and heads turned to look at them. 'That's wonderful news. I'm so happy for you, but even more happy for the kids you're going to help.'

'Thanks. No idea how I'm going to fit it in with work, Ramona and Tristan, but I can't wait to get started.'

'You'll manage and you'll be awesome.'

'How's Snoodles?' Deb asked.

'Did someone mention the beast?' Oscar said, leaning into the conversation.

Quinn laughed. 'He's his usual handful.'

'Hopefully the bone I left him tonight will keep him from destroying my leather couch any further,' added Oscar.

Deb was about to ask after Mrs D when a hush fell over the crowd and the band stopped playing. Everyone looked to the stage to see a tall slim woman in an outfit that looked like a cross between a dressing gown and a space suit, but somehow worked. Even before she introduced herself, it was clear this was the famous Ms Rose.

'Good evening, I'm delighted to see you all here tonight to celebrate our end of semester fashion show and the exceptional designs of your daughters. This semester has been all about the fashion of last century. The girls paired up and each duo documented the trends of one decade and then designed a gown specific to their era. It is my greatest pleasure to introduce Sian, Leila, and the 1900s!'

The crowd joined Ms Rose in applause as she stepped to the side of the stage and a girl in SLC uniform approached the podium and introduced herself as Leila.

'These girls are super talented,' whispered Quinn as the 1940s gave way for the 1950s and Ramona stepped up to the podium.

Oscar and Elijah whooped and cheered.

'Lucy and I chose to publish a magazine, showcasing our decade,' she explained. 'Anyone who would like to see our magazine can view it at the end of the night.' Then she launched into each year, offering highlights and interesting facts. Ramona was in her element and Deb couldn't have felt prouder. Tristan squeezed her knee under the table, and she met his smile with one of her own. On his other side, Elijah's eyes were glued to Ramona and he was hanging on her every word.

When Lucy modelled their gown, she carried herself as if she'd been born on the catwalk, and she looked absolutely stunning in the black sleeveless dress with its tight bodice and full skirt that swished against the floor as she walked. A deep crimson train made of chiffon wrapped around her waist and fell in two dark slashes to the floor. It was hard to believe this creation came from the minds and hands of two teenage girls.

Deb glanced over to Jake, and they met each other's eyes, both of them fighting tears of pride. Their whole table gave the girls a standing ovation when they were finished.

When the final pair had presented the 1990s, Ms Rose took the stage again to present the awards. Sydney and Nyra won best gown for the 1960s with their dress made almost entirely of hot pink tulle, which had more ruffles than a toilet paper cover doll. Deb saw both Lucy and Ramona congratulate them as they walked past and was glad to see the winners smile back. They might have got off to a rocky start and would probably never be bosom buddies, but Deb had been glad to hear that the bullies had apologised to Lucy and stopped tormenting her and Ramona.

The girls from the 1920s won best research, and Deb crossed both her fingers as Ms Rose announced the overall prize. 'Although all my students have worked hard this semester and this was an extremely difficult decision to make, I'd like to congratulate dream team Ramona Fast and Lucy King. These girls have passion, dedication and a drive that will take them far in this industry.'

She went on a little longer and then finally invited the girls to the stage to accept their award.

'Woohoo,' Deb shrieked louder than anyone in the hall and pumped her fist in the air, so full of pride she thought she might explode.

'Thanks again, everyone, for coming,' Ms Rose said. 'This concludes the official part of the evening, but we do hope you'll stay for light refreshments.'

'Mum,' Ramona said, rushing over to their table, 'what did you think?'

'What did I think? I ... I'm speechless. You're both amazing,' she said, drawing her into a hug.

The others stepped up to congratulate them and Deb gave Lucy a hug as well. 'You looked gorgeous up there. What talent you both have!'

Lucy beamed. 'Thanks, Deb. Maybe Ramona and I can work together one day.'

'That sounds wonderful,' Deb said to the girl who'd become almost like a second daughter these past few months.

'Brought you a selection of treats,' Tristan said, appearing with a plate as Lucy went off to join Ramona and Elijah.

'Thanks.' She smiled. 'You truly are the man of my dreams.'

'Dammit,' he replied as he yanked his phone out of his pocket. Although on silent, it was flashing like a Christmas decoration. 'I'm not supposed to be on call, but it's the clinic. I—'

'You answer it,' Deb said, picking up an arancini ball.

It was then that she saw Ramona wasn't with her friends anymore but sitting next to Oscar at the table, their heads bent towards each other as if they were in deep conversation. Although she knew it wasn't right to eavesdrop, she couldn't help herself.

'I wish you were my dad,' Ramona said.

Deb's heart squeezed as he took her daughter's hand.

'You'll never know how much I wish the same, but I'm sure glad we found each other, and I'm going to do my damn best to be the best uncle you've ever had.'

'I've never had an uncle,' Ramona remarked.

'Well then, I guess I'm already ahead.' He kissed her on the forehead and looked up when he caught Deb watching them.

'Room for one more?' she asked.

'Of course,' he replied, pulling out the seat next to him.

'Thanks.' She sat and offered them her plate of food.

Maybe that DNA test hadn't been the worst thing that could happen to them after all.

Acknowledgements

Honestly, it takes a village to write a book and I'd like to take this opportunity to thank mine:

Team home—Craig, who keeps me grounded and never has any doubt that I can finish a novel, if only I'd stop whinging about it! My three gorgeous sons, Hamish, Lachlan and Archie, who inspire and motivate me daily to keep publishing because they keep eating and growing and that stuff is *expensive*. My mum, Barbara, who makes sure my boys have clean uniforms when I'm too busy writing (and a whole lot more—we're all lucky to have you). And my fur babies: Gibson, who amuses me with his grumpiness—I love you even if you hate me; Addie, who keeps me company lying by my feet beneath my desk while I write; and Budge, our cantankerous eleven-year-old budgie, who provided some inspiration for the birds in this book. (If you're still alive by the time it's published, it will be a freaking miracle.) And to Rose who provided so much love *always* and passed away while I was writing *The Work Wives*. RIP my darling girl!

Team office, aka the wonderful team at Harlequin/HarperCollins Australia—thanks always to Sue Brockhoff, who champions me and supports me and continually encourages me to strive to make each book better than the last. To Jo Mackay, who provided a wonderful sounding board when I was first brainstorming this book. To Annabel Blay, for giving such detailed insight on my first draft and for coordinating the production from manuscript to final book. To my amazing editor, Lachlan Jobbins—I'm so glad we got to work together again. I love that you can lift me up and make me feel like a fabulous writer, while also providing invaluable critique to make my books better. Don't think I'm letting you go again! And to Di Blacklock, another editorial whiz who gave such helpful instruction and once again made sure this book wasn't longer than the bible. Thank you. To Jo Munroe and Josey Bryant, marketing and publicity extraordinaires—thank you for working so tirelessly to get this book out to the masses. To Daren Holt and Kat Chadwick thank you *so* much for my new cover direction. I couldn't love it more!

Team LA—to my agent, Helen Breitwieser, who has been my cheerleader since almost the beginning of my career. Thanks for all you do. I think it's about time we had another Mother's Day together, don't you!?

Team mental health—I make no secret of the fact that the last few years have been tough on my writing (not pandemic related, I don't think). Maybe I was suffering a bit of burnout but the doubt, imposter syndrome and anxiety threatened to get the better of me for a while. Knowing I couldn't just give up writing for numerous reasons, I went to see my doctor, who I've been going to since I was twelve. Dr G sent me to a psychologist and put me on anxiety medication, which has lifted the fog and allowed me to find the joy in writing again. Writing isn't always easy, but I believe most of the time it should be fun, since if I'm having fun, so (hopefully) will my readers. I also want to give a massive shout-out to the gentle, kind, giving, wonderous author that is Holly Ringland. I'm so grateful that I met you that weekend at the Capricorn Coast Writers Festival. It was just the right time I needed to meet someone like you ... actually scrap that, you're one of a kind—it was just the right time for me to meet *you*! You taught me so much in such a short space of time and continually inspire me with your wisdom. The world is lucky you also have another book out right now!

Team readers—whether you've been reading me for years or this is your first, *thank you*! Without you I couldn't a) live my dream b) feed my family and c) write off fun research trips on tax. If you're not already, join us in The Rachael Johns' Online Book Club on Facebook where we have endless fun chatting books all year round.

My work wives, aka my writer friends—there are *too* many of you to name, but special shout-outs to Rebecca Heath, my sprinting partner and critique buddy; to Anthea Hodgson and Fiona Palmer, who I escape with on writing retreats as often as we can; and to all the other wonderful authors I call friends and chat with on a regular basis.

Special mentions go to Jackie Claridge for helping me research some office stuff (you gave me way more than ended up in the book, but I really appreciate it), Rowena Preddy from *Brand You* magazine and podcast, who gave me the title for this book when she interviewed me last year, which sparked the idea, and Debra Fast who bought naming rights to a character in a charity auction *years* ago. Thanks for your patience—I hope you like what I've done with your namesake.

Book Club Discussion Questions

- Do you believe in fate?
- Deb keeps a big secret from Ramona. Do you think she should have told her the truth earlier?
- Deb and Quinn became best friends at work. What do you think they have in common? Have you made any close friends through work?
- Have you ever tried online dating? Any horror or success stories?
- Have you ever taken a DNA test? Were the results surprising?
- Both Deb and Quinn are in jobs that pay the bills but are not their dream careers. What is your dream career? Are you doing it?
- Are some people just born bad?
- Mother–daughter relationships can be complicated, especially in the teenage years. What are some of your favourite books or movies that explore this dynamic?

- Quinn becomes good friends with her neighbour. Are you friends with yours?
- Do you think the title *The Work Wives* suits this book? If not, what might you call it?

talk about it

Let's talk about books.

Join the conversation:

 facebook.com/harlequinaustralia

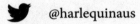 @harlequinaus

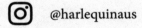 @harlequinaus

harpercollins.com.au/hq

If you love reading and want to know about our
authors and titles, then let's talk about it.